Dallas

Special Edition

The Bull Riders

Maisey Yates

Dallas

Content Note

Sarah's past includes childhood SA. This is a heavy subject, and one I didn't take writing lightly. There is no graphic description, and all of it occurs in the past off the page.

Chapter One

Dallas

I don't have a death wish. I just like to flirt with death for around eight seconds on a Friday night.

Every so often that old song drifts through my head as I climb into the chute. *Mamas, don't let your babies grow up to be cowboys.*

Good thing my mom doesn't give a shit about me.

My stepmom is a good woman, though, and she doesn't deserve to worry about me. Hell, my dad is a decent guy, for all that he didn't know about me until I was fifteen. He took me in after years in foster care, tried to finish raising me right.

He did his best.

I'm just fucked up.

Fucked up enough that this is how I get my kicks, I guess.

I'm sitting on the edge of the chute, and I lower myself

down onto the bull, grabbing hold of the harness and slipping my hand beneath the leather strap.

"The next rider up is a champion. Number two in the world right now, folks, just twenty-four years old, from Gold Valley, Oregon, riding a little bull called Tundra. Give it up for Dallas Dodge!" The crowd cheers and I adjust the leather strap, my heart pounding in my head, my whole body shaking from the adrenaline pouring through my veins. A better high than any shit out there.

Though, it's not unlike shit you buy on the street. You could think you're buying straight shit, and it could be laced with Fentanyl and send you straight to an early grave.

Tundra might be my bad batch. He's pissed at me, that's for sure. Which is his whole job. I'm supposed to ride him; he's supposed to buck me off.

I'm never sure who the crowd is chanting for.

If they want me to get my full eight seconds, or if they want the bull to throw me, and tear me a whole new one for good measure.

This is Rome and we're the gladiators. Though we aren't prisoners of anything other than our own bullshit.

I think about my stepmom then – who surely didn't want me to grow up to be a cowboy. My dad. My half-siblings. All the people who love me back in Gold Valley.

Then Sarah.

I always think about Sarah.

It doesn't matter how many years it's been since she got sent back to her mom, since we were separated in that last foster home, I think about her. Especially in these moments.

I touch the brim of my hat.

Those who are about to die salute you.

The bull bucks underneath me, and I nod to the men holding the gate. They release, and it's on.

It's either the fastest or slowest eight seconds imaginable. There's not much in between. And I'm feeling it tonight. But I know what I need to do. I let out a breath, my body sinking into the rhythm. The movements. I'm hoping that I get a high enough score. That the bull doesn't ruin this by being too kind to me. But then, he reverses his movements, planting both front feet down and shifting from a fluid twist to short, shocking movements. Good. That's what I want. I want to compete. I want to win.

There's nothing but me and the animal then. A fight for dominance. A fight for that win.

If my friend Colt Campbell scores better than me, I won't mind so much. But if that bastard Maverick Quinn gets a high score, I swear—

And then the time is up. I did it.

I follow the movement of the beast and jump off, landing on my feet, stumbling forward as the bull goes the other way.

The roar of the crowd is deafening. But I don't take a bow.

I adjust my hat, look up, and begin to walk back toward the gate.

And that's when I see her. Right there. I would think I was hallucinating except...

In all my memories, and my imagination of her, she's not *this*.

When I think of Sarah, she's that little girl who has nightmares. Who has to hold onto me at night in order to fall asleep. She's the one person I want to protect more than anything in all the world. The person that I begged my parents to find, but they never could.

The last time I saw her, she was being carried away by a social worker, while she screamed and fought, and my foster parents held onto my arms, trying to keep me from stopping them. I pulled so hard I ended up with fingerprints on my arms, bruises where they'd kept me captive while I tried so hard...

I never saw her again.

Until now.

I know it's her, and yet it's not her.

Because this isn't a vulnerable little girl standing there staring me down from the bleachers. No. This is a woman. She must be nineteen, twenty years old. Twenty, I think. I try to remember when her birthday was in connection to mine, but everything is jumbled up. I remember the little parties that I threw for her, but not the time of year. I guess you only remember the things that matter.

It's like everything goes silent. Like it all stops. The edges of everything go fuzzy, but not Sarah.

I can't hear her. But I see her move her mouth. "Dallas."

And then, I suddenly catch movement out of the corner of my eye. The bull is running straight toward me. And I have to jump up to the side of the gate to escape, the bull fighters doing their part to lure the animal away while I climb up and over, back into the chute. And when I look back up, I don't see her anymore. Did I hallucinate her? Was it a dream?

No. That can't be. I've spent all these years looking for her. Ever since I was fourteen. It's been ten years. I can't lose her again. I can't. My team is trying to talk to me, but I don't want to hear it. I know my score is posting, judging by the sound the crowd makes, it's good. But I think it's the best. Suddenly, it doesn't mean a damn thing.

My heart is pounding, my legs unsteady, it's always like that after a ride. But this is different. This isn't about the ride.

"What the fuck are you doing?"

Colt is standing there, arms crossed, watching me.

"Don't you have a fucking ride to get to?" I ask.

"Yeah. In a second." He's watching me, like he knows me. I guess he does. I guess he does know me and knows something is up. Fair enough since he's been my friend ever since I moved to Gold Valley.

"I have to... I saw somebody that I know."

"Oh. And?"

"I have to find her."

"Some Buckle Bunny?"

I want to growl. I want to grab them by the throat and tell him never to call her that. For all I know, she is a Buckle Bunny. And it isn't like there's anything wrong with that. But not her. All my protective instincts rise up inside of me, and I want to fight.

"Okay," Colt says, holding his hands up like I'm keeping him there at gunpoint. "No jokes."

"Come up with good jokes next time."

Colt shrugs. "You seem rattled."

"I'm not rattled. But... I just saw someone I've been looking for, and then I lose sight of her. I can't let her get away."

"Sounds ominous," Colt says, eyeing me closely.

"It's not, I'll explain later. I'll catch up with you after your ride."

I don't need to be talking to Colt that way. He's my best friend. Has been ever since we started riding together four years ago. A couple of bored kids in Gold Valley, Oregon, looking for something to do. We found it. And we made a name for ourselves with it. Made a whole lot of cash too. Made our moms cry.

But right then, though, I wonder if the whole point was this. If it all brought me right here. To her.

Or, you hit your fucking head and you have no idea what's happening.

Maybe. Maybe I did.

I haul myself up over the guardrail into the bleachers. And I start walking down toward the section that I saw her in. I'm creating a stir. I don't particularly care.

I'm avoiding all the people gawking at me, trying to take selfies in front of me. In any other circumstances I might stop and flip them the bird so they have that as a keepsake from tonight.

Then for some reason, I turn around.

There she is. Not up on the bleachers anymore, down by the chutes. I grit my teeth, haul myself right back over, and there we are. Three feet apart from each other. She's staring at me, wide brown eyes that are so familiar to me they might as well be my own.

"I don't know if you remember me..." I almost can't make sense of what just came out of her mouth. *I* might not remember *her*? I've spent so many sleepless nights worrying about her. Wondering where she is. Driving myself crazy.

Now she's here. She's right here.

Without thinking, without giving any allowance for the fact that I'm sweaty and full of dust, I reach out and I pull her into my arms. "Sarah," I whisper, my hand on the back of her head. I must look like a crazy person. But I feel like a crazy person.

"Dallas."

Chapter Two

Sarah

I want to cry, but I can't. I can't cry because this isn't what I'm here for. An emotional reunion, a rekindling of the friendship we once had, the promises we made to each other as scared, desperate kids who needed something to cling to —that's not what I'm looking for.

I can't afford to let my guard down. I can't afford to melt into him.

I can't break. Not yet.

But I *want* to cry because I can't remember how long it's been since anyone's touched me. Because I can't bear for anyone to touch me, not anyone but him. It's been that way for as long as I can remember.

Ten years.

Ten years this man has been gone from my life. He was a boy then. Everything to me. He haunts me. My dreams, my days, my nightmares.

I remember far too clearly the first day that I met him.

I was eight.

I'd just gotten removed from my mom's care. She won't leave the man that's been touching me, and even though he's going to prison, nothing about her behavior suggests that she can be trusted to take care of me.

I'm shut down. I'm lost. Everything is dark. My life has never been easy. But it got remarkably worse when Chris came into my mom's life. And as a result, into mine.

Now I know you can't trust everyone. I know the people who say they love you will choose themselves over you every time. That men are vile, disgusting creatures whose hands bring hurt, discomfort and disgust.

I don't trust anyone. Not the foster family I've just been introduced to, not the social workers who have been trying to help me. And before that, not the people I was in temporary placement with. But for some reason the minute I see him… It's like everything is different. I feel safe when I look at him. He's about twelve, I think. Tall and safe looking. When I have nightmares, he comforts me. He's the only person I can bear to be touched by. True then, true now. Like no time has passed.

For years, he and I were bonded. For years we moved to the same foster homes. When they tried to separate us, I wouldn't eat. I wouldn't even come out of my room. He would run away from whatever home he was in.

He would always come find me. Wherever I was. It didn't matter.

Dallas Dodge was the one thing I could count on. In a world that had treated me cruelly, viciously, he was the one kindness.

I remember one of our foster families lived on this big, rural property, and Dallas and I used to sneak away and lie on a grassy hill that had a view of Portland, down below, and a view of the stars up above.

Someday I'll have my own place. My own life.

I remember whispering that to him one night, up there, like I was whispering a prayer. Better to talk to Dallas than God. At least I felt like Dallas listened.

I know you will, Sarah. You can have anything you want.

Our social workers ended up trying to group us like biological siblings, because they didn't know what else to do with us. The goal was never to separate us, because of the mental duress that it caused.

And they didn't.

Until my mom was given custody back. It was my nightmare. She took me away from him, from the one person I felt safe with. She brought me back into her chaos and self-destruction.

I didn't love her. I didn't want to be with her. I wanted to be with him.

That was all I wanted. All I cared about.

The way she punished me for that. For years.

The things that she called me.

I trusted him. With everything I was. And my mom acted like he was my *boyfriend*. Like that was the only kind of connection she could understand. I was twelve. She said that I was a whore for him, obviously, because of the way I laid around mourning the loss of him.

I wanted to yell at her. I wanted to tell her that she would never understand the feelings that I had for him.

Because she doesn't understand love.

Love that can be bright and pure and wonderful. Unselfish.

But all the words got jammed up in my throat when she

said that. I could never talk to her. I still don't really know why she wanted custody back in the first place. She changed our last names – she said it was to hide from one of her exes.

It didn't protect me from the one person I needed protection from.

All it did was hide me from the only one I wanted to find me.

Because I know he looked for me. I dreamed of him finding me, and then I found him. I'd been looking him up continually for years – he's not a social media guy, which doesn't surprise me. But then his name came up connected to the rodeo.

I've been holding that discovery close for two years. Knowing he was out there, feeling afraid to actually *see* him. I was afraid he'd forgotten me. That our connection was more powerful in my head than for real. That it was all in the imagination of a sad, lonely little girl, and a famous, successful bull rider wouldn't even remember me.

I was afraid of that. So afraid I didn't go to him.

Until Chris got out of jail.

I tried to comfort myself with the knowledge that my name was different, that it would make it harder to find me.

Then he found me. And now he's stalking me. Lingering outside the diner I work at. Doing little enough for the police to help me, and doing enough to make me feel terrified.

He came to town two weeks ago, and then I saw an ad for the rodeo. It didn't feel coincidental. It felt like he'd come to save me again, and I need that.

I need *him*.

Then he releases his hold on me, and I take a breath. I can't believe it's him.

He's looking at me like I'm a ghost.

"I've been looking for you," he says.

For the past ten years I've felt broken, like my heart shattered into tiny, unfixable pieces. I can feel them mending now.

"I...I knew you rode in the rodeo and then I saw you were coming into town and I needed to come see you."

"You live here?" he asks.

"Yes," I say.

That's the simple answer. The whole story of where I've been since we last saw each other is much longer.

"Let's go get a drink."

I look away, feeling suddenly embarrassed, and I don't know why. "Oh, I..."

"You aren't old enough to drink, are you?"

"Well, the..." I don't know why that makes me feel small and silly. Young. I never feel young. I feel tired already. I work as many hours as I possibly can to afford my apartment, taking as many college courses as I can online while I try to get to a place where I can go full-time. I've had to take care of myself for so long, I don't just feel like an adult – I feel old.

But I'm not allowed to go into a bar and order a beer. I bet if I tried to buy a beer the cops would involve themselves in my life. I can't get them to handle my stalker, though.

"The diner I work at is open late," I say.

Though I don't love the idea of going there because what if he's waiting for me?

You'll be with Dallas.

"We don't have to leave now," I say.

"Why not?"

"Your...the rest of the event."

"I don't care."

I'm more important. He doesn't say that, but I feel it. I feel it warming me from the inside. No one has ever treated me like I mattered. No one except him.

"I can't believe you're here," he says, looking at me like I'm a ghost – but maybe a good one.

"Neither can I."

He's happy to see me. For the first time in so long, I feel something like hope, and that's going to go a long way in healing all these tears in my soul.

I'm a terrible cliché, and I know it. I want to get into social work because of my experiences in the foster care system. Genuinely, I can't think of anything else to do. The foster care system is what I know, inside and out. Good social workers are a gift.

Bad, detached, disinterested ones can quite literally be the death of you.

I talked to my old case worker about this when I decided to go to college. She warned me that I was destined to repeat my same situation, over and over in slightly different ways, with different children, trying to do better than what was done for me.

Trying to repair a system that's as broken as the people in it.

But what else is there? Leaving kids like me to drown.

I'm drowning now.

Reunification with bio parents is good for so many people, but it wasn't good for me. Instead, it stripped me of the support system I did have and left me vulnerable to the man who victimized me.

No. I'm not vulnerable. I have options.

I have Dallas.

I decide I don't want to take Dallas to *my* diner, because not only do I not want to chance seeing Chris, I don't want to get asked questions by my coworkers tonight. Those questions will be unavoidable eventually. But not now.

I suggest that we walk to the Withered Cactus, which would be my favorite non-bar place to go to late because it has some nice food, but isn't pretentious. Which just means it won't break the bank if I want to go get some hipster food with a fried egg on it.

Sometimes I do go out.

Or at least I did.

"Sarah, I... I worried about you every day."

His eyes are almost glittering as we sit there underneath the green neon sign, shaped like a cactus, obviously. I don't want to tell him about my life. I just want to sit like this for a while. I just want to hear that he missed me. That he cares about me.

Oh, God, just knowing someone cares is a whole new feeling. It's like coming home after being away for a lifetime. If this is all I get out of tonight it might almost be enough.

"I didn't want to go with her," I say.

He hadn't found me. It was the one time he didn't. I was angry at him for a while, but that faded with time. I let him be one of my very few good memories. I have one picture of him, and I keep it framed. It's moved to about five different homes with me.

He's with me wherever I go, whether he knows it or not.

"I know. I know. Afterward, I went off the deep end, kind of. But then they... They found my dad."

I can't help but wonder what the deep end was, but that thought is completely derailed by the revelation about his dad.

"What?"

He laughs, a short, disbelieving sound. "Of course, you wouldn't know about that."

"No. I don't know anything."

"It turns out my mom never told my dad about me. She lost custody of me, and they didn't pursue him until I exhausted all my options. After you were gone I... I kind of lost it. I ran out of options. There were no more places that would take me. Not even group homes. But that's what led me to my dad."

"Your biological dad?"

"Yeah. He's great."

"Really?"

"He was really young when my mom got pregnant. Then she told him she lost the baby, and left town. By the time I showed up at his place with my garbage bag full of all my shit, he was single and living in a really nice place, so it was...an upgrade. He hooked up with my stepmom not long after that."

"Huh."

It's such a funny thing, and I don't really know what to say. He has a dad. A respectable dad with a career. I don't know what I thought. But I guess I just figured that Dallas spent the rest of his childhood in foster care. I knew his mom had lost custody for sure and certain.

Something that never happened to me, to my detriment.

"Yeah. Right when I moved in, he started kind of having a thing with this woman, his business partner. And his best friend. Anyway, she's my stepmom. Really, she's the only mom I know – she's great. I have an amazing family."

Envy that I don't see coming stabs me square in the chest. I'm not really sure what the envy is about. Him finding a family, or this family having him for all these years while I just didn't.

It makes me burn.

Maybe it doesn't matter exactly what it's from.

"I'm really happy for you," I say.

I never imagined him with a home. With a family. When I saw that he was in the rodeo I wrote some ridiculous fairy tale in my head about how he'd gotten there. Taking a job on a ranch with some cowboys after he got spit out of the system and discovering he had a talent for...riding bulls. I don't know how or why anyone realizes they can do that or decides to *see* if they can. But he doesn't fit my idea of the fantasy I had of him.

He's Dallas, but he's not.

There's something more complicated about him, something in the way he holds his shoulders, his jaw.

He orders us some French fries and drinks, and I realize I haven't eaten all day. My nerves consumed my appetite, and the only thing I gnawed on were my fingernails. I couldn't do anything but anticipate this moment, and I'm starving now, but I also think if I tried to eat, I'd throw up on his boots.

The trouble is, it's hard to make small talk with a man who held you while you shook and cried as a traumatized child. A man who both knows me in ways no one else ever has, and also now doesn't really know me at all. It's hard to make small talk when there's so much heaviness hanging in the air, and the truth of why I'm here.

"Why did you come tonight, Sarah?" he asks.

He can feel that I'm holding back, and I don't have it in me to lie to him. There's no point anyway since this is why I'm here. I just hate bringing it up. I hate exposing myself.

I wish I could tell him it's because my life is so great and I just wanted to give him an update. That I could be this whole, complete person like he is. With a career and a family.

But no. I'm a broken little girl inside, still looking to Dallas Dodge to fix me.

"My...my mom's ex. The one who abused me and went to prison. He found me. He knows where I work and where I live. I've been trying to get away but I don't...I don't have anyone else. I don't have any options, I...I'm screwed, Dallas."

I sound as weak and pathetic as I always have with him. No one else knows this version of me. Since moving here, I've mellowed out a little bit – on purpose. I've been a bitch, quite frankly, in my life after Dallas.

I've kept people at arm's length; I've been needlessly hostile. I've made an art form out of not collecting friends.

After I crashed and burned out of my last job, I knew I needed to make some changes, which I've done to the best of my ability in the time since then, but I know it's been an imperfect process.

But I'm not being brave for the sake of it now. I sound scared, because I am. I sound like I need him, and I do. It's been too long without him, and I want to melt into him. I want to beg him to protect me. To hold me. To keep me.

He looks at me with those blue eyes I've never forgotten. But he's different now, too. Not a boy anymore, a man. And there's more than just comfort in those eyes. It's so intense, I look away. But he reaches out, and he takes my chin in his hand, forcing my gaze up to him.

He's so familiar, but so different now. His face chiseled now, his jaw dusted with golden stubble. I can't breathe, and I don't know if it's fear or hope making me nearly choke now.

"Sarah, you're coming home with me. Tonight."

Chapter Three

Sarah

He's so definitive that I know he's not joking. Not that he would joke about this anyway.

Not the Dallas I knew back then, anyway. I realize I'm assuming a lot, but I have to believe our soul connection-or whatever the hell it is–matters even now. With all the time and distance, I have to believe it matters.

"I feel pathetic," I say. "But I don't know what else to do, I don't know where else to turn..."

"You don't need another option," he says. "You have me. You can turn to me. You did the right thing."

I feel warm. Like I've been scratched behind the ears, which is the most bizarre comparison I can ever come up with, but I feel it.

And I just feel *happy* in the weirdest way. Like I might be able to take a full breath. Like I might be safe.

"Do you need any more to eat?"

"No. We don't need to order anything else."

"Have you been eating?"

I'm undone by that question. It's been so long since anyone has looked after my well-being.

Years.

I do have people in my life, but I don't let them in. They don't really know me. They don't know about this, about how much I'm struggling. About how I'm losing sleep, about how I can't eat. He's the one person I felt like I could trust with this information. He's the one person that I felt safe with.

"Not really. But I will. After this. Now, at least I don't feel like there's a giant rock sitting in the bottom of my stomach."

"Tell me everything. From the beginning."

"Okay. You know the story of what happened. How he was arrested and put in prison for what he did to me."

"I remember."

"Well, my mom got custody again while he was in jail. And she changed my name. Our names. To outrun one of her ex-boyfriends. Another abusive asshole. To *her*, not to me, of course. But there was always a thing with Chris to her that was just...it didn't matter what he did to me. She just couldn't let them go. She never could. So when he got out of prison... She contacted him."

"You're kidding me."

"No. And at that point, he had her contact info, and for all I know she just gave him mine. I don't know what he wants from me. But I can tell you that he's never wanted anything from me that I wanted to give him."

He looks wild then, like he's ready to commit a murder or turn the tables over, or both. He reaches across the table and puts his hand over mine. His palm is rough, his fingertips callused. The heat it generates when he touches me is a shock. Usually, touch freaks me out. Usually, I can't stand it. But right now, I need it.

There's a shift in his demeanor, his eyes going dark, the blue harsh like a flame. "That motherfucker better never touch you."

His voice is low, much lower than it was when I last saw him, the words echoing inside me, filling all those hollow, aching places that have been so pronounced for all these years.

His words are what I've needed this whole time. What I haven't gotten– not from anyone. He's on my side.

"I can't get any protection," I say. "I've tried, but the police won't help. He hasn't *done* anything. That's the problem."

He scowls. "Menacing? Harassing? Stalking?"

"I agree. But I don't have sufficient evidence of any of that. It's my word against his."

"Your word against a pedophile's word."

"You know that nobody cares," I say. "You know that, as well as I do. We know it better than anyone. There aren't any real saviors coming for kids like us. We don't matter. It's amazing, rare and..." I take a sharp breath. He and I both know that the way the world *should* work has nothing to do with reality. "That he was imprisoned at all is a minor miracle. I guess I can't expect any more than that."

"You should be able to. You should be able to expect all the protection in the world."

"That would be nice. But..." My throat aches, and suddenly, I don't want any more of the French fries. "When can we go home?"

I don't know what home is for him, I realize.

Gold Valley. The announcer said it before he rode

tonight, but I'm not totally sure where that is. Somewhere west, toward the coast, I think.

"I have another event tomorrow night. But I swear to you, right afterward, will drive out."

The idea of going back home to my apartment tonight makes my stomach hurt. And he already said that I was going home with *him* tonight...

"You're going to come to my motel room."

"I am?"

"Yes."

His tone is blunt and uncompromising. It's not a suggestion, it's a command. I don't remember Dallas being quite this bossy. But I don't remember his voice being this deep, or his hands being this rough.

A lot has changed for me. And clearly, a lot has changed for him.

"Is this insane? Because you don't really know me anymore." I feel compelled to point this out. I'm not trying to talk him out of taking me with him – I want to go with him. But it feels like someone has to be rational.

I don't *think* it's insane, but the problem with being a traumatized kid who has turned into an adult with few support systems is that sometimes I don't know when I'm being weird. There's nothing quite like having a light conversation with your friends and making a joke about the parental neglect you've experienced, which makes you laugh, only to realize they're all staring at you in abject horror.

Story of my life.

"I know you," he says, those blue eyes looking into me. "I've always known you."

Again, I'm fighting back tears, and I'm not a crier. Life hasn't given me that luxury. It's hard, and I've had to be harder. I had to put walls up around myself, around my body, around my heart. The only person who's ever gotten close to getting around them is Dallas. Because he's always been a taller wall, a stronger wall, all around me.

These last few years without him have felt hard. Rough. Like I'm constantly in danger of being dashed against the rocks.

Being back with him now is like the sweetest gift.

"I think I'm ready to go," I say.

"I'm parked over at the Expo."

"Would it be okay if we just leave my car there? That way…"

"He won't drive by the motel and see your car in the parking lot?"

"I just don't know where he is. I feel like he's everywhere. I know that isn't true. He's not a criminal mastermind. He's actually a dumbass." Anger spikes in my veins, sharp and hot. "I hate that more than anything. That he's such a dumbass, and he's managing to make me afraid again. I'm not a little girl anymore. He shouldn't be able to scare me."

"Hey," Dallas says. "Everything's hard enough without you being hard on yourself, okay? He knows you're scared of him because he made you that way, and it's not weakness for you to be afraid of someone who victimized you, who hurt you. But just so we're clear, I'm not scared of him. And I'm armed."

Dallas stands up, walks over to the register, and pays our bill. I take a deep breath and join him a moment later, walking with him out the door. It's warm outside, the air dry and crisp. Crushed glass stars glitter in a deep velvet sky, and for a moment, I let myself bask in the miracle of it all. I found him. He knows who I am. He *cares* about who I am. He wants to protect me.

Someday, I'm going to have to make it up to him for all of this. But right now, I'm just too broken, and I hate that more than I can say, but I'm a fighter. That's the truth. I've been fighting ever since I was a little girl, and I'm smart enough to know when the fight has gotten away from me. If there's a life preserver out there in the middle of the ocean, you just grab onto it. You can't worry about whether or not you're sharing an equal load with your rescuer.

He stuffs his hands in his pockets, and I followed him across the street, back toward the Expo. The parking lot is almost entirely empty now, and my car stands out like a sore thumb. We walk past it, headed back around the big arena to where there are stalls, stables, and trucks with horse trailers. It seems like this is where a lot of the cowboys choose to stay, but apparently not Dallas.

"You don't sleep here?" I ask.

He shakes his head. "No. I don't have a horse with me."

Right. Because, of course, the ropers, the barrel racers, they have their own animals with them. Whereas a bull rider like Dallas draws his animal before the event. At least I'm pretty sure that's how it works. I'm not a rodeo expert, but I did a little bit of cursory reading on it when I found out that's what he did.

A little online stalking to feel closer to him felt benign. Again, I'm not great with how normal people connect.

"I like a comfortable bed."

I can't help but wonder if there's more to it than that. If what he really likes is to have a place to take a woman back to. I can't explain the feeling that gives me. A strange sort of hot sensation that burns in the pit of my stomach.

It makes me want to growl like a bothered animal.

He belongs to me, at least that's how it's always felt. When I knew him, he was young, and none of that stood between us. But now I'm acutely aware of the fact that he's a man, and an attractive one. Normal women were probably chomping at the bit to climb all over him. To beg for the cowboy to ride them.

I just want to grab onto him, sink my nails into him so he has to stay with me forever.

That isn't normal. That's batshit crazy, and if he had any idea how intense I'm feeling inside he'd probably have regrets about letting me go with him. A lot like finding a baby raccoon on the side of the road and discovering later it's rabid.

I'm rabid. But maybe I can keep that part of myself hidden, at least for a while.

"This is me," he says. If he has any idea of what I was thinking, he doesn't indicate it. Instead, he simply opens up the passenger door to his pickup truck, and I climb up inside. He closes the door, and I'm enveloped in the silence. The safety.

I want to weep with relief.

He gets in the driver's seat and starts the engine. The truck roars to life. It's a *nice* truck.

"I take it the rodeo has done well for you," I say.

"Yeah. I've done all right for myself." He's minimizing it, I know. Probably because I'm pitiful, and he doesn't want to brag.

I realize that I know very little about his life. I had no idea that he'd found his father, not all this time.

"What's your... What's your family like?" I ask as he pulls the truck out of the parking spot, and onto the driveway that will take us out of the Expo grounds. "I'm just curious. I... This whole time I imagined that you'd stayed in care. I was heartbroken when I had to leave you behind."

"Yeah," he says, his voice rough. "I pretty much lost it when you left. And after that was when my dad found me. Like I said. I think I made his life hell there for a minute. But I didn't really know how to be loved. I'm not sure that I do still, but I have no interest in making my dad's life hell. Especially not when... I mean... My stepmother's amazing. And the kids... My half-siblings, it's great to have them, even though I'm not home with them. And they're still little. Four and six."

"Oh," I say. "They *are* little."

"How about you? You have siblings?"

"I think so. I think a couple of them are in care, but I'm not sure. I think my mom has a couple other kids she lost custody of, but they were older than me so I don't know them. As far as my bio dad, I just don't really know him. I don't know for certain, but I feel like I heard that he had some kids."

"You haven't done one of those DNA tests?" he asks.

I huff out a laugh. "People with lives as dysfunctional as mine know better than to do those."

He makes a speculative noise in the back of his throat. "You don't want to find people you're related to?"

I don't really know what to say to that. Obviously, finding his family has been a great thing for him. But I can't imagine it being the same for me. Not even remotely. Everything I know about my family suggests they're nothing more than a bunch of dirtbags, and I can't really trust that any random person wouldn't just be... A disappointment at best, dangerous at worst. Because that's my experience. You can't trust just anyone.

In fact, you're better off not trusting anyone at all.

In high school I read that ducklings will imprint the first thing they see move, which means they identify their source of comfort, care and safety, and they never look at anything else with that kind of trust.

That's me with Dallas.

I'm a fucked-up duckling who imprinted on him when I was eight.

I saw him, and I just *knew*. I knew that he was my survival, my safety, my comfort, all in one. From that first moment, everything in my soul recognized that he was mine.

Not romantically or anything like that. Just real and true and deep.

But other than that, I don't trust anyone.

"It's just right up here," he says, gesturing to the small roadside motel right off the highway. I should've known it wasn't anything fancy. There are fancy places here, but they're the sort of place you vacation in with your family, not the kind of places you just crash for a couple of nights.

Sisters is small. Cute, but small.

He pulls his truck to the front of one of the red doors and gets out. I follow him, like the sad little duckling I am.

I have a backpack with me that contains one night's worth of stuff. Because I'm hopeful in the face of adversity, I guess, and I wouldn't have said that I was an optimist of any kind, but bringing the bag suggests I might be.

Or maybe I'm just desperate, and I was going to attach myself to him like a rabid raccoon-duckling I am.

"Home sweet home," I hear him say through the window of the truck, and I smile. I get out and close the door behind me. It locks, and then I walk up to the door, walk inside ahead of him.

There's only one bed.

A strange memory twists through my stomach. We used to sleep in one bed all the time, but again, I'm pretty sure now that's weird. And I might be weird, but not so weird that I don't know that.

"I'll take the floor," he says.

He's a step ahead of me as far as the one-bed weirdness goes.

"No," I say. "You don't have to sleep on the floor. This is your room. I'll sleep on the floor."

I'm not going to suggest we share a bed.

We're not kids. Not only that, I don't actually know him. As he closes the motel room door behind him, I'm struck by how foolish this is on the surface. I knew Dallas when he was fifteen. To say that I know him now is a stretch. I knew him way back then and have a sense that I can trust him based on my own gut feeling, which is probably not the most reliable. Though it does tend to be suspicious, I suppose. So, I have that going for me.

I set my backpack down in the corner, and I look at him. The truth is, I've just gone willingly into the motel room of a man I really don't know. *Me*. Who literally has every reason to be suspicious of and generally dislike men.

Yet, here I am.

I don't feel panicked, though. I feel something else. Something I can't quite define, and don't necessarily want to.

I feel weak and trembly, but I don't want to reflect on what that feeling might be.

"You're ridiculous," he says. "You're not sleeping on the floor. I'm a gentleman, Sarah. And that's simply not something I'm prepared to allow."

He's standing there with a cowboy hat on, a button-up shirt, a big belt buckle, and blue jeans, and he does not look like a gentleman. He looks like a manufactured fantasy of classic masculinity, wrapped in this *protectiveness*, this *care* that I know for a damn fact you don't usually find on this kind of man.

"You can't be this nice to me," I say. "It's not sustainable. I'm going to get spoiled."

He scowls, his handsome face contorting. I see new lines next to his mouth, between his eyebrows. I like his more mature face. "What the fuck does that mean?"

"It's nothing. But you know... It wasn't a good thing that I went back to my mom."

He nods slowly. "I'm sure. Sarah I... You're the only person who really *knows*," he says. "I love my family. I love my family, and they have no idea what it's like to be in the system. They have no idea what it's like to experience that kind of uncertainty. You know. You know what it's like to have to pack all your stuff up in a plastic garbage bag. To wear the same pair of shoes until they're falling off your feet. Until you have blisters on your toes, because nobody remembers that they need to get new supplies for you. You're the only person in the fucking world that I know who has any idea what I've been through. It's just really great to see you again. You can have my bed. You can have whatever you need."

I take a deep breath. "I forgot what it was like to have somebody on my team."

"Fuck," he says.

Then he's closing the distance between us, wrapping his arms around me. I'm enveloped in his heat. In his warmth. The security of him. He's so much taller now. More solid. He's like a wall of muscle and comfort. Everything I've ever dreamed about, honestly.

His arms. His touch.

Him.

It has never, ever been more than a deep desire for security. But right then I feel the stirring of something else, something low in my stomach, and I shove it to the side.

And I just let him hold me. I let myself feel secure. Which is something I simply don't have a lot of experience with. Something I gave up on ever feeling.

He releases his hold on me. "I need a shower."

I swallow hard. "Yeah. Of course."

There's an open suitcase sitting on the other side of the bed, and he reaches down and grabs his clothes out of it. I perch myself on the end of the bed. "Should I... ask for extra blankets at the front desk?"

"I'll handle that," he says. "I don't want you walking out of here, and I don't want you answering the door for anyone while I'm in the shower."

"I don't think I'm in that much danger," I say.

"But you don't know that," he says.

The truth is, he's right. I *don't* know that. I haven't known for sure the whole time, that's why everything feels so terrifying.

I don't know what kind of revenge that man wants on me. If it's just to make me feel small, helpless again, if he wants to hurt me. I don't know. Foolishness would be tempting finding out for sure if I'm in danger.

Dallas disappears into the bathroom, and I hear the water running. I open up my backpack and take out my pajamas. I decide to dress quickly while he's in there. My pajamas – such as they are – are a pair of oversized men's sweats. But nobody ever sees what I sleep in, so it's never mattered whether they look nice or not.

Though I think as I look in the mirror, they definitely don't. Which seems a little bit sad now. Not that I care what

Dallas thinks about my pajamas, I guess. His shower is quick, and I find myself imagining the steps he's taking when he gets out. Drying himself off and getting dressed.

I do my best to shut my brain off as those thoughts get a little bit too intimate.

The door opens, and he steps out. The first thing I do is laugh. He's wearing a pair of black sweatpants that look identical to mine.

"Well," he says. "That's a greeting."

"Not meant to be offensive," I say.

But then, my eyes moved to his chest, which is bare and sculpted, and I find it harder to tear my eyes away than I should. I can honestly say I've never been this close to a half-naked man who looks like him.

I've never tried to be. Men are, and have been, low on my list of priorities. Which isn't to say that he isn't singular. Because that's certainly part of it. His is an above average physique. Even I, with my minimal experience, can recognize that.

"I'm going to go get blankets." He reaches down into the suitcase and takes a white T-shirt out, shrugging it on. I realize that I'm watching his every movement with the sort of forensic care. Which is weird, but I try not to worry too much about that. Or maybe worry isn't the right word.

"Lock the door while I'm out," he says.

He slips on a pair of slides, and heads out the door, and is gone for about ten minutes. I pace around the room, and I don't let myself look in his suitcase, because that would be creepy. I'm struck again by the level of intimacy he's allowing. Letting me, a functional stranger, stay in this room with him. But I suppose as a woman, the risk is greater on my end.

He says that he has a weapon.

I can imagine it. He seems like that kind of guy. There's a quiet strength about him. Something that many might mistake for being easy-going. There always has been.

There's also always been anger in him, below the surface. Anger that I could sense because it mirrored my own.

I'm tempted to go through his suitcase, but I'm not *that* feral. Only rabid. So, I don't. I just sit on the end of the bed with the motel silence bearing down on me. I can hear trucks on the highway, and my heart throbs as I imagine Chris somehow figuring out where I am. My car isn't in the parking lot.

Still, panic is beginning to rise up inside me, and I don't want Dallas to see me having a full-blown meltdown in his bedroom.

When the door opens, and Dallas appears, the enormous amount of relief I feel is enough to make tears sting my eyes. We haven't been together for so long, but suddenly I feel calm. Like maybe everything is going to be okay, and I can't remember the last time I felt that.

He has a bundle of blankets in his arms, and he smiles at me as he throws them down on the floor, like it just isn't a big deal that he's giving the bed up for me. Like he's happy to do it.

"Get your rest. You probably haven't been sleeping very well," he says, as he spreads the blankets out.

He's right. I haven't been getting rest. He's right, I can't sleep because I'm afraid that Chris is going to find me. I'm afraid he's going to hurt me.

I'm afraid he's going to make me that eight-year-old girl that I used to be. Powerless, trying to get someone to believe me. Being hurt and abused by the people I should be able to trust most.

I've worked so hard to make a life for myself. To let that stuff go. To not be defined by something I didn't choose. It's the most unfair part about being a victim of anything. That somebody takes you and imposes all their darkness onto you.

That a grown man had the power to make a young, innocent girl feel afraid of her own body. Afraid of every man. Afraid of being touched when touch is so desperately needed. He isolated me. And in the end, that might be the worst of it.

Except this. Except for him terrorizing me now.

"Thank you," I say, snuggling underneath the blankets and curling up into a ball.

Dallas reaches up to the bed and takes a pillow, and suddenly, it reminds me so much of who we were back then. Suddenly, I don't feel so terrible. I was always safe when Dallas was there. And happier too. He lies down on the floor, and I stay firmly planted in the bed, even though I'm tempted to lean over and look at him one more time.

I don't. Instead, I lie there until his breathing becomes even. Until I know he's relaxed enough to sleep, because that's how I know it's safe. Maybe that's weird. Maybe it's against all kinds of survival wisdom. But I don't care. I fall asleep listening to Dallas breathing again. And for the first time in a long time, I feel safe.

Chapter Four

Dallas

Competition day always starts early for me. I've got to get a workout in. There's a tiny, sad gym in the motel with weights, and I use those until the mildew in the walls begins to smell a bit strong. It's not the nicest place. I can afford better, but it's one of those things – why? I've made a lot of money in the circuit.

My winnings total over a million dollars, but someday I'll have to use that money for something.

To buy land, to buy a house.

This intangible fantasy of getting what my dad has. Though part of me lives in abject fear of that. I've never had a relationship. Not a deep one. I had a girlfriend in high school, which came to its natural conclusion at graduation. She went off to college across the country, and I went to the University of Oregon for a year. I just felt like I didn't know what I wanted enough to be there. Then I decided to pursue bull riding.

It was a miracle that I graduated high school, much less getting into college, honestly. My education was so interrupted all my life. I moved around a lot, I didn't have any support, and honestly, I didn't take it very seriously. It seemed pointless. Futile, even. I knew as a kid that I wasn't college-bound. In fact, I had a hard time imagining making it to adulthood. Life with Bennett changed that.

When I found my dad, the whole world opened up to me. But the problem is, I'm still carrying a lot of baggage, and none of it's his fault. I know he feels terrible about it. He didn't know about me for the first fifteen years of my life. His relationship with my biological mother was something he always regretted. The way that ended, the way that he lost touch with her, all of it. It's crazy to me to think that by the time my dad was my age he was a dad, even if he didn't *know* he was a dad.

I remember getting to be about my mom's age when she had me. Sixteen, fuck. It gave me a lot more sympathy for her than I ever had at any other point in my life. Honestly, I just always thought that she should've sucked it up and raised me. Taken care of me, because anything would be better than bouncing around foster care.

But I know differently than that now. I know that, because the greatest failures in Sarah's life were really the system having custody of her. Her mother put her in the most dangerous situation she could have. She created all these problems that Sarah is still dealing with. So yeah, I no longer come down on the side that parents should try to keep their kids no matter what. But man, when I was young, I was sure angry about it. I felt like she gave up on me.

Maybe part of me still does. There's got to be some reason I'm out here doing this, instead of following in my dad's footsteps.

I could be a veterinarian.

That would be respectable.

I guess I still could if I want to spend all that time in school. I have the money. I'm running along the highway, and I increase my pace as I turn around, heading back toward the motel. Sarah is safely locked in the room, and I want to take her to get some breakfast before we head over to the Expo. I like to spend the day getting myself totally familiarized with the surroundings – even though it's day three of the rodeo, I need to do my walk-through. Need to let the place sink into my bones.

I'm superstitious.

Hell, anyone who does this ought to be.

You're at the mercy of fate. Of an animal who genuinely doesn't care if you live or die, and whose life wouldn't change if you did die. I find that reassuring in some ways. Maybe reassuring is the wrong word. It reminds me of how small I am, though. How much I don't matter.

I try not to carry around too much main character energy.

That just puts a whole lot of pressure on everything you do, when in reality, all the little choices that you make on a given day don't matter all that much. Just don't go around hurting other people, that's what I figure. There's no cosmic deity who gives a shit as to whether or not I take a left or right on my run this morning.

I knew people who thought like that in high school. Who thought that they needed to consult God about every single thing they did, from what they were going to have for breakfast in the morning to who they were going to take to prom.

Maybe it's my background, but I figure God is a little bit

too busy to weigh in on your prom date. I've seen what real problems look like.

My lungs are burning by the time I make it back to the motel room, and I'm sweating. I pull my shirt off right as I walk in, and glance around the room, not seeing Sarah anywhere.

I hear the shower running, and I grimace. Because I really need the shower. I'm disgusting. I have a low tolerance for that, and I draw that back to a childhood that carries traces of neglect. Sometimes the water wasn't turned on, so it wasn't like I could have a bath every day. Now I like to be clean all the time, which is kind of a bummer given my chosen career. There's a lot of dust, a lot of sweat. I don't mind it for a short amount of time, but that's it. It's probably a control thing, really.

Issues. They're my generational wealth. The inheritance that I got from my mother.

I feel a little bit of guilt when I think about her.

Marnie. I know her name. I don't really know what happened to her after she lost custody of me.

But I do know that she was a teenager. I do know that she didn't have support, and while I know she also chose not to seek support from my dad, I can't know for sure what all was going on with her when she made that decision. Life is complicated. I've tried to be a little more understanding as the years have gone on.

The door to the bathroom opens, and Sarah emerges, dressed in a different outfit than the one she had on before. A sundress with little yellow flowers. Her dark hair is wet, beginning to curl, and her cheeks are pink from the warm water. It's weird, cognitive dissonance. Because I know her. I've known her in this capacity for a long time, even though there were years between. We were like siblings.

But now, when there's a woman getting out of my shower, it's usually because I had sex with her.

So, my body is reacting to this moment in weird ways, and it makes me feel astronomically guilty, because I also am so familiar with her background of abuse. The last thing that she needs is a guy thinking things about her when the situation isn't sexual at all.

It feels like a violation of her, and I take that little, blooming feeling of tension in my stomach, and pick it off aggressively like I would pick a dead blossom off a plant in my stepmom's flower bed.

"Morning," I say.

"Morning," she says, looking away from me, and I'm suddenly very conscious that I'm half dressed.

"I need a quick shower," I say.

She nods. "Yeah."

I grab my clothes out of my suitcase and head straight into the bathroom, closing the door and locking it behind me. The water is warm instantly, because Sarah just used it, but I need cold water coming in from that run. I spend the next five minutes standing underneath a punishing spray before soaping up, rinsing and getting out and dressed as quickly as possible.

When I come back out into the room, Sarah is folding the blankets on the floor. Something about that makes me smile. That she's trying to make it easier for whoever has to clean up after we go.

"Breakfast?"

"Oh. Sure. Actually, if we could go to the diner that I work at, Daisy's, that would be good."

"Sure," I say.

"I'm going to have to quit. I feel bad leaving them in the

lurch, but my boss does know about Chris. I mean, not the whole story, but she knows that he's been harassing me."

"She won't be surprised, then."

"No. Also, if he shows up around there, they don't let him stay. They can't stop him from loitering across the street or anything like that, but they don't let him into the diner."

I nod, and we pack everything up in the motel room, loading it all into my truck and heading to the diner.

I've been to countless diners across the country, traveling with the rodeo. This is the sort of place you find in Anytown, USA. A vague 1950s flair, booths covered in thick red vinyl. A bar with chrome stools. For lunch, they have hamburgers and milkshakes, for breakfast, bacon, eggs, and toast drowned in butter, which is exactly what I want out of the most important meal of the day.

We're greeted by Sarah's boss, who looks at me like I'm an alien, which makes me wonder more about her life here.

I guess she doesn't bring men to breakfast here on a normal day.

What does a normal day look like for her?

I spent years with her, and now she's a stranger who feels like home to my heart. But I don't know what she likes for breakfast, or what kind of men – or women – she dates. I don't know what her favorite foods are or where she likes to shop, or what music she likes.

"We have a table right in the corner," the woman, who I assume is Daisy, says.

"Thank you," says Sarah. She clears her throat. "This is my... My friend. Dallas. We were in care together."

Daisy's demeanor shifts. "Oh. Well, that's... Nice to meet you."

I nod. "Nice to meet you, too."

It's funny. Because I don't tell people about my time spent in foster care. I have a family, and so when we talk about families, I just talk about mine like I was always there. I don't get into what happened before I found Bennett. But I wonder if Sarah has to tell people because she still doesn't have a family around her, and it raises questions.

"I just want to thank you for everything you've done," Sarah says. "But I'm... I'm leaving town. With Dallas. I need to get away because –"

Daisy nods. "Of course. But you know that you always have a job if you need one."

"That's so nice of you."

"Where do you live?" She directs that question at me.

"Gold Valley," I say as we walk across the diner and go sit in the booth.

"I have a friend who lives there. Sammy Daniels. She makes jewelry. If you need a job, Sarah, I could put in a word with Sammy. She's pregnant, so I know she's looking to cut her hours at the store."

Sarah looks completely shocked by this. "I... well, that would be amazing."

"I'll give her a call. You've been amazing here, and I'm really sorry to see you go. But I get why. I just wish there was more I could do."

"You've done so much for me," Sarah says.

"I wish I could commit murder for you," Daisy says.

We sit down in the booth, and she doesn't even look at a menu; she just orders a standard breakfast, and I do the same.

"I'm still surprised when people take care of me like this," she says, looking down at her hands as Daisy goes off to the kitchen to put in our order.

"You deserve it," I say.

"You don't really know if I deserve it. You don't know me. Oh, we're going to have to get my things out of my apartment."

"What can you leave behind?"

"Most everything."

"How about this? We'll come back in a month or so and clear everything out, then you can get it all. But let's not trigger Chris thinking that you're leaving. Let's give it some time."

She nods. "That's smart."

"Just get your essentials. We'll do that before we head to the Expo."

We eat our breakfast, which is better than the average diner, I have to say, and say a muted goodbye to Daisy. I'm appreciative of this moment, and the fact that she understands everything needs to look as normal as possible. For Sarah's safety.

I'm glad that she's had a community around her that will protect her, even if law enforcement can't or won't.

The next stop is her apartment. I don't know what I expected from it. But somehow it isn't that. It's small, above a garage in a small neighborhood. "The main house is a vacation rental," she explains. "So, there are different people here all the time."

"Good thing Chris didn't figure out how to rent that place," I say, my chest getting tight. There's a look of horror on Sarah's face at the suggestion.

"Yes. Very good. And I worry that he would've figured that out eventually."

We head up the narrow staircase and go inside. I fight the urge to go in in front of her like it's a cop movie, and make sure it's all clear, but I am scanning the place as we enter, thinking about what I'd grab to use as a weapon if that asshole is in here waiting.

I don't see anything out of the ordinary, though.

Her house is neat. Perfectly organized. Something about that makes me feel a rush of emotion. The strong kind that I'm not accustomed to feeling, but that I've been steeped in ever since I saw Sarah for the first time yesterday.

"You got your house," I say.

"And he's taking it from me," she says softly. "I wish that I were braver, Dallas."

"Hey," I say, moving over to her, grabbing her shoulders and squaring her toward me. I'm not sure if I should do that. I don't know if I should touch her without asking, but she doesn't shrink away from me. "You're brave. He's insane. He's a bad person, Sarah, and he's already proved to you that he doesn't care about hurting you. In fact, he wants to. You can't put anything past someone like that. He's the worst, most vile sort of person. Anyone who would hurt her child, then go on to mentally torture her as an adult is someone that you should be scared of. It's basic survival. You and I both know survival."

She sighs, the sound heavy. "I just wish I didn't have to. I wish she could mean nothing to me. I wish that I didn't have to carry around the weight of his sins. But he's... he's fucked up my entire life. It shaped me into who I am. And I *hate* that. I can ignore it when he was imprisoned at least, but now he's out, and it's like he's a ghost of my past, hunting everything that should be mine."

Her eyes are filled with tears, but they're angry tears. I reach up, and I catch one with my thumb as it begins to slide down her cheek. "I can't take that away. I never could. But I'm not a little kid anymore, either, I promise you this. If he comes anywhere near you, I'll kill him."

"Dallas..."

"You think I'm kidding, but I'm not." I look at her, and I make a vow, burn it into my heart as I speak it out loud. "I'll kill him, and I'll deal with the consequences later."

Because he deserves it. The man who wounded her like this isn't even fit to be called a man. He's little more than an animal; people shoot rabid dogs for less, and this man should be shot just like that.

She packs up slowly, and I can see a sadness in her movements.

My heart is heavy for her.

But I realize there's nothing I'd rather do than be here with her right now. Then try to help her carry some of the weight of this. She has a little sideboard in the corner of the room, and there's a small picture on it. My heart jumps in my chest when I realize what it is. Us.

"Where did you get this?" I ask as I look at it. She must be ten, I'm maybe thirteen. I'm pulling the edges of my smile out as wide as possible by hooking my fingers into my cheeks, and she's wearing a princess hat, leaning against me, smiling, eyes glittering bright.

"I think we got it after a birthday party?" She looks at me, her brows pleated, a little crease between them.

"I don't remember." I walk over to the sideboard and pick up the photo, pressing my fingertips over our smiles. It's in a little circular frame with gilded edges, like a precious object, and that does something to me.

"That photo has moved with me into a lot of different apartments," she says softly.

"I don't have any pictures of you," I say.

"I just have this one. I think I stole it from you when I had to go back to my mom."

The strength of our connection feels profound in that

moment. I remember the grief. The horrendous grief of losing her.

"I'm never going to lose you again," I say.

It's a promise.

"Well, I'm not planning on running away."

She walks over to me and takes the picture out of my hand. Hold it against her chest. Then she carries it into her room, where her suitcase is sitting on the foot of her bed, and puts it inside. She closes the suitcase and zips it up. "I think that's what I really need for now."

"You're going to move in with me," I say.

"I am?"

I realize I haven't explained anything to her.

"Yeah. I have a place on my dad's property."

She blinks. "Your dad has property?"

"I told you. He's a veterinarian. He's... He's pretty well-off, actually." I don't know why I feel a vague, creeping sense of shame about that. About having money. About having things. Except, I knew so many kids in the same situation as Sarah and I, and they didn't get this kind of hand up in life that I got. And what have I done for anybody? This is the first thing. The first opportunity that I've had to do something meaningful with the gift that I received being taken in by Bennett Dodge.

"I am so thankful for you," she says. I feel like that's not even a thing for her to say. She shouldn't have to be grateful to be taken care of.

But life's not fair. *Life's not fair*. I've been given this gift, this gift of a family, and she hasn't been given anything. That really isn't fair.

Sometimes I think I have survivor's guilt.

That I get mad about that, because why should the survivor get the luxury of guilt?

I shove all that to the side, and I go into the bedroom and take her suitcase for her. I don't even let her start to protest, and we lock the apartment back up and head to my truck.

"After tonight's event, we're driving to Gold Valley. It's a little bit of a haul. But we just need to get out of here."

She nods. "I just want to go home with you."

Chapter Five

Sarah

I don't know what to expect today at the Expo. I'm being given a behind-the-scenes look at the rodeo, and I can't say that I ever really fantasized about having one. But here we are.

My heart feels bruised from everything that happened this morning. From having to quit my job, showing Dallas my apartment, and facing the reality that I'm leaving it. We parked my car there, so that it would look like I'm home. Part of Dallas's plan to keep Chris from realizing what's happening.

I hate that he's forcing me out. I hate that the little life I built for myself is being absolutely demolished by the hovering specter of Christopher Murphy. I know that he's small.

I know he doesn't matter.

I know that he's the worst sort of person.

Someone who doesn't deserve loyalty, who doesn't deserve to be at the forefront of anyone's thoughts.

I know that, and yet he has the power to make me afraid.

I don't focus on that, though. Instead, I focus on my surroundings. It's an organized chaos, animals and rodeo officials everywhere. Everything is a lot more regimented than I could've ever imagined. The riders are randomly assigned the animals that they have for the events, so there's a coordination effort that happens in back offices, I certainly never imagined. There are judges, the bull fighters, who I usually think of as rodeo clowns. There are men on hand to help open the gates, to get all the animals where they need to be.

Dallas gives me an overview of everything, and for a little while, I'm taken out of my life. Out of all of my issues. It's amazing, if I'm honest.

There's a refreshment tent in the back, serving meals, barbecue mainly, and beer on tap. Again, I remind Dallas that I can't drink yet. He laughs and gets us a couple of waters and two plates of barbecue goodness- brisket, potato salad, and baked beans. "I don't drink before events," he says, holding up the water.

"Hey! Dodge."

We both turn at the sound of someone calling out to Dallas. There's a tall, handsome man with dark hair heading our direction, a blonde woman at his side.

"Sarah," Dallas says. "This is Colt. He's another one of the bull riders. And this is Stella, she's a barrel racer."

Stella is beautiful. Athletic and compact, with bright blue eyes and freckles scattered across her nose. The strange flood of possessiveness that I feel, standing next to Dallas, is not entirely unfamiliar to me. It reminds me of being a kid, whenever a new foster sibling would come into the family, or when Dallas and I would get moved to a new house, and I felt the need to make sure that all the other kids knew that even if he was nice to them, they weren't special to him. Not like I was.

It's such a weird, childish feeling, and yet mixed with something that doesn't feel childish at all, that I don't want to look at too closely.

"This is Sarah," he says. "I... I knew her back when we were kids."

He doesn't introduce me as his foster sister. I guess I'm not, currently. But it's still noticeable that he edits out the truth of our relationship, and I'm curious about why, but I also can't ask right now.

"Nice to meet you," says Stella, who is as bright and lovely as her beautiful face suggests, and I am irritated by it.

"You here for the event?"

"She's coming back to Gold Valley with me," Dallas says, and again he offers no real explanation, though this time I'm relieved.

"Oh, Gold Valley," says Stella. "I've been there a couple of times. It's really pretty."

"Yeah, it's fine," Colt says. "Boring."

"It's not boring," Dallas says.

"That isn't what you thought in high school. Anyway, maybe it's because I grew up there. Spent my whole childhood in that place," Colt says, turning a chair around backwards and sitting straddling it, looking at me with a smile that I'm sure most women consider charming. He's extremely handsome, in every way that one might measure that metric. His jaw is square, his dark eyes are compelling. He's got the kind of easy smile that transforms his entire face from a brooding intensity to the brilliance of the sun.

But he just doesn't do anything for me. In general, no one does.

That's another thing that's been taken from me.

Because touch has become weaponized. And all these years later, I haven't figured out a way to make it not something that just reminds me of violations of trust. Anyway, I've never wanted to get close enough to a man to try and work through it. I don't mean physically. Emotionally.

That's one reason Dallas has always been so important to me. Touching him has never felt scary.

I look between Colt and Stella, and I wonder if there's something romantic between the two of them, though it doesn't seem so. And now that I'm not being weird and possessive about Dallas, I can't see any special connection between him and Stella either. She's not gazing at him with any sort of admiration. Which I find kind of insane, because every time I look at him, I'm flooded with admiration.

Colt suddenly grimaces, and Dallas follows his gaze. "Oh, good, the bad guy has arrived." Colt looks murderous. I don't need to be a keen judge of people to read that.

"Who's that?" I ask.

The hairs on the back of my neck stand up, and I tell myself not to be dramatic, because it's not like there's an actual bad guy roaming around the rodeo, but I don't take accusations of men being bad lightly. For obvious reasons.

"Maverick Quinn," Stella says, leaning forward. She jerks her head back, and I follow the motion. It's like people part as this man walks into the food tent. As if everyone knows better than to be in his way. There's a confident swagger to the way he walks, and a wall of unfriendliness. I recognize it. The man is a walking red flag, but he's also a walking tribute to trauma. I can clock it from this far away. The rest of them don't see it, but I do.

I can also see that he's toxic. No doubt about it.

He's wearing a black cowboy hat, a black shirt, and black jeans. He has a dark, heavy beard, and there's a malice to the smile on his face that suggests he enjoys all that darkness. Playing in it, making others have to contend with it.

Stella shivers just slightly, and I realize that Colt and Dallas aren't on her radar at all. For a reason.

I guess everybody has inclinations toward making a little bit of trauma in their lives, even if they don't come by it naturally.

"I'll be back in Gold Valley too," Colt says. "If all goes well tonight."

"In what way?" I ask.

"Well, we have to get high enough scores tonight to qualify for the championships. Or we don't, and we have to keep going to try and scrape up enough points at some of the smaller events. But the ideal will be to finish out on top."

Dallas laughed. "That's always the idea."

"I have to keep going," says Stella. "Because mainly I'm just trying to win money. They don't have a championship like that for barrel racing. It doesn't get the same kind of attention."

I frown. "That doesn't seem fair."

"Welcome to sports," Stella says. "None of it's fair. But that's not why I do it. I do it because I love it."

"So," I say, looking around the tent. "If you all don't compete for the rest of the year, that must make the rodeo boring in other cities."

"That's flattering," Colt says. "But yeah. The best riders are out before the season is over. There's no point tempting injury for points you don't need."

"Yeah. Better to go rest up before you try to go win big at the championship."

"Have you ever won before?" I ask.

Colt and Dallas laughed. "No. That's a million-dollar pot all on its own," Colt explains. "If I win that, I'm out. Retiring."

"Liar," says Stella. "If you were just here for the money, you would have been gone a long time ago because you really do have enough. You want the clout."

Colt shrugs. "I suppose so. But I'd like to test that theory by winning the championship."

"You have to compete with me," Dallas says.

"You both have to compete with Maverick," Stella points out.

"Plus, everybody that comes outside of this regional circuit," Dallas says. "You get into the championships and you're competing with global stars. It's a lot harder."

"And the bulls are meaner." Colt grins at the prospect.

I don't like the sound of that, but I realize that Dallas isn't asking my permission to do his job. Nor should he. But it makes me nervous, knowing that he does something so dangerous. I'm also kind of in awe of him.

I don't feel especially brave. I feel like I have a small life geared toward my safety, and that hasn't even actually kept me safe. He's out there. Wild. Brave.

"I have some pre-riding rituals I need to do," Dallas says, looking a little bit sheepish.

"What?" I ask, amusement making me smile.

"I don't usually have to explain it, because these two get it," he says, gesturing to Colt and Stella.

"Yeah. I have some things I need to do, also," Colt says. "You have to appease the gods."

"The arena gods," Stella says, hand on her heart. "You get a little bit superstitious. Because you win after you do a certain set of routines, and then you want to make sure you keep doing it."

"And you never want to repeat something that you did before you had a ride that went badly, or before you got injured," Colt says.

"Do you get injured?"

"I broke my jaw last year," he says. "I got hit in the side of the face by the bull's horn. I'm lucky he didn't tear my face open. If he'd hit me with a sharp edge, I'd have gotten cut open from jaw to nose."

I put my hand on my stomach. "That sounds horrible."

"Yeah. But it's great," Colt says.

Dallas smiles. "I just need to take a few laps around, then... other things."

I tilt my head at his vagueness. "Is it bad luck to tell me what your superstitions are?"

"I don't know," he says. "I've never spoken them out loud. Which means I won't be doing it today. *Afterward*. Afterward, we'll have the conversation."

He doesn't leave me alone without making sure that I'm settled. He puts me in the corner of a space that's something like a green room and gives some information to a woman who seems to be in charge of the area. After that, I'm given water and offered food continually throughout the day, while I wait for the rodeo to start. Then I'm ushered to amazing seats that give me a prime view of all the proceedings.

Until last night, I'd never been to a rodeo. This is quite literally my first one.

Today, it feels no less electrifying as I sit there watching as rodeo royalty rides out on their horses, flags held up in the air and streaming behind them. There's a stirring rendition of the national anthem, followed by *Friends in Low*

Places, which I don't know, but everyone in the crowd seems to know. I feel like I'm missing an important piece of the culture with that one.

The bareback bronc riding is first, and that's enough to get my adrenaline pumping, my pulse ratchets up, and doesn't go back down. Not during the calf roping, the steer wrestling, or the saddle bronc riding. Barrel racing is right before the bulls, who are the grand finale of the night. I'm captivated by the fierce, strong barrel racers. How they guide their horses with speed and precision.

When Stella Lane is announced, I jump to my feet and cheer for her. Like she's been my best friend for years, and not just a girl I sat and had lunch with. All her strength is on display as she steers her horse around the barrels, leaving each one standing, every turn tight and fast.

Her score puts her in second place, and she's grinning from ear to ear when she finishes.

I'm disappointed for her that she didn't get first. I thought she was better. Not that I know anything. But still.

When it's time for the bull riding, I actually feel dizzy.

Dallas could get hurt.

That gut feeling that gives me is heavy, and the weight lodges down in my stomach. What would happen if he did get hurt? I would take care of him, obviously.

Well. He has a family.

He also does this all the time without me sitting here. Manages to navigate his career just fine. But Colt's story about breaking his jaw is reverberating inside my head, a reminder that injuries are probably extremely common in this line of work. I swallow hard and wait. The first rider gets bucked off the bull in less than a second. I gasp, even though I should probably be cheering for his downfall since that makes things easier for Dallas.

I don't want to see anyone get hurt.

The next rider up is Maverick Quinn, and in my heart, I root against him. I can see why he's the beloved villain of the circuit. There is something magnetic about him. The animal that he's on gives him a fierce fight, but he stays on for the full eight seconds. Jumping off and turning his back to the crowd as he walks back out. Every footstep shows that he thinks he's the best, his stone-faced refusal to acknowledge the people cheering for him giving the impression he believes the adulation is his right. His score is high enough to put him in the top, for now. But when Colt and Dallas talked earlier, it sounded to me like they expected that. To be somewhere in the top three along with him, and that's what they need.

I want Dallas to win.

There are three other riders I don't know, and only one of them manages to get a score. Then Colt is up.

His bull bursts out of the gate, explosive movements and twists and turns, jerking his body all around. But he stays on. It's the most intense ride that I've seen tonight, and he completes it beautifully, eight seconds flying by quickly before he jumps off and pumps his fist in the air, hyping up the crowd and drinking in the attention with a giddy kind of joy that feels infectious.

If Maverick is the villain, Colt feels like the affable golden retriever mascot. Colt moves into first place, ahead of Maverick. Now, only Dallas is left.

I'm not sure I can watch. Honestly, I feel like I might throw up. I don't know how anybody does this all the time. How they watch people they care about put themselves at risk like this, and then there's the element of competition on top of everything else. It isn't enough to just not die. You have to win, also.

Well, I don't need him to win.

But he wants to win. That matters to me. It matters to me a lot.

I can see him, on the back of the bull, adjusting the straps beneath his hand. Adjusting his positioning. His body jerked violently as the animal kicks in the chute. But his face is determined. Set. He's ready, and I can feel it echoing inside of me.

I can still feel him. Like we're still connected by an invisible string. The same one that has always tied us together.

He draws a breath in, and I match it. Then, the gate is open, and the bull bursts out into the arena. He isn't doing quite as much as Colt's, which gave him a wild ride. But it's still intense, Dallas's body jerking hard with every movement, and I wonder what the hell that does to your back after enough years.

It makes me weirdly angry. Watching this animal do that to him. Watching him put his body through it, his precious body that I care about so much. It's so weird.

But then, we've already established that I'm weird. Most especially about him. Possessive and definitely not logical.

The seconds are moving too slowly. I can't breathe. And then, we pass eight. He made it.

He jumps off the bull, and the animal turns around and goes straight for him. I stand up, shouting something. He jumps up on the side of the arena walls and narrowly escapes getting clipped by the horns. The bull fighters are doing everything in their power to lure the animal away, but it's far more interested in digging a chunk out of Dallas than in going quietly back into its pen.

Finally, two men on horses come out, and one lassoes

the bull right around his horns, pulling at him insistently while the bull stands there, four feet planted on the ground, pulling back away from them.

The other rider moves around the back, and finally, with some reluctance, the bull moves back into the chute.

Dallas jumps off the wall, the crowd cheering wildly, and finally, I can breathe again. He waves and looks up at the scoreboard. They rank him second, and I can see the irritation on his face with his friend's name above his. But he's qualified. As far as I know. I'm selfishly so pleased, because that means he'll be home until the championships. I don't know when those are.

I have him now. And I don't have to watch him do that again. I feel sweaty, drained, like I'm the one who just finished riding a two-ton animal.

I know where to find him because I did it last night. I walk out of the stands and head around to the side of the arena. He's back there, letting out a hard breath, taking his hat off. Colt is standing next to him, grinning like a fool. Maverick is nowhere to be seen. As annoyed as Dallas is to come in second to his friend, I imagine it's nothing compared to how irritated Maverick is coming in third to two people who don't like him.

Of course, that's all speculation based on my assumptions about the dynamic between everyone. But I'm unerring in my assessments most of the time.

I don't plan my next move. My body just acts, launching across the space between me and Dallas. I wrap my arms around his neck. "You're amazing."

Chapter Six

Dallas

I secured my place in the final, which should feel more triumphant than it does.

I suppose it's nice that Colt won. Mainly, though, all I can think about is Sarah running up to me in the aftermath of the ride, wrapping her arms around me. She's sleeping now, has been since the clock ticked past midnight, leaning against the passenger window as we cruise across the state, from Sisters to Gold Valley. It's almost a six-hour drive, and even though we hightailed it out of there as quickly as possible, it's going to be past two in the morning by the time we pull into my parents' place.

Just being with her gives me a strange sense of calm.

She shifts, and — seatbelt still on — reverses position, lying across the truck seat, her head in the middle, her hand on my thigh. She's not awake. I take one hand off the wheel and push my fingers through her hair. She makes a sleepy, satisfied sound, and suddenly I feel like everything is right with the world. In a way that it hasn't been for a very long time.

I turn on the radio and crack the window, anything to keep me alert, and she stays resting against my thigh. When we roll past the familiar welcome sign that says *Welcome to the Gold Valley,* I feel like I can take a full breath.

I have her. She's home with me.

The family ranch is a little ways out of town, and for some reason, this time when I turn up the familiar dirt driveway, I'm reminded of the first time I was ever here.

Fifteen years old, with my social worker, Grace, who was really and truly one of the best people I ever encountered in the system. Patient with my nonsense, and with a genuine desire to help. Maybe it's being with Sarah that makes me think of the past. Because I've driven up this road countless times since then. It's become my home, in such a profound way that sometimes I don't remember life beforehand. Sometimes my life before this feels like it doesn't matter or doesn't exist. Except for Sarah.

Now that she's here... all is well. Kind of. I'm not going to be able to let go of that man harassing her, and I swear I'm going to make sure he ends up back in prison or dead before all this is over. If he touches even one hair on her head, he's a dead man. That's a fact.

I don't play when it comes to my family. Sarah is my family.

She was my family before Bennett Dodge ever was. Before Kaylee became my stepmother. Before my half-siblings were born. She was my purpose, my reason before all of this.

I drive around all the familiar potholes on the driveway, bypassing my mom and dad's place as I head around the back of the property to where my cabin is. I pull up to the front and turn the engine off, putting the truck in park.

"We're there," I say, touching her face.

She looks up at me with sleepy eyes, and my stomach goes tight. It's like an engine inside of me revving up. An intensity building that I don't have a name for. It's not like anything I've ever felt before. It's not attraction, purely. It's also not *not* attraction. And I don't want to feel that. Not for her. Not when she needs safety. Stability. Not when she needs me to be safe.

She sits up, wiping at her eyes. I get out of the truck and go around to her side. I reach across and unbuckle her, gathering her up into my arms. She hangs onto me as I carry her up the steps and into the house. I have a second bedroom here, I just never use it. But it's furnished. My dad lets family stay in it when I'm gone. I lay her down in the bed and close the bedroom door firmly behind her. I'll get everything out of the truck in the morning. For now, I just need to sleep.

Morning comes far too quickly. I can hear all the roosters crowing aggressively from my mom's chicken coop.

Great. I groan, rolling over and putting my pillow over my head for a second. Then I remember that Sarah is here.

Sitting up, I fling the covers off. I rub my face as I stumble out of my bedroom and into the living room. I went to bed in my jeans and T-shirt. That's how exhausted I was.

I stop when I get to the dining room. I can see my front door, and there's a note on the window.

I go and I open it, looking down and seeing a tray with a covered platter, and a vase of flowers in it. Then I snag the note off the window.

. . .

Your dad looked at the doorbell camera footage from last night when you got home and saw that you had a guest. Breakfast for two.
-Mom

I shake my head. I should've known they would be tracking my every move – in a loving and nonjudgmental way, of course because that's how they are. Knowing my dad, he just wanted to make sure that I got home safely. I don't usually bring women back here. Not that I never have, but it's definitely *not* a common enough occurrence for anyone in my family to have opinions about my sex life.

I used to push him with comments about it. And hell, I was a little shit when I got here. Almost sixteen and I'd spent the last year so angry without Sarah. I'd gotten into my share of trouble – stealing things and vandalizing businesses. I'd started sleeping around because sex was free, and it gave me a feeling of emotional closeness to the person, even if it was just for a while.

I changed when I got to Gold Valley. Changed thanks to the love my dad and Kaylee showed me.

They're wrong here, though.

Sarah has nothing to do with my sex life, and I'm going to be making sure my family is aware of that as soon as possible.

I grab the tray and bring it inside. I lift up the cover on the platter and make an audible sound when I see the stack of pancakes.

I put the vase in the center of the table and take out the plate of pancakes. She also included a little jar of preserves and one of lemon curd. A bowl of heavy cream, some fresh berries and some maple syrup.

She's a great woman, my stepmom. Mostly, I think of her as my mom. I don't really have another one. If I ever think of her as my stepmom, it's because I'm caught up in thinking about the past. But I just call her mom.

I hear a stirring sound behind me, and I turn to see Sarah standing in the doorway. "You made breakfast?"

"No. My mom did. My *stepmom*. Kaylee."

"Oh," she says, walking into the room and looking at the beautiful spread. There's a strange emotion on her face and I can't quite place what it is.

"What?"

"Your life is just so beautiful," she says, looking around the little log cabin. It's rustic, but I have to admit that it's charming.

I try to evaluate it like I'm seeing it for the first time. The floor is wood, with a geometric patterned rug in dusty blue colors sitting in the blank space between the living room and the kitchen. The walls are split logs, treated with a varnish that makes them look warm and shiny. The cabinets in the kitchen are stained cherry, a nice contrast to the walls. I've always liked it.

"Is this a working ranch?" she asks.

"Nah. Not really. We have horses, which..." I realize that she doesn't know about my journey after foster care, my journey to the rodeo.

Connecting to my dad was a surprise when I moved here, but the connection I found to horses was an even more unexpected development. It's such a deep love that goes down to my bones. That's become part of who I am. Another thing that's hard for me to remember a time when I wasn't like this.

The before and after feels so strong right now.

"Lucy was my first horse," I say, grief making my chest

heavy. I've mourned her like a family member since she died four years ago. She wasn't just a horse, she was my way into this new life. The first thing I was really comfortable loving here.

"How long did you have her?" Sarah asks, her voice soft.

"Five years. She was older when I moved here. We almost lost her in the first few months I was here it was kind of my intro to ranch life. It's when I got to see my dad in action. He's a great vet. He loves animals and…I discovered I love them too. He had a couple of Australian Shepherds when I moved in, too – Pepper and Cheddar. He got a new puppy after I'd been here a while, Dougie, and he's still around and old. Then he got puppies for the girls once they were old enough to handle them. Though, we could debate whether or not they're actually taking care of them at all, so when we head over to the house it's going to be chaos."

"Girls?" Sarah asks.

"Yeah, my little sisters. Cara and Lucy."

"Wasn't Lucy your horse?"

I feel the back of my neck get hot. "Yeah, I…named her. After my horse. Which, when you say it like that, it seems kind of weird, but at the time it made sense."

She's smiling at me, and it makes me want to look away from her. I don't, though, so our eyes just hold for an uncomfortably long time and my chest feels sore.

"So yeah, there's Lucy, who's four, and Cara, who just turned six. Well, and the dogs."

"That sounds like a nice big Christmas," she says, her smile looking a little bit dreamy. "It is. Come on and eat. We're not going to be able to avoid my family very long. I think they've jumped to some incorrect conclusions about your presence."

She frowns, going over to the table as I go to the kitchen and fire up the coffee maker. Caffeine is important.

"In what way?"

"I think my dad saw me carrying you inside on his security camera. You know, it goes off whenever somebody approaches the house. It's practical because I'm gone all the time. I don't think he means to use it to spy on me. Or maybe he does.

Truthfully, Bennett's not the kind of dad to be too up in my business. We're close, but my dad respects the fact that I lived the first fifteen years of my life without family. That doesn't mean he gave me total freedom during my teenage years. Quite the opposite

But he held on loosely with certain things, because what's the point of being overprotective when your kid had already been through a host of traumatic things by the time he was five? It was never about him overprotecting me, overcompensating. He gave me boundaries to let me know he cared.

I do wonder sometimes, though, if he's a little more overprotective than I realize. Because he was up last night at some point, making sure I was home.

And hadn't texted or anything to let me know he was waiting, or to say that he was worried. He's not the type to get up in my business like that, but maybe my dad worries about me more than he pretends to.

I feel weirdly warmed by that.

The coffee maker is running too slow, and I pace around in front of it while Sarah serves herself pancakes.

"These are amazing," she says, focusing on eating, which I can't start until I have my coffee.

I realize that I left my phone in my room, and I go to grab it, because honestly, I wouldn't put it past my mom to show up and knock, desperate for Intel. So, it's better to just text her.

I grab my phone off my nightstand, and I see that I do, in fact, have two unread text messages.

I look at Kaylee's text first.

> I left breakfast for you and your friend out front.

And then my dad's.

> Sorry, ratted you out. You're probably going to get interrogated later.

I press the message and give Dad a thumbs down, while I go back to my mom's message and give her a thumbs up.

Then I return to the kitchen just in time for the coffee maker to finish running. I pour a cup of coffee for myself and one for Sarah, bringing it over to the table. I've never actually had breakfast with a woman in my house before. Another way that Sarah is special. As she should be.

Because she's still one of the most important people in my life, even with a ten-year gap between meetings.

"Well, my family isn't planning to invade, but we should go over to the house and meet everybody soon." I pause. "How much do you want them to know?"

She looks down at her plate. "You can tell them whatever. I mean, you might as well tell them the truth. You have siblings, what if he follows us here..."

"First of all, that's not going to happen. He's not tailing you, and we left your car for a reason. We left a lot of things for a reason. Didn't make a production out of moving out. We're six hours away. But also, he'd be rolling up on a whole Dodge militia. My dad has two brothers, and his sister is pretty mean if I'm honest. And when I tell you, they're not going to take kindly to you being threatened, I mean it."

She blinks. "Oh. Of course. You have this whole big family."

"Yeah. I do."

"It's really amazing, Dallas. Whenever I thought of you, I was so worried that you were still alone. When I left you were still in foster care."

"Yeah. I already mentioned that it kind of pushed me over the edge when you left. But all that is what led to finding my dad. They got desperate. They didn't have anywhere else to put me."

"Losing me really did that to you?" She looks hungry for the answer.

I get it. I know that feeling way too well, and she hasn't had the family I've had these past nine years making everything better.

Reunification is supposed to be a good thing. It's supposed to be the kind of thing that a kid in care dreams of. But in her case, it was a nightmare. It didn't give her anything good. The irony that she lost support when she went back to her mother is definitely not lost on me.

"I knew you didn't want to go back to her. I think if you'd been happy, things would've been different. I think I would've felt different," I say. "But I knew. I knew you didn't want to go back to her. I knew you wanted to stay with me. I couldn't do anything. I felt so powerless. Being just a kid, trapped in the system. Not able to do anything. So, I lashed out. At everyone. At everything. Because it was the only thing I could think of to do. Or maybe it wasn't even that calculated. I was just angry. Angry that I lost you."

"Well. You have me again," she says.

We eat the rest of our breakfast in silence, and then I decide it's time for me to go talk to the family.

"Why don't you wait here?" I suggest.

"Really?"

"Yeah. Just let me deal with it."

"I'd like to meet your family." She's looking at me with suspicion, and I wonder if I hurt her feelings. Definitely not my intent.

"I'm not hiding you, I promise. I just don't want to throw you in the middle of all the chaos."

"I'm fine. Honestly. I am staying on your parents' property, and I do feel like I should at least make an appearance. Otherwise, it's going to be weirder."

I laugh. "Well. True enough."

"Just let me go get dressed. I don't actually want to meet them in pajamas." She grimaces. "If you can call my sweats pajamas."

I think there's something cute about them, though I don't say that. She's swamped by the fuzzy black pants, and it captivates me more than it should.

New kink unlocked? God, I hope not. Not only do I not need more issues to go with my issues, I don't need to be panting after Sarah. My – hell, I don't even know what to call her. My best friend. My charge.

Lord.

I go and take a quick shower, changing out of my road clothes and getting the grime off me. I broke all my own hygiene rules yesterday in the interest of getting home as quickly as possible.

When we meet up again, she's wearing another one of those floral dresses she seems to favor.

"We can drive over, but it's about a six-minute walk if you don't mind."

"I think I'd like to walk," she says. "Just so I can see... I mean, we rolled in the dark last night when I was mostly asleep."

"Yeah."

I gesture for her to follow me out of the cabin, and we're greeted by the aggressively cheerful sunshine. The front of the cabin is clean, but minimally landscaped. There are a couple of planter boxes that Kaylee keeps up, but that's all. It's surrounded by tall pines, and the scent of the wood, the soil and the trees is rich and sharp, as they bake in the sunshine.

"It's beautiful here," she says. "And quiet."

"Sisters is probably a pretty quiet place to live."

"Yes. Definitely." She kicks a stone in the path. "The town gets really busy, particularly during summer. A lot of tourists."

"Yeah. Gold Valley is the same. There's a historic Main Street, which is where Sammy Daniels' jewelry shop is. I'll drive you by later. I mean, if you want to talk to her. You can also let it sit for a few days."

"I'm going to have to figure something out. I can't mooch off you forever."

Wrong. That's the word that rises up inside of me. The truth is I know it. I would take care of her for the rest of her life and I'd do it with a smile on my face.

"You have a place with me as long as you need one," I say.

"Well, that's... That's really kind of you."

We walk down the gravel road that leads back toward my parents' place, and she lifts her face toward the sun, the way the light catches her hair, stopping me short for a moment. I can see glimmers of the girl that she was, but she's different, too. I'm so sorry that she's going through all of the bad things that she's been dealing with, but I'm also proud of her. She didn't have the family that I did. She didn't get rescued. Everything she's done so far, she's done by rescuing herself, and I think that's incredible. I think she's incredible. I don't say that, though; instead, I just keep pace with her.

My dad's house is neat and clean. He's like that. Well-ordered and generally dependable. The house is a crisp white, and he has it repainted frequently to keep it looking perfect.

It makes me smile to see it. With all of its hanging flower pots and wide, tidy porch.

The front door bursts open, and two dogs come running out, with one old dog walking slowly behind. I can hear my sisters squealing at the chaos they've caused, and I hear their feet stomping on the hardwood as they run away from the scene of the crime.

The pups – who are a couple years old now but still act like squirmy babies – Jimmy and Blondie are racing around Sarah like they're trying to do a ritual, while Dougie sits down on the porch, wagging his tail and looking up at me.

Sarah is laughing, but also clearly doesn't entirely know what to do with the dogs. "Beasts," I snap. "Go inside."

The dogs stop, look at me, and race back up the porch stairs and into the house. Dougie doesn't move. I walk up the steps and bend down, scratching him behind the ears. "Hey, buddy."

Sarah walks up the steps slowly behind me.

"You can pet him," I say. "He's a good boy."

Sarah looks reluctant but bends down and gives Dougie a brief pat on the head. She seems slightly uncomfortable around dogs, which I suddenly want to change. I don't have a pet right now because I'm gone too much, but when I settle down, I'm going to have a lot of them.

I suddenly remember being an angry teen boy, who had never had much care in my life, being dropped into this new planet where people didn't just care for each other, but animals too.

I can remember getting assigned to the care of Kaylee's animals, back before she and Bennett were even dating.

"I don't like animals," I say.

"Why?" Kaylee is looking at me without judgment, which I know I don't deserve.

"They're pointless."

"That's the most ridiculous thing I've ever heard. Animals are important. Even if you don't like them as pets, don't tell me you've never eaten a steak. In which case, you definitely appreciate animals in one way at least."

"I don't understand pets," I say.

"There's nothing to understand. They keep you company. They love you. You love them."

"I still don't get it."

"Okay. Show me where the stupid dogs are."

"I don't have any stupid dogs," she says, still not angry, not taking my bait.

"Really?"

"They're good dogs, Dallas."

I smile as I think about that, about her. About how my family has changed my life in so many ways. I was little more than a feral animal when I came here; it took making me a bit more human for me to be able to appreciate the pets.

I look up and notice the door is still standing wide open. "Come on in," I say. "Door's open."

Right as we walk in, Mom comes out of the kitchen, her

strawberry blonde hair up in a bun, her smile warm. If she's surprised to see Sarah standing there, she doesn't really show it.

Oh God. She thinks that I've brought a woman home. In that way. I've never done that before. And it's so far off my radar right now that it didn't occur to me that she might think this is me making some kind of announcement.

"Bennett," she says. "The prodigal has returned."

"Hey, small fries," I say. Lucy has red hair just like Kaylee, Cara has brown hair like our dad. Both are filled to the brim with energy in ways that make me feel old, honestly.

"Dallas Dallas Dallas Dallas Dallas." They run my name together all in one shriek with no breath in between.

"Children children children children, I say back.

Which is when my dad comes into the room, surveying the situation. From the girls, back up to me.

My dad looks too young to be my dad, mostly because he is. He and Kaylee are in their early forties. That's what happens when you become a teen parent. Sometimes it feels a little bit strange to be in this house. Even though they've never made me feel like I'm not exactly the same as the other kids, I don't fit in the same way. Lucy and Cara are the kids he meant to have. Kaylee is the woman he chose to have children with, to spend his life with. My mom was some early fling, and early heartbreak that faded into the background, and never would've come up again if not for me.

Even though I know they love me, and I don't question that, it doesn't mean I'm not different. It doesn't mean I don't occupy a whole different space in the family. One that's unique to me.

"This is Sarah," I say.

I know there are a lot of Sarahs. But still, they know who Sarah is. I told them all about her. It's Kaylee who realizes first. Kaylee who gasps, hand going to her chest as she walks right to Sarah and pulls her in for a hug. "Oh. You're Sarah." She steps away from her. "Sorry. I shouldn't have just hugged you like that."

Sarah looks shocked. "Oh. It's okay."

"You're *his* Sarah."

Sarah's cheeks turn pink. "I'm... I was in foster care with him."

"He told us all about you," Bennett says, looking grave. "How did you two find each other?"

"She came to the event this weekend." I give them a quick summary of everything that's happening. I don't need to go into details about what happened with Chris; all they need to know is he went to jail for abusing her. That he's out now and menacing her.

"You'll be safe here," my dad says, his voice definitive. "You're part of our family now."

Chapter Seven

Sarah

I can't believe this. That these wonderful people in this beautiful house are just accepting me. Like I belong. Saying I'm part of their family.

It makes me want to cry. In fact, I'm only barely holding it together. Between the pancakes this morning and now this. They're just accepting me, and it makes no sense to me why. Nobody ever has.

Nobody except Dallas.

And now this man, who is definitely Dallas's father, I can see it in his eyes, the way that he stands, the shape of his jaw, is telling me that I'm part of the family. It's like a rare gift. Certainly, for someone like me, who has felt like I didn't have anyone for all this time. And now I have... These people.

I swallow hard, my throat going tight. "I don't want to put anyone at risk –"

"No one here is at risk," Dallas's dad says, crossing his arms. And I believe it. The same as I believed it when Dallas said he was armed. These are strong men. Men who will defend their own.

And for some reason, they've decided I'm their own.

"I just want to thank you," I say, holding back an onslaught of unfamiliar emotion. Usually, I'm so contained. But everything has been dismantled over the last few months. And most especially the last few days.

Maybe it's the fact that I feel safe that everything is coming close to the surface. I'm starting to discover I can't hold back my feelings anymore.

"You don't have to thank us," says Kaylee. "I know how much you mean to Dallas."

How much I mean to Dallas.

I suddenly feel unequal to that. We haven't actually known each other for the last eight years. It doesn't feel especially fair for him to be carrying around the weight of feelings he had for me when we were two lonely kids. He's not a lonely adult.

I am.

I've sort of elbowed my way into his life, this rich, full life, with siblings and parents, friends, his whole wonderful career. I have aspirations. But that's all they are.

Aspirations of a life that I should be able to have when I can devote more time to school. When I can stop running. When I can heal a little bit.

But he has those things. Maybe he doesn't need me dragging him down. I don't know why people being nice to me is sending me into a spiral. I guess that speaks to how unfamiliar it is to me.

"I'm going to take her down to town," Dallas says. "Give

her a tour of the place. Her old boss offered to give her a job reference with Sammy Daniels."

"Oh," Kaylee says. "Sammy is great. She's a friend."

More connections. Connections between all these lovely people.

I'm an interloper. I get that.

"Oh, and thank you for the pancakes," I add quickly.

"Of course," Kaylee says. "Though, I thought... Never mind."

"Yeah," Dallas says. "I know what you thought."

"You have to admit," Kaylee says, "there's no way we could've guessed that you finally found her."

"She found me," Dallas says, looking at me, and for a moment, it's like everything fades away. Everything and everyone. Except for him. His blue eyes.

I look away, because suddenly it's just too much to bear.

"Oh yeah," Dallas says. "I won. Well, I didn't win first place, but you know, I qualified for the finals, so I'm home for the next few months."

Kaylee shrieks and grabs him, jumping up and down while she hugs him. "Dallas. You didn't say, which made me not want to ask."

"It's a superstition," Bennett explains. "We're not supposed to ask him about any of it, he tells us when he's ready. It's also why we weren't allowed to go to the last event. He makes an exception for championships. Otherwise, he doesn't want us traveling to go watch."

"You don't let your family come see you ride?" I ask, completely shocked by this information.

"It's not that. But they traveled from out of town one time to see me, and I lost horribly. Not only that, I got pinned up against the wall, and I broke two ribs. So yeah, I decided that having them show up isn't the best. Anyway, the girls hate it because it's so loud."

"They don't hate it. We put headphones on them, and they do just fine."

Dallas sighs. "All right. But it's still bad luck. Except championships."

"Why isn't it bad luck at championships?" I ask.

"Because he never wins them," says Lucy, who has been standing in the corner in the kitchen this whole time, and apparently has been paying closer attention than she let on.

Kaylee laughs uproariously, and Bennett covers his mouth.

"Well," Bennett says finally. "She's not wrong."

"Thanks, guys." Dallas grimaces. "You ready to go?" he says to me.

"Sure."

"Why don't you both come over for dinner tonight?" Kaylee suggests.

Dallas looks at me, and I nod. "Okay."

He ushers me out of the house, and I can hear the family talking behind us, even as we step out on the porch and close the door. "So that's them," he says, stuffing his hands in his pockets and walking down the steps.

I follow after him.

"Well. They're amazing." I find myself getting choked up again, which is just ridiculous. "I'm so happy for you. I mean, you have your family."

He laughs, a sort of short, uncomfortable sound. "Thanks. I'm happy for me too."

We walk slowly back to the cabin. It's beautiful, the trees are lush and green, there's more moisture in the air here. Not quite as dry as the high desert climate to the east.

"How far away is Gold Valley from the ocean?"

"A couple of hours," he says. "Not far. We can go if you want."

"I'd love that." I look around. "So, what do you do when you're back here?"

"Mostly, I do work on my uncle's ranch. Wyatt has a big spread not far from here. My other uncle, Grant works there too, my Aunt Jamie has a ranch with her husband, Gabe, but they do plenty at the Dodge Ranch. My dad is the weirdo who has another career beyond ranching."

"So, you're all cowboys?"

He chuckles. "I guess so. Wyatt used to ride in the rodeo. He's kind of how I got started, much to my dad's chagrin."

"Oh my God, I bet your dad was so mad."

Dallas laughs at the memory. "You have no idea. Lindy, Wyatt's wife, her brother was a bull rider too. Anyway they had some animals at the ranch – I can't even remember why or how, but they encouraged me and Colt to give riding them a try. We were sixteen? And so dumb."

"No way, did your dad try to murder them?"

"I think he did. He was chasing them with a Burdizzo all around the ranch. Colt and I thought it was hilarious."

I frown. "What's...a Burdizzo?"

"I believe the generic term is an emasculatome."

I mouth the word and try to figure it out.

"It's for making bulls into steers, Sarah."

My eyes go round. "Oh!"

"But even with all the threats and yelling...you couldn't keep us away after that, and ultimately my dad was never going to keep me from something I wanted to learn. I think he was just glad I was outside touching grass instead of being on the Xbox all the time." He smiles. "Plus, it gave me something in common with my extended family."

"Are you guys close?"

"Yeah. Really close. My grandpa doesn't live in the state anymore, but he and his wife come and visit a lot too."

"You have such a big family."

"I know. It's still kind of strange, if I'm honest. It's almost like two different people have lived my life. It's hard for me to really remember what it was like to be that kid."

"I guess having me around is kind of a strange reminder."

"It's not bad," he says. He stops walking and turns to me. "I hope you know how serious I am when I say I never forgot about you. My life is great, that's true. But it's felt incomplete without you in it. I mean it."

He turns away from me and starts to walk ahead, and I'm winded by what he's just said.

I don't fully know how to process it.

"Let's get in the truck and go to town," he says.

He's eager to get past the sincere moment, as am I.

I get into the passenger side of the truck, while he gets in the driver's seat, turns the engine on.

"This is a really great truck," I comment as he pulls out of the driveway.

"Yeah. You'll notice I don't really feel compelled to spend a lot of money on motel rooms when I travel. But I want to drive in comfort."

"I can confirm that it's a pretty great place to sleep," I say.

"Good to know, honestly. Maybe I can save my money and just sleep in the truck next time."

I rest my elbow on the ledge of the window and look out at the passing scenery. I've never been here, and in fact, I can't say that I've ever been very conscious of Gold Valley as a place.

But it suddenly feels like home to me.

I don't know if it's because of the man sitting beside me or his family... I don't know. But I'm going to go ahead and let myself just be happy for a minute. Because when was the last time I let myself have that? I catch a sharp breath as soon as we drive into town, the red brick buildings are so quaint and lovely.

He's right, it's not entirely unlike Sisters, which is another old west town with roots in Gold Rush history, but where Sisters has wooden buildings, Gold Valley is brick. There are old ads painted on those walls, for blue jeans and coffee beans, and bronze statues of the horse, a cowboy, and a bull bucking just like in the rodeo.

"Welcome to my home," he says, looking around as we drive slowly down the streets.

"God." I laugh. "I'm so fucking jealous of you."

He looks at me, a rueful smile on his face. "I don't know what I did to deserve it," he says. "Getting this, I mean. It doesn't seem fair. Honestly. I'm no better than any of those other kids in care. I just happened to have a dad out there who wasn't total trash, and..."

"No," I say. "I don't want you to feel bad about it. I'm glad that you have it. But I just..." I can imagine living here. I can imagine the idyllic teenage experience it must be." There's a lull in the conversation, until I speak again. "Tell me. Tell me about being in high school here."

He laughs. "I played football. We used to go to Mustard Seed Diner, and Gloria made the best milkshakes. Well, she *still* does. It's my favorite."

"I want to go there."

"I think that can be arranged." He gestures to the left. "There's a park up there called Doc Griffin. Back in the day, we'd get milkshakes from Mustard Seed, shut it down, then go hang out at the park. Just a group of rowdy kids, causing not all that much trouble, because there's not much trouble to get into here." He grimaces. "I mean, there was the time we built a still up in the woods behind my dad's house."

"You did?"

"Yeah. I blame Colt for that."

"So, you knew Colt back then."

"Sure did. He was one of my first friends when I came to town. He's a great guy."

"Stella?"

"Oh, we met her when we got into the rodeo."

"Did she date either of you?"

He frowns. "No. Why would you ask that?"

"I'm just trying to figure out how two bull riders ended up befriending a barrel racer. It seems like an unlikely crossover."

"I don't think so. Stella is an adrenaline junkie, so she loves getting as close as possible to the more extreme sports. Plus, she's just cool. A lot of nights we hang out, play poker after the events."

"Really?"

"Yeah. For obvious reasons, things went a little differently this last time."

"Well, I'd love to play with you guys sometime."

"That can definitely be arranged since Colt is back in town, too."

There's something so aggressively normal about all of this. It's all very Friday Night Lights. Very quaint and homely in a way that I've never experienced, even living in small towns over the years.

"Where did you go to high school?" he asks.

His mention of my past sours my stomach and casts a pall over this beautiful, small-town fantasy I'm in.

"Oh. Portland. It's so weird, because Portland is a pretty big city, but it felt too small for me. I moved to Sisters because at least it was *actually* small, and I didn't know people there."

"Why Sisters specifically?"

"Honestly? I found the apartment there, and I just went. I didn't really think about it. I've been living there for the last two years."

He pulls the truck up against the curb, right in front of a cute little store with a sparkling jewelry display in the front. I know that this is Sammy's shop.

"I feel weird. Like maybe I should call the store first."

"You don't need to feel weird. Not only is Daisy calling ahead, but my mom knows her."

In my life, that isn't a positive. If my mom knows somebody, that means they're a person I don't want to know, and if they are a person I want to know, then I don't want to use her as a reference. It's such an interesting thing to have his network. Especially working the way that it does.

But I'm grateful for it.

I get out of the truck and step onto the sidewalk. The breeze is warm, and the town is bustling. There are little groups of people wandering down the sidewalks, popping into different shops, laden with bags. I spot a bookstore across the street, a toy store, and a bridal shop. There's an Italian restaurant and a saloon at the end of the block.

"When you turn twenty-one, I'll take you to the saloon."

"My birthday is in a couple of weeks."

"Really?"

I look down. "Yes."

I can't remember the last time I celebrated it. I'm not sure I want to, but somehow I know he'll want to.

"Then I'll definitely take you to the saloon."

"Great."

That feels so normal. Like such a normal thing to look forward to. I can't remember the last time I celebrated my birthday, and I guess I should celebrate turning twenty-one. I hear it's supposed to be fun. But nothing in my life has ever been all that fun.

Now that Dallas is back in my life, though...

He leads the way into the shop, and I'm dazzled by the surroundings. It's small, but lovely. There's a girl about my age working behind the counter. "Welcome in," she says.

Just then, a woman comes out from behind a curtain stretched over a doorway. She has long, curly blonde hair and a serene demeanor. "Hi. I'm Sammy. This is my store. Oh. Dallas," she says, as soon as she recognizes him. "I think your mom said something about you coming back into town."

"Here for a few months, anyway."

"That's great."

He clears his throat. "This is my friend, Sarah. I think Daisy called about her?"

"Ah. Daisy. Yes. I'm in an entrepreneur group with her. She did mention someone who was looking for a job. Is that you?"

"Yes," I say. I look down and notice that the woman has just the slightest baby bump. "I don't have any experience working in a retail store like this. Mainly, I've waited tables. But I'm moving to town and –"

"She's a good friend of mine," Dallas says.

"I do need help. Ryder and I have three kids, and a fourth one on the way, and honestly, I'm just exhausted. Between making the jewelry, going to the different trade shows... running the storefront is a little bit much. I have Allison working most days, but she's also going to school."

"Yeah," the girl says. "But I have my schedule worked pretty well around all of this."

"What are you going to school for?" I ask.

"Oh. Nursing."

"That's cool," I say, and then I'm not sure what else I should say. I don't really know how to do pleasantries and small talk and making friends. I especially don't know what to do right now when I feel a desperation for both the job and befriending Allison. So I look at Sammy. "Well, if you have a position, I would love to see if I'm a good fit."

"I have a feeling you would be a great fit," Sammy says, and I don't know why she's so confident in that, but that confidence makes me want to be certain that I don't let her down. Maybe I can build connections. Maybe I can make myself a community. I started to do that in Sisters. I was making slow progress with it. Learning how to be less of a feral animal and trying to actually be friendly to the people around me.

Maybe that didn't end up exactly the way I wanted it to, but maybe here... Maybe here it can be different.

"Can I get your details, your phone number? Then I can look at my schedule and get you set up for your first training day."

"That's perfect. Really, I so appreciate this."

"Not at all. *I* appreciate it."

"So do I," says Allison.

I wonder if maybe we can be friends. I did make some friends at the diner, but none of them were my age. I haven't had the chance to make a lot of friends my age. I glossed over my high school experience when I talked to Dallas earlier. But the truth is... It wasn't very happy. I struggled. I struggled to connect to people. A lot of it's on me. But I was so *angry* about everything that had happened to me.

I've started a few new lives in the years since then, and I'm not sure that I've been particularly successful at any of them.

I'm left feeling so behind where Dallas is.

And I try not to overthink that.

I leave my information with Sammy, and we walk back out onto the street. "Want to take a stroll through town?"

"Sure," I say.

"That's going to work out perfectly," he says.

I can count on one hand how many times I felt like something in my life was going to work out perfectly. But he's right about this. It's perfect timing. A perfect gift.

"I'm going to school," I say. "Very part-time. Like one class at a time. I want to get into social work. So, I'm taking some psychology classes, sociology."

"You're going to be a social worker?" he asks.

"Yeah. I mean, you and I both know, better than anybody, that it makes a huge difference when you have someone who actually cares. And if you could have a social worker who understands being on the other side of the table? I want to believe that I can make a difference."

"Of course you can," he says. "Of course you can make a difference. I think that's a great idea. Maybe you should just go to school for now."

"No. I have to work to be able to pay for it. I can qualify for some financial aid, but I have to be able to live and–"

"I'm serious when I say you can just stay with me. I'll feed you."

"I can't do that, Dallas. That is the kindest, most generous offer anyone has ever made to me, but I cannot take advantage of you like that."

"It's not taking advantage of me."

"I know you feel that way. But I would feel differently."

"You're the best, Sarah, but I don't know that I'm willing to take your opinion into consideration here."

I laugh. "I'm the best? What leads you to that conclusion?"

"My instincts," he says.

"And your instincts are above reproach?"

"I'd say so."

I look at him, my stomach tightening when his eyes meet mine. I'm going to be twenty-one in two weeks.

I've never been kissed. I'm glad that wasn't part of my abuse. It was wrong and disgusting, and what he did felt like abuse. Felt like trauma. Maybe that's a weird thing to be grateful for, but I've been to some therapy sessions where people talked about how their abusers manipulated their feelings – mental and physical – formed bonds with them. I can't imagine how hard it would be to undo damage like that. Mine is hard enough.

I don't count what happened to me as having sexual experience. What I had done to me was assault. It hurt. I didn't want any of it. The problem is that it ended up categorizing sex and sexual contact as something distasteful and frightening. And so even though in many ways I don't feel like I have true sexual experience, it did taint the idea of it for me.

Touch is frightening to me, first and foremost.

It's complicated. I'm acutely aware of my experience, though, standing next to Dallas. Feeling this strange, hollow sensation in my body when he looks at me. Feeling compelled to move closer to him.

If maybe I'd met another man, if maybe I'd done this kind of thing before, I wouldn't be feeling this now. Because there's no way I can afford to bring attraction into my relationship with him. He's the single most important person in my life, and I just got him back.

He's the only person in my life who cares about me, really. There are so many other people now who care about me by extension of him, and I can never, ever follow this tightening in my stomach down its natural path. I can never, ever let that grow into anything.

I'm horrified that I'm even thinking about it now.

I was young when he was taken away from me. But not so young I didn't understand that I was beginning to think he was beautiful. That the love that I felt for him was beginning to turn into something all-encompassing. Something that wasn't just family.

There wasn't anything either of us could or would ever have done about it back then. We are adults now, though. And just allowing my thoughts to go there at all feels dangerous.

I start walking again, anything to put a little bit of distance between us. "Historically, I haven't been the best. I feel like you should know that."

"What do you mean exactly?"

"I mean, people were mean to me in high school, but if I litigate that with any kind of honesty, my verdict is that I was the bitch. Because I never wanted anybody to befriend me so closely that they wanted to come to my house. I never wanted anyone to get so close to me that they might ask about my past. I'm over that. I've started overcompensating by telling the people around me that I was a foster kid, and an abuse victim right at the start. Even though I also hate wearing all that on my sleeve, the alternative has been that I live in a weird shame spiral I can't seem to get out of, and then I can never get to know anyone. I graduated from high school having literally never been invited to a party. Having never made friends with anyone. I moved out of my mom's house before I turned eighteen. I moved out of Portland right after I graduated. I moved to Wilsonville, and had a difficult time there."

"What did you do there?"

"I worked at an auto parts store. It wasn't a great fit. Men were always trying to get close to me, and I didn't like that. I quit shortly after I started. I moved to Sherwood and started working at a diner, so that's what set me up on that path. I decided to move to a smaller town to pay lower rent. Ended up in Winston, then in Sisters about six months later. I started doing school online, I started working at Daisy's. I'd managed to keep anyone from getting to know me too well. I was just starting to change that when Chris showed up in Sisters."

"I have a hard time imagining that you were mean to anyone," he says.

"I was. Especially in high school. I was. You said that you lost it after I left, but I didn't fare much better. I ran away from home once, but my mom made me too afraid to keep doing that. Because the first time I got dragged back, her boyfriend hit me and then made it very clear that if I kept behaving like that, my mom wouldn't protect me if he decided to do...other things to me. And when men say things like that, I pay attention."

"Your mom is a monster," Dallas says, looking at me with hard, blue eyes.

"I mean, I definitely could've made things easier for myself."

"No," he says, his voice uncompromising. "She's a monster. Because not only did she fail to protect you, she used that failure to manipulate you later. She kept men around who were more than willing to hurt you, whether it was doing her bidding or not. You deserved better."

"Thanks. I agree. It doesn't change anything."

I feel guilty about that the minute the words exit my mouth. I'm showing him a little of my sharper side. The ways that I've kept people distant from me, but I know he means well, it's just that if I had a nickel for every time someone heard my story and said that things should've been different, I could've financed my college education by now. Wishing that things were different, knowing that they should've been, doesn't change anything.

I suppose it's not fair. Because people freaking out when they hear what happened to me annoys me too. People ignoring it. But then also the hyper-empathy, like they might cry hearing about my past irritates me too, and maybe the problem is me. As far as being able to have friends, as far as being able to connect with anyone.

Maybe it's still me.

"I know it doesn't change anything," he says, his voice low. "But you need to know it. Really know it. You need to feel like you deserved better."

"Why. So, I can make it better? Like it's my responsibility to fix all the bullshit?"

"No," he says, reaching out and grabbing me by the chin. All the breath rushes from my body. I can't move. I can't think. I can't do anything but stare into his blue eyes, warring with a feeling in my chest that's too big for me to breathe past. A feeling that I wish I wasn't having. A feeling that I want to alchemize into anger, but I can't. Because he smells so good, and he's just so beautiful. And quite apart from anything else, he's Dallas Dodge. The one man who's ever meant anything to me.

"It's not because I think that you're responsible for fixing anything. It's because I'm afraid that somewhere inside yourself, maybe you think you deserve it. And when you tell me things like... How you weren't nice to people, when you frame it that way, I worry that maybe you blame yourself for where you are. You shouldn't. I say it, because what I want you to know is how egregious it is. We both deserved better. But God, you deserved so much more than what you got."

I take a deep breath and move away from him, swallowing hard, turning away. Trying to minimize the feeling that's making me shake. "I appreciate that. I know that. There's just no point going over any of it, okay? There's nothing I can do about it. It happened. And I'm not excusing my behavior. Yeah. I'm traumatized. A lot of people are traumatized. But I think it's taken way too long for me to figure out what to do with that trauma. I think it's taken me way too long to try and figure out how to connect with people." What I don't tell him is that I still can't bear to be touched.

Even his mom hugging me earlier today bothered me.

I didn't want to say it, I didn't want to react, because I know the problem is me. But I feel like I'm frozen in time, stuck with all this baggage that I can't do anything about.

I can feel as bad about it, or as angry about it as I want, but it doesn't change the fact that I'm the one who has to live with the consequences of all of this, and so I'm the one who has to just... Get over it.

But it's a lot harder to do than it should be. That makes me angry. Because I wish–I really wish–that I could just make it go away. But it's always there.

I turn away from him. It's safer than standing there like that. I don't know which of us needs the safety. Me or him. I don't usually feel unpredictable. I'm very boring, and very self-protective, but right now I feel shaky. Right now, I feel like an unknown even to myself, and that has me frightened. Terrified of what I might do to implode this gift that I've been given. This new network, this new family with Dallas. With Gold Valley.

As we get into the truck and head back toward his house, I remind myself of exactly who he is. Who I am. And why it's so important that I never forget.

Chapter Eight

Dallas

Sarah retreats to her room for the better part of the afternoon, until it's time to go to dinner at the family house.

She emerges looking beautiful. So beautiful that for a moment I have to pause to catch my breath.

One of the first things I noticed when I saw her at the rodeo was how pretty she's gotten.

Her dark hair curls just slightly, framing her face. Her cheeks are round and naturally rosy. She has a dimple on the left side of her face, and that is the part of her face now that reminds me most of her face when she was a kid. But it's changed along with the rest of her. The context of where it sits now feeling less cute, and more enticing.

She is not very tall. She only comes up to my shoulder, her frame petite, her figure neat and lovely. I really shouldn't be looking at her figure. That is the very last thing I should be looking at, and I make sure to force my eyes up to hers the moment they're tempted to drop to examine her body.

"My mom said she made spaghetti," I say.

"Oh. Sounds good," she says.

Not like it's fancy. But I've always loved that about Kaylee and my dad's cooking. Neither of them are world-class chefs or anything, but it just feels like family. Family in a way I never knew before I moved in with them.

I want so badly for her to feel the same thing. For her to have the same experience. Even though it's late for her. She's almost twenty-one.

Life really isn't fair.

"What?"

"What?" I respond.

"You're scowling."

"Oh. It's nothing. Come on. Let's walk over."

"Doesn't look like nothing," she says, following me out.

"I was just thinking about how life's not fair," I say.

"We both know that," she says. "In fact, I would say that it's the primary drumbeat of our existence, wouldn't you?"

I look at her, she's smirking, her expression impish. But I know that she's also serious enough. She's not wrong.

"Yeah. That is true. But that doesn't mean I can't be mad about it sometimes. Especially not when I look at you."

"I don't really want you to be angry when you look at me," she says, hopping down the last step, her yellow dress floating up, exposing her thighs. And I look away as quickly as possible. "Doesn't seem very nice."

"That isn't what I mean," I say.

I keep pace with her, as she forges ahead. I'm trying to imagine her in the way she described herself. She claims that she was mean to people. Difficult. I don't see any of that.

"Sarah..." She looks back at me, but she doesn't break her stride. "Sorry. I just can't imagine you being mean to anyone. I'm not sure that you see yourself accurately."

She laughs. "Dallas Dodge. Don't you remember when you first met me? Don't you remember how I bit people?"

I laugh. I didn't remember her biting people, but now that she mentions it, I do recall there was a biting incident early on at the first house I moved into with her. But, if I also recall correctly, it's because that kid was bothering her.

"I don't think you did anything wrong."

"Generally speaking, when you're the one who bit someone, the authorities don't take your side in the dispute."

"You didn't bite without just cause."

"I don't think it matters why you bit, it's frowned upon to sink your teeth into others."

"You didn't rend any flesh."

"Ha! Well. I might have, actually."

"Tell me you didn't have a good reason."

She shrugged. "Okay. I had a decent reason. Still, I over-reacted. And it isn't that I didn't have a reason to. I don't need you to validate me. Or my trauma. I know where it comes from, and I know why I have it. But I'm just saying, the only reason I quit being quite that feral was because of you. I felt safe when you were around, and I didn't feel like I had to protect myself quite that intensely. All of that was undone when I had to go back to my mom. I was only ten. Everything that felt safe and okay with you, it just felt broken and awful when I was with her. I felt like I was right back where I started. Like I had to defend myself from every unseen danger, everything that might be lurking in the shadows. Everyone felt like a threat."

"But you seem..."

"It's you. It's you. You make me feel safe. It's amazing how things change when you feel safe."

We don't speak for the next few minutes, as my parents' farmhouse comes into view. We walk up the steps to the porch together in silence, and I open the front door without knocking. The smell of garlic bread hits me right when we walk in, and my stomach growls.

Sarah is looking hungry too, and I suddenly want to learn how to cook. I'm on the road so much that there's no occasion for me to do it all that often, and when I'm back home, I let my mom feed me. But I want to take care of her. That realization is deep, grabs me low in the gut. I want to do everything that I possibly can for her. I want to take the pain of our separation and fix it. Make it all go away. Turn it into something glorious and golden.

If I can do that by learning how to make a meal for her, then, I will.

"Hi there," Kaylee says, poking her head around the doorway. "Dinner is almost on the table. You can just go inside." She gestures toward the dining area.

When we walk in there, I laugh, because Lucy and Cara are sitting there clutching one fork in each fist, their hands planted firmly on the table, toothy smiles on their faces. "What are you two doing?" I ask.

"Waiting for food," Lucy says, her expression not changing.

"Did you see this in a cartoon?"

Cara frowns. "No."

At the same time, Lucy, whose expression is still frozen, says, "Yes."

Sarah looks amused if a bit uncomfortable but sits down next to me at the table.

"Do you like horses?" Lucy asks the question very seriously, her eyes trained on Sarah.

"I don't really know any," Sarah says.

"I'm named after a horse," Lucy says.

I laughed. "Yeah," I say.

"My big brother named me."

She sounds proud of it. And that feels like an ice pick right to my heart. In the best way. But that's one thing I've learned over the past decade. Love hurts. Even if it's in beautiful ways. But feeling anything for people, for animals, for a community, has the potential to wound you. Even in happy moments. For me, it's because I'm always so aware of what I didn't have for all those years, and about all the people who still don't have it. Like Sarah.

Yeah. This one hurts a little bit because I'm thinking about Sarah.

Kaylee comes in a moment later, a bowl of pasta in her arms, and my dad follows with two trays of bread balanced on one arm, and a bowl of salad.

They work in tandem, setting the dinner down on the table, smiling at each other as they do, and this is another moment where all this love hurts just for a moment.

"Glad you could join us," Bennett says.

"Yeah. No worries."

Though, as soon as we dish up all the food, they begin interrogating Sarah. What she does for a living – which quickly turns into a discussion about her aspirations. The fact that she had success earlier with the job hunt, and for a brief moment, glances back to when she and I met in foster care.

My dad looks down, then back up, his expression grave. "I know that we don't know each other. But I've always been appreciative of you. When Dallas told us about you... I realize how much you took care of him for all those years when I wasn't there. I have a lot of guilt. A lot of guilt around the fact that I wasn't there for him in those early years. But you were. It means a lot to me."

Emotion rises up in my throat, tightening it, threatening to strangle me. I feel like a basket case. I know it's all of this with Sarah, the past being so close to the present. It's not a bad thing, not necessarily, but I'd kind of like a reprieve from it. I don't need to get emotional over everything from my wild little sisters to my dad being sentimental, and a piece of garlic bread that just tastes like home.

But I am. It's that kind of night.

We finish up dinner, and my mom gets out dessert, a giant bowl of the richest banana pudding you've ever tasted. It's a copycat recipe from some famous bakery in New York, and she always complains about how criminally easy it is to make, particularly given how much that's in it. The fat in the pudding is my friend, not my enemy, and I've never met a dessert that I thought was too sweet, which makes it my absolute favorite thing. I know she made it for that reason.

I take a helping that's probably too generous, and Sarah scoops herself a small amount.

"Thank you," she says softly. "Again. I don't know that I've ever really had a family dinner before."

Her words are soft, devastating in their simplicity. I see Kaylee's eyes welling up, but she looks away, does her best to hide her reaction. I look at Sarah, trying to see if she's aware of just how horrible an admission that is. I also get it. Because yeah, we got included sometimes in the houses that we lived in growing up. But we always felt acutely out of place. Either with the other kids that were sitting there at the table, with the parents, or with ourselves. It was just a dark time all around. And then in all the years since, I know she's felt so isolated. So Goddamned isolated.

"We're glad you're here," my dad says, his words firm and definitive, glossing over the emotion of the moment, and I'm grateful for that.

She doesn't need to be made to feel like an alien. We don't need to have moments that highlight how different our pasts make us from other people. They are inevitable, and they happen, but it's always weird when they do.

In this house, people at least understand that.

"Do you want to play a game?" Lucy asks.

And that's how we find ourselves embroiled in a cutthroat game of Chutes and Ladders, which Sarah has never played before, but catches on too quickly.

As her game piece gets launched down the slide for the third time in a round, my sisters screech with delight at her fate.

"This is not a fun game," Sarah says, pushing her fingers through her hair. I reach up, grab her wrist, and try to unbury them. "Don't tear your hair out," I say.

She looks up, and suddenly I'm very aware that I'm holding onto her.

I let go, and I press my hand down to the top of my thigh, letting the heat from her touch bleed away.

We go straight into another round, and this time Sarah wins, and she puts her arms up, laughing in victory, while the girls swarm her.

Their instant comfort with her makes my chest ache, and I catch her eye again, then my mom and my dad's. They both smile at me, and I look away. Because I don't want them to get any untoward ideas about this. About *us*.

Though, I guess it doesn't really matter what they think. She's family. I can see it now.

She just is.

We finish about the time the girls need to head up for their bathtime, and Sarah thanks my parents profusely again for the meal.

"Of course," Kaylee says. This time, she doesn't touch Sarah. I noticed that she didn't seem to react negatively when the girls grabbed onto her. Which I mentioned as soon as we are out of the house, walking back down the road.

"It was okay, the kids grabbing you like that?"

"Oh. Yeah. Kids are fine," she says. There's a brief pause. "I guess I didn't know that until tonight. But they are."

"You haven't spent very much time around kids, have you?"

She shakes her head. "No. Which is maybe not a great thing since I want to be a social worker. But somehow in my head that feels like a different thing. Because I already know those kids. Those kids are me. What I don't know are kids like your sisters. Who just have a lovely house, and wonderful parents. Who just have this beautiful, sweet life. It's really... It's really great."

"Yeah, sometimes I envy them too," I say.

She laughs. "No. That's not it. You can't be jealous of children."

"Sure you can," I say. "I feel it all the time. Every time I feel like I'm part of this family, but also not quite." I growl, because I really didn't intend to get into this. This is the kind of thing I never say out loud. It's not fair. That's the thing. "Don't listen to me. It's dumb."

"Not dumb. It's how you feel."

"But I know my dad feels bad about it, and it's not his fault. Yeah, I didn't spend the first fifteen years of my life with my family, but I have them now. Sometimes... Sometimes I feel it. Sometimes I feel it in the way the girls just feel so safe and secure. That a family dinner is normal for them."

"I kind of brought the room down with my comment."

"You didn't bring the room down. One thing about my parents is that they're used to grappling with my past. It's not like we ignore it. But there are certain things that I just tend to keep inside myself, because I don't think it's fair to project onto other people. Least of all my dad, who already feels bad enough about the way everything went down."

"You can still feel wounded without blaming him. You can still feel like it's unfair without being mad at him. Hell, you can still love him and be mad at him."

"I can't be mad at him," I say.

"Why not?"

"Because it's not fair. I already said that."

"Remember the whole conversation we had earlier today about life not being fair. Cuts both ways. You know, I am kind of mean sometimes. Because I'm traumatized. I'm going to do the wrong thing, say the wrong thing, and feel a whole lot of sharp, difficult feelings, and a lot of times the people around me aren't responsible for it. They didn't ask for it. A lot of the time they didn't earn it. But that's the same way my abuse is. Sometimes I'm what's not fair about life. I guess I've kind of accepted that in some ways."

I've never thought about it that way before, and I stop walking for a second, considering that. "Well. I think there's something to be said for not wanting to make anyone else's life needlessly difficult."

"Sure." She shrugs. "I'm not saying go out of your way to be a jerk about everything. I'm just saying, as much as we've had to flex to survive, other people can flex around us sometimes. You don't have to suppress everything."

"Is that one of your psychology classes talking?"

She laughs. "Maybe. Why didn't you go to school, Dallas?"

"I didn't like it. I just remember being in Eugene, doing classes, walking around campus, feeling like I was playing pretend. Like none of it was real. Like I wasn't real. Definitely like I didn't deserve to be there. I think I mainly got in because of the essay I wrote about the first fifteen years of my life."

"You deserved to be there," she says. "You're smart."

"Well, I didn't feel like it. Also, I didn't like sitting still. I'm happier doing this. Anyway, I've found all the financial success I could possibly need in the rodeo. Guess I didn't need school."

"Maybe not. But it's okay if you wanted it."

I think about that for a moment. "Maybe a version of me would have. One who grew up in that house. With my dad. I bet my sisters will go to school. Maybe they'll even be veterinarians. But they'll have the luxury of having been raised in one place. Of having always known they were secure. Loved. Of having people praise the work that they do, make a big deal out of it. I love my family so much. I'm glad that I'm home. Gold Valley is my home."

"But you feel on the outside of it sometimes."

My jaw aches. "Yeah. I do."

We arrive back at the cabin, and I open the door for her. "Want to watch a movie?" I ask. I don't want to go to bed just yet, and I'm not sure why. Things feel a bit uncertain. They feel unsettled. Maybe because all this stuff has been dredged up to the surface.

"Yes. I do." Her eyes go bright, and I know what she's

going to say before she even says it. I've set myself up. "I think we should watch Lord of the Rings."

I groan. She was obsessed with that movie when we were kids. If we were ever in a household where we got to have some modicum of control over what was on TV, she would put on Lord of the Rings.

She smiles, wicked. "Please, Samwise Gamgee. I need you to come on this journey with me."

"How the fuck did I end up being Samwise?" I ask, moving into the kitchen and rooting around to see if I have a bag of microwave popcorn somewhere. I do. She's already fiddling around with my TV, toying with the remote and pulling up the settings to see where the movie is available.

Luckily, I have the service it's streaming on. Well, luckily for her. I am an unwilling participant in this trip to Mordor.

"Because I'm Frodo," she says. "The One Ring is all my trauma, I need to cast it into the fire, but I don't really want to. The longer you carry it, the more you start to think it protects you, even though it causes you pain."

I grimace. "That is a little bit on the nose, and something you've undoubtedly thought about before."

She laughs. "Yes. I wrote a paper on it, actually. In one of my classes. A lot of times we carry trauma around for longer than we need to and it does become a weapon, a shield. I recognize it. I haven't figured out how to cast mine into the fire, though."

I pop the bag into the microwave, and press the popcorn button, which I know you're not supposed to do, but I don't care, I'm lazy.

I lean against the cabinets and stare at her while she curls up on my couch.

"Go on," I say. "I'm interested."

"I'm really angry, Dallas," she says, suddenly very serious. "About all the things that happened to me. I'm angry they affect me, I'm afraid to let them not affect me. Because I..." She looks away. "I still don't let anyone touch me."

Her voice is soft, so soft that I almost can't hear it. I'm not entirely sure I understand exactly what she's saying.

"People you don't know," I press.

"No. Nobody. I don't let anyone close. I... I'm so angry, because it's the ring. Around my neck, right? But I put it on my finger too many times, I've used it to keep people at a distance. I've used it to remind myself that the world isn't safe and I can't trust anybody. Now I don't know how to get rid of it. I'm just carrying it, and it's a burden, and I'm basically Gollum." She's referencing the character who loses all his humanity chasing after the ring, which transforms him into a vile disgusting creature.

There is nothing vile or disgusting about Sarah.

"You're not like that," I say. "Sarah, you've been through a lot. Don't be so hard on yourself about what you haven't been able to let go of on top of everything else."

"But it's killing me," she says. "Literally. I'm lonely. I want to feel normal. I don't want dinners like that to be an anomaly. I don't want connecting to people to be something I don't have experience with. I'm almost twenty-one, I would damn well like to go on a date."

I grit my teeth and pull the popcorn bag out of the microwave just before it stops, because I can hear that the popping has slowed down, and I'm sure it would burn if I left it.

I shake the bag as I walk over to the couch. "Yeah. You're young."

"You say that like you're an old, wizened man, and not

twenty-four," she says, reaching out and poking me between the ribs with her thumb and forefinger.

"Ouch!" I drop the bag of popcorn as I reflexively moved to cover myself. She steals it, opens it up, laughing like a little troll.

"I told you I was Gollum," she says, tearing into the bag and stealing a handful.

"You suck," I say, taking the remote and pushing play on the movie.

"I know," she says.

I regret making a joke about that, because I fear on some level she thinks that's true.

I'm not all that interested in this movie, and I've seen it too many times, which leaves my mind to wander over to her. I look at her profile, watch as she watches the movie like she's never seen it before, her eyes wide with fear when Frodo is nearly captured, smiling when the Fellowship of the Ring is formed.

"There's just something about the story," she says wistfully. "That if we all just try to do what's right when it's really hard, we could change the world. Defeat the bad guys. Make friends and boil potatoes."

I swallow hard, and for the first time I really understand what she gets out of the story. Because for a little while, it's possible to look at very real problems through this lens of fantasy. See a world where good does triumph over evil simply because it's good, and it has to.

She wants a date.

That creates an uncomfortable shift in my chest.

She doesn't let anyone touch her.

Except me.

She touched me herself, reached right out and jabbed

me in the middle of the discussion, and she doesn't seem afraid of me at all.

Maybe I could...

No. No. I pushed that thought to the side. It's a complete betrayal of her. Of everything she is for me to think something like that, to even begin to think something like that.

She's Sarah. I'm taking care of her. She trusts me.

She trusts me enough to tell me about all these things. To sit with me in a darkened room, sharing this space, sharing air, sharing her favorite movie.

I would never, ever do anything to compromise that. Never.

I love her. With everything I am. Every fiber of my being, and I always have. I haven't always known what love was, and I still might not know exactly what that emotion looks like in every form in my life, but I believe in it. I value it.

Because every time I've ever been loved my life has changed for the better. Every time I've ever loved someone.

Even if sometimes it hurts a little bit.

The movie is long, and I'm surprised I don't start dozing off. But I know it's because of her. I know it's because I feel like I'm making up for lost time. Precious moments and memories with this person who slipped through my fingers for so long. Maybe it's strange, but she and I have never had the option of being normal, so I don't feel any shame about it. I take joy where I can find it. Right now, it's in this. The simple pleasure of sitting there with her. And if I feel like moving closer to her, I don't need to do that. I can just sit where I am. I can just watch her enjoy the movie.

I can get plenty out of her happiness.

Just being in the presence of it. Soaking it in.

She looks at me, narrows her eyes. "What are you doing?"

"Staring at you."

"Why?"

"I need to make sure you're real."

Her shoulders jerk, a sharp breath sounding a little bit like a gasp. Then she looks away, sticks her hand into the popcorn bag, and starts watching the movie again.

"Did I say the wrong thing?" I ask.

"You just... You sound sentimental."

"I am sentimental," I say. "Pretty damn sentimental, actually."

"Why?"

"Because life has given us plenty enough to be jaded about."

She snorts. "True. But I'm never jaded when it comes to Lord of the Rings."

"And I'm never jaded when it comes to you."

"You have to stop saying things like that, Dodge," she says.

"And why is that?"

"Because. You can't make a wild animal into a house pet."

Except she's never really been a wild animal with me. But I don't say that, because for some reason she needs to be protected by this narrative. But I'm too nice to mention it. Far too kind to ask her why she's hiding behind the One Ring.

"Whatever."

She throws a piece of popcorn at me. And I smile.

"Yeah. Whatever."

Chapter Nine

Sarah

I'm starting a new job today, and I've started so many new jobs that you would think at this point it wouldn't make me nervous. But everything feels high stakes because I feel like I'm a representative of Dallas, and all the things that he's vouched for.

Because he said that I was going to be good at this, so I really hope that I am.

I don't have a car, so he drops me off in front of the store in the morning, promising to pick me up in the afternoon.

I feel clingy.

Like a kid getting dropped off at her first day of kindergarten, though honestly, I always loved it when whatever adult was in charge of me dropped me off somewhere. A few hours of freedom away from whatever dysfunctional situation I was in? Yay!

This is different. But I guess it's like a normal kid might've felt in those circumstances.

"What if I screw this up?"

He smiles, and that smile tugs at something inside me.

He's just so... This past week has been the happiest in recent memory. Really, since I had him in my life before. I have forced him to watch the entire Lord of the Rings Trilogy, and he didn't even really complain. He complained more when I would make him watch it when we were kids. He has a comfy couch and popcorn. My room is cute, and his family is wonderful. His sisters are the sweetest things.

That I'm happy is actually the thing making me nervous, I think.

Because I don't really know how to deal with happiness. There's always an end to it. At least in my experience. Flashes of joy like this are always too brief.

"You won't screw it up. Even if you do, I'll be on your side."

I get out of the car, making an exasperated sound. "That's not helpful."

"Sorry. I can't be endlessly sage. I'm going riding with my dad. I'll see you later."

"Yeah," I say, closing the door behind me and standing there on the sidewalk, looking at the cute, red building, gathering up my courage to go inside. As soon as I walk in, there's a feeling of calm. The whole environment of the store is tranquil. But I know immediately that a big part of that is Sammy herself. She comes in from the back, a dreamy expression on her face. "Good morning," she says. "I'm so excited to get started with your training."

"Oh. Good. I... I'm nervous."

Sammy waves her hand. "You don't have to be. There's really no mistake you could possibly make that would make me throw you out the door. It would have to be malicious. And I don't think you're malicious."

I shake my head. "No. I'm not."

"I didn't think so. Everything is just basic retail stuff. Have you done retail?"

"A few years ago. But it was auto parts, not fine jewelry."

"Well. That is different. I think the only specialty thing you might need to know is that we do forever bracelets here. You use a micro welder to put them on. But we won't start you off with that. I don't do all that many of them."

"What are they?"

"Jewelry that you always wear. I mean, you can get it taken off, but the idea is to wear it all the time. I have one," she says, holding her wrist out. "With my husband and kids' initials on it. I'll be adding another little charm once this one is born."

"Oh."

Forever jewelry. It's a weird concept to me, and one I can't wrap my head around. The idea of being so certain of your connections with people that you would get jewelry with their initials on it permanently anchored around your wrist is pretty wild to me. Like tattoos, which I also don't really understand. Because nothing is permanent. Not a place, not a person. The only thing that seems to be permanent is trauma.

What a hilarious realization.

I almost roll my eyes at myself, but don't, because then Sammy will think I'm crazy, or rolling my eyes at her.

"So, how do you know Dallas?" Sammy asks, ushering me back behind the counter. I worry a little bit about the answer, because I know that he doesn't talk about his past as much as I do. He doesn't like to throw his trauma out there like poorly conceived self-defense, which I'm personally such a huge fan of.

"I... I don't know how much you know about his life before he came here..."

"I know that he was in foster care."

"Yes," I say, relieved. "That's where I know him from."

Her face softens, but it's not the kind of pity that I'm accustomed to seeing. This is recognition. "Oh. Well, I'm sorry about that. I'm also a member of the dysfunctional family club. And my husband is a member of the orphaned club, so I have a lot of sympathy for anyone who grows up without stability as a kid. Regardless of the circumstances."

"Oh," I say. "Were you... In foster care?"

"No. I wish." She pulls a face. "Sorry. That seems really insensitive."

I laugh. Because no. It doesn't. Not to me. I get that it would to some people, but as difficult as that was, it was far better than being in my mother's custody. "No. I get it. The worst thing that happened to me was being sent back to live with my mother. After which she kind of dropped off the radar and kept me out of the system, and that wasn't actually a good thing for me."

"Well, I understand that. I moved into a caravan on my parents' property when I was a teenager. I aggressively befriended my now husband, who lived on the ranch next door, and he was my... well, he was my everything. My lifeline, my only connection to a family that was somewhat stable, and his family wasn't exactly traditional."

I'm fascinated by Sammy. Obsessed with her, even. She's so open and ethereal, funny and strange all at once.

While I do spend most of the day getting trained, it's filled with interesting conversation. She tells me all about how her husband raised his siblings and his cousins in a blended family after their parents died in a plane crash.

And how she weaseled her way into the family, finding it much happier than she found her own home.

There's something so *hopeful* about it, about her. She's settled and happy; she has a business and children.

I deliberately avoid thinking about her relationship with her husband, and how the connection that she always had with him reminds me of...

No. I push that aside.

Allison comes in midway through the day, a scowl on her face.

"What's wrong?" I ask.

"Oh. Nothing. Just my... my it's my stepbrother. It's not a big deal."

She doesn't offer more information, and I don't press. I sort of wonder if she wanted me to, if she wanted an excuse to talk about it, but I don't play those kinds of social games. I'm not experienced enough with them. So, I just kind of have to take her at her word.

I still hope that I'll become friends with her. *That*, I would like.

At lunchtime, the door to the shop opens, and I'm shocked when Colt walks in.

"Colt?"

"Sarah," he says, grinning. "I thought we would run into each other at some point. Didn't expect for it to be here."

"Oh God," Allison says. "What are you doing here?"

"Gentry asked me if I would bring you your lunch, you ungrateful varmint."

Well. Clearly, their relationship isn't a delightful, cordial one of a happy blended family. I pick that up from all the context clues.

I'm just so insightful.

"Why didn't he do it himself?"

"He got called out to fight a fire."

Her face immediately shifts to an expression of concern. "Oh."

"It's fine. He would let you know if there was anything dangerous."

Colt leans on the display case, and Allison shoos him. "Don't do that. You'll leave an elbow print above the jewelry."

"When did you start working here?" he asks me, ignoring Allison.

"It's my first day," I say.

"Well. That's great. And how is living with Dallas?"

"Oh. Also great," I say, and my face feels a little bit warm, in spite of everything.

"My mom has a little rental cottage in town, if you ever want to live closer. If you ever need anything. Just let me know."

Allison looks between the two of us, and I feel suddenly awkward. I can't tell if Colt is trying to flirt with me. As part of my issues with certain social nuances, I have trouble figuring out if a man is actually interested in me when he's normal and nice, and not a creep.

I'm used to five-alarm hair-raising experiences that make me want to shoot a man in the chest rather than lean in. That's not this. But I'm also not entirely sure what to do with this.

"Here's your lunch," he says to Allison, passing it over the counter to her. "I've been told it's a steak sandwich. You can chew on that instead of trying to gnaw my arm off for being nice."

"You're never nice," she mutters.

"See you later," he says to me, and walks out the door. Allison's cheeks are vaguely pink.

"You know Colt?" she asks me.

"He's friends with Dallas."

"Yeah. My...Colt is my stepbrother. Our parents married each other when Colt was about sixteen. He's the same age as my brother, Gentry. Gentry, Colt, and Dallas are Gold Valley's own Three Cowboy Musketeers. Gentry doesn't do the rodeo thing, though. He's a wildland firefighter and a rancher."

"Oh. That's... cool."

"Yeah. Except it scares me. But it's still not as stupid as what Colt does."

"Colt won. The last event. I was there."

She rolls her eyes. "Oh. Believe me. I know. He would never miss an opportunity to brag about an achievement."

"You don't like him?"

There I am again, so great with context clues.

"He's arrogant. And kind of an asshole."

That hasn't been my experience of Colt, and I think that it's interesting she thinks so. But maybe there's something I'm not seeing.

"He's being nicer to you because he thinks you're cute," she says.

I feel that in my solar plexus, and I'm not really sure why.

"Oh," I mumble. "Well...."

She huffs. "Colt is nice when he likes women. But he's a user."

"A user?"

She huffs an uncomfortable laugh. "I'm trying to be delicate, he's a slut."

"Oh," I say, laughing. "Don't worry. I'm immune."

She laughs. "They all say that. I'm inoculated against him. I've known him my whole life, which has dimmed the charm somewhat."

I don't say anything, but part of me feels like that's not strictly true. I file that information away, because one thing I'm not going to do is step on my new friend's toes.

And I really think she might be my friend.

Chapter Ten

Dallas

It's a beautiful day, and I'm so glad to be out riding in it, that for once I'm not thinking about everything that's going on with Sarah. She's at work, and while I was a little nervous dropping her off – because *she* was nervous – now I'm just thinking about the moment I'm in.

The trail is glorious, this one winding up into the mountains, around the property, giving a beautiful view of the valley below.

Gold Valley.

The mountains in the distance look blue, the patchwork fields different shades of green. You can see Main Street from up here, cars driving up and down, looking like little toys.

"I'm glad you're home," my dad says.

I turn toward him, where he's stopped his horse a foot or so from mine. He's not looking at the view. He's looking at me.

"Thanks. I'm glad... I'm glad to be here."

"I'm also really glad you brought Sarah. I'm glad that you trusted us with her."

I snort. "Who else would I go to? You're the most important people in my life."

My dad swallows hard, looks away. "I'm glad to hear that. I've been thinking... You know, I realize there are a lot of things I've never told you. Because when you came to live with me, I was so focused on being the best dad I could be. I was trying to tread that line between being a good father, a father that could get you through school, and give you guidance, and... Remember you had that one English teacher threatening to fail you junior year?"

I frown. "Yeah."

"I don't think I ever told you that Kaylee and I went down there and read him the riot act. Told him that he was being ridiculously hard on you, ignoring all the improvement that you made, and all your hard work. But I know that with you, we just told you that you had to be respectful and do the assignments."

"I... I didn't know you did that."

"I know. Like I said, I've been thinking a lot about that stuff lately. And especially with Sarah here, I've been thinking about a lot of the conversations that we've never had. I don't know if you can ever really know how much I regret not being in your life for those first fifteen years. Having the girls has only made it worse."

I'm shocked by that. I was sure that having the girls just fulfilled his desire for a family. Gave him all the things that he wanted. I was sure that his having the girls would erase the pain that he felt about me, if he felt lingering pain at all.

"Why?" I ask.

"Because I'm so aware of what I missed with you.

When Cara was born, I... it was a really happy time. But all I could think about was when you were born. How I wasn't there. How I didn't get to hold you. When she took her first steps, I just thought about how I missed yours. All the things I wasn't there for. Your first words, and kindergarten, and... you throwing soggy Cheerios on the floor."

My chest feels tight, and I feel uncomfortable with the shared emotion. "Come on, Dad. You don't really miss soggy Cheerios."

"I fucking do, actually. I'm really sorry that I never cleaned up yours. And I realized I needed to tell you that. Because as parents... we want to protect our kids. We want to make things seem effortless and easy for you, but that's foolish. Because your life was not effortless or easy before you came to be with me. And I think that you should know how much I regret certain things. How much I care, still, about everything I missed."

I'm not sure what to say to that. Because I've been thinking about all these things too. "I just figured... I figured Lucy and Cara felt a lot more like your real kids to you. Because it's the family that you chose. I..."

He looks like I just stabbed him in the chest, and I regret saying it. I really do.

"Forget it," I say.

"No," he says. "I don't want to forget it. That's how you feel. But it's not true. You're my real family, Dallas. You're my son. I'll have an ache inside of me for the rest of my life because of the years that we missed, because you are so important to me. Missing a single moment would've been hard enough, but I missed fifteen years. I wasn't able to protect you all the time I wanted to. And really, I owe Sarah my thanks. Because she kept you safe, I know she did. All those years that you were away."

"She didn't keep me safe," I say. "She was little."

"Emotionally," he says. "She was your family."

Well. I can't deny that.

"I'm not mad at you," I say. "You know that, right?"

He looks at me, and I can feel the regret. Like everything he's just explained is somehow radiating out of him, transferring itself directly into my chest. I feel the complication of it. I feel the love, too.

"I know," he says. "But that doesn't stop me from being mad at myself, and I don't need you to try and make me feel better."

I shift on the back of the horse. "Shouldn't we try to make each other feel better?"

"I'm your dad, Dallas. So, whatever it is you need, I'm here for you. It's not equal. It doesn't need to be. I'm supposed to take care of you."

I nod. "Yeah. You do."

More than that, he's given me so much of who I am now. I feel guilty, about all the things I haven't been able to heal. I think about what Sarah was saying, about carrying it around like an enchanted ring. It would be easier to just get rid of it, it would be easier if good things wiped it all away, and it would certainly be a better tribute to the man who has given me so much.

But that's not how all this works.

"I didn't know how to ride horses before you," I say. "I didn't even know that I loved them. I never had a dog, I didn't see the point. I would never be where I am now if it weren't for you. I feel like... I know me not finishing college wasn't the best."

"I never cared personally whether you did college or not, I just wanted you to have the option. I didn't want you to take anything from yourself before you were old enough to realize what you were doing. I might not have reacted the best to that."

"You were fine," I say.

"Yeah, but I wasn't happy with you, and I take it you figured that out."

"Sure. But whose dad isn't a little disappointed in them?"

"I'm *not* disappointed in you," he says. "I'm not. But sometimes maybe I overcompensate by being a little intense because I want you to have everything. Hell, look at you. You're a bull riding champion."

"Yeah. I am."

"I mean, that's not all I want for you. Being an absurdly young father means that I could be a young grandfather."

I grimace. "Please. I'm not even remotely to that point."

"I know," he says. "I do. I just mean that I want you to have a family. To fall in love. Whatever that looks like for you."

"That's what you thought was happening when you saw a girl on my front door camera," I say.

He snorts. "Sure. It's not what's happening?"

"I told you. She's like family. I just want to take care of her. All the things that you just said you wanted for me, that's what I want for her. I want her to have a good life. More than that, I want her to be safe. I want her to feel safe."

"It's awful to watch someone you care about go through this kind of stuff. I mean, I don't have experience with exactly this. But you know, Kaylee had a pretty rough life, and we were friends when we were younger."

I shift uncomfortably because it feels like he's turning the conversation back to the possibility of romance between

Sarah and me. Though, I know he's just telling me about his own life.

"Yeah. But she's here now."

"Yep. And she has you."

Instead, we finish up the ride, and I look at the time and realize I need to go down and pick Sarah up. Eventually, we're going to have to go back to Sisters and move her out of her apartment, get her car, and get everything that she needs. But right now, it's okay that I'm the one who's going to pick her up. But I'm the one who's going to take care of her.

I shower, get dressed and headed to town, and as soon as I drive in, I see Sarah standing out in front of the shop. With Colt. He's leaning against the side of the building, chatting to her like she...

Like she's one of his Buckle Bunnies. I know the posture. I know his game.

Well. That's not fucking happening. He doesn't know anything about her. She probably doesn't want him talking to her. She might even feel...

I pull my truck up against the curb. I know that I can't come barreling out looking angry at one of my oldest friends, but I feel angry.

How dare he? How dare he assume that Sarah wants his attention? His ego is out of control.

"You come in first in one big event and you start thinking you're pretty big stuff?"

I think I've managed to keep my tone conversational, but a little bit confrontational.

Colt steps back and looks at me, chuckling. "Well, I don't know. I would leave that verdict up to Sarah."

Motherfucker.

"Yeah. I think Sarah's fine. She doesn't need to give you a Best in Show ribbon just because you want one."

"Wow."

"Colt is fine," Sarah says, shooting me a strange glance and moving nearer to me. "If I didn't want to talk to him, he would know. But I've enjoyed it. Thanks for keeping me company, since Dallas was late."

I looked down at the time. "Dallas is only ten minutes late."

"I appreciate the company all the same," she says, not looking at me.

Well. Well, that's just fine.

"I was thinking I could take you to dinner," I say.

"Oh. To Mustard Seed?"

"Sure," I say. "In fact, we can just walk from here. See you later, Colt."

He gives me a look that I can't quite pull apart, and I decide that I don't really care if I do. "This way," I say.

She turns and waves at Colt, and as soon as we go around the corner she looks over at me. "What was that?"

"What?"

"You were kind of mean to your friend."

"I didn't want him to bother you."

"Who said he was bothering me?"

"Listen, Sarah, I know that you don't like men to be in your space, and I know you don't like to be touched. He doesn't know any of that, and he was being presumptuous."

"Yes, Dallas, you do know all that, but I'm also perfectly capable of taking care of myself. I have been, in fact, for years, and if I wanted Colt away from me, he would've been away from me. But I like him. He's nice."

"Oh. He's not... he's not nice."

"You're the second person to try to warn me off him

today, though I think the first person was trying to warn me off because she has a crush on Colt. Do you have a crush on him too?"

"Please. If I were going to bed down with a rodeo cowboy, it would never be a bull rider. Those pricks are bad news."

"So, does that mean you're bad news?"

"To most everybody except you," I say.

And then I feel bad about it. Because I shouldn't be saying things like that to her. I'm not even sure which way I meant it, or who I was trying to insult. What I was trying to prove.

I just feel out of sorts and unhappy after seeing that interaction. Sarah, for her part, is clearly annoyed at me, but also kind of amused that I'm bothered.

I can see that amusement in the evil little smirk on her face, and I remember that more playful side of her from when she was a kid, and how it used to drive me nuts. Because whenever she was like that, I knew she was up to no good, and all that no good would eventually become my problem. She was always the kind of kid who would start something so that I could finish it. And I can see that, now that she's not feeling quite as stressed, now that she isn't actively afraid for her safety, that's definitely still part of who she is.

"So, what? You want him to flirt with you?"

"He seems harmless," she says. "So why not? Get a little practice in."

Practice.

I don't like the direction this conversation is going at all. In fact, I hate it. She needs to get established here. She needs to get to where she's feeling secure. I don't want her to be so traumatized that she could never date anybody, but

I also don't want her dating Colt, who certainly wouldn't be much use in healing her trauma.

No. Maybe that isn't fair, it's not like Colt isn't a decent guy, he is. But he's definitely a one-night stand kind of guy, and that's not right for somebody like Sarah. Somebody who's been hurt like she has. A man would have to take his time with her. Check in with her, make sure she was okay. He'll have to know her. And that just isn't Colt.

I push all thoughts about what I think my friend might need sexually aside. Because that's a weird thing to be pondering. And then I gesture for her to cross the street toward the little yellow building where we're going to grab dinner.

"Well, well, well," Gloria says, looking up from the register when we walk in. "Look what the bull dragged in."

"Hey, Gloria," I say.

She crosses the space and wraps her arms around me, giving me a hug. "Long time without seeing your sweet face, Dallas Dodge."

"Yeah. I'm home for a couple of months."

"And who's this?"

"This is my friend Sarah. She's..." I need to just start saying it. There's nothing to be ashamed of and acting like there is puts some of that shame onto her too, and I hate it. "She was my foster sister. Back before I came to live in Gold Valley. Back before Bennett found me."

"That's a wonderful reunion," she says, beaming at us. "Your dinner is on the house."

"No way," I say. "You don't have to give me dinner."

"I want to. You're a good kid." She winks at me.

Sarah and I sit down at one of the tables. The dining room in Mustard Seed is tiny, one little square room, the floor covered in bright copper pennies that have epoxied into a high-gloss shell. There are quirky fork sculptures — silverware fashioned into creatures with googly eyes—hanging from the ceiling, whimsical and unsettling all at once.

By the end of the month, the seniors at Gold Valley High School will have their names written on the window, celebrating their achievement. It's hard to believe it's been six years since my own name was there.

Hard to believe that I'm here now with Sarah.

Yeah. It's all pretty damned hard to believe.

I order us two cheeseburgers, two orders of sweet potato fries, and two chocolate milkshakes, and I'm going to leave Gloria a tip that totals the cost of the whole meal, she can't stop me.

Sarah takes a bite of the burger, her eyes rolling back in her head. "This is delicious," she says.

"Yeah. Best in town. There are some fancier places, but to me, nothing beats this."

It might be the nostalgia. There's so much tied up in this place. It's where we ate after Dad and I decided to become a real family. It's where my name was written after graduation. Where I sat with friends who became even better friends, and went on my first date in town. Showing this to her is pretty much the best I can do as far as sharing the life that I've been living since we lost each other.

"I just have a lot of memories here."

"It's great." She takes a bite of one of her sweet potato fries and chews thoughtfully. "I had a good day at work. Thanks for asking."

"Sorry. I had an overprotective older brother moment."

The words feel a little bit... off. Like I might be lying, but I don't mean to lie. And I can't think what else I would mean. What else it is.

I don't think about it too deeply. I just take another bite of my hamburger.

"Tell me about it," I say.

"You decided to be weird and controlling instead of asking me how my day at work went, you were rude to Colt—"

"That's not what I mean. And I think you know that. I mean, how was work?"

"Oh. It was good. Sammy makes all the jewelry in her store, which is really cool. And she does this permanently installed jewelry, and that's something she's going to teach me how to do. I got to watch her do a bracelet for someone today. It was interesting. It's definitely different than working at an auto parts store."

"That's great."

"I think so," she says.

But I'm still going over my reaction to Colt talking to her. It was me being overprotective. Because I do know her. And I think that's reasonable.

I'm *totally reasonable*.

We finish dinner, and I leave a stack of cash on the table. "This is the opposite of a dine and dash," I say. "We've got to get out of here before she realizes we paid."

I jump up from the table quickly, and Sarah follows me. She does an exaggerated sneak once we get out the door and onto the sidewalk, and I smile at her ridiculousness. I pretty much forget everything that happened with Colt after that.

Because it doesn't really matter anyway. She's fine. That's what's important.

It's the only thing that matters.

Chapter Eleven

Sarah

I hear Dallas come in and decide it's time to tell him we have plans for the evening.

"I think you're legally obligated to watch The Hobbit with me tonight."

"I think I'm not."

I look up from the kitchen table, where I've been working on some homework for one of my classes. It's been a week of working at Sammy's, of being with Dallas, I'm feeling like my nervous system might actually be settling down.

Nothing has been weird since that incident with Colt, when Dallas was acting like my angry older brother.

I'm not sure Dallas knows how ludicrous it is that he thinks he has to worry I might get taken in by some wolf in sheep's clothing. No one could be more cynical about men than I am, and genuinely no one could be less likely to fall for something they don't want to fall for.

Whether or not I want to fall for it is a question that I've been wrestling with ever since that day. Colt is interested in me. Physically. Dallas knows him, which means that he's... safe. In spite of how Dallas reacted.

And I really want to cast this ring into the fire. So to speak. The fact that I've never had a romantic or sexual relationship is getting uncomfortable. I probably have a couple more years before it gets super weird. But given I'm not attending a Christian college, it's already a little odd. And here's one thing I know from experience, when you're already weird, and you let things go on without correcting them, you only begin to get more brittle and set in those ways. You end up saying things like: I've never really had a family dinner.

It makes everyone uncomfortable. The last thing I need is to bring all of my own issues into a sexual encounter I have to admit that I'm a laughably old virgin who also has pretty severe trauma around touch. Those are things I don't want to explain. There are details I don't want to get into. Somebody like Colt is maybe kind of ideal, honestly. He doesn't seem to possess enough interest in who I am as a person to become a problem.

Maybe that's mean. He's perfectly nice, but I get the impression that what Allison said about him is true. He's here for a good time, not a long time, and there's just enough of a connection with him. Just enough. It feels almost reasonable.

But that's a whole tangle for another time. It's my birthday that has me thinking all of this, in addition to Colt being flirtatious. I've seen him a few times when he's been passing by the store, and I don't think he's passing by accidentally.

So yeah. I can see an opportunity there. But I'm also

still weird and fearful and completely unsure of what I want, or even more worrisome, I don't really want it. I've never wanted it. And I feel like I need to in order to get on the path to being a functional human being. To actually banish my trauma once and for all. Maybe Colt's penis is my Mount Doom.

I frown.

"What's wrong?"

I didn't realize that I was broadcasting my thoughts. "Nothing," I lie.

"Fine. I'll watch The Hobbit with you if you're going to pout like that. I can't bear it."

Well. There. My response to something totally unrelated got me my way. Fine by me.

"It *is* my birthday week," I say. "And I think you should have to do it for that reason alone."

"Okay," he says. "I think that's fair enough. Though, I think you can agree that you've made me watch an awful lot of this."

"Yeah. Maybe."

I bat my eyes at him, because I feel like being ridiculous, and even though he can't read my mind, I want to move my thoughts further and further away from where they were. Because I don't want him to have any inkling of what I'm thinking about.

"Popcorn, please," I say.

He sighs and looks long-suffering as he immediately moves to make my request a reality.

I owe him dinner. I'm not the best cook, but I think I should make him something. I got my first paycheck last week, and I've been hoarding it. But now that I know all my bills are paid, I should go grocery shopping, do something to support him. Given how much he's supported me.

I definitely owe him many bags of popcorn.

He puts it in the microwave, and I make my way over to the couch, abandoning homework. I'll have to finish that paper by tomorrow, but that's fine. It's interesting because I was always resentful of homework when I was in school, but now that I'm working so hard to be at school, to make my way toward my goal, I feel a lot different about it. It's a privilege to have it, honestly, so even if sometimes I don't love it, I'm just glad that I'm able to do college.

It's cold in the room, so I decide to go to my bedroom and steal a blanket, which I then wrap around myself as I curl up on the couch.

Dallas walks in front of the couch, looks at me, and flings the bag of popcorn onto me.

"Hey," I say, scrambling to unwrap my hands from the blanket. "That's mean."

"I'm actually very nice."

"Yeah. So nice."

"I'll even put the movie on for you."

"Thank you," I say.

He smiles, and I feel like happiness washes through my entire body. It's such a weird feeling, not one I've ever felt before.

Maybe it's being settled. Because that's definitely new. When we were kids, I had started to take for granted that he was my safe place, but even then, we were moving around. I guess it's only been not quite two weeks, and it's a little bit dramatic, I've also certainly been in places longer, but it hasn't felt like *this*. Like home, like family. Like long dinners and silly kids' games. Like safety, Comfort, and ease.

And all of that with my wonderful friend, who is the most beautiful man in the entire world, and it makes me feel proud just to look at him. Makes it feel like my heart is going to burst through my chest. Makes me feel like maybe everything is going to be okay and anything is possible.

So yeah. I guess what I feel is happiness.

Even with the popcorn bag thrown on me. Anyway, I don't mind, because then I tear into the bag and begin to eat far more than my share, which has been our MO with popcorn.

"I was thinking, on your actual birthday, maybe we can get a few people together that you've met here to come to the saloon."

I frown, stopping chewing mid-mouthful of popcorn. "I don't know very many people." I grimace. "I also don't really do birthday parties."

"Well, I think you should. Twenty-one is a big deal."

"I don't know about that. I mean, I guess it's kind of a big deal that I've survived this long."

I do hear myself. I know that what I just said sounds a little bit sad. I know that. That surviving is different than living. At least, I know it in theory. But all I've ever had are little tastes of living. Like a shot of flavor on your tongue, a piece of cotton candy that makes a direct hit, a burst of sweetness that's gone too soon.

"Maybe that will be my twenty-one-year resolution," I say. "To live."

"As opposed to?"

I realize that he can't read my thoughts, which is slightly jarring, because a lot of the time it feels like he can. "Surviving. I guess the two of them are probably different."

"Yeah," he says. "I would guess so."

I think about him. About how he's chosen to do such a risky job for a living, even while being given a life that is safe, secure.

"Why do you put your survival at risk when you don't have to?"

He looks at me. "What?"

"Well, I was thinking. Thinking about how you don't have to do a job like the one that you do. You could die, and for what? We were always at risk when we were kids. Much higher risk than most. But now... You don't have to be."

"I don't really think of it that way. I guess it goes back to what you just said. You have to live. Instead of just survive, and that means thriving instead of thinking about strict survival. I ride because I love it."

"I think maybe you're a liar," I say.

"I don't..." He looks away. Then he lets out an exasperated breath and sits down on the couch beside me. "Let's just watch the movie."

"Why? Because now you're frustrated with me?"

"I'm not frustrated with you."

"Well, then you're frustrated with yourself. You don't want to think about your issues."

"I don't have issues," he says.

"You really are a liar."

"I'm not. I just... All right. I do. And I feel really stupid talking about any of them with you, just like I feel dumb talking about them to my dad, even though I did about a week ago. After you and I talked."

"It's okay that you didn't get out unscathed. If anything, it makes me feel a little better."

"I think it looks ungrateful."

"It doesn't. I promise. Well. I don't promise. But you're allowed to be complicated."

"Thanks," he says.

And then he does hit play on the movie, because obviously he's a little bit tired of me pushing him.

I don't really know why I'm doing it. But maybe that's it. Maybe he makes me feel a little bit less lonely. I don't want them to be totally okay, because I'm not okay. I'm a broken mess, and if Dallas isn't a little bit of a broken mess with me, then I don't really know what I am. That's tough. And I feel more than a little bit mad about it.

The familiarity of the movie washes over me, distracts me from my darker musings. But as much as I love this journey through Middle-earth, Dallas is not enjoying it quite as much, and he starts to nod off, his blond head dipping as the movie wears on.

I smile and throw a piece of my blanket over his lap. His head falls back against the back of the couch, and eventually he slumps against me, heavy and far too warm, so I don't really need my blanket anymore.

He ends up lying down, head in my lap, and I look down at him, studying the lines of his face with my eyes, taking this opportunity to look closely at him.

I lift my hand, my fingers hovering over him. I touch a lock of his hair that's fallen onto his forehead, and sweep it away. This feels safe. Because it's Dallas. Because he's asleep. Because I can look at him, how beautiful he is right now.

Looking at him hurts. My chest, my stomach.

Not in a bad way.

It's just the way that he is.

I let out a slow, shaky breath. I think about Colt. Will I actually let him touch me? Kiss me?

I look at Dallas's lips. Thinking about them pressed against my skin makes me shiver with a kind of sensual longing I didn't know I had the capacity for. I have such an intense, visceral reaction to it, and it isn't negative.

I don't know anything about being kissed. Feeling desired. I don't know anything about mutual wanting.

And my eyes fill with tears as I think *maybe* I could feel all that someday. Maybe.

I move my hand away from Dallas's face, and I don't move away from him.

I just relish it. His body against mine. I let it be something that feels soothing. I don't think about sex. But my heart is still beating fast, and I can feel need gathering at the center of my thighs, because apparently I can be basic. Apparently, I can be just like other girls. Apparently, I can feel need and desire, and maybe I'm not such an alien after all.

Maybe I can be normal. Maybe I can live, instead of just survive.

I feel something that I think might be longing. Yearning. I don't actually want to get better acquainted with that feeling. Because I know what it's like in other contexts. To want something that you can't have. To wish that things could be different. I'm caught up in that feeling now.

What if he and I met at school? In this beautiful town. What if I had a family, a functional mom and dad, and we ate dinner around the table every night?

Except he probably still wouldn't have asked me to be his date to any school dances because he's too much older than me. Because there's a reason he was always like a surrogate older brother, and not a potential boyfriend, and that doesn't even have anything to do with me and my issues.

He was too much older *then*, it doesn't feel like it *now*. He's just too important to me. He can't be my experiment. Not ever. And I ignore how hollow that makes me feel.

How sad it makes me. Because I have enough. Enough to live. I don't need to be greedy. I have Dallas. As my best friend. My beautiful, wonderful best friend, and that's enough.

It's certainly more than I ever expected to have.

Chapter Twelve

Dallas

"I want to do something nice for Sarah's birthday," I say, lingering in my mom's kitchen long after dinner is over.

"When is it?"

"It's tomorrow."

She rolls her eyes. "Dallas," she says. "A little advanced warning would be good. We could have a party for her here."

"I told her I'd take her to the saloon. Because she's turning twenty-one."

She looks at me. "And you've cleared this with her for real?"

"I have. And I invited a couple of people."

Inviting Colt made me feel edgy, but I did it, because it's not about me, it's about Sarah, and he is one of the people that she's met. I also invited Allison, who I believe is bringing her brother Gentry, and Gentry is probably bringing his friend Lily, since wherever he goes, she goes, and it's another opportunity for Sarah to meet a woman who lives in town.

"All right. So, what do you need to make it special?"

"I don't know. A cake. I've never baked a cake."

She smiles at me. "Okay, well, let's go to the store. I can get you a cake mix. You can make it here. Isn't she studying at your place tonight?"

I nod.

"All right. So, let's get to baking."

She drives me to the local grocery store, and I choose a strawberry cake mix because it's pink. And glittery sprinkles. I definitely go overboard with candles and decorations.

I've never made a cake, and I have no idea how to even decorate one. But I just grabbed everything I thought looked like Sarah.

Pretty and princessy.

Maybe I'm thinking of her when she was younger. But she didn't have enough birthday parties. She didn't have enough good things, and I want to give them to her. I want it more than I want anything in that moment.

Kaylee has a soft look on her face, something that seems a lot like contentment, and it makes my chest feel bruised. She adopted me officially years ago. She's really the only mom I know. And I'm really lucky. In the mom stakes, they don't get much better than she does. She was good at giving me tough love when I needed it, even before she was dating my dad.

"I think you did a great job," she says, insisting that she paid for the basket of groceries, which I think is outrageous.

"I'm an adult, Mom," I say.

"Not to me really," she says.

And then she makes me put the cart back, which feels fair.

We drive back to the ranch, and she proves to me that making a box cake really is very simple, and I don't have to be intimidated by it. I just have to follow the instructions.

"I know you don't love following instructions," she says.

I roll my eyes at her.

I play video games with the girls while we wait for the cake to bake and then cool. They have my old Xbox from back in the day, and it's crazy to me that they find it even remotely relevant, but they are children. It's been a long time since I've played video games. My poor dad bought the Xbox for me to blackmail me into liking him, I'm pretty sure.

I didn't need it.

But I did have a lot of fun with it.

When the cake is cool, Kaylee doesn't help me at all as I decorate it.

It becomes a free-for-all. Pink icing dripping everywhere, glittery sugar sprinkles and pearlescent chocolate beads in random spots over the top of it. Then she hands me a bag of bright pink frosting for piping, and I write *Happy Birthday Sarah* in the most hideous handwriting you've ever seen.

"What do you think?" I ask.

She puts her arm around me and gives me a squeeze. "I think you're probably the best friend she could ever ask for."

That warms me, even though I'm also aware she didn't compliment the cake itself. Either way, I feel a deep satisfaction in my soul. I know the cake is ugly. But it's for *her*. If I could've put my heart in the middle of it and somehow not die, and have it not be gross, I would've done that.

"She means a lot to you," Kaylee says, and it doesn't feel loaded when she says it. I don't feel like she's trying to convince me that my relationship with Sarah needs to evolve into something else. It's like she actually sees and recognizes the connection.

"Yeah. I think... I think she's the first person I ever loved."

"That's really special, Dallas."

She means it. She's not placating me or just trying to make me feel better or whatever. She means it.

And I agree.

Because Sarah is the most precious person to me. Maybe because I know how difficult everything has been for her. So, I hope that I can give her a birthday that feels a little bit nice. It won't make up for everything, but it'll be something.

Chapter Thirteen

Sarah

I decide to go with a white dress with pink flowers for my birthday party. And I put on more pink eyeshadow than normal, and some glitter on my cheeks, because I am the birthday girl, after all, and I can't say that that's ever really meant anything to me.

But Dallas says it's a big deal for me to turn twenty-one, and so I'm going to treat it like a big deal.

Maybe I'll even order a drink.

A pink one.

I smile a little bit as I think about that.

I walk out into the living room where Dallas is standing, wearing a black T-shirt and blue jeans, a black cowboy hat. His shoulders are broad, so is his chest, his waist narrow. He's a solid wall of muscle. I already know that from all the times I've hugged him. His body is warm, and I remember the heat from when he fell asleep on my lap the other night.

I remember how it feels to be pressed up against him. I look down at his hands.

I've associated a man's hands with pain for a long time. Pain and fear and disgust. But when I look at Dallas', I don't feel any of that. I imagine what they would look like, big hands gripping the fabric of my white dress.

No. I shove the thoughts away, and I smile.

"I'm ready for my party."

"Good," he says. His eyes flick over me, like he's looking at something mundane. I can't read the expression on his face, but it's almost like he's trying to be too casual, and I'm not sure why I think that.

"Ready to go?"

"Yes," I say.

We get into the truck, and as I'm buckling, I look over my left shoulder and spot a platter covered with a tall, metal lid.

"What's that?"

"A surprise," he says.

"A *surprise?* I get a surprise?"

"Yeah. Because it's your birthday."

"Well, that's nice." I see a little package back there too, with a pink ribbon on it, and I'm secretly pleased that the ribbon is pink because it is my favorite color, even though I try to pretend that it isn't. Because just like in my little fantasy where I think about Dallas and I meeting at school, I sometimes imagine who I would be if I didn't have to be tough. If I didn't learn that being a girl is dangerous. If it hadn't made me hate the things about me that were feminine or soft.

I think I would really like everything to be pink. I've really embraced the summer dress, because in recent years I've tried to disentangle my hatred and loathing about the past from the way that I feel about my body, from the way that I feel about clothing, but there are still things that linger, I wonder who I would be if I felt like I had the freedom to be feminine and pretty all the time. To experiment with makeup and high heels. To look sexy, even. I can honestly say I've never attempted it.

He pulls the truck up to the curb, I get out and so does he, collecting the pan, and placing the little present on top.

"Come on," he says.

And then we walk into the bar together. The bar is a funky place, styled like an old-fashioned saloon, with a large liquor cabinet behind the glossy bar top that looks ancient. "Laz," he says, greeting the tall man behind the counter, with a big smile and a pine tree tattoo on his forearm. "Good to see you."

"Good to see you too, Dallas.

"This is my friend Sarah. It's her twenty-first birthday."

"Oh well, we'll have some drinks on the house for the birthday girl."

I smile, because the attention doesn't feel creepy or wrong. And maybe some of that is because he has a bright gold wedding band on his left hand, but it just feels friendly, and I feel safe because I'm with Dallas.

"You can think about what you want," I say.

"Something... Fruity?"

"That sounds good," Dallas says.

"I don't know. I'm probably the only person with a background as sketchy as ours who didn't do any underage drinking."

Dallas looks at me. "Probably."

We go over to a table in the corner, where he sets all the things down. "Why didn't you drink?"

"I always felt like I needed to be in control."

"Fair enough. You don't have to be in control tonight, though. I am your designated driver for the evening. And I'll be taking care of you. You can do whatever you want."

I'm about to demand a cake reveal when Colt, Allison, and two people I've never met walk into the bar as a group. They see Dallas, though, and smile and wave.

"Hey, Sarah," he says. "This is Gentry and Lily. And you already know Colt and Allison."

"Hi," I say.

"We're just doing the very important work of deciding what Sarah is going to have for her first drink."

"Well, that's very important," Lily says.

"I had Laz make me a strawberry daiquiri," Allison says. "My birthday was three months ago."

"Is that sweet, and is it pink?"

"Yes and yes."

"Then I guess I'll have that."

"I'll order for you," Allison offers cheerfully.

"Dallas," I say, elbowing him. "Show me the cake."

He looks a little sheepish, then hesitant, but pulls the cover off the cake, revealing quite possibly the most garish, hideous thing I've ever seen. The frosting is dripping, the top layer is sliding slightly to the left, and there's too much of the pink sugar glitter, with larger, rounder pearls that seem to have been placed on top of the cake at random.

I know instantly that he made it himself.

I also know that it's the most incredible thing I've ever been given.

In spite of myself and all my prickles, my eyes fill with tears.

"Dallas," I whisper.

Colt turns away from the bar, two beers in his hand, and

comes over to the table. "Where did you have that made? I'll make a note to never go there."

"I made it," Dallas says.

"Oh," says Colt. "Well. It's nice."

"Fuck you." Dallas scowls.

"You made that for her?" Allison asks. "That is so sweet."

"Oh, that's *so sweet*," says Lily.

"It's an ugly cake, guys." Colt is being honest, but mean.

"It's sweet," says Lily. "No man has ever made a cake for me."

"Me either."

"No man has ever gone on a date with you," Gentry says to his younger sister.

"Rude," says Allison.

Now I'm wondering what's in the gift box.

I can't begin to guess because I don't have a gauge for the kind of gift Dallas would buy. Well, not what adult Dallas might buy.

I can remember him getting me a bracelet out of one of those little machines you put a quarter in and you get a little plastic ball with a trinket inside. He was so proud that he got that for me, and I treasured it, until another kid who lived with us broke it.

She took delight in it. Like crushing something that I loved might heal something inside of her.

I punched her in the face.

I don't know whether to cry, smile or shrug at the memory. It's one of many just like it. We've lived a life full of bright little moments in the middle of a lot of sad things. Living around the sad things that other people are grappling with, and it makes for a lot of complicated memories.

I'm tired of complicated. Sometimes it feels like all I'll ever be is a tangle of knots I can't undo.

Well. That's a cheery birthday thought. The alcohol is seeming like a better and better idea as time ticks by and I start getting lost in my thoughts.

My drink arrives, and I'm excited by it. I sip, and the buzz goes to my head. It isn't the law that's kept me from drinking, it's my fear of losing control. On what it could mean for me. But I feel safe here. With him, with his friends. It almost makes me giddy.

The other girls order drinks, and for a minute there, I feel like I might be normal.

The more I drink, the more I feel *normal*. The more all of those tangled, knotted, complex memories fade into something diffused. They're not so sharp. They don't have any power over me.

There's music playing on the jukebox, and I stand up, shimmying my shoulders. I have terrible rhythm even when sober, and now, edging toward tipsy, I know that it isn't improved. "Care to dance?"

I turn and see Colt standing there, handsome and offering, and why not?

Why not?

Yes, normally, a man's touch would make me recoil. But I want to change that. I want to change *me*. So, I take his offered hand, and it's fine. Everything is okay. I'm not panicked. My body is loose, and I feel good. This is how things should be. You should feel good more often than you feel bad. You should be happy.

You should be able to go out with friends and have a good time, and have a birthday party. All things that I've never been able to do. God, I *want it*.

I want this to be fun.

So, I let him twirl me in a circle, and I laugh when he draws me up against his chest, facing away from him as we sway, and he spins me out again, and I twirl in a circle like I am the birthday queen, and I really would like to be.

The song slows down, and he brings me close, and there is a slight difference in the way he's looking at me now. If I wanted to sleep with him, I think I could. But maybe I should start with smaller goals.

Maybe I should just think in terms of a kiss.

A *kiss* wouldn't be so bad.

I feel a little bit sorry for him, because he's more guinea pig than man to me. An experiment more than an object of my desire. But my inhibitions are loosened, and I like the way I feel. My motives might not be pure, but then, maybe his aren't either. He's a man who's free with his favors, as far as I'm aware, as far as everyone has led me to believe, so it doesn't need to mean anything to him.

And that, I feel, is a good thing for me.

He puts his hand on my face, and I don't hate it.

"Hey," Dallas says, suddenly breaking the spell. Breaking through the haze. "You should come eat some cake."

He's sitting at the table, half a bar away from us, shouting like a fool. And I know he's sober because he's the designated driver.

"Right now?" I ask.

"Yeah, you better go have it," Colt says, releasing his hold on me, his expression wary. "I don't want to have a bar fight."

I feel dizzy, that drink hit me harder than I realized, and I'm not mad about it. Because I feel great. Genuinely so good. Except now I'm a little mad at Dallas. But I sit down at the table, and he pushes the cake over to me. His expression is sullen, and I don't think I've done anything to earn that.

He takes two candles out of a bag and puts them on top. A two and a one. I'm momentarily mollified by this gesture. He lights the candles with that same flat expression.

"Sing," he says.

They all do, but everyone is now stressed out by his behavior, and so am I. Because he's not enjoying himself, that much is certain.

He cuts the cake, and scoops a large, pink piece onto a plate for me.

"It's strawberry," he says.

"And God dammit I'm gonna like it," I say, mimicking his tone. Because I'm kind of over it.

He's being a grump, and I don't know why, and yes, the cake is a nice gesture, and the candles were lovely, but he's pouting, maybe because I'm not paying attention to him? And that feels childish.

"I'll eat the piece of cake in a minute, come and dance with me, Colt?"

"Sure," he says.

"I have a present for you," Dallas says, taking the small box and handing it to me. I'm standing there, holding Colt's hand, mid-step toward the dance floor, and Colt is thrusting that pink ribboned box at me like it's got a bug in it.

"Oh. Do you?"

"Open it," he says.

"Open it..." And that's when I lose my temper. It could be the alcohol. Because I just feel weird. Loose, reckless, a lot more distilled to my essence than normal. Normally, I would be anxious. Normally, I would be thinking everything through, turning it over, examining it from every angle.

I would be panicking over Colt's hand being in mine, and I would be bothered that I had upset Dallas.

But I'm not thinking anything through, I'm just feeling, and that seems fair. Because it *is* my birthday. I suddenly remember that song about it being *my* party, so I can cry if I want.

I don't want to cry.

I want to yell.

I let go of Colt, snatch the gift, then grab Dallas by the hand. "Outside," I grumble, dragging him out the back of the saloon into the street. The door slams shut behind us, and we are left out in the muggy, overly hot evening.

The sun has gone down, but the atmosphere has retained all the warmth like an oven that hasn't quite cooled yet. It's baked into the brick of the building, radiating around us, but it's not as hot as my temper.

"What is the matter with you?" I ask, waving the present at him.

"With me? You're drunk, and you're off dancing with Colt. He should know better."

"He should? What does he have to do with anything? I chose to dance with him."

"You're drunk," he says. "Do I really need to explain to you how consent works?"

Rage floods me. "Oh. Fuck you. I am *well aware* of how it all works, thank you. I am a woman, walking in the world, a woman who has been severely traumatized by men and their appetites, and I don't need your concern to pop up at my twenty first birthday party, you absolute dick."

"Sarah—"

He feels bad now, I can see it in his face. I know he wishes he hadn't said that. That he regrets it. I don't care.

I'm going to make him regret it harder. Because how dare he?

"Don't you know that I've been living by myself for years? That I've been taking care of myself. I've been isolated and sad, but I've been safe. And tonight, with you in there, dancing with your friend, you know that I'm safe. You don't have to ruin it. Because you're..."

Overprotective. That's what it was. For one moment, I look at him, at his beautiful face, those glittering blue eyes, and I wish it were jealousy. I really do. But all this is some misguided attempt at protecting me. All this is Dallas treating me like a child.

Like the child no one ever treated me like when I was one.

I don't need to be coddled now that I'm twenty-one years old. I've done enough hiding. I've done enough psychotic protecting of myself.

"I don't need your misplaced pity," I say. "Your misplaced honor. This is supposed to be *my* night. And if you have so many issues with Colt, you shouldn't be his friend."

"That's not it. It's not that I think there's anything wrong with him, it's just that–"

"You think there's something wrong with me!" I explode. "That's it. You can't deny it. Because what he's doing would be fine with any other woman, but you think that I'm some kind of fragile little fairy that isn't allowed to do this. But I want to. I'm tired of this. I'm tired of being locked away, put up on a shelf, I do it to myself, and I don't need you to do it too. Keep your fucking present." I throw it at him then. Absolutely launch it at his head.

He tries to catch it, the box bouncing against his palms, before hitting the sidewalk.

"Sarah..."

"No. Go home. I'm going to finish having my party with people who don't know me. That's the problem, Dallas Dodge. You know me, and it's supposed to be a good thing, but you've turned it into something I hate. Maybe this doesn't work. You and me. Maybe it doesn't work because you still think I'm a kid. Maybe it doesn't work because you'll never let me live because you only ever see me as a victim. I don't want to live that way."

"That is pretty fucking amazing," he says. "That you came to me looking for protection and now you're angry when I offer it."

"I think you're smart enough to understand the difference between me being afraid of the pedophile that tortured me when I was a child versus having a dance with your friend at a bar. But if it's all the same to you, go fuck yourself."

I turn around and try to open the bar door, but the back door doesn't open from inside, and I scream and kick it. Then I stomp away from Dallas, going around to the front of the saloon, pushing the door open and coming inside. Colt, Gentry, Allison and Lily are at the back staring keenly at the door when I storm in.

I'm breathing hard, and I look at the cake, and I have two options. I can burst into tears, or I can order another drink.

"Bartender," I say. "Another daiquiri, please."

I wipe invisible tears off my cheeks and make my way back to where the group is.

"Are you okay?" Allison asks.

"I'm okay."

"You need a place to stay tonight?"

I nod. "Yes. I do."

It feels scary, it feels a little bit painful, but I need some distance from Dallas. I feel a little bit bad about how I handled that. Which is why I need that drink to come faster.

Guilt is not for my birthday.

I can deal with the guilt tomorrow.

Chapter Fourteen

Sarah

Apparently, it's not only guilt that comes with the bright light of day, but a hangover. I've heard that some people don't remember clearly the things that they do when they're drunk.

Very sadly for me, I have a clear recollection of everything that happened last night.

I'm staying in the guest bedroom at Allison's cottage in town. It's an adorable place, one that she's renting from Colt's mom – her stepmother, I've discovered – at a reduced rate, at least I think that's what she said when we stumbled inside out of Gentry's truck. She was more than a little tipsy herself.

I roll out of bed, and put the floral cover back in place, before stumbling out into the kitchen area. The cake is sitting at the center of the table, half demolished. I have a vague memory of us, drunk, eating that while we both complained about men.

Her complaints are largely about Colt. And it occurs to me that her hatred of Colt feels just sharp enough to be something a lot more problematic. Yes, he's her stepbrother, and that would be pretty messed up. But I'm not judging. I'm so messed up. If I'm right, though, she's very good at hiding her feelings. Maybe even from herself. Even if everything last night hadn't been so bad, being certain about that makes me also certain that Colt is not the one for me to do my experimenting on.

But that isn't my biggest problem.

The door across the hall opens, and Allison comes out, blinking furiously like a mole that's been pulled unceremoniously from its burrow.

"Morning," she says, sounding muffled.

My head pulses. "Oh. Good morning."

"Last night was kind of crazy," she says.

"Yeah."

We don't speak as she makes coffee, and we both sit down and sip it quietly.

"Did anyone text Dallas?"

"Yeah. Gentry let him know where you were."

"Good," I say, because as mad at him as I am, I don't want him to actually worry about me. I sigh heavily. "I'm going to have to get back home. But I don't have a car."

"I can take you," Allison says.

"Really?"

"Yeah. I don't mind. But I do need to... maybe take a shower first."

"Fair."

While she does that, I sit there and stare at the wall, my thoughts tripping over themselves. I was ridiculous and overreacted last night, but he did too. I shouldn't have thrown anything at him, though.

I've actually never been overprotected.

Not by anyone but myself.

So even though Dallas was ridiculous, I should have been a little bit... I don't know. More grateful? Grateful that somebody finally cares what happens to me at all?

That thought makes me growl. What an obnoxious situation to find myself in.

Allison emerges a few minutes later, and we load up into the truck. I put my hand on my forehead.

"Is he always that jealous?" she asks.

I huff a laugh. "He wasn't *jealous*. He's overprotective of me. That's it."

"I'm not an expert, but it looked like jealousy."

Jealousy. Like maybe he wishes he were dancing with me, not Colt. Like maybe he wants to touch me...

Just thinking about it makes me breathless. But where would it even go? We're so dysfunctional. I don't even know what sex would be like for me. What if we have sex and I hate it? Or he kisses me and I punch him in the face?

What if my rabid raccoon self scratches his eyes out and feasts on them while I growl in the corner?

Worse, what if I love it and I get obsessed with him and I can't get enough of him? What if I send myself back to the hell that is longing for Dallas Dodge without ever being able to really have him? But this time with sex involved. This time with him in my life, but not...

What do I want?

I have too many questions, and no answers to any of them.

So it's best to just not think about this at all. And certainly not act on it.

"Trust me," I say. "It's not. And even if it were, he wouldn't be able to do anything about it. I wouldn't do anything about it." I clutch my seatbelt. The edges of it dig into my hands. "We're in kind of a weird codependent relationship. I'm not sure what the answer to that is. I'm not sure what we can do to be healthier or better or... but I don't want to lose him. So, I need to apologize for everything that happened last night. Because I really should be more grateful for him. He's the only family I have, and I let my temper get the best of me."

A decade apart didn't change how we relate to each other. We were a mess then, we're a mess now. We don't know how to be without each other, and we're territorial, but we don't know what to do with each other either. Sure, when we were kids, we didn't fight. I've never fought with Dallas before. But there was always this sharp-edged intensity.

"I'm really not an expert on this kind of thing," Allison says.

"Well, nobody is, because Dallas and I aren't an established normal thing."

"He's not your only friend," Allison says. "I'm your friend."

I try to hold back a smile. I still feel all kinds of difficult about last night, but it's amazing to hear somebody say that. That I'm her friend.

"Having said that," she continues. "I get that he's more than that."

I take a sharp breath. "He's... Dallas."

I'm not sure how to explain it any better. I'm not sure that I can.

Tension and nerves tighten my stomach as soon as we pull up to the cabin. "Thank you," I say. "For everything."

"Of course."

I trudge up the steps slowly and give Allison a wave

right before knocking on the door. I haven't been knocking, because I lived there once. But it feels weird to just walk in now.

It takes a couple of minutes, but the door opens, and I'm greeted by Dallas, who isn't hung over, but is shirtless, wearing only a pair of blue jeans, his hair sticking up at odd angles, his jaw covered in stubble.

"Hi," I say.

"Hi," he says, regarding me closely. He's probably trying to figure out if I'm about to launch myself at him and tear his throat out with my teeth. Fair, honestly.

"I'm sorry about last night," he says.

I'm shocked. Personally, I thought that I was going to have to grovel. Because I did throw something at him. Instead, he looks tired, unhappy, and he's done the apologizing first.

"Oh, I…"

"I shouldn't have said that to you. About consent. That was really fucked up. I don't have any right to bring up things in your past and act like I'm trying to protect you. I… I'm trying to protect you. But I also got angry, and none of that is fair."

"Can I come in?"

"Oh," he says, pushing his fingers through his hair. "Sure."

He steps away from the door, and I squeeze past him. My breath catches. He smells good. Like some kind of spicy soap, and him. His body is hard, sculpted, and I am far more fascinated by the shape of him, by the hard cut lines of muscle on his torso, than I should be.

"I made you that cake," he says.

"You did."

"I bought you that present. But you danced with him."

I blink slowly. "I... Yeah. He asked me to."

"You don't like being touched or anything. So, it never occurred to me to ask you to dance."

If I'm not totally crazy, he's upset I was paying attention to another man when he went to all that trouble for my party. When he says it like *that*, it makes me feel bad, actually. It doesn't mean that he wasn't out-of-pocket, he was, but I was too.

"Yeah, I know." I look away. "But if you had asked me to dance, I would have danced with you."

"Maybe next time I'll ask."

"I'm very sorry that I threw the present at your head."

"You didn't *hit* my head."

"Regardless," I say. "I was being a little bit over the top."

"We both were," he says.

We stand there and look at each other, and my heart throbs.

We're both just so messed up.

He means more to me than anyone else in the entire world, and I almost ruined everything. And he pretty much did the same in return. Neither of us knows how to act. Neither knows what to do with big feelings and big moments.

And that's with all this caring and between us.

No wonder I have so much trouble making friends. My rabid self takes over.

The wrong thing happens, and I just want to shove snarl and growl and froth at the mouth until everyone leaves me alone.

I want to protect myself.

What he said was messed up, and he knows why, but I didn't have to react that way. I know him. I'm willing to forgive him for it, so I also didn't need to completely lose it last night. We don't really trust each other, because we don't trust ourselves, I guess. It's exhausting. To live in this traumatized body that's constantly vacillating between fight or flight...

It's exhausting to be me sometimes, and that is a pretty whiny thought to have before ten AM the day after my birthday.

But here I am. Having it.

"Do you want the present?" he asks.

I blink. "What?"

"I have the present still. If you wanted."

"Of course I want it," I mutter.

Only a psycho wouldn't want their birthday present, even after all that.

He nods and leaves the room. I wonder if he's going to come back with a shirt on, as I sit there and examine the muscles on his back, the way they move as he retreats. He returns, still bare-chested, holding that box. It looks no worse for wear after what happened last night. It's faring better than me, basically.

He reaches out and hands it to me. I swallow hard as I begin to work the ribbon through the loops. I slide it off slowly, then take the lid off. Inside is a wide, flat black velvet box.

I've never gotten anything in a box like this, and I'm not exactly sure what it is. I lift it out, and open it up, and my breath catches. It's a necklace. Not just any necklace, but one from Sammy's store. White gold with rose gold woven in to make blossoms on the ornate chain. I also know exactly how much it cost. It's an original piece, made by hand, as everything she does is. One-of-a-kind.

I could pay my whole year's rent with this.

"I..."

I look up, and he's staring at me with intensity that makes my breath catch.

"I don't know what to say," is the only thing I can force through my tightened throat.

"You don't have to say anything," he says.

"Turn around."

I obey him, as he slips the box out of my hand, and sets it down on the kitchen table. I take in a jagged breath, and I feel his heat behind me. His large hand wraps around my hair, sweeps it over my shoulder, fingertips brushing the back of my neck. I shiver. And my heart begins to beat faster. I don't move, but I hear him touching the necklace, the box. The slight clinking of the jewelry as he undoes the clasp. Then he brings it around to the front of my body, the chain settling on my skin as he works to close the clasp. A long piece of chain dangles down the back, and he runs his finger along the length, letting it settle against my skin link by link, making me shiver. He's still close to me, hasn't moved.

"It's perfect," he says.

"You haven't even seen it yet." My voice is a whisper. I can barely make it work. My throat is so tight I can hardly breathe.

"Show me," he says.

I turn around, and he's so much closer than I expected him to be. My entire field of vision is filled with blue. Those blue eyes. Then my gaze dips down to his mouth. I'm suddenly seized with a hunger that I wish I didn't understand. I do understand it. I've experienced it in a disconnected fashion before, like I'm standing on the other side of a glass door, and I can't break through to the other side. Like my body is hungry for something that it won't allow me to have. My jailer and protector all at once. But this time, there's no pane of glass between myself and my desire.

This time, it isn't theoretical, nothing that I suspect I might feel some day if the right man is in front of me, nothing that I think I might be able to conjure up if I close my eyes and throw myself into it, regardless of how I actually feel.

I want him.

I want him to kiss me. I want him to touch me. If Dallas Dodge wanted to strip my clothes off me and lay me down on the floor, I would let him do it. I would *more* than let him do it, I would beg him to.

That thought hits me like a flashbang. An intrusive thought. One that escaped the basement that I locked it in, ran outside and screamed as loudly as possible before I could shove it all down back inside.

He lets out a harsh breath, steps away from me, and I'm afraid that he can read my mind. That the temporary insanity of it just flashed through my thoughts was written across my eyes. I'm shaking. I'm throbbing between my legs, and my entire worldview is suddenly twisted, turned on its head. I touch the necklace.

"Thank you," I say, taking a step away from him, and then another.

"Of course."

"I don't really blame you for being mad, I guess. I didn't even know all the trouble you went to. How much money you spent."

"It's not... It's not that. It's not..."

But he did all that for me, and I did dance with another man, and if he wanted to kiss me, the way that I was thinking about kissing him only a moment ago, I can see how that would be outrageously offensive.

But he doesn't. He said so himself. He wants to protect me.

Without thinking, I reach up and touch his cheek. Then I lean in quickly and press my mouth to his.

His breath is sharp, indrawn, and for a brief second, he presses his large hands to my lower back and just holds me there.

Then we part.

It's a sweet kiss. One that could easily pass between friends, family. Except for when he put his hand, on my lower back. But that might've been an innate response learned from all the women who have kissed him before, and nothing quite so purposeful.

A humbling thought.

"Thank you," I mumble, my lips on fire, my heart beating recklessly. I'm dizzy. I've never kissed anyone before at all. Not like that, not in any regard. So even though it was just a little peck, it's still rocked my whole existence.

He clears his throat. "I... yeah. I... you're welcome."

If he had been planning to say something more eloquent, it's lost. That's fine, because I probably wouldn't be able to hear it over the buzzing in my ears.

"I've got to go. I'm... I'm doing some work over at my uncle's today."

"Oh."

I'm disappointed. I want to get things back on track with the two of us. I want to do something normal. I want to watch the next installment of The Hobbit. I want him to tease me and throw popcorn bags at me. I want to go for a walk with him, eat dinner with his family. I want to do something to smooth over the last twenty-four hours, that kiss definitely *wasn't* it.

"I can bring you something back for dinner."

"Oh, I'd like that."

"You have the day off, right?"

I nod. "Yeah. I'm probably going to catch up on homework."

"Good. Sounds good."

And then he turns and leaves me standing there, my lips still burning. I guess we fixed everything. I'm not sure why it doesn't quite feel like it.

Chapter Fifteen

Dallas

Usually, going to my uncle's ranch is one of my favorite things. But my head is somewhere else. I really messed things up last night, and it isn't so much *how* I acted as *why* I acted that way.

When she kissed me earlier today, it was like an electric shock to my system.

I bought you that present. I made you that cake.

I might as well have sat down on the ground and thrown a tantrum at her. Hell, I practically did last night.

I did all that for her, and she paid attention to another man, because he was flirting with her, and I wasn't.

But she kissed me.

A little peck on the lips that would mean nothing for most women, but from Sarah...

I know how precious touch is to her. The problem is, what I really wanted to do was grab the back of her head and keep her from pulling away. What I really wanted to do was deepen the kiss, part my lips, and claim her mouth as my own...

Fuck.

"Fuck!" Right as I finish thinking the expletive, I bring a hammer down on my thumb, pretty much smashing it all the hell and obliterating every thought in my brain. Maybe it's a good thing. Maybe I should be grateful.

Grateful for the pain.

"You good?"

I look over my shoulder to see my uncle Wyatt standing there, staring at me in amusement.

"Totally fine," I say.

"Has it been this long since you did any real ranch work, rhinestone cowboy?"

"No," I say.

"Rhinestone cowboy," Uncle Grant says. "Good one."

"Oh, be nice to him," my dad says.

"Why?" Grant asks. "Because he's a champion bull rider millionaire?"

"No," Dad says, reaching over and bumping the cowboy hat on my head. "Because he's just a little kid."

"All right," I say. "All of you settle down. You're worse than all the kids."

And there were a lot of kids. I'm pretty much beset by little cousins at this point. I don't mind it. But I'm the oldest by quite a bit.

I didn't know Wyatt before he was with his wife, Lindy. She was apparently married to the biggest jackass on the planet, and my uncle was her knight in shining armor. To hear him tell it.

And she lets him tell it that way, so I have to assume it's close enough to the truth.

They all have what I want. This kind of stable, happy

life, complete with the right kind of person by their side, who makes them better.

"Did you break it?" Wyatt asks me.

I forgot about my thumb for a second.

"No," I say, looking down at my swollen thumb. "It's not broken. It just hurts."

"Well, I'm about done for the day anyway," Wyatt says. "It's getting too warm. We can stop by the house and have some beer."

"Oh. I've probably got to get back. I promised Sarah that I'd bring her some dinner."

Grant and Wyatt exchange a glance. "Sarah?"

"His friend," my dad says quickly.

"Thanks, Dad," I say. Though a bit dry, since the way he said it almost made it sound even more like she was my girlfriend than if he hadn't said anything at all.

"You're getting on in years," Wyatt says, clapping his hand on my back. "It might be time for you to settle down."

"Yeah, no," I say, but I'm thinking about Sarah, and the way her lips felt against mine.

"I got married young," Grant says. "I don't regret it."

I know for him it's complicated. But I can understand that.

I knew Uncle Grant before he married his wife, McKenna. But he was married *before* that. I never knew his high school sweetheart, who died of cancer not long after they got together. I don't know his whole story, but I do know that he was pretty much a monk until he met McKenna. I remember that version of him. Prickly and difficult, and he's basically like a different person now. He has little kids, he's in love. He smiles now, which he never did before.

"That's great. But I'm kind of doing the rodeo thing right now, and…"

"I think the bull riders get too much action for him to consider settling down is what he's saying," and I turn and look at my dad with what I know is an incredulous expression on my face, because I can't even believe that he would acknowledge such a thing.

"What?" he asks.

Sadly for him, I know more about his personal history than that. I know how he dated a woman named Olivia for years and she was making him wait till marriage to have sex. My dad is *not* an anonymous hookup type.

The truth is, I'm not really either. I've done it, but it doesn't make me feel great. I've done it, but it makes me feel lonely and a little bit sad.

"Let him have fun," Wyatt says. "Having spent some time playing the field myself, I endorse it. Because then you really know what you have when you finally do settle down. Also, you never know, the woman for you may not be ready to be yours yet, so you have to wait sometimes."

I think about Sarah. About that kiss.

About how young she is, and how much shit she's already been through.

"Lindy was married when I met her," Wyatt says. "When I saw her for the first time that night she walked into that bar, I thought my whole life had been turned upside down, and then she was off limits. But eventually, she wasn't. Eventually, that feeling I had the first time I saw her, it made sense. It wasn't really love at first sight, I guess, but it was a recognition of something. That something grew into love. When it was time."

I snort and try to use the force of it to take some of the

weight off my chest. "That's your endorsement? Play the field while I wait around for some woman to be into me?"

"Worked for me," he says.

I grimace, but there's something about what he said that keeps on tugging at me, and does the whole way home.

There are clouds gathering just over the top of the mountains, which isn't my favorite thing.

You would think that a little bit of rain in the middle of summer would be nice. But if it gets too dry, we just end up with heat lightning and not quite enough rain. When that happens, a lightning strike can set the forest ablaze, which isn't ideal for anyone.

It's getting more and more humid, the air heavy with the scent of impending rain. I pull my truck into the driveway and just let it sit. I decide that I don't want to go into the house, not just yet. There's something inside me that feels raw and edgy, and I'm thinking way too much about the kiss for my own liking.

So I get out of the truck, and walk down the trail that leads to the swimming hole just behind my dad's house.

I strip my shirt off, my jeans, my boots. I leave my black boxers on and throw myself into the water. I submerge myself in the icy cold, hoping that it will wash away all the confusion inside of me.

It's not working, not so far.

For a moment I hold my breath, and I imagine letting the water drag me down. I feel like I'm floating in space, but I'm not alone. She's there. She's always there.

I find myself kicking back up to the surface, breaking through and gasping for air.

The thunder rolls overhead, ominous. I don't need to be in a fucking swimming hole during a thunderstorm. That's asking for trouble.

But then, that's what I'm doing, isn't it? Asking for trouble.

I grit my teeth and I swim toward the shore. I get out, and I collect my clothes. Strip my underwear off, put my jeans on. My skin is slightly soggy, and it's not the most comfortable thing. But I grimace and pull on my T-shirt. I need to go get dinner. I made the excuse that I couldn't stick around at my uncle's place because of dinner, but my head is just so full of so many things, that I didn't even do that.

I feel like I'm spinning out. Everything I did with her yesterday was wrong.

I don't know how everything with her can feel so right in so many ways, and I can still be so wrong. I don't know how I can want to protect her and then also say the kinds of things I said to her yesterday. I don't understand what she does to me.

When we were kids, our relationship was fraught and intense, yes, but I felt like that was because of the world around us.

Maybe we're just shaped into fraught and feral things.

Maybe there is no coming back from it. No changing it. Maybe it's too late for us to become anything better. Maybe it's too late for us to become anything healthier. Maybe between the two of us, it will always be bad patterns.

But then, I think about us watching Lord of the Rings. Then, I think about the two of us together, at my parents' dinner table, and when we're alone, and I think maybe we can't be entirely broken.

How can anything that feels that good be broken?

I suck in a sharp breath and walk back down the road toward the cabin. The sky opens up, water drops landing on my neck, my shoulder, rolling down my back. The air is thick with heat, and now the smell of rain, the scent of the pine trees soaking in all that much-needed moisture.

I put my head down and let the rain pour over me.

By the time I get back to the cabin, I'm soaked to the bone.

I need to go inside and change, then I need to drive down and get us a rotisserie chicken from the supermarket, or something. But before I reach the porch steps, the door opens, and Sarah comes out.

I stop right where I am, looking up at her, the rain rolling down my face. I see a fire in her eyes. Something determined. Something intense. I see her make a decision. And then she flies down the stairs and up against my body. I catch her, on instinct, wrapping my arms around her waist.

Then she stretches up on her toes, and she kisses me.

Deep and long and slick in the rain. This isn't a kiss between friends.

She's changed the rules.

She's changed everything.

She's changed me.

Chapter Sixteen

Sarah

My heart is pounding in my ears so loudly that I can't even hear the rain anymore. I'm dizzy. It's something that I have only ever experienced when I was terrified before. But I'm not terrified now.

I'm *kissing* him.

When I made the decision to do this, about five whole seconds ago, I thought that it would be a relief to finally kiss someone.

But now that it's happening, I realize that it isn't about kissing someone at all.

I'm kissing Dallas. That's what matters.

Dallas. His mouth is on me, his hands holding me steady, his body rock hard in front of me. I put my hands on his cheeks, his skin slick as I slide my thumbs across his cheekbones, bring my hands back around behind his head, and push them through his wet hair. I tilt my head, part my lips, and he growls, pushing his tongue into my mouth, the sweet, slick friction making me tremble.

I'm not a stranger to sexual desire, divorced from others.

I have a vibrator, and I know how to use it. I've done a lot of personal reclamation of my body. I spent a lot of time learning to love it, care for it, not be resentful of it, and figure out ways to make it feel good.

But it's nothing compared to this.

He moved his hands, and I don't know where they're going to go next. And I'm not frightened.

I was so afraid for so long that the feeling of the unknown would remind me too much of being a confused, scared child. But it doesn't at all. Because it has nothing to do with this. I knew that intellectually all this time. I knew that abuse had nothing to do with this. But I was still so afraid. So afraid that it would poison a beautiful moment, so afraid that it would put me back somewhere I didn't want to be.

But now, I'm just with him. I'm being held in his strong arms, and there is nothing other than this. Nothing other than our need for one another.

It's undeniable.

He feels it too.

His mouth is firm and sure on mine, and he guides our movements. His kisses are expert, and I know mine aren't. I'm driven by my desire, and there's something like a rush of satisfaction when I realize it's not desire just for the sake of it.

I want him.

There has been a feeling inside of me that was too big to be contained from the moment that I met Dallas. I didn't know what to do with it. I didn't know where it was supposed to go. It made me wild. It made me feel safe, it made me feel afraid, it made me feel like I might die if I lost him, and there was never a word for it. Never a place that I could put it neatly.

But finally, *finally* I feel like I have a way to express it. A way that feels big enough. Strong enough. A way that matches the intensity that has existed in my heart for him for so many years.

Of course, it could only ever be his. All his.

That thought makes me feel like I'm falling. Like I'm sailing through the abyss, because it's a terrifying, awful, wonderful realization.

That part of me will always feel like I belong to him no matter what. No matter where I end up, no matter where he goes. No matter what happens after this kiss ends.

I will always feel like half of a person without Dallas Dodge and that is both ugly and beautiful all at the same time.

Is it love or is it trauma? It's very hard to say.

But it's real all the same.

I'm getting wet out in the rain, from his touch, water drops rolling from his hair, down my face, or maybe I'm crying. It's probably both.

And it's appropriate anyway. Because this is like having a drink of water after eternity in the desert. I've been lonely, isolated, separate, different, for so long. And right now I feel like I'm part of him.

I don't want it to end.

Then, he pulls away from me, holding onto my face, looking at me, those blue eyes all I can see. "Sarah," he rasps, his voice rough. "What's going on?"

"I don't want to talk."

"But we have to," he says.

I shake my head. "No. I don't want to talk. I want to

feel. Dallas, for so many years I've been afraid of feeling. But I'm safe with you. I know that I'm safe with you. We can talk afterward. I don't need it to be safe. I don't need any decisions to be made. I just need this. I need you. I need you to..." I reach up, and grab hold of his wet T-shirt, holding onto him tightly. "I need you to take me. Like you would if I were a girl you met at the rodeo. I need you to treat me like you would anyone, because I'm just so tired. I'm tired of myself. I'm tired of feeling like there's something different about me that I never, ever change."

He's holding my face, fingers blunt against my skin, his eyes intense. "I can't do that. I can't treat you like someone else. Because you're you, Sarah. I'm never going to treat you the way I would someone random. You're never going to be a stranger to me. But I'll make you feel good. I promise you that."

He picks me up, and I wrap my arms around his neck, burying my face against his shoulder as he carries me up the front steps and into the house.

He closes the door behind us, and for the first time I'm aware that he's clutching a sodden bunch of fabric in his hand against my body. He throws it down onto the floor with a soggy, soft sound.

I frowned in the direction of the black bundle.

"I went for a swim," he says, setting me down, albeit much more gently than what he just threw on the floor a moment earlier. Then he reaches back behind his head and strips his T-shirt off one-handed, and my mouth goes dry.

His body is gorgeous. I've been entranced by it more than once since coming to live with him, but this is the first time that I really let myself openly admire him. This is the first time that I've really allowed myself to admit that it's sexual desire. That I'm looking at him like that because I want to touch him, kiss him, lick him, even.

My desire is suddenly so intense, so completely all-consuming that I feel like I'm standing outside of my body for a moment, staring at myself. Like I split myself off because I can't handle the intensity of just being inside that body that has been transformed into a well of need that exists entirely for Dallas Dodge.

I'm still wearing his necklace.

Maybe that's what changed me.

Like he put it on me and I suddenly realized that I belong to him. Really and truly.

All of a sudden, I'm right back in my body. Needy, desperate, trembling for him. All of a sudden, there is no escape from that feeling. I'm so aware of everything. How hard my heart is beating, the way that my breasts feel heavy, my nipples tight. The aching throb between my legs, and how slick I am with my need for him.

He moves toward me, cups my cheek, and kisses me, this time much more gently, but no less impactful.

I want to beg him. For more, for less, for everything. I want to promise to do everything he wants. To be whatever he needs me to be. His perfect girl.

I just want this to go on forever, as much as I need it to stop.

I'm overwhelmed. And yet I also feel the best I ever have.

Every fear that I've ever had rises up inside of me, I fear that this won't be able to last, that he'll leave me. That I'll lose him again. I push it aside. Because right now, we are together. Right now, I have Dallas. And that's more than I ever thought I would have, ever again. I didn't think that I would ever find him. I didn't think that if I did he would care about me. I never thought that I would end up in his arms.

The feeling inside of me is so big the only thing I can compare it to his panic, except unlike a panic attack, I wanted to go on.

But my breathing is shallow, my heartbeat erratic, my body trembling.

"Sarah," he whispers against my neck. "Can I touch you?"

He looks up at me, his eyes meeting mine.

I nod, wordless.

"No, baby," he says. "That's not good enough. I need to hear you say it."

"Yes," I whisper, the word coming out strangled.

He makes a sound like relief, and moves his hand to cup my breast, his thumb skimming over my tightened nipple before pinching it. The answering pulse between my legs nearly makes my knees buckle. He continues to touch me. Working magic on my skin like a sorcerer in possession of wicked spells. Like a sensual wizard.

There is no sex in Tolkien. I think that's partly why it's the kind of fantasy that I've always enjoyed.

Right now, I'm enjoying it.

Right now, I feel like I am on a whole new kind of adventure. Maybe by the end, I'll be able to cast the ring into the fire. Or maybe I'm being overly optimistic. Maybe I just need to stop thinking altogether. And just feel. Because I trust Dallas. One thing has always, always been true. He's going to keep me safe.

He's going to make it okay. He's going to give me what I need. He's always known what that was, even when I didn't.

That's been part of our dynamic forever. It was always going to be him. Part of me wants to say that. But I'm the one who said I didn't want to talk. So it's best if I stick to that. If I can't follow my own rules, then I won't be allowed to make them. I'm okay with that right now. Honestly, I would prefer to live under Dallas's rules. I would prefer for his hands to be my whole world. Honestly, this is the safest I've ever felt. Even as I tremble in his arms. Then, he slides his hands down my waist, my hips. And pushes the hem of my dress up my thighs. And then it just isn't my breasts that he's touching.

His hands find where I'm wet and slick for him. And he's touching me there. Making me feel glorious, wonderful things that just don't hurt at all.

I whisper yes against his throat as he continues to stroke me, his fingers touching me intimately before he pushes one deep inside of me.

I whimper, and he stops. "Is that okay?"

I nod, having a hard time using my words. I'm having a hard time shaping my thoughts into language.

But he stops, and I know that he's waiting for me to tell him for sure that everything is fine. I told him to treat me like he would anyone, but in the moment, I'm glad he's treating me like this, not because I want to be treated like I'm fragile. But because it makes me feel special. Like he's entirely aware of who I am, and it matters.

In that first feverish haze, I thought I wanted to be just like all the other women he's been with. But I want to be special.

Oh, that sad, small part inside of me that always wants to be special. But I don't let it make me feel bad, not now.

I embrace it.

As part of the moment. As part of who I am, and part of what we are.

His hand begins to move again, his finger pushing deeper inside me, his thumb slides over my clit, perfect, the rhythm he establishes sending waves of need through my body.

And before I know it, the wave of my climax crashes over me. My entire body shaking as I cry out his name. As I cling to his shoulders, I experience my first orgasm with another person.

Tears are streaming down my face. But they aren't sad tears. I'm just so happy. So happy that it's him. So happy that it's us.

And for a brief, wonderful moment, I feel like everything might be okay. I can't remember the last time I ever had that feeling. And then I do. With shocking, blinding clarity. It was the first moment I met Dallas.

A scared child, moved into my first foster home, barely verbal. Completely taken apart by everything that had happened to me.

And then I saw the strongest, most handsome boy I'd ever seen in my life. And I was so sure that he could slay every dragon for me. That he was my rightful king. The one who would take care of me and save my whole world.

I lift my head, and our eyes meet. He's trembling. Just like I am. And there's an expression in his eyes that I can't quite read.

"Sarah," he says. "Can I take you to... Can I take you to bed?"

"Yes," I whisper.

There is no hesitation. This is right. This is mine. This is what I was always supposed to have. This is the thing that

I thought I wasn't worthy of, that I thought I was too broken for, and I still get to have it. Because of him.

Because one day I met the most beautiful boy in the whole wide world, and he never, ever forgot me.

And that is an epic story by every metric.

He takes my hand, and he leads me slowly into his bedroom. My heart is thundering, but now I know for sure it isn't fear. No. I'm not afraid of anything right now. Because I'm with him.

"You never done this before?" he asks.

I shake my head, and then remember he wants me to use my words.

"No," I say.

"Okay," he says. "I have. Quite a few times."

That annoys me, but I realize he's telling me that to put me at ease. I realize he's telling me that so that I know that he knows how to take care of me. So I choose not to be up in arms about it.

"I'm going to make it good for you," he says. "But if at any point you want to stop, if at any point you don't like what I'm doing, then you just tell me. You're not going to make me mad, you're not going to hurt our relationship, do you understand me? Nothing could ever do that. Because we're not like that, okay? We're not like anybody else. We always find each other, don't we?"

I nod, and then he kisses me. He kisses me and I nearly tremble to pieces. Because it's really happening. His hands go to his belt the buckle, and I reach between us and touch him. My breath escaping in a gasp. He's so hard, and... Very, very big. I feel him through his wet jeans like an iron rod. And there's a minute there where I feel some very real trepidation.

"Don't worry," he says. "I've got this."

"Oh, are you used to walking women through their first time?"

"No," he says. "I mean, not since my first time. But I do know what I'm doing."

Yes. He knows what he's doing. And that is a good thing, I remind myself. A good thing that I'm going to benefit from. So I try to relax into him, and he continues to work his belt free, and I let out a shaking breath. He pulls his belt through the loops of his jeans, undoes the snap on them, and then lowers the zipper.

He doesn't have any underwear on, and suddenly I realize exactly what the fabric was he threw on the floor in the entryway.

Then, that realization just doesn't matter. Because all I do is stare at him, my mouth dry. I'm not sure that I ever thought I would be able to find a man beautiful.

I find him beautiful.

His body is a glorious testament to all the ways in which masculinity can be something good and caring and protecting. Strong.

And I want him.

Over me. Under me. Inside of me.

"I want you," I say.

Because I know that matters to him. Because I know he wants to hear me say it out loud.

"That's good," he says. "Because I want you."

And then, there's no more talking. He pulls me into his arms and kisses me. He pulls my dress-up over my head and reaches behind my back, unhooking my bra with deft, practiced fingers. And he's right, I appreciate it.

Then he lays me down gently on the bed, stripping my underwear off, looking at me in a way that makes me feel beautiful. His desire makes me feel good. His desire fills me with confidence. It makes me feel new. It makes me feel like I own every part of myself. I've done a lot of work on my own. I'm proud of how strong I am. But I've always needed Dallas, and I'm not ashamed of that at all.

He was the missing piece to this. And I'm completely okay with that.

He moves to me, kissing me, hands going between my thighs again as he strokes me, bringing me back to that state of oblivion. Where I'm not thinking too deeply about us, about the past, about what I haven't done, or what is left to do now.

I'm just lost. In feeling good. In feeling his.

Tears prick my eyes, and I close them, clinging to his shoulders as he pushes a finger inside of me, then a second. As he brings me to the edge before kissing his way down my neck, drawing one nipple into his mouth and sucking it in deep. I arch my back up off the bed. It's wonderful that it's Dallas. But this intimacy... It's...

And then he kisses his way down my stomach, and I know exactly what he's planning on doing. He forces my thighs apart, and he's past asking. He lowers his head, and he licks me. Right there.

He looks up at me, all that blue. That familiar blue, as he starts to eat me like I'm the most delicious dessert he's ever had.

All I can do is surrender.

All I can do is give myself over to the incredible sensations he's creating in my body. I didn't know that it could be like this. I didn't know anything could be like this.

I knew that the body could endure a whole lot of indignity. A whole lot of pain. A whole lot of suffering.

But I had no idea that it could endure this level of pleasure. I didn't know that I had the capacity for this.

I am made new by it.

All of a sudden, there is no end to the beauty in the world. I was so world-weary and cynical for so long, I felt like I'd seen too much of life. Now I think I haven't seen enough. I realize that I don't know much of anything. I feel small, gloriously so.

There are miracles out there, and I haven't even scratched the surface of them. But now I know of their existence thanks to Dallas Dodge's talented, wicked tongue.

He pushes two fingers inside of me as he continues to tease me with his mouth. The slow, aching rhythm building a new climax inside of me that's deeper, more intense than the one that came before.

And when I come this time, I cry out his name, my arm thrown over my eyes as my back arches up off the mattress, as I try to keep myself from flying into millions of pieces.

I'm not sure that I succeed. Maybe I've shattered completely. Maybe I'm going to blow away on the wind.

That feels reasonable. And fine.

Because he's still there. And that's all that matters.

He kisses his way back up my body, lips skimming over my breasts before he licks his way up my neck and claims my mouth again. I taste my own pleasure on his lips, and there's something deeply beautiful about that. That the evidence of how much I want this, of how much I enjoyed it is right there, between us. Undeniable.

He pauses for a moment and grabs a condom from a drawer in his nightstand. Then he tears it open and rolls it onto his thick length. I watch, transfixed as his large hand grips that gorgeous part of him. It's so erotic, and I had no idea something as basic as protection could be so...sexy.

He presses his forehead against mine, his hand moving to my hip as he spreads my thighs wide, positioning himself between them. I feel the blunt head of his cock up against the slick entrance to my body, and he begins to push inside of me, slowly, achingly so. There's an apology in his blue eyes, I see it. But he doesn't speak. He's sorry that it hurts. That he's stretching me.

But I'm not.

Because it makes it feel real. It makes all of this feel real. And it's a different kind of pain than anything that's come before. Because I want this. I want him buried as deep inside of me as he can go. I want everything. All of him.

And then he's there. As deep inside me as he can go. And it's like everything makes sense. Like he was always meant to be there.

Mine. *Mine.*

Inside my body.

I want to cry, but I don't, because I don't want to freak him out, so I bite my lip to keep it back. And I just let go. I surrender myself to the experience. To the feeling of him moving inside of me.

To everything.

And I find myself scaling that mountain again. I find myself on the verge of coming.

I cling to his shoulders so tightly, so tight that I fear I might draw blood because my nails are digging into his skin but I can't let go of him, because it's all too much. And not enough.

It'll never be enough. That terrifies me. Even as I'm standing there on the edge of the cliff, right on the verge of another orgasm, I'm so afraid. That this won't be enough, that I'll never get enough of him, that I will never ever be able to fill the void that's inside of me. I'm a black hole.

Of all the love that I never got, all the love that I want.

Of the great and terrible need that I have felt ever since I first saw Dallas.

Stay with me. Stay with me.

Love me. Love me.

I cling to him, and I squeeze my eyes shut, and I scream as my orgasm rips through me. And that scream almost turns into a wail, but I catch it.

It's done. We've done it. It's over.

And I feel like curling up into a ball and sobbing.

I'm half despair and half hope. I don't know which is worse. The hope, I decide. Because at least despair is something I'm familiar with.

Then Dallas gathers me up in his arms and holds me against him. "Wait here for a second," he whispers against my temple.

He goes away for a moment, and then I hear water running in the next room. He comes back sans condom, and stands there in the doorway and looks at me.

"God." He bends over at the waist, hands planted on his knees, and I'm not sure he's praying or swearing. He's out of breath like he just ran a marathon. "I think you almost killed me," he says.

Warmth trickles through me. I almost killed him?

"You sent me to another planet," I say.

He lifts his head, and grins. And I see him. My friend. My Dallas. Suddenly I feel like everything's going to be okay. Like it really might be.

"Come here," he says, not waiting for me to come here, bending over and gathering me into his arms and picking me up. My skin against his feels so good. He's got hair on his chest, and it's a little scratchy against my breasts, and I like it. His muscles are tight, hard. Beautifully defined. I lift my hand and touch him, just there on the chest. I want to explore him. I want to do what he did to me, I want to take his cock into my mouth and swallow him deep.

I want to taste him everywhere. And I hope there will be an opportunity for that. Because I don't want it to just happen once and then never again.

He carries me into the bathroom, and sits me on the edge of the counter while the bath runs. It's a deep, clawfoot tub that I haven't seen before, because I haven't gone into his bathroom before.

"This is cute," I say, looking around. There's a small, square shower in the corner, with glass doors. But it looks barely big enough for one person, let alone two.

"Oh yeah. This bathroom got a remodel a few years ago, but you can only do so much with the room this small."

I drink his body in as he fusses around with the tub. His thighs are thick and hard, and I never really thought about checking out a man's thighs, but I'm definitely doing it now.

It takes a while for the tub to fill, and he continues to check the temperature judiciously, before he lifts me off the counter and brings me down into the water with him.

For a moment I wonder if it should be weird to be intimate like this with someone I've known for so long. If the change should feel more jarring.

Then I decide I don't care.

I hum with contentment and lean my head back against his chest.

This feels both entirely new and entirely settled all at once. Like my body recognizes his as home in a way that feels profound.

"So," I say, putting my hand over his forearm, watching my finger as I trace a line along the dip in his muscle there. "You have a lot of experience."

He snorts. "There's a whole thing. Rodeo groupies. We call them Buckle Bunnies."

"That feels problematic, Dallas."

"I think it can be. I definitely think there are issues within that culture. With the way they get treated and how some of the guys see them. But I'm pretty new to the whole thing, I mean, relatively. And ever since I've been in the rodeo, videos and stories about hook-ups with athletes have been going viral."

"And?"

"You just have to accept that if you're going to fuck around, your junk could end up posted somewhere. Or, the story of what happened. I don't need that kind of threat to make me a decent guy, but I'm just saying I think that has changed the culture a lot in sports. It used to be, even the married guys were flinging it around here, there and every-where, but now, with social media, half the time their wives are as famous as they are. If they got up to shit, women would just message the wives and tell them. I think that changes the power dynamic a little bit. So yeah, I think there's sort of a cachet thing that comes along with bagging a rodeo rider, and I'm not going to say I haven't enjoyed that, but I don't think it's quite as unsavory as it used to be."

"All right," I say. "As long as everything is sex positive." I elbow him in the ribs, and he shifts underneath me, and I become deeply aware that his cock is getting hard again. I wiggle against him, and he wraps his arm tightly around my waist, keeping me from moving.

"Stop it," he says. "You can't be tempting all that again."

"Why not?"

"Give your body a chance to recover."

"Dallas, I'm never going to recover from that."

I jump as I feel the sharp scrape of his teeth on my shoulder. "Good," he says.

My stomach goes tight, my heart thundering hard. I feel marked. Branded. I'm good with that. I really am.

All I've ever wanted in my life is to belong to someone who actually wants to care for me.

If his teeth could leave marks that last longer than my trauma I'd be okay with that.

He reaches for a washcloth, gets it wet, soaps it up and rubs it over every inch of my body, taking extra time between my legs.

By the time we get out of the tub, I'm panting, and I'm annoyed at him, because he's the one who said we couldn't do it again.

"I think that we should watch the last part of The Hobbit."

I frown. "I don't want to watch The Hobbit."

"Oh no," he says, reaching up and planting his palm on my forehead. "Are you okay?"

"Stop," I say, wiggling away from him, and he picks me up around the waist and carries me into the bedroom, my legs dangling as he sets me down, reaches into his dresser, and pulls out that pair of sweatpants that's exactly like mine. He hands them over to me. "Wear these. I already know they're your style."

"I could go in the other room and get mine."

There's a possessive light in his blue eyes. "I want you to wear mine."

I put them on, and they're a lot roomier than mine, so much so that I have to cinch the waist almost all the way. I'm standing there in pants that are more like balloons, and he throws me a white T-shirt. I put it on, and I'm deeply aware that my nipples are visible through the fabric. I can tell by the way he's looking at me that was the plan.

"So," I say as he turns away from me and finds another pair of sweats in his drawer. Gray. And when he pulls them on, I still see the muscular, gloriously round shape of his ass through the fabric.

"You *were* jealous."

He turns to face me. "When?"

"At my birthday party."

He blinks. "Yeah. I thought that was clear."

"You said you were being protective."

"I lied."

"Why did you lie?"

"Because I don't know what the fuck to do with this."

It's raw and honest, and it hurts my feelings a little bit. But I also understand. Because the two of us were like hit dogs yesterday, and that really is a worry. I don't think either of us really knows how to conduct a relationship. I'm not sure if we could even do that. With the two of us. Because we are already something. Something steeped in... fucked up shit.

I don't know if something that comes from a desperate, unhealthy attachment can ever become something normal.

I really don't know if *I'll* ever be anything normal. Based on my response to having sex with him, I would say no. Because I wanted him to stay inside me forever.

And now that some of my need has subsided, I can see that my reaction was a little bit over the top. But it lingers.

"All right. Fair enough. I just... I don't like Colt, to be clear. I mean, I like him, but I don't... I don't want him."

He lifts a brow. "Then what was all that?"

"I just wanted to feel like I wasn't broken. For a little bit. He's nice, and it seemed easy. I really would like something easy." I look at Dallas. "I'm not sure easy is available to me."

"What's that supposed to mean?"

"Well. Are we easy?"

He snorts. "No. Definitely not."

"There you go."

"You don't want him," Dallas says.

"No. I don't. You're the only man I've ever wanted."

Chapter Seventeen

Dallas

Fuck.

I am way more satisfied by that statement than I should be. My whole body is buzzing. I'm still in disbelief that it even happened. Sarah. My Sarah. I take her hand and lead her out into the living room, and I let myself enjoy how cute I think she is in my sweatpants. How sexy I think the white T-shirt is. Especially with nothing on underneath. I allow myself to really let myself call it what it is. I want her. I want her, and I think she's the most beautiful woman I've ever seen.

I sit her down on the couch, and I frown. I go back into my room and grab a blanket. I wrap her up in it, making it tight, like I'm securing a burrito.

"What are you doing?"

"I want to take care of you," I say. "And I didn't go get dinner, so you have to suffer through whatever I have on hand."

"Haven't you ever heard of girl dinner?"

I frown. "No."

"Girl dinner is the fine art of piecing together a meal out of seemingly unrelated things. Since I'm incapacitated, I'll give you directions if you tell me what you have."

"Okay."

A truly hilarious series of events ensues after that. But we end up with the platter with cheese, crackers, cold cuts, some grapes, half a loaf of sourdough bread, artichokes and olives, and a mason jar full of M&Ms.

"Perfect," she says as she works her arm out of the blanket, and I begin the process of starting the movie.

She snuggles up against me, reaching for a piece of bread and taking a fierce bite of it. "I'm starving," she says. "Who knew that orgasms burned so many calories?"

"I don't know what to say to that."

"Just say you'll do it again."

She looks up at me, her eyes hopeful. I hadn't actually thought about what was going to happen next, but now that she says that, I of course know for sure that there's no way it won't happen again. I suddenly feel overwhelmed by the responsibility of her. I have to keep her safe. I can't hurt her. And I'm... I don't know what to do. I don't know how to have a relationship like this. The stakes feel so high, it feels so overwhelming.

It's stupid, because I know without a shadow of a doubt that I would kill for her. I've already told her I would. If Chris were here right now, I would take him out. If I thought that he would harm one hair on her head, I would destroy him. I don't feel overwhelmed by that. I don't feel uncertain about it.

I would die for her. I feel certain about that too.

But living with her, making a relationship with her,

trying to bundle up all this intensity and figure out how to make it something real, something that will last, something that won't blow up and hurt us both, that feels much more uncertain, and it makes me feel unsteady.

"I'm not letting you go," I say, touching her hair, brushing it out of her face. There's a soft smile on her face after that. She leans back against the couch, clutching her bread against her chest like a talisman.

I want to believe that I can fix her. That I can help her be the one to cast the ring into the fire. I guess I do want to be her Samwise Gamgee. I just don't have any confidence in my ability to do that.

She leans against me, and I run my fingers through her hair, smiling as I do. I remember driving into town and touching her like this while she slept. My heart feels sore.

And then my phone buzzes in my pocket. I reach in and take it out, and see that I have a message from my dad.

Busted on doorbell camera.

"Fuck," I say.

"What?" She asks, twisting her neck to look over at me.

"We got caught making out on the doorbell camera," I say.

She blinks, looking shocked for a moment, then a crack of laughter escapes, and she covers her mouth. "Oh. That's... Oh well, I guess. But is that... Uncomfortable for you?"

"No," I say." I try to think about whether or not that changes anything. If that makes a difference. No. It doesn't. All right, I spent a minute trying to explain to my family that it wasn't sexual between the two of us, but what does it matter if it is?

My relationship with Sarah is different than any other relationship I've ever had. Different from any relationship I will ever have.

It's fitting, honestly, that we did this.

Because we belong to each other. She's mine. If she was ever going to work all this out, it was going to be with me. She trusts me. And I felt a lot of guilt about whether or not it was all right for me to want her while protecting her, but she wants me. The minute she changed things, the minute she flipped the script and ran into my arms, it became all right. It became more than all right.

Meant to be, even. Because this is where I need to be, I can feel it. As close to her as possible.

I relate, very suddenly, to the dragon in the movie. Guarding my treasure. Protecting it at all costs, and in order to do that, I need to be as close to her as possible. So no, I don't care if my family knows. I don't care if everybody knows.

We've never been able to define what we are, so why start now?

She wiggles against me, and I tighten my hold on her, tossing my phone down onto one of the couch cushions that we wiggled onto the floor when we were getting settled. I don't need to deal with my family right now. I don't need to deal with anything outside this room.

The movie is still playing, but she angles her head upward, and I can't resist, so I lean in and kiss her. I kiss her, deep and long, slick as her tongue finds mine and tangles with it.

I push my fingers through her hair, and I drink her in. All that she is. All the desire that I feel for her. Then I lift her up from where I have her wrapped in the blanket, struggling to unwind her as I move her onto my lap. She giggles, freeing herself from the blanket and settling herself so that her thighs are on either side of mine. I'm getting hard, and can't hide it in these sweats, but I don't really care.

I need her to know how badly I want her.

She strips my shirt off, quickly, and runs her hands over my chest, down my stomach. "Can I... I want to explore you," she says, her voice shy, her cheeks pink.

Sarah really isn't shy, and there's something so endearing about me being on the receiving end of this bashfulness. That pretty blush.

I reach up and touch her cheek. "My body belongs to you."

I didn't realize how true that was before this moment. My body is hers. I'm hers.

That simple truth has existed between us from the moment we first set eyes on each other. It's true now, even more than it was then.

She smiles softly, leaning in and kissing my neck, down my chest, becoming more and more bold as she strikes a trail from my pectoral muscles down my abs. She stops at the waistband of my sweatpants, and presses her hand over my hardening cock.

"God damn," she says. "You are so big. So beautiful."

I grit my teeth, my hips practically coming up off the couch. Am I that basic? Yeah. I'm this fucking basic. Her saying that to me is enough to nearly send me over the edge. God, I want her. I want to grab her and strip those ridiculous sweats off her, bury myself inside her, hard, fast, no more exploration, no more teasing.

But she wants this, so I'm going to give it to her.

Because whatever Sarah wants, she can have. At least, whatever I have to give. And she can have my body. Hell, she can devour it if she wants.

She pulls the waistband of my sweats out, down so that my cock is free, and she curls her fingers around my hard legs, squeezing.

"I really don't know what I'm doing," she says, large golden eyes staring into mine.

"I don't need you to know what you're doing," I say, my voice a desperate rasp. I cup her chin, and she bites her lip as she looks away from my gaze, down at the most intimate part of me.

"I want..." She leans in, flicking her tongue lightly across the broad head of my cock.

It's like heat lightning in the mountains.

A flash of fire and danger that threatens to spark a whole conflagration inside my body.

I reach out, grabbing hold of her hair, and this time, when I sift her hair through my fingers, I stop and make a fist. Then I tug, hard. She gasps, letting her head fall back for a moment as I hold her steady, because I don't want to come all over her face without clearing that first. I don't want to come this fast.

I want this to go on forever.

My spirit is willing, but my flesh is very, very weak.

We both pause for a moment, and she looks at me, our breathing erratic, but in sync somehow.

"Please," she says.

That she's pleading to take me into her mouth kills me, and I release my hold on her, let her bring her delicate mouth back down onto my aching flesh.

Then she sucks me in deep, and the combination of swear words that come out of my mouth is so creative, so filthy, I think even Uncle Wyatt would be a little bit disappointed in me.

Then I'm lost. In her.

I know that it's Sarah. The entire time.

I'm captivated by the fact that she's been everything I've needed for so many years.

Suddenly I feel hollowed out, aching and bitter about the ten years we were apart. But maybe we needed those years apart. So that we could come back together like this.

I let my head fall back, luxuriating in the wet suction of her mouth, the way that her hands are skimming over my body as she teases me, torments me.

"Fuck," I say, my hips rocking up off the couch, and this time I grab hold of her hair and pull her away for me for good this time. My body hates me for it, but it'll thank me later.

"I don't want to finish like that," I say.

"What if I want to. What if I want to swallow you?"

God damn. I think she might kill me. I'm so turned on, I think it actually might be fatal. I can't see straight. I want all this. I want everything. I want to fuck her until we can't walk. Until neither of us can talk because we burned our voices out screaming. I want to come down her throat, but first, I want to be inside of her again, really inside of her, so the extracurricular activities are going to have to wait. Because I need to be with her. In her. For real.

"I need to get a condom," I say.

She nods slowly, and I get up off the couch and go into the bedroom. My heart is thundering hard, and I shed all my clothes completely as I fumble around in my nightstand for another condom. Then I walk back out of the bedroom, and there she is, in the hallway. Completely naked. During that time, she took off all her clothes, and she's standing there against the wall, hands behind her back.

The only other time I've had a feeling that comes close to this is when I'm about to ride a bull.

A mean one. In a championship tournament.

When it's going to be the ride of my life.

Heart raging, body on the edge, hands trembling.

The feeling isn't gentle. It's not easy.

I wouldn't want it any other way.

I don't want sweet, easy, romance. I want this. I want to be cut open by it, scarred by it. I feel like this is what I'm always looking for. Every night out in that arena, I'm looking for this. To feel something. Something undeniable that cuts through all the bullshit.

This is it.

I stride toward her, aware that I must look as on edge as I feel. I reach out, grab the back of her neck and haul her toward me, my mouth crashing down on hers, the storm that reps between us a beautiful catastrophe. I press her naked body to the wall, her small, round breasts pressing against my chest, and I growl. I fumble with the condom, roll it onto my cock, and lift her thigh up, thrusting hard inside of her body, pinning her against the wall as I thrust into her.

She grips my shoulders, crying out, arching against me, and shuddering every time I thrust home.

"Mine," I growl. "Mine."

She whimpers, clinging to my shoulders as I push us both to the edge of sense, the edge of reason.

"Mine."

Stay on for eight seconds, Dodge. No glory if you can't finish the ride.

I grit my teeth and try to hold back. I need her to come. I put my thumb between our bodies, rubbing her sweet little clit as I continue to thrust inside of her. Deep. Hard. *Please.*

"Come for me." I'm begging now. I don't care.

She gives me what I want, beautifully. She trembles and shivers in my arms as she comes apart, biting down hard on my shoulder as she quakes. And then I give up all control. I wrap my arm around her waist, lift her entirely off the floor as I thrust inside of her, losing myself in the rhythm, in my pleasure. In my need. When I come, my knees buckle, and I press her against the wall, my arm planted next to the side of her head, as I try to keep myself from falling over.

"Dallas," she whispers, pushing my hair off my forehead. I open my eyes, and meet hers. "Sarah."

She kisses me, deep and fierce. And then I suddenly hear a roar come from the other room.

Dragons. That movie is still on.

I laugh. "Well. I finally figured out how to distract you from hobbits."

"An orgasm will do that," she says.

"Christ," I say, scrubbing my hand over my face.

She laughs. "I'm not quite God, Dallas. But I'm close." Then she poked me in the ribs, which she keeps doing, and I grab her arm and pull her up against me.

"You need to be punished," I say. I'm teasing her, but I'm starting to get turned on again.

"I wouldn't say no," she says.

I lean in and bite her lip. "Really?"

Her cheeks turned bright red. "You do have a lot of experience, don't you?"

There is actual insecurity in that, and she's throwing some barbs at me, maybe to put some distance between us. I get it. I was lost in the moment there for a second, but the reality of the whole situation isn't... Not scary.

"I told you. I do. I'm not ashamed of it. I've never cheated on anybody. I've never had a relationship. I've never tried to, not really."

"Because you don't want one?" she asks.

"No. I do. Someday. Look at my family. They're great." I let out a sigh. "Are we just going to stand here talking about this while I still have a condom on my dick?"

She looks down, her cheeks turning an even brighter pink.

"I don't know. You're the one standing there."

"Sarah," I say. "Behave yourself. I walk past her, and go into the bathroom, discarding the condom before coming back out. She's standing in the bedroom doorway.

"Get in bed," I say.

She lifts her chin, looks at me mulishly. "I'm not tired."

"You're such a brat."

So I walk over to her, then down, pressing my shoulder against her rib cage as I lift her up off the ground, draped over my shoulder.

"Hey!"

Then I flip her over onto her back, depositing her firmly at the center of the mattress. "If you want to fight with me, get it out. Let's do it then. If you want to put distance between us, go right the fuck ahead. Scratch me, little cat. See what you get back."

She frowns, and I swear, if she were a cat, her claws would be out. "I'm not picking a fight."

"You are. I know you. You're pushing at me, because... this scares you."

"I'm not scared." She's scowling at me ferociously. "I fucked you twice."

"No. I don't think you're scared of my penis. I think you're scared of everything else." I sigh heavily, coming down next to her on the mattress. "I'm not *not* scared of it. I don't know how to do this, Sarah. I figured I would meet somebody, maybe in ten years. Think about settling down."

She looks offended. "So there's some mythical woman out there who's good enough for you?"

"I have a mythical idea in my head about a family. Something that's like what my dad has. Yeah. That's true. I've always thought that I would... No. Not always. Since I was eighteen or so. I figured I would do the family thing. Wife and kids and all of that. But you know, someday. When I feel ready."

"I'm twenty-one," she points out, like I didn't just give her a party in a saloon.

"I know," I say. "And you need to go to school. You need to figure yourself out."

"Yeah," she agrees. "I do."

"This is a mess," I say. "You came to me because you were in distress, and that's not a great start to anything. How long have you been in fight or flight?" I ask, reaching out and wrapping a tendril of hair around my finger.

"Every day for as long as I can remember," she whispers.

"I'm not going to hurt you," I say. "I promise. This doesn't change what we are."

"What are we?" she asks, her dark eyes searching mine for assurance I don't know I can give her.

"Just the most important people in each other's lives. Just..."

I want to say everything. But I also don't quite know where to push and where not to. I don't want to scare her away. I also don't want to make a mistake and promise something that I can't deliver. Because thinking about a wife, kids, family, in some theoretical future way off in the distance doesn't feel scary.

Because the woman isn't real, the kids aren't real.

Right now I'm actually staring at the one woman I think

I would want to marry, knowing how badly she's been her, knowing how high the stakes are for me to be the best husband to her... That makes it feel like a totally different thing. It makes it feel like something I might not have the wherewithal to accomplish. Not because I don't want to, but because...

I return to that fight we had in the alley behind the saloon. Because I don't know what to do with my feelings. Especially when they're big.

They're really big right now.

I want to make all kinds of promises. But I know that promises that end up broken or worse than promises that are made at all. And maybe I need to do something I'm not good at. Which is just sitting in a feeling instead of trying to immediately turn it into an action item.

She reaches out and grabs my hand, draws it toward her mouth and bites my finger. Then looks up at me with ridiculously innocent eyes.

"You still bite," I say.

"Only really special people."

"God damn, girl."

"Affectionately?" she asks, eyes round.

"Fucking affectionately," I say, drawing her up against my chest. The weight of her feels right in my arms, her body soft and glorious against mine. Maybe I don't need to know the future. Maybe I just need to know right now.

"Dallas," she whispers. "Do you remember when we were kids and you held me in bed at night?"

I smile. "I do."

"It's the only time I ever felt safe."

My chest feels tight. Overwhelmed by the weight of that emotion. "Sarah, it's the only time *I* felt safe," I whisper, the reality of that hitting me hard.

She touches my face. "Well, you're safe now, too."

I close my eyes and take a deep breath. And I feel something change inside of me. I don't know what it is. I don't know if it's healing or breaking. It hurts.

Love hurts, I think. Even as I fall asleep.

Chapter Eighteen

Sarah

When I wake up in the morning, I know exactly where I am. Dallas' bed, in Dallas' arms. I want to cry. I'm not sure why. I feel small and delicate, nice. I kiss his wrist and then slip out of his arms. I have to get ready for work. He has to take me, but that's just going to have to happen.

I sneak off to my room, and choose the dress that I'm going to wear today, then I slink back down the hall toward his room. When I, he's just sitting up, the covers fallen around his waist, his body... Oh, his body. It's so nice to just be able to look at him, openly. It's so amazing that I can. I'm not carrying this big weight on my shoulders anymore. This thing I haven't done. This thing I haven't been able to get past. I did it. With Dallas. Twice. It was amazing, and I loved every second of it.

I want to do it again as quickly as possible. But sadly, I have to get ready to go.

"Keep looking at me like that and there's going to be trouble," he says.

I smile. "Well, I like a little bit of trouble."

"Don't you have work?"

"I do," I say piously, holding up my clothes. "I'm just going to take a shower. In your shower."

That turns out to be not the best idea (except it's an awesome idea) and Dallas joins me, and derails the whole thing. I have every intention of taking him into my mouth and making him mine, swallowing him, but instead he drops to his knees, drapes my leg over his shoulder and eats me out until I am screaming.

My voice echoes off the walls, and I feel like I should be embarrassed.

Embarrassed that he is eating up every bit of evidence of my need for him, making me into his creature, but all I can do is enjoy it.

When he's done, he licks his lips. "You are delicious," he says.

I suddenly don't care as much that there have been a lot of other women. Because he thinks I'm delicious. And he's mine.

I'm a possessive, wild creature. Rabid, as I've always known. So, this doesn't really surprise me. Because I was always like that with him. I wanted everyone to know that he was mine. That maybe he was nice to them, but he would never really be theirs. Not in the way that he belongs to me.

I guess I still cling to pieces of that. At least where he's concerned.

I get my clothes on, and I find my dress laughably demure in the face of everything we've just done, and then I slip into the truck, buckling before Dallas gets in. He's frowning at his phone. He grimaces, sending a text before getting into the driver's side.

"What?" I ask.

"Oh, my dad was wondering if I could help with something over at my aunt Jamie's ranch. They're all going to do something with some of the horses there. But I need to pick you up. My mom said that she could do it..."

"That's okay," I say.

I'm trying to weigh whether or not that's going to be embarrassing. She does know, after all, she must, considering we got caught on the camera last night. But there's also something I want to talk to her about, and that would be a good time. An organic time.

"Are you sure?"

"Yes," I say.

I've been staying with him for a minute now, and we've had a few dinners with his family. His stepmom is really nice. A quick drive back from the store with her will be totally fine.

"All right," he says. "I'll arrange it."

When he pulls up to the curb, I almost get out immediately, but he grabs my arm and pulls me in for a kiss. I'm dizzy by the time we part. "Wait there," he says.

He gets out of the truck, and rounds to my side, opening the door for me. I have that same feeling that I've had a few times since he came back into my life. Part of me wants him to stop. Because if we're ever separated again, if ever we're not like this, I'm going to miss it. I would almost rather not know how nice someone can treat you. I would almost rather not know that things could be like this.

It's weird and sad, I grant, but I'm a little bit weird and sad.

But right now, I don't have the capacity to tell them to

stop. I just want to enjoy it. For a little bit, I want to enjoy feeling like I'm special to somebody. In every way.

He puts his hand on my lower back and walks me across the street to the store. "I'll see you around dinnertime," he says.

I nod. "Okay."

Then I open up the door and step into the store. The air conditioning is welcome, as is Allison, who is standing behind the jewelry counter looking at me. "So, you two made up."

"Oh," I say. "Yeah."

"I take it he was jealous."

I smile, slow and wide. "Yeah," I say.

I have a friend. That makes me giddy. I have a friend and I can tell her about this.

"I had sex with him," I say. Then I realize that sounds weird. And I'm not sure people say it like that. "I hooked up with him?" I frowned, trying that instead.

"Oh," she says.

"The Hobbit and chill?"

"Well, that's... Nice."

"I think it was nice. It was... I wouldn't call it nice, actually," I say. "It was more intense than that."

"In my experience, sex is..." She scrunches her face up. "I don't know. Fine?" She shakes her head. "I prefer the romance part."

I'm suddenly intrigued, because clearly she has more experience in this than I do. Well, most people do.

"There hasn't really been any romance." But then I think about him wrapping me up like a burrito, and feeding me dinner. Putting on a movie that I love. Bringing me to bed with him. All of that felt pretty romantic. Oh God. I don't love that. It scares me. I don't think I want romance with him.

I did the thing that I wanted to do. I chose to have sex, I enjoyed it, I ripped the Band-Aid off. And he's Dallas, so it was special, and I can't imagine being with anyone else, but that doesn't mean that... That doesn't mean it's romance. He's my Dallas, and it is what it is, but it's not... He wants to get married someday. We're too young. And I don't even know if I want to get married. I really don't know if I want to have kids. I would almost say that I don't. Pretty aggressively.

"Well, we're not... I told you already, we have a very specific relationship. It's trauma based."

Allison's forehead pleats. "That doesn't mean that's all there is to it."

She's not wrong. That isn't all there is to us. It's never been all there is.

"I know," I say. But I don't know what else there can be, and eventually, I have to have an actual life and not live off of him. Not be fully codependent."

"Didn't you spend ten years away from him?"

"Yes." But I was never as happy.

Is that just loving somebody? Is that actually okay? I don't know the answer to that.

"I think I want to stay here," I say. Which is the first time I say that, and maybe Allison is the person I should say it to. Except she's my friend. I really want her to be my friend. "I like it here. I like... You, and him and... His family."

I've never loved a place this much. I've never loved people this much. But I'm so very aware that Dallas is my connection, and if I fuck it up in some way then... I'm not going to have anything.

I've had him ripped away for me before. I've had the only source of stability I've ever had ripped away from me. And just when I thought I was settling in – I wouldn't say I was filled with joy or anything, but I was settling in – in Sisters, Chris appeared and...

I'm spiraling a little bit now. Which is understandable considering I just had mind-blowing sex, and things felt good for a minute. I really don't know how to let things feel good. In fairness to me, life has a pattern of being kind of a bitch.

It likes to punch me in the face when I feel like everything's going to be fine.

"Was it the best you've ever had?" Allison asks.

"It's the *only* one I've ever had," I say.

She looks at me, wide-eyed. "Really?"

"Yeah, I... Again, it's the trauma of it all."

"Oh," she says. "I thought I should just get sex over with, kind of like ripping off a Band-Aid. Because I... I just used to have a stupid crush on someone I can't be with. And I figured if I could demystify the physical act then it wouldn't be that big of a deal. And I did. It was really good for me, because now I know that it's not going to change my life to have a certain man in bed, you know?"

I don't know. Because my life is changed. I feel sad for her. Sorry. Also, I'm not stupid, and I'm pretty aware that she's talking about Colt which...

I get why it's impossible. And I get why she doesn't want to admit it.

"I was going to do that," I say. "Rip the Band-Aid off, I mean."

"With Colt," she says.

So we're both thinking about him. That makes me feel pretty solid in my assessment on her feelings for him.

"Yeah. With him. But honestly, that just seemed like it wasn't fair. I didn't really want to. Also, I actually think he's a really nice guy, and I didn't want to use him."

"I don't think he would've minded being used for that purpose. Believe me when I tell you, Colt Campbell is for the streets."

"Well. Yeah. I won't doubt your judgment on that, considering that you've known them a lot longer than I have. But you should... You shouldn't sleep with people that you don't actually want."

She smiles. "It's not like I'm sleeping with *everybody*. But I like relationships. They're nice. I haven't been in one for a bit. School is keeping me too busy."

"I'm here to tell you that window-shattering sex does exist."

She scrunches up her face and frowns. "I don't know that I like that information."

I blink. "Why not? I'm telling you that orgasms exist that can make the sky break open and rain down upon you, and you're mad about this?"

"I already told you I..."

Right. She wants to minimize it. It makes her feel more comfortable. I worry for her then, that her person might be Colt. Might be the one person that she's not going to allow herself to have.

"The person... Why can't you be with him?"

"First of all," she says. "I'm over it. I don't have the same crush that I had in high school. Second of all, because it's complicated." She looks away. "You already know," she says.

I nod slowly. "Yeah. Well. I do."

"It's weird. Right?"

I shake my head. "No. It's not weird. I'm also a very bad judge of that, because I'm extremely dysfunctional."

She laughs. "Well, that actually works for me. You want to be my friend who enables me?"

"I really do. I really do want to be your friend. You can trust me with that information. I'm not going to tell anybody. Not even Dallas." I love the idea that I have a secret with a friend. "I'm bad at figuring out romantic relationships, honestly, but I'm just as bad with friendship."

"You're pretty good at it, actually," says Allison.

I spend the rest of the shift feeling like I'm floating. It's amazing how intense the formation of a friendship feels. Similarly fraught to this whole thing with Dallas, if I'm honest. Okay, maybe not quite so intense, but it's definitely not nothing.

When Kaylee comes to pick me up, I feel like I'm on the verge of peaking in my happiness. Everything feels like it's working together. Like it's normal and functional and great. And yes, that underlying sense of the possibility of everything being torn away from me also exists. I can't escape that. But I'm choosing to embrace the good.

"How was your day?" Kaylee asks as I settle into her car.

There are car seats in the back with Cheerios ground into them, and I smile.

"Where are the girls?"

"Oh, they're with Bennett. He went to help deliver some puppies, and they went with him. If they don't come home committed to at least two of the puppies in the litter I'll be surprised. Bennett is such a pushover when it comes to his kids and animals."

"Dallas really likes animals too," I say.

Kaylee looks at me, and I can see that she's debating whether or not to push the topic of Dallas now that he's been brought up. I also see when she gives in. "So things are going well with Dallas?"

"Yeah," I say. "Great."

"I think it's really wonderful that... That you found each other," she says.

I feel a little bit panicky, because I don't want her to attribute something to it that isn't there. Commitment or vows that we haven't made.

"I would really like to figure out how to make him dinner," I say.

This is the thing I wanted to talk to her about.. Though it feels a little bit more high stakes now. Especially because she knows everything. Though I've been spending time with their family a lot over the last few weeks and I feel comfortable enough with her.

Maybe less comfortable now that I'm sleeping with her stepson, but still.

"You would?"

"Yeah, I... He's been taking care of me, and I want to take care of him."

"That's really sweet."

"I just want him to have everything he needs. I want to be able to give it to him. He's my best friend." Though that doesn't feel quite right. "He's my..."

"I know that you care a lot about him. He cares about you too."

I nod and look out the window.

"I'm not a great cook," she says. "Bennett and I split kitchen chores. I'm competent, I can definitely show you how to make some things that Dallas likes."

"I'd like that," I say.

"We don't have very long until dinnertime, but I can help you make something quick to take back to the cabin for dinner. He really likes stroganoff made out of condensed cream of mushroom soup. It's easy. Takes about twenty minutes, and we only need four ingredients."

"That's something I can do."

"All right. I'm going to take you to the grocery store."

She takes me to the tiny little store right near the jewelry shop, and guides me in choosing what I'm going to need. Then she drives me back to the main ranch house and gets me set up with the very basic directions for the meal. She's not wrong. It's very easy. Just browning hamburger and putting salt on it while I boil noodles.

"I know there are more elaborate recipes," she says. "But Bennett isn't the most adventurous eater, and so I have a lot of really basic recipes that are tailored to him, and as a result, Dallas loves it."

"He told me that you and Bennett got together really quickly after he came to live with him."

She nods. "Yeah. It was kind of the catalyst for Bennett and me finally getting together."

"Finally?"

She sighs. "We were friends for years. My family was really dysfunctional. I mentioned that, didn't I?"

"No," I say. But between her and Sammy, I'm starting to feel more normal with my own dysfunction.

"He was the best. We bonded together as kids over how much we loved animals. Got ourselves through veterinary school. I was so jealous when he started dating Marnie. God." She sighs. "He told me when he lost his virginity to her." She looks a little murderous even now and I love her for it. "What I didn't know is that she got pregnant."

"Oh," I say. I would've died. I realize that now. If Dallas got another woman pregnant? I think it would actually kill me.

"Yeah. Then she lost it, so she said, and... Fifteen years later, that baby came back as Dallas."

"And in all that time you never..."

"Never. He dated a woman named Olivia for a really long time, I hated her." She laughs. "That doesn't sound very mature, I realize. But I just... That was tough."

"So Dallas brought you two together."

"Yeah. God, he was a pain in the ass. And I loved him. Immediately. It's been the best gift for him to be my stepson, honestly. He's mine. Just like Bennett is. Just like the girls are."

I hear a note of steel in her voice, and I can tell that she's warning me in a way. Not to hurt him.

I don't want to.

I also don't have a gauge of how to do much of anything else.

We strain the noodles, mix in the meat, the soup, and some sour cream. Then, I have a big pot of creamy-looking noodles that I'm personally quite uncertain about, but I'm confident Dallas will enjoy, so it's good enough for me.

"Thank you," I say. She smiles at me, and I have the strangest longing at the center of my chest. I wish she could be my mom. Like I wish I had any maternal figure in my life. Anyone who cared about me the way she does, Dallas. It's another reminder of how high the stakes are. Because any good person I have on my periphery is because of him.

She gives me a ride back to the cabin with the food, and I thank her again profusely for the lesson.

"We'll do it again," she says. "I'll give you a whole list of meals that you can make for him pretty easily. She's quiet for a moment, then looks at me. "I know how scary it is. Loving someone who means so much to you, and having the relationship shift and change. I didn't feel like I could make a move with Bennett, because I thought that I would break it if we kissed. If we had sex. I was so afraid of what would happen, and I knew that I wouldn't be able to stand life if he wasn't in it. I have a lot more experience with life now. I realize that it doesn't have to be that way. If you and Dallas can take this and find a way to be together forever, that's amazing. But I also know you're young. If it isn't right now, it doesn't mean it never will be. If you do this for a while, and then you don't, it doesn't mean it was a mistake. And it doesn't mean you can't still love him in all the most important ways."

It's beautiful advice. And it does something to soothe the fears inside of me, and yet I feel like it's not quite... True. Of us. There's an intensity between me and Dallas that just feels like it has the potential to be something toxic if we're not careful. We need to be careful.

I say goodbye to Kaylee, and take the pot of stroganoff into the house with me. I waffle on what to put on before he gets home. And then I choose a new dress, one he hasn't seen me in today, I feel like I'm cosplaying some kind of traditional 1950s housewife, like I've never aspired to be, and never will be. What am I doing?

I don't have an answer to that question. But when Dallas pulls into the driveway, it takes actual restraint for me to not run out the front door and fling myself straight into his arms. If I could crawl under his skin to be closer to him, I would, and that is an extremely concerning sentiment. I recognize that.

My breath catches as he opens the front door.

He looks first at me, then at the pot of food on the table. "You made dinner?"

"I did," I say, and I want to jump up and down like

those excitable dogs at the main house. Because he's home. He's here.

I feel like I'm outside of myself again, terrified at how overjoyed I am to be with him. Terrified at how intense all this is, and also completely unwilling to stop it.

Like we're driving in a speeding car not paying attention to the speed limit, and I guess if we hit the wall, we're going to do it together.

"Well that was... That was really..." He crosses the room, eyes intent on mine, and wraps his arm around my waist, pulling me in for a kiss. "You changed your dress," he says.

"I did," I say. "For you."

"It's pretty," he says, grabbing hold of the flowy purple fabric. I could've gone with a short dress, I know he would've liked it, but I went with a maxi dress because I thought pretending to be demure might drive him even crazier.

I want to drive him crazy. "I'm informed that this is one of your childhood favorites," I say, going and taking a couple of bowls down from the cupboards and bringing them to the table.

"You colluded with Kaylee," he says.

"I did," I say. "I colluded with her completely. I mean, since your family saw us making out on camera anyway."

He laughed. "Yeah. Apparently."

"I hope you didn't get crap for that today."

"No. Clearly, my dad didn't tell my uncles or my aunt. Otherwise, I would've been getting ribbed all day. But I wouldn't mind."

"You said you've never had a girlfriend before," I say. "Not that I'm your girlfriend."

He nods slowly. "I haven't. And that doesn't quite sound like the right term for you, you're right."

I balance on the knife's edge between being hurt and complimented by that. Because I could take it either way.

I decide to be complimented as I take a ladle and scoop a portion of noodles for him and for me into our respective bowls.

"Why not? Because you're really very functional," I say.

"I did *kind of* have a girlfriend in high school, but you know it was one of those things. Where it's high school. And you know it's not going to turn into anything."

"That's not never having a girlfriend," I point out, jealousy nipping at my shoulders.

"It's not in the sense that it... We both knew that we weren't going to marry each other. We just wanted to have dates to prom. You know? We wanted to... lose our mutual virginity."

I hold back a hiss, but I need to not be vile about him sharing the parts of his life I wasn't around for. The truth is, so much of us is tangled up in all the trauma that's happened to me before and since he came back into my life. I need to be able to listen when he talks about himself.

I flash back to something he said last night. That sleeping with me was the only time he felt safe.

I know that his mom lost custody of him, but I know very little about what his life was like before that. He's never really talked about it. It's only just occurred to me. I filled in all kinds of blanks in my head. Because I know what happens to me. Because I know enough to make up decent stories about what might've been.

I take a bite of the stroganoff, and wrinkle my nose. "It's a bit monotextural," I say.

"What?"

"I find it a bit mushy."

"Really? That's why I like it. It, like, blew my mind the first time she made it for me."

"Were you immediately happy to be with them?"

"I was... It's complicated. I was. But I was also afraid that I was going to fuck it up by being myself. Because at that point, I had just torpedoed every single relationship in my life. At that point, I was a professional at making a mess of things, and I didn't know if I could make something work just because I wanted to." He sighs. "I was pretty much a stereotype. I was... Angry and difficult because I didn't want to go, but I didn't want to admit that I didn't, and I was afraid that if I acted too hungry for it, I would lose it. I was afraid that if I admitted even to myself that I wanted this to be my permanent home, then it would be gone. Just like that." He snaps his finger.

"I understand that," I say.

It's pretty much my whole life. What I know is how to alienate people. Keep them at a distance. I even instinctively did it with him after the second time we had sex. Because it started to feel real. Because I started to worry about the future. Like I have been doing off and on ever since. I realize, with no small amount of alarm, that I am basically teenage Dallas even still. At my big age.

Because it's both, isn't it? At twenty-one, you're still young, but also, you are an adult, and you really should have some of your shit worked out.

"Well, and you must have been afraid of being abandoned, like your mom abandoned you."

I'm trying, gently, to see if he wants to share that information.

He nods slowly. "She was never really around," he says. "But it's amazing how awful it felt when she was gone

215

forever. I went back and forth for a little while. Mainly, she would get charged with neglect, have to take some parenting classes, and do a clean drug test. For a while, she could pass those tests. And then she couldn't. And then she stopped trying. Then she signed her rights away, which I think..." He sighs. "I think that she was probably trying to do the best thing for me. Because I think she wasn't able to care for me at the time. But I didn't realize that. I was an independent kid, because I had to take care of myself, but the thing I hated most was being at home at night by myself. I would always imagine that someone was going to break in. That there was a bad guy who was going to take me. It was scary. When I went into care, there was family, there were always people home at night, but a lot of times the other kids were... You know. When I went into my first home, I was the smallest kid there, and one of the older boys beat me up. Like a hazing, I guess."

"Oh."

"I was five. So after that, whenever I got moved into a new home I didn't really feel safe either. The first time I met you, it made me think of myself. Being the smallest one in the home, being the one who was vulnerable. I didn't want you to be vulnerable. I wanted to take care of you. Protect you. Because I didn't have anyone to protect me, I had you to keep safe. And it felt... good. But what I didn't realize was how connected it made me feel. How safe. Like I had a family. Like I had *someone*. For the first time in my life."

"I never realized that I did that for you. I knew you did it for me, but I just thought... I want to take care of you, too," I say.

"You do take care of me," he says back.

"With my mushy dinner?"

He laughs. "I like the mushy dinner. But yeah. And in more ways. He pushes his empty bowl aside, and stands up, walking over to me and capturing the back of my head, bending down and kissing me.

He lifts me up out of the chair, pulling me into his arms. "I think I want to have you for dessert," he says.

He turns me away from him, bends me over the table, moves his hands up to cup my breasts and I gasp. We were just having a moment. Kind of an emotional one, and now he's feral, but I wonder if this is one of those things. If it's the only way he knows how to deal with a nice moment. And honestly, I don't have a problem with it.

Because I don't know how to deal with one either. This feels... It feels good because I don't have any more words, and I don't know if he does either. It feels good, because I can give him this, I can give him my body. Even if I don't know how to give him any more assurance. Even if I don't know how to make any promises to him.

He begins to gather up my skirts, growling as he does, and I feel validated, because somehow I knew he would enjoy this.

And then, the growl becomes fearsome.

"You don't have any panties on," he says.

Pleasure pulses through my center as I give thanks for that other feminine instinct I had.

"Somehow, I didn't think I would need them."

"You really didn't," he says.

I feel naughty. I feel feminine. Dirty, wild and wonderful. And it feels okay.

I feel healed in ways I would never have imagined were possible. He moved his hand down between my thighs, stroking his fingers through my slick folds. The white-hot lightning bolt of pleasure that ascends through me, making me gasp. He pushes two fingers inside of me, working them in and out of my body, and I arched back against him as he presses his hand between my shoulder blades, forcing me to bend at the waist, my hands now braced on the top of the table.

"I'll take my time over this later," he says, a promise. Brave and real. "Right now, I just have to have you."

I hear him tear a condom packet open, hear him messing with his belt buckle. Then he positions himself behind me, and pushes himself deep inside me as I'm there, bent over the table. He wraps his arm around my waist, and he begins to fuck me, hard and fast, claiming me over and over again. It's everything I've ever wanted. Everything I never knew to fantasize about. His thrusts are sure, insistent. And perfect.

This should feel impersonal, with me facing away from him, but it doesn't. Because I'll always know when it's Dallas touching me. When I was a child, he was the boy that I depended on, and now that I'm a woman, he's the man that I need. Perfect for every facet of my life, for every facet of me.

It's not just bodies. It never will be.

It's us, and that matters. I'm scared of how deep it is. I'm scared of how this makes me feel. But I'm even more terrified of what my life would look like without it. Without him. And so I give in to the enormity of it, and I let my need swallow me whole.

I let him claim me, over and over again. Until we're both shaking. Until I come hard around his cock, and he grips my hips and follows me over the edge.

He rests his head against my back. "Was that okay?"

"Everything you do is okay," I whisper. I reach behind

my back, grab his hand, then I turn around I kiss his knuckles. "More than okay."

He looks at me, and I am undone. The past is there in those blue eyes, so is the present. I'm afraid to look at that glimmer of the future there.

Could we...

I let myself imagine it. Right there in the moment. A wedding ring on my finger. Wearing a white dress and walking down the aisle toward him. A little boy or girl with his blue eyes looking back at me.

That's all so insane.

Something I would never have fantasized about before, ever. But he makes me want it. He makes me want this so much.

More than that, he makes me believe that maybe I can have it.

Even if we didn't get married. Even if we didn't have children, a lifetime of living together, watching movies, making popcorn, having sex, it's a more beautiful future than I've ever imagined for myself. I want to believe that it's possible. But something holds me back from asking for everything.

Maybe because I'm still figuring all this stuff out inside of myself. Maybe because it seems ridiculous that my feelings could be so intense after such a short amount of time.

A short amount of time? It's a lifetime.

We very quietly clean up after dinner, and it's so domestic, particularly given that he just screwed my brains out with me bent over the table a moment ago.

"So, how was work?"

In contrast with the absolute carnal wreckage we just created, his benign question makes me howl with laughter. "It was good," I say.

"What's so funny about that?"

"It's very normal next to that."

"That could be normal," he says.

It's the closest thing to a declaration that I think either of us can give right now. It's right in line with my thinking.

The truth is, I know that I love Dallas more than anything. I know that I don't want to let it go. But trying to think all that through, trying to battle all the razor wire in my soul makes me feel like I'm being gouged and torn from all angles.

Makes me feel like I might be destroyed.

I can feel what I have to do. Cast that ring into the fire. Let go of everything. Trust in him, trust in us.

But right now that just feels too damn dangerous, so I just let what he said stand. I let him take me to bed, and I let him kiss me all over. I let him lick me until I'm screaming his name, and then I take him in my mouth and let him pour all of himself down my throat, because he's mine.

And I love everything about him.

It feels cowardly that I can't tell him.

But I've always been afraid.

I wish so much that I weren't always afraid.

Chapter Nineteen

Dallas

It's been another long day working at my uncle's house, and they're planning a big family get-together in the evening. I'm tired, and I just want to see Sarah, but my dad suggests that I go pick Sarah up from work and bring her by. I think it's not a bad idea, in fact, I really want to. It seems like a great opportunity to get to introduce her to everybody and... well, I'm damned proud of her, I realize.

I'm proud of everything she is, everything she's been. Everything she will be.

I'm proud of our connection.

What began with me being slightly hesitant to share our relationship and how we met around town has turned into something else. I want people to know. I want them to know that she matters to me. That she's important. I want them to know that she's the one who got me through everything.

She makes me feel prouder of myself. Where I came

from, where I've gotten to now. Makes me feel like I have less to prove.

I didn't realize that's what I've been doing. Trying to prove myself. Trying to make myself acceptable. But in going over things with her, the way that I dropped out of college, the feelings I have when I win at the rodeo, when I go out and ride, I've realized the truth. I'm *always* trying to prove something, and when I was in school, I didn't feel like I could prove it, so I quit.

For some reason my soul doesn't feel that same restlessness now.

She makes me feel more settled. Makes me feel like I'm all right. I mean, she's here with me, isn't she?

I roll up to the front of the store, and she steps outside, waving goodbye to Allison.

"Did you have a good day?" I ask as soon as she gets into the truck.

Just looking at her makes me lose my breath. I don't know if I'll ever get used to her.

"Yeah," she says.

She looks slightly distracted. But happy.

"Really?"

"Yeah. I'm just thinking about things. Nothing bad. Just life."

I wait to see if maybe she'll share some of that with me, but she doesn't. I'm not sure if she wants me to pry or not. I don't press.

"I know you just got off work, but there's a big get-together over at my uncle's ranch. I was wondering if you'd want to come by."

She looks at me, biting her lip. "That's a lot of Dodge."

"It is. You don't even know. It's going to be the entire

Dodge family, plus spouses, plus kids, and surrogate family, which includes my dad's ex."

"What?"

"Have I told you about Olivia?"

"No, but Kaylee did."

"Yeah. Well, my dad dated this woman Olivia for a long while, and then she married a family friend, and I think all is well now. I mean, it's been more than ten years."

"I mean, it must be well if everybody all hangs out at barbecues."

"They do. But yeah, my family is big, and it's a lot of a lot. But they want you there. And I would love for you to come."

She looks down. "I've never been invited to anybody's family barbecue before. That's really cool."

"Really?"

"Yeah. Really. I like the idea of being included in that."

"Well of course you are. You are family, Sarah."

I reach across the seat and take her hand in mine, and hold it the whole drive back to my uncle's ranch. We drive underneath the sign, and she looks up, a strange smile on her face. "Get Out of Dodge."

"Oh yeah. That's the name of the ranch. Punny."

"Yeah. Very."

"I think my grandpa named it. I wish he were here; he's great. He's a livewire, even at his age. I never met my grandma, his first wife, but his wife is the best. She's the only grandma I know, and I love her. It's great when they come to visit, but they live in New Mexico most of the year. I know there was a little bit of family difficulty between Wyatt and him, especially, but they're fine. I just think they all get along better when they're not living on top of each other."

"Fair enough. I've always imagined that family is complicated." She laughs. "I have to imagine it, because my family's not complicated, they just suck."

"True."

The grills are going when we arrive at the main house, smoke filling the air, and there are long tables with fixings, sides, and rolls laid out in a pavilion. The ranch staff is also there for the big barbecue, and it actually looks like a giant party. I wonder what it looks like to Sarah. I can remember how it felt to me as a kid who was so used to having nobody. Being surrounded by so much family felt wild.

"This is... This is amazing," she says.

"Yeah. Isn't it? When I'm done with the rodeo, I want to buy a spread of land of my own. Maybe I'll have cows, like my uncle. Or maybe I'll do horses like Aunt Jamie. I don't know. But I love the idea of having a place that's mine. I know when I was a kid, I never even dreamed that far ahead."

Sarah shakes her head. "I just thought I'd probably die before I turned eighteen."

I reach across the cab and touch her cheek. "Here you are, though. They didn't break you, sweetie."

She puts her hand over mine and smiles at me.

Then we get out of the truck, and are immediately swarmed by a pack of small cousins. "Here we go," I say.

I growl, and the small kids scatter; that's what they were waiting for, after all. They want the drama.

Wyatt and Lindy's kids hang back, a little bit too cool for all this, given that they are edging close to that deadly preteen era. I don't hold Sarah's hand as we walk over to my family, only because I don't need everybody breathing down our necks and asking about marriage or anything like that. Some of them would behave, but a number of them wouldn't.

I know them well enough to know that. It can be part of their charm, but not right now.

"Hey all," I say.

"This is Sarah. She was my foster sister back when I was in care. We finally reconnected, and... She's been staying with me."

The greeting she receives is warm and boisterous, and I move her through the ranks of everyone, introducing them, but I know already that all the names are going to get lost in the shuffle. There's Wyatt and Lindy, Grant and McKenna, Jamie and Gabe, then Luke and Olivia, and Beatrix and Lindy's brother Dane, who aren't my blood family, but might as well be. Then there are all the kids, and ranch workers besides.

Lindy is the kind of polished and poised that I can see Sarah finds a little bit intimidating.

I'm sure most people do. But McKenna is scrappy and still has all the sharp edges she had way back then.

"McKenna is one of us," I say, because I know she won't mind.

"In what way?" Sarah asks, looking at me.

"A foster kid," says McKenna.

"How did you... How did you end up here?"

"Gold Valley has foster kids," Dallas says.

"It does, Dallas," says McKenna. "But I'm not one of them. I was passing through, all down on my luck. Homeless, actually, and I ended up staying in one of the cabins on the property. Grant found me. He was a humorless piece of work back then. But, rather than calling the cops on me, he offered me a place to stay. A place to work. And I'm just so charming he couldn't resist me, and he fell in love with me."

"Wow," says Sarah. "That's quite the story."

"We kill at Two Truths and a Lie," Grant says.

"I bet."

And I know that Sarah has found a quick friend in McKenna, unsurprisingly. I've always been close to her, too. Because she gets it. She had to do some dicey things to survive, and she made it.

Food is served quickly, and it's easy to pile too much onto the large paper plates sitting on the table. Once we've finished, Sarah gets absorbed into my aunts and ends up getting dragged back to the house to bring desserts back down.

That leaves me with my uncles.

"So," Wyatt elbows me, "I hear that you and your friend have recently become friendlier."

I turn around and give my dad a hard glare. "We just don't have secrets now?" I ask.

My dad spreads his hands. "Can it really be called the secret when you get caught kissing on a doorbell camera you know is there?"

I snort. "I can't say that I was really thinking about the doorbell camera at the time."

Wyatt claps me on the back. "Fair enough, kid."

"She seems really sweet," says Uncle Grant, which is deeply Uncle Grant of him.

"She can be," I say. "But you know, there's a little bit of something wild to her."

"Well, that's not a bad thing."

Grant smiles at that, and that's something else I know he really gets. "I'm glad I got to bring her here today," I say. "Because she just doesn't have family."

"And look at the family you have to give her," says Wyatt.

"I don't know if..."

"Come on," Wyatt says. "You don't know what? You don't know that you're in love with her? Because it's pretty damned obvious from where I'm sitting."

"Yeah," my dad agrees.

"Excuse me," I say. "What happened to letting people figure their own stuff out."

"Have we ever claimed to do that?" Wyatt asks. "I thought it's pretty well-documented that we are up in each other's grills whenever possible."

"That is, as I understand it, the blessing and curse of living in the general area of your family. And working with them," Grant says.

"Well, all right. So yeah, that would be great if I could just give her everything. Everything. Everything she's ever wanted, everything she's ever... The family and all that stuff. But I don't know what she wants."

"Ask?" my dad suggests, sounding incredulous.

"Yeah, right. So I just say: what exactly do you want in the future?"

"Yes," Wyatt says. "Which I get seems revolutionary to you in your twenties, but it seems a little bit more obvious when you're in your forties."

"Well, thanks for the tip, old man. But, I don't want to scare her away. Like I said, she's a little bit feral."

"I'm not Wyatt," Grant says. "Hell, I'm not even your dad. My experience with women isn't vast. But, I do know a thing or two about building trust with someone who doesn't trust anyone or anything. You just have to show her that you're always going to be there. Your words are never going to mean as much as your actions."

I think about that. I've given her a place to live. And we have a long history together, even if there were years in between where we didn't see each other. She knows she can trust me physically. If the last few days have proven anything, it's that sex works right between the two of us. But I do feel like there's something missing. Romance. Something sweet and nice for once. We have our friendship, we sit together, and watch movies. But I want to give her... Everything. I want her to look at me and think that all the possibilities for what she wants in her life can be with me.

Oh God *dammit*. I *am* in love with her.

"Well, I need to do some kind of grand gesture, I think," I say.

"Yes," my uncles, my dad, and Luke and Dane all agree on that one.

"Such as?"

"You take her into the bathroom at the Gold Valley saloon," says Luke. "You know, when you get lucky and there, you carve your name in the door."

"My *dad's* name is in there," I say.

I look over at my dad, who looks away from me.

"That isn't romantic," Grant points out.

"Worked for me," says Luke.

"I don't need help with sex." I stare Luke down, because I refuse to be embarrassed that I've gone and said that, and I know he doesn't think I have the balls to lay claim to that here in this group.

"Good for you," he says, giving me a grin.

"I'm just saying, that's great. Just fine, thank you. But yeah, I might need a little bit of help with the romance."

"Well, we can help."

Chapter Twenty

Sarah

It was just the best time at the ranch last night, visiting with his family. I've never felt so surrounded by so many wonderful people. Hell, I don't think I knew that many wonderful people existed in the world.

Dallas went back to his uncle's ranch for the day, and it was my day off, so I stayed home and studied.

I've also been thinking about a conversation I had with Allison yesterday. Part of me wants to stay with Dallas forever – it's been so wonderful existing like this. Frozen in this moment in time, but I can't keep doing it. Once I quit paying for rent in the apartment and sisters, I'll be able to get a place here.

The rent is actually a lot higher in Gold Valley than in sisters, but Allison's stepmom owns a few properties in town, and she has a tiny little cottage – the one that Colt mentioned when he first came into Sammy's jewelry shop – and that's available to me if I need it. Which is honestly so nice. I feel like I probably need to do that. I probably need to live on my own for a little bit.

It doesn't mean that Dallas and I can't still be together. But I feel like some independence would probably be a good thing. Or maybe I'm just looking to put a little distance between myself and the intensity that I feel every time he looks at me.

This is uncharted territory. To want things this badly. I've never been one to harbor big dreams of the future. Getting to a place right can even allow myself to admit that I want to be a social worker is kind of a big deal. Goals have felt like my enemy for a long time, because when I was a kid, I didn't have any control over anything. Wanting things felt pointless.

But I'm starting to want. Really big things. Really scary things.

Kaylee really homed in on those worries that I have when she talked to me the other day. Like I'm worried if I do the wrong thing now, now that we've made our relationship physically intimate, there'll be nothing left of us. That if I ask him for more than he wants to give, or we try for everything, and we fail, we'll be left with nothing. She seems to think that isn't necessarily true, but I just can't imagine Dallas and me being anything other than an extreme.

Because even though our foundation is friendship, it was never a healthy friendship. It was always a trauma bond wrapped up in a scarcity mindset and set on fire with fear and isolation. We've always been unhealthy.

Wrapped around each other in a way that feels intimate, intense, and that was even before we introduced kissing and sex.

Yeah. I don't know that balanced, healthy friendship after an implosion is going to be us.

But I really hate the idea of not having him, so I don't know… I don't know what that means. I'm trying to figure it out.

Trying to figure myself out. I wonder what my life will look like, when I'm not on the run. This has been such a wonderful thing. I've been able to really rest. To meet people, connect with them. To find parts of myself I've never really been able to see before because they've always been obscured by trauma.

I'm grateful to him for that.

My gratitude, my willingness to fling myself into his orbit and absorb into him, isn't really the issue, though. I stand up and stretch, feeling like I've been absolutely rotting for the whole day, barely moving from the kitchen table as I completed my assignments. And right as I stand, the door opens, and Dallas comes in.

It's getting dark outside, I've only just noticed. And my stomach is growling.

"I have dinner plans," he says.

"Oh. Well, that's great. Because I'm starving, and I didn't think of dinner."

"Come on." He looks impish, and most definitely like he's up to something, which I'm definitely interested in.

He extends his hand, and I walk toward him. I take it, and he pulls me to him, lowering his head and giving me a kiss.

"What's happening?"

"You'll see," he says.

He helps me into the truck, and I go willingly. And then we drive up one of the dirt roads on the property that I haven't been down yet.

It winds up into the trees, and up higher still. Until we arrive at a grassy hillside, and my heart lurches. There are lanterns set up in a circle, and what looks like a picnic basket, and a blanket spread out on the grass.

"What is this?" I ask.

"A grand gesture."

"Dallas..."

He kills the engine, puts the truck in park, and gets out. Then he rounds to my side and opens my door. "Come on. I'm giving you romance."

Romance.

Allison told me that she prefers the romance to sex. I unbuckle, and he grabs me by the waist and lifts me out of the truck, holding me against him. I'm not sure I can say I prefer romance, but it all feels part of the same thing. Like he took the physical intimacy between us and made it bigger, more expansive. Like he added a new thing that we are. Because we are movies and friendship and trauma and protectiveness, sex and orgasms and romance, now I guess.

I think there's something amazing about that.

He leads me to the blanket, and sits me down.

"I'm not a wine expert," he says, "but my aunt owns a vineyard, and she is. And she gave me a bottle of what she says is one of their most popular wines."

I don't know anything about wine either, but this feels so... Fancy. Like something from someone else's life. Can this really be me? Sitting with this man who is so beautiful when I look at him, I could barely breathe, with a beautiful view, glowing lanterns, wine, and a picnic basket? It doesn't seem like it. There's lovely food in the basket – also from his aunt's winery- and he hooks his phone up to a Bluetooth speaker, and we even have musical ambience surrounding us.

"Please tell me you don't do this with every woman you hook up with?"

"Never," he says. "Just you. Because I want... I've never wanted so much to give someone everything. It's like life was to you. I know what you actually deserve, and I want to make up for everything you didn't get."

"That would be pretty tricky to do. Might as well climb up there and grab some stars and bring down a handful for me."

"I would if I could."

He means that. I can see it.

The truth is, I bet if you brought stardust down to earth, it would lose all its shine.

But that doesn't stop the feeling in my chest from expanding, so big that I can scarcely breathe around it. So big that I don't know what to do with it.

The wine is wonderful, I wasn't sure how I would feel about wine, and the food is delicious. We eat in silence, and there's something comfortable about that.

I look up at him, at the way the waiting sun shines against the angles of his face, those glowing blue eyes in the twilight.

"You know you're amazing, don't you?" I ask him.

"Funny," he says. "I was going to say the same thing about you." When we finish eating, he reaches out and takes my hand, pulls me up. "We missed the chance to dance on your birthday. I do want to miss it again."

I nod, and he pulls me up against his chest, then twirls me in a circle. I look up and watch the stars all blur together in the sky.

And when we finish dancing, we lie down in the field, just like we did back when we were kids, staring down at the city and trying to dream up futures that weren't quite so dark.

Here we are. With each other.

Dallas and Sarah back then couldn't have dreamed up anything quite this sweet. Quite this miraculous.

This is magic.

But I wonder if, much like the stars and stardust brought to earth, if the sun shines too bright on it, if it leaves its heavenly position, it'll all disappear.

I wonder if something this beautiful can possibly last.

Because I'm still me.

I'm still Sarah Anderson.

The foster kid. The abused little girl. The woman who's running away from old ghosts.

I don't know if Sarah is allowed to have nice things. Not for keeps.

But what a beautiful temporary this is.

So I close my eyes, and sway in time to the music, feel the way his body is pressed against mine.

If all we have is beautiful temporary, then I'll revel in every moment. Until it fades away like stars with the sunrise.

Chapter Twenty-One

Dallas

The weeks slip by, and there comes a point where we can't wait any longer to go get Sarah's things.

We've been in a bubble. We meant to leave it a month, but we let one roll into two. She's still been paying her rent – but she had warned her landlord she'd be moving out. Now the landlord is getting edgy because they need to know when they can find a new renter which is fair enough. So we need to break the bubble.

I don't mind driving her everywhere, I really don't, but there's no point her paying for an apartment she's not living in, and it would be better if she had everything she needed.

She's tense when we load up for the trip to Sisters, and I don't blame her. I almost can't believe she's the same girl that I met there a couple of months ago. Because so much has changed since then.

She's changed. She's happier.

I like to think some of that has to do with me.

What's truly amazing is how much *I've* changed. I used to have this idea of what the most important things in my life were. I used to feel like I had a certain amount of anger, self-destruction to work out before I could claim anything like a normal life. Now I don't feel that way.

I feel like there are no mountains left to climb. I've found my home, my homestead, and I want to settle down.

But I'm also very aware that Sarah is twenty-one, and has lived her life with terror, trauma, and the ghosts of her past following her around.

I've had a decade to heal, and while there were parts of me that were still bound up, in a lot of pain, finding my dad, having that chance at normal, at support, it's meant a hell of a lot more to me than I think I've even given it credit for. I can see how it changed me over time.

She hasn't had that. She's been scrapping and fighting the whole time. Healing has been theoretical. She hasn't had the support system I've had. Support systems make all the difference. Mine sure as hell did.

I know she's going to need time. I know she's going to have to go on her own journey. I just feel impatient.

I rent a small moving trailer that my truck can pull, which should fit all her stuff. Once we get out on the road, she rests her elbow on the window and turns her head to look at me.

"Just so you know, Allison's stepmom has a cottage in town that I'm allowed to stay in. I mean, I can rent it. And it's affordable for me. I think they're giving me a really good deal."

"Huh?" Her words are a shock at first, and then, as I process them, like a stab straight to the chest.

She wants to *leave*?

"Yeah. I... I don't feel right about mooching off you. And

really, it seems like the right thing to do for me to get my own place. I mean we've been... whatever this is, we've been doing it for a little over a month and nobody would have the person they're fucking move in after a month."

The *person she's fucking?*

Like that's all we are? Like that's all it is. She eats dinner with my Goddamn parents. I don't know what she's doing, and I really don't like it. I tell myself that I can just calm down and listen to her, and we can discuss it more in depth later, but... I put the brakes on, and stop the truck right in the middle of the long, lonely highway. "What are you talking about?"

She looks around. "Why did you stop in the middle of the road?"

"Why are you saying crazy shit?"

"It's not crazy shit. I moved in with you because I was in a desperate situation, and you've been great, but I don't need to take advantage of you like that."

"Do I look like I'm being taken advantage of?"

"We haven't discussed it, Dallas, and that's why I'm bringing it up. I want you to know that I have other options. I feel like it's really important that you know that."

"Well, I know it. But I don't like it. I want you in my bed."

"I know you do. I can still be in your bed sometimes."

"No," I say.

"Don't," she says. "Don't be inflexible and ridiculous. I have to... I'm trying to do school and work and figure myself the fuck out. I *need* to figure myself out."

I feel like I'm bleeding out here in the middle of the desolate highway, like I'm losing her all over again. "You can't figure yourself out with me?"

"I can I just... I feel like I'm your parasite. I latched onto you with my sharp little teeth and I'm feeding off you. Like I don't function if I'm not with you, and I know that we spent ten years apart. I know that. But it just feels like I'm pathetic without you, and I don't want to feel pathetic. I don't want to feel dependent."

My heart is pounding in my ears. "Being in a relationship with someone is not being dependent."

She looks away from me. "We haven't really discussed what we are."

"What do you *think?*"

I feel defensive, and raw, and that's not the right way to behave and I damn well know it. She deserves for me to be gentle. For me to listen to what she's trying to say, but I feel hurt, and it makes me want to lash out.

"Sarah," I say. "Haven't I made it clear that you're not a burden?"

"Yes, but... Dallas, we are from dysfunction alley. Okay. And it all just feels a little bit too neat, don't you think? Like we're falling into a pattern rather than actually making a choice. Like this feels like the easiest thing for us to do. And I just feel like... You told me that you want to get married someday. There's this theoretical woman that you're going to meet in your thirties, when you're both older and you're established and... you know, I think that's smart. I don't know what I want. Honestly, until recently, the idea of getting married... It never even crossed my mind. Much less having kids. I'm just not there at all."

There's a car coming up behind me on the road, and I have to start driving again. The only sound is the tires on the asphalt, and there are a lot of things I want to say. A whole lot of things, but they would require me exposing myself, and I don't want to do that. So I keep my mouth shut. And I just drive on.

"Don't be mad at me," she says, her voice small. "I'm not... I'm not ending anything."

"I know," I say.

I didn't know. Suddenly, I feel like I can breathe a little better, even though I'm still angry.

"You're acting upset."

"Yeah. I'm upset. Because you talked to Allison, clearly, and you didn't talk to me."

"She's my friend. And this *is* me talking to you. Don't be petty."

"I'm not petty."

"You're a little bit petty."

My abandonment issues have issues, and this is scratching at all of them, and she's right. She didn't say she wanted to break up.

She's also right — under no other circumstances under which I would ever be cohabitating with somebody after this short amount of time.

But she's not just anyone. She's special. She's trying to turn this into a normal relationship. When it just isn't.

Then I think about what my uncle said. About how he had to wait for his wife. She was married to another man. I can't even imagine that. Her marrying somebody else. Her belonging to someone else, the idea of letting somebody else touch her makes me feel like committing a murder. But maybe there's something to what he said. That sometimes you have to wait until the right moment. The right person will always be there. Hell, we found each other after ten years. Maybe we just need ten more.

That makes my stomach feel sour.

Yeah, she's not breaking up with me, but she's putting distance between us. I don't like it.

"Please don't be mad," she says. "I just want... I think

it's important for me to figure out how to stand on my own feet."

If I look past my own shit, I can see that. I can understand what she's getting at. What she thinks she wants.

And I have to try. I have to try to listen. And maybe I need to figure out how to say the things that are rolling around in my chest like knives, stabbing me. But I'm just afraid that I'm going to end up stabbing *her*.

Liar. You're afraid that you're going to expose yourself and then get hurt.

I ignore that. I focus on the road.

"How many different houses did we live in together?" she asks.

I tap my hand on the steering wheel. It's a weird segue, but I'll allow it. I sure as hell don't know what to say about anything else.

"Seven," I say.

"Wow. Over three years."

"Yeah," he says. "It was brutal."

And without even having to pull it apart, I can understand why she needs her own place. I can understand why she needs something that feels like stability for herself. A life that's her own. And I have to be secure enough to let her get grounded in that so that she can get grounded in me.

"Every new experience was so scary," she says. "But not you. You were there and you were safe. Did I ever tell you that... he molested me for six months. Until a teacher at my school noticed that something was really wrong with me. I wasn't eating, I wasn't social anymore. And I got really upset when people touched me. Even accidentally. He would come into my room at night... everything he did hurt. It made me feel gross and dirty and bad. I..."

"You don't have to tell me," I say. I tighten my hands on

the steering wheel. "But you *can*. It won't make me think there's anything wrong with you. It won't change how I see you."

My eyes sting as I stare ahead. I could blame the bright light of the sun, but it's emotion. Rage. Hurt. I hate that someone did this to her. I hate him. If I ever get my hands on him...

"I know," she says. "It doesn't feel like a terrible secret with you. It never did. I was never afraid of how you would react. Ever. I saw you, and it was like... I thought... *There you are.* There's this other piece of me. That knight in shining armor I always wanted to come rescue me. The one true king. I knew you had to be out there, and then there you were. Another part of my soul that had been missing for me forever."

"You were eight," I say, my voice rough. "You didn't think all that."

"I absolutely did." Then she says, so softly I almost don't hear her. "I would have been such a romantic if life hadn't made me scared to dream."

I clench my jaw, tightening it, my teeth grinding. It hurts to hear her say that. I want to give it all back to her. Everything.

I swallow hard. "When I saw you... I could see that you'd been hurt really badly." I look out at the middle distance, trying to keep my voice from breaking. "One time, I... at one of the homes I lived in, I befriended a litter of feral barn cats. It took a while for them to let me pick them up. They scratched me at first. Bit me. You reminded me of a little feral cat. One who wanted care but didn't know how to have it. And hell, I didn't really know how to give it. I wanted to. You know what a gift it is to be a kid with nothing, to suddenly have someone else to care for. To love."

"I think I do now," she says softly.

The difficult issue of her moving out is tabled as we both sit in those feelings. Whatever happens with us, our connection will always be one of the most profound things I've ever experienced. Hell, I'm convinced it's one of the most profound things in all the world. So whatever else there is, there's that.

We listen to music for part of the drive, and by the time we roll into the hotel that we're staying at, it's getting to be about dinnertime. We got a nice place on the edge of town, tucked away in the trees, the biggest lodging in sisters, and one that puts the little roadside motel we stayed in to shame. But that's the thing. I have money, and I might not spare an extra dime to make myself comfortable, but I'll give Sarah whatever she needs.

Will you? Are you being petty when she's telling you what she needs.

Yeah. I kind of am.

I want to say something to her about it, but I can see that she's getting antsy.

"You want to order dinner?"

"I actually just want to get my stuff, get it loaded up, grab my car and be done with that place. I need to. Like I just need to... I just need to be done."

"Okay."

I stash our stuff as quickly as possible, and we get back into the truck and take the fifteen-minute drive to her apartment.

We pull into the driveway, and I look around. There's no one around, the street clear.

It's clear that Sarah doesn't want to linger. She heads straight up the stairs and unlocks the door, and we both head inside.

She insists on team lifting furniture with me – which is hilarious. She's no help at all. But it's cute. If she'd just stay with me she wouldn't need furniture.

I'm especially bitter taking her bed apart.

"You're a dark cloud," she says.

"I want you with me," I say.

She steps toward me and touches my face. "You have me, Dallas."

Across time. Across town. I always had her. But somehow I never felt like I could get close enough. I feel so desperate and needy every time I look at her.

I want her to wear my ring. To live with me. I want her in ways I can't explain.

The corner of her mouth tips upward. "What?"

"I think if I told you I'd scare you."

I go back to disassembling her bed. It's the very last thing. We get it all packed away and I shut the trailer up and turn away from it.

Then pause.

I have a strange sensation prickling the back of my neck. I stop, and I listen. I don't hear anything.

But the vibe is suddenly off. Like the air changed.

I don't like it. I turn around, and there's a car across the street that wasn't there before. And there's a man sitting behind the wheel.

Oh *fuck*.

I just know it. In my gut.

"Sarah," I touch her arm. "Is that him?"

She startles and turns, her eyes wide. "Oh, oh no, Dallas..." Suddenly, I see her, my fierce, glorious Sarah become small again. I see her become that little girl that I wanted to protect.

That little girl this man hurt.

I imagine her the way she described herself all those years ago. Not eating. Not letting people touch her. The way that I met her, fierce and feral biting and scratching, doing anything she could to keep yourself safe.

And the rage that pours through my body is murderous.

"I'll handle it," I say.

"No. Dallas…"

"Wait in the truck," I say.

"Dallas no…"

"Now," I say.

Something in my tone gets through to her and she obeys me, stepping up into the truck and getting inside. I reach into my pocket and lock the doors. She's safe. That's what matters. This isn't her battle, not now.

She has me to fight for her.

She'll never have to fight again.

I start crossing the street, and he gets out of the car.

He's a small man.

Doesn't matter how tall he actually is. He *small*. He's no kind of man. He's looking at me like he thinks he can fucking menace me. But as I get closer, I see fear in his eyes, because he's used to frightening children. Women. People who are smaller and weaker than he is.

It is time for him to tangle with somebody his size. It's time for him to know what it means to be afraid. To be the one begging for mercy.

"I want you to know," I say. "I'll send you straight to hell and never lose a minute of sleep."

He opens his mouth to start to speak but I don't want to hear a single word he has to say. I never want to hear his fucking voice. I don't want him to become a person. I don't want him to try and justify a damn thing. He's a worm. A lowlife, he deserves nothing.

And so I catch whatever he was going to say with my fist, plowing it straight into his teeth. When I feel them give, and I feel a deep sense of satisfaction.

He rallies to try and block my next punch, but he can't do it. I hit him in the side of the head, then hit him again for good measure. He falls to the ground, legs splayed wide, and I stomp his knee with the heel of my cowboy boot, satisfied when I hear a snap. "If you ever show your damned face anywhere near her, ever again, I'll kill you. You understand me?" He's whimpering, unintelligible. Because, of course, he is. Because he's scared now that he has to face a man.

"You better never look for her, but you better wonder if I'm looking for you, you understand me? She doesn't belong to you. She never did. You fucking useless waste of space." He tries to speak, the sound strangled. "Not a word from you. You don't get to speak. If you try to involve the cops I'll tell them you started it. Yeah, your word against a woman's seems to work out well for you, but try it against me. See how it goes. The worst thing that could happen to you is they do nothing, and then it's just you and me still out here."

I can tell he hates this. That I've made him feel small and helpless. I revel in it. I hope she sees it.

I'd ask him to beg me for mercy, but I never want to hear his voice.

I'd ask him to beg for mercy, but I wouldn't give it. It's in his best interest to leave now, so I don't finish the job.

"Leave," I say. "Never, ever let me see you again."

He whimpers, and climbs back into his car, laboring to move with his broken leg, but his pedal leg isn't busted so there's no reason he can't get his sorry ass out of here.

I'm sure shock will help with that, and it'll be a painful bitch when it wears off. At least I hope so.

I stand there, watching as he drives away, until I can't see him anymore, adrenaline pumping through my veins.

I turn and see Sarah, sitting in the truck still, frozen. Her face is white, tears streaming down her cheeks. I watch as his car disappears down the road, and only then do I get into the truck with Sarah, pulling her against my chest as she shakes and cries.

"He's never going to bother you again. He's never, fucking ever going to bother you again, do you understand me? You're going to go on and you're going to have a life. The life that you want, that you need. And I'm always going to protect you. Always."

"Dallas," she whispers, wrapping her arms around my neck. "Thank you."

"He's had that coming for years."

"Yeah," she says. "He has. What if he reports you to the police?"

"It'll be his word against mine. And I don't think he's going to like that experience. I also think he's not going to involve the cops, because last time he went to prison. But it's why I didn't kill him. I can't be with you from spending the rest of my life in jail."

She laughs, a watery sound. "Well, I don't want you to go to jail."

"Me neither. But I would. For you."

"I'd rather if you stayed out here and lived with me instead."

Chapter Twenty-Two

Sarah

I'm still trembling when we get back to the motel. I can't believe what just happened. Dallas has blood splattered on his white shirt, some streaking his forearms, and his expression is grim. He said that he would do that for me. He said it from the beginning. He meant it. He would kill for me. I'm glad he didn't. I'm glad he didn't make it so that he would be separated from me. We have all my things, I'm out of the rental. That part of my life is over. And I really do believe that Chris is never going to show his face again. Because at the end of the day, he's a coward. He's an absolute coward.

Seeing Dallas reduce him like that, took him from being the monster that I always believed him to be, and showed me what he really is. A sniveling, weak, disgusting human being, who can barely lay claim to the species.

He's nothing. And he has no power over me anymore. I hate him. I always will. I will never forgive that piece of shit for everything he put me through. Some people are monsters.

Some people should rot in hell.

And he's one of them.

I'm very clear on that.

I'm also free of him. Detached from him. He has no claim on my life. That's not the same as forgiveness. It's simply a choice not to let him occupy any more of me. Ever again.

We pull up to the front of the secluded hotel, and I'm also grateful that Dallas picked this place, because there's a secure gate to get in, with a code, and the parking lot isn't visible from the road. I really don't think he'll come after us, but part of me needs that added layer of security. Just for my own peace of mind. While we're in town at least.

He pulls up to our little cabin, and we get out, he unlocks the door, his hands steady. I follow behind him, and then he turns around, fury and fire in his blue eyes. He deadbolts the door, and then grabs me, hands cupping my face as he kisses me with ferocity. His hands are sticky with blood, and I take hold of them, pulling them away from my face, holding them between us. "Thank you."

"It's what I always needed to do."

"Thank you," I whisper.

He backed me toward the bathroom, reaching inside the shower and turning it on. He strips off that blood-splattered shirt and throws it onto the floor. He looks feral. Like my warrior. The one I always dreamed of. He looks like my hero.

He looks like Dallas. The bull rider.

The love of my life.

The love of my life.

Maybe we need time and space, and maybe I need my own place. Or maybe... Maybe I just need him.

Maybe nothing else matters because while we were the unluckiest children in so many ways, we found each other. And in this world, in this life, that makes us lucky. We have something different than what anyone else has. We have something beautiful and strong, forged in this impossibly fucked up fire.

We are infinite.

The stars that keep on shining, despite it all.

We were meant to be. I thought a long time ago that I'd accepted my weirdness. But part of me has always been looking for a way to feel normal. A way to feel like what I'm doing in a given moment is right, and easy and good.

I don't care anymore.

I want him.

If it makes no sense to anyone, oh well. I want to marry him. I want to have his babies. I want to belong to him in every possible way.

And I'm done pretending I don't want it. I'm done trying to be measured and balanced and normal. I am obsessed with Dallas Dodge. I love him, and I'm going to have him.

He strips my clothes off me as he finishes taking off his own, drags me into the shower, the water washing the blood off his hands, his forearms, the water running pink down to the floor.

And he's still kissing me.

"I love you," he whispers against my mouth.

I'm undone.

Completely unraveled, like he pulled a thread that had been holding me together for all these years, one that I needed gone. So that I can be remade. Into this new thing, with a new life, new hope.

"I love you," he growls. He pins me against the shower wall, big hands roaming over my body, thumbs rough over my nipples. "I fucking love you, Sarah Anderson. You've been mine from the moment that I saw you. And I knew, I've always known that I would kill for you. That I would die for you. But I think even more important, I will live for you. Be whatever you need. I will... If I could cut myself open and show you everything that's inside of me, the way that I feel about you, everything, I would. If I could make you understand like that, I'd do it."

"I understand," I whisper. "I do. Because it's the same in me.

"I love you," he whispers, as he thrusts inside me, my hope, my heart, my Dallas. "God, sweetheart."

And he begins to move, deep and sure within me, I'm clinging to his shoulders, crying out with pleasure, when I realize I didn't say it back.

"I love you," I say.

He grips my face, kisses my mouth. "I want you to live with me," he says. "And I know I shouldn't say that. If you need to live on your own, I respect that. If you need distance. I'll let you have it. But I don't want to give it to you. I want you to live with me."

"I don't want distance either," I say. "I want us."

"I want you to marry me."

"I want that," I whisper, emotions making my words thick. "I do. I don't care if it seems healed or healthy or balanced, because we don't need to be anyone else. There's no guidebook for surviving the shit that we've survived. There's just this."

He shudders, and he continues to move inside me, and

my own climax hits me like a freight train. He goes over, his head falling back on a guttural sound as he comes deep inside me.

"I'll pay for you to go to school," he whispers against my neck. And you can't complain about it. You have to let me. You have to let me take care of you. It's what I want."

I touch his face, the water running down his skin. "You have to let me take care of you. Because it's what I want."

"I will," he says. He holds my chin, his eyes gazing deep into mine. All I see is blue. "Sweetheart, I've had so many good things over the last decade, but it was never quite right. Because there was never you. It's like there was a missing piece. And now here you are."

I'm not afraid anymore. I just trust him. I'm choosing it. To dive headlong into this whether it's logical or not, to forget that I've ever been hurt. To forget that life is scary, because I want Dallas more than I want anything.

I imagine myself standing on a precipice, over a magma-filled volcano, a gold ring in my hand, representing every trauma, every issue that I've ever had. And I picture myself just letting it go. So that I can hold onto Dallas. "I love you."

"I love you too."

Chapter Twenty-Three

Dallas

It's harder to complete all my championship rituals when my mind is firmly fixed on what will happen afterward. Win or lose, I have a plan.

And something burning a hole in my pocket.

I don't intend to lose tonight. My family is in the stands, my dad, my mom, Lucy and Cara.

Sarah.

My whole world is out there. I just have to complete this one ride. One ride, and I win a million dollars, and I know exactly what I'm going to do with that money. The land I'm getting, for me, for her.

One ride, and I can finally claim world champion status.

It'll be my last ride. I've already decided. Win or lose.

I'm no gladiator in an arena. I'm not romanticizing risking my life, not anymore.

My heart is pounding hard, and I climb into the chute and onto the back of the bull. He jerks beneath me, and I slip my hand beneath the leather strap, adjusting, adjusting, trying to make sure that everything is right.

I imagine my family. And then, just like I always do, I think of Sarah. Only this time, she's not some distant fantasy. This time, she is not something I lost a long time ago.

This time, she's mine.

The chute opens, and the bull runs out. Spinning, tossing, turning. This is my last ride, and I'm the last of the night. The score I have to get to win is huge. If it's not me, it's going to be Maverick Quinn. I don't have the stomach for that. But if I lose, he goes home the champion, but he's still him.

And I get to go home.

I picture her face as I hang on, as the bull tries his level best to end me. Then the timer passes eight seconds, and I leap off the animal. I know the score is going to come up. But I don't even look. Instead, I look up in the stands, I look to see where Sarah is, right on the railing, looking down at me, cheering. And I run straight to her. Run straight up the wall, climb the railing, and make my way to her. Then I reach into my pocket, and I take out the ring box.

Something I picked out with Sammy's help. Because she knows exactly what Sarah likes.

We had a lot of talks about what she needs to do in life, how she wants to finish school, how she wants to work for a few years in social work before she has kids, and I'm on the same page. But this, this we both decided we didn't have to wait on.

I open the box, and get down on one knee.

"Dallas," she says, shaking my shoulder. "You... You're the winner."

But all I can see is her. "Yeah. I am. But only if you marry me."

"Yes," she says. "Yes." The crowd is cheering, and we're up on the screen, so I'm not even really sure if they're cheering me being the champion, or us getting engaged. And I don't care which. I know what I'm cheering. I know what matters to me. The money matters, because I know that I'm going to be able to take care of her. Give her whatever she wants.

Be whatever she wants.

But I've been at peace with myself ever since I found her. I don't need a win, a ride, an award to make me whole.

It's just her.

I put the ring on her finger, and then I pick her up in my arms and kiss her as I take my hat off my head and put it on hers. Her arms wrap around me as I twirl her in a circle, my chest so full I feel like my heart might just burst.

She's mine. My girl. My Sarah.

Always. Forever.

This is just the beginning.

I don't have a death wish. I have a beautiful life to live.

Check out the rest of The Bull Riders series! And read on for the bonus novella, Imagine Me and You!

Imagine Me and You

For the readers - those who have been here since the beginning, and those who are here now. You're the reason for all these books. Thank you.

Chapter One

"I'm literally out in the cold, Jace. I need you."

Jace Colter looked at his best friend Samantha Parker, who was indeed on his porch and freezing her small, perfectly round butt off. Which was a damn shame in his opinion. Because it was a perfect butt. Completely perfect. Not that he'd noticed. At least not that he should have noticed, but he had.

And then he looked down at her companion. Not too far down. Even sitting, Poppy was one big-ass dog. A giant mound of hair and drool that, Samantha was always quick to point out, was a purebred Newfoundland. As if that somehow excused the drool.

It didn't. Not in his opinion.

He and Poppy had a tentative truce when he was over at Samantha's place, but the idea of letting her, and her huge paws, in *his* house on *his* couch was enough to make it feel like his skin was itching. Like he already had dog hair embedded into his clothes. Dog hair he would never, ever get out.

"Start at the beginning."

"Can we come in?" she asked, hazel eyes huge, her red hair creating a ginger halo around her head thanks to the porch light. As if on cue, snowflakes started falling behind her. She looked like a pitiful angel.

"Yes," he growled, standing to the side and letting Samantha hop over the threshold.

Poppy followed, no encouragement needed, as she tended to do. Poppy was as insistent as she was shaggy. She always wanted him to pet her. Stroke her. Things he could never, ever get away with doing to her owner. Not that he would try. Samantha was his friend and this sudden surge of lust, whatever it was, that had crept up on him over the past couple of months was just damned annoying. And completely impractical. And not something he could do anything about.

Ever.

Samantha bent down and started taking her boots off. She knew him well.

Jace had no problem getting his hands dirty working his ranch, but he didn't track that dirt inside his house. His operation was an organized one: a place for everything and everything in its place.

He had a major outfit here with horses and cattle, and letting loose ends hang could result in devastating consequences. Jace didn't allow loose ends, and he didn't screw up. Ever.

"Let me get a towel for your dog. And then you can explain to me why you're standing here looking like a dramatic reenactment of the Little Match Girl."

Jace stalked off to the laundry room and took a towel from the dryer, then walked back into the entryway, where the dog was currently dripping on his wooden floor. He tossed the towel to Samantha, who bent and started working on Poppy's massive paws.

"My lease is up," she said, straightening. "Poppy sit." And Poppy did. "And basically, no one in town will rent to me as long as I have her." She gestured to her massive, hairy companion. "And I can't buy anything yet. Not until I can do taxes for the year. Because that's when my income from the bakery will count," she added, her face glowing now. "Two years in business."

"That's great, Samantha—it is. But it doesn't really answer the question of why you're here."

Except he had a feeling it did. And he had a feeling he knew just what she would ask of him. And he had a feeling he really, really wasn't going to like it.

"I can do my taxes in January. I just need a place to stay, with Poppy, until then."

"So, you need a month. A whole month."

"Yes, and Jace, you're my best friend and I didn't have anywhere else to go and I knew you wouldn't turn me away and—"

"Take a breath, Sam," he said, his head pounding as he tried to sift through the jumble of words she'd just let spill out of her mouth.

"You have a lot of room here, you would hardly notice me. And I would cook for you."

Samantha looked at Jace and tried to will him to feel her desperation. She was sure if she tried hard enough, she would be able to make him understand her distress. He'd been her best friend since high school, and fourteen years after they'd first met, he was still her best friend. Her rock. Her support. He was all things stable and good, and given her upbringing, he was everything she needed.

Not that her adult life had been a whole lot more stable,

except there was Jace. Always Jace. And Poppy, whom she was not, under any circumstances, getting rid of, even if it meant sleeping in a snowdrift in eastern Oregon in December.

Because friends took care of each other, no matter what. And Poppy was her friend. And Jace was her friend, so she expected him to extend her, and thus Poppy, the same courtesy.

He wouldn't let them freeze in a snowdrift. Though he looked as if he was considering it.

"What would you cook?" he asked.

"Stew. And bread. I would bake you bread. And pies. Lots of pies. All the pie you could eat."

He cleared his throat and shifted his weight. "Generous."

"Well, yeah, I thought so." Jace had plenty of room. His two-story, Craftsman-style home had gorgeous, exposed wood beams in the ceiling, making the space feel huge and expansive. His fireplace had a huge couch in front of it, and it really would just be sad to sit there alone. And a dog should definitely lie on the rug by the fire too.

He also had four bedrooms and he didn't need them all. He could certainly spare a corner of his house for a small redhead and her not-so-small dog.

"She's not allowed on the furniture," Jace said.

"Thank you!" She flung her arms around his neck and buried her face in his skin. And for a moment, she couldn't help but be conscious of just how hard and muscular his body was. Or of the fact that his skin smelled like soap with a sheen of sweat over it, thanks to the long workday.

No. She wasn't going there. Jace was her friend. Her attractive, hyper-masculine, sexy friend. But just her friend.

She had her occasional forgetful moments, often fueled by the scent of his skin or an unexpected smile that seemed to break through all the walls surrounding her heart and hit her square on.

But she knew friendship was the best place for them to be. He was her pillar. And without him...without him she would fall.

Which meant no risking the solid relationship they had for a little spark that was probably one-sided. Heck, it was almost certainly one-sided. If Jace wanted a woman, he didn't sit around and wait. He went out and got her. Temporarily. Jace was a fling guy. And while she was sure being flung by him would be a good time, it wasn't what she wanted.

Samantha was a bit more reserved in her relationships, but even with the great caution she exercised, they always seemed to sink like a bad soufflé. Nope. Definitely not moving Jace from FriendZone to BoyfriendZone. In her case, BoyfriendZone was always temporary, and it always ended in disaster.

She'd had all the relationships-ending-in-fiery-hell-storms-of-doom that she could possibly take for one lifetime. And not just with boyfriends. She hadn't spoken to her mother in years. Jace was her rock. And cracking the foundation she built her life on was just not going to happen.

"Jace," she said, pulling her face back so she could study him. He wasn't smiling, but had a weird kind of intent look in his eyes.

"Yes?"

For just a second, a little tiny second, she thought about leaning in and brushing her lips against his. A friendly thank you. An expression of gratitude.

But that would be stupid. And it wasn't the kind of thing they did.

"Yes, Sam?" he asked again, his voice a little deeper, a little huskier than normal. Oh, my.

She pulled out of his embrace. "I'm going to make you some cupcakes."

Chapter Two

Somehow, Jace had ended up with two guests for dinner. One beautiful. One decidedly not and lying far too close to the table for his liking.

But Sam had made dinner, in addition to the cupcakes from earlier, and that meant he couldn't flip his lid over the damn hairy dog sprawled out nearby while he was trying to eat.

"Guess what," Sam said, beaming, her round pale cheeks downright cherubic. Ironic, considering she made him think of sin, not salvation.

"What?"

"I had German chocolate cake leftover at the bakery. And a lemon cream pie. And now they're in your fridge."

He took a bite of homemade bread. "I appreciate it." He really did. Samantha was the best baker around, in his opinion. She'd also been the best personal chef, the best hairdresser, and the best dog groomer. Not necessarily in that order.

Samantha was always bursting. With ideas. With talent.

It was the settling that was hard for her. The follow-through. But then, given her upbringing he could hardly blame her. By the time she'd come to Bend at the age of sixteen, she'd lived in nine states and twenty-one cities. She and her mother had rented the apartment above the mercantile where Jace worked, and he'd clicked with her instantly.

It had started, he could admit now, as a case of insta-lust like a corn-fed country boy had never known before. She was new and bright. She wore eclectic clothes and had hair that seemed to glow in the sun.

When she'd turned seventeen, she'd shown up at his parents' house, much like she'd done tonight at his own house, in tears, telling him she didn't want to move. That her mother had found a job in Washington state and was going north.

Mrs. Brown, who owned the mercantile, had let Sam stay on in the upstairs apartment. She had a way of taking in stray people and making them feel like they belonged. She'd done the same for him when she'd given him his first job.

Mrs. Brown let Sam live there rent free so she could finish school, so she could remain in the town she felt a part of.

It was too bad Jace hadn't bought the store from Mrs. Brown when she'd offered, or Sam could have stayed in the old apartment. But when she'd been ready to retire and spend half the year in a warmer climate, his ranch had just been getting off the ground and he hadn't been willing to take his focus off of his new enterprise for a moment.

It was, by extension, his fault that Sam and Poppy were bunking with him. Not that he minded Sam's presence so much.

Unless you brought the sexual frustration issue into the

picture. Though even when she wasn't staying with him, she did a pretty good job of sexually frustrating the ever-loving hell out of him. Just last week they'd curled up on her couch to watch an action movie. And she'd put the damned popcorn bowl. In. His. Lap.

The ceramic shield over his cock was the equivalent of a Kevlar vest pitted against a 30-06 rifle. Not. Fucking. Helpful.

The constant promise of a hand job with no satisfaction. And she'd had no idea. She'd been all involved in the movie while he'd sat there with a hard-on so intense he was a little afraid it would break the popcorn bowl.

Yeah, so...he was already in hell where she was concerned.

Now hell had moved in. Complete with hound.

His own little ginger specter of sexual doom.

And none of that was fair because Samantha needed a friend. But not a friend who was hiding an erection that wouldn't quit and casting aspersions on the round suppleness of her breasts.

Not right now. Which meant getting a grip on himself—literally in the shower if need be—and moving on without blaming her for what a sick freaking puppy he was where she was concerned.

"And tomorrow I'll make you pancakes for breakfast," she practically chirped. In truth, it had been a long time since a woman had made him breakfast. But usually when one did, it was a much-needed refueling after a night of sex. Not so for tomorrow's pancakes.

He repeated that to himself. Enough times and his body might get the message.

"Great, but you don't have to pay rent, Sam, in money or in foodstuffs."

"No, I know. But I figured that I should do something. If not for you, Poppy and I wouldn't have anywhere to go."

He knew better than to suggest she not tie her fate to her pet. That would get the batter of his morning pancakes sneezed in.

"So where are your things? Do you need help moving?"

"All of my things are in the delivery van."

Samantha's only vehicle was a giant white van with colorful decals on the side and the words *Samantha's Sweets* emblazoned on the side in swirling letters.

"Even your furniture?"

"No. I got a storage unit for that. Which, come to think of it, Poppy and I probably could have slept in if we'd gotten desperate."

"Yeah, right, like I would have let you sleep in a cold, mouse-infested storage unit."

"Mice?"

"I mean, I'm not that heartless, Sam, not even when it comes to dogs."

"Mice? As in actual mice?"

"You're welcome to stay here as long as you need."

"Are they going to have babies in my couch?"

"What?"

"The mice," she said, hazel eyes round.

"You sound concerned. I thought you liked vermin."

"I like dogs," she said. "And cats. And...fluffy vermin like hamsters. I draw the line at anything with a naked tail. No mice, rats or possums."

"Hairless cats?"

"Ew, no."

"See, I think I could get on board with a hairless cat. The kind of pet that doesn't leave pieces of itself all over your house."

She smiled, that impish smile that took him straight back to high school. And made his heart and body react just like the boy he'd been, not the man he was. The man who had decided, years ago, that Samantha was his friend and nothing more, in spite of occasional lapses in sanity.

Like when she stuck her hand into a bowl of popcorn that happened to be positioned on his lap.

"Yeah sure, but it's a cat. So it would probably bring pieces of other animals into the house for you to find."

The idea disturbed him, which was doubtless what she intended.

"The dog doesn't do that, right?"

She cocked her head to the side, her smile widening. "Not usually."

"If it brings a rat into the house, I'm throwing it out into the barn."

"The rat?"

"The dog."

"The dog isn't an *it*. She is a she and she has a name. As you well know, since I have owned her for five years and you've been in my life for every single day of those five years."

"Fine. If Poppy brings a rat into my house, I won't hesitate to kick her furry, purebred behind out to the barn. How about that?"

"You would let her in your barn?"

She had him there. "The stable. In a stall."

"What if she barked and scared your horses?"

"Samantha, you're making the image of you in a storage unit not seem that bad. I'm sorry," he said before she even had a chance to react to his jackassedness. "That was uncalled for and I don't want you sleeping in a storage unit on a nest of baby mice."

"Jace, I know you worship at the altar of bleach and disinfectant spray. I have a certified kitchen and a food handler's card, plus, I passed my last health inspection with a score of ninety-nine. So I don't think you really have to worry. I shall not desecrate the temple of cleanliness."

"I'm not that crazy, Sam. I'll deal."

"Darling, Jace, I've known you since we were sixteen. You *are* that crazy."

"It's better to care about being clean than to be attached to your dirt."

He cringed, knowing they were having a shared memory. Of his childhood home, the piles of things, his mother 's over-attachment to all of it. Her inability to throw one damn thing away.

For a while it had spilled over into his room. Until he'd reclaimed it. Until he'd thrown out every piece of garbage and disinfected every corner and told her anything that crossed the threshold was going in the dumpster. He had to have a haven, or he would have really gone insane.

But he'd had his bedroom. He'd had the store and Mrs. Brown. And he'd had Sam.

His room and the store had provided escape. Mrs. Brown had provided the tough love, the guidance, the financial help when he'd wanted to start his beef ranch.

Sam had provided the smiles. The laughter. Sam made everything feel a little bit lighter. A little more colorful.

It was just ungrateful to begrudge her or Poppy a place in his home. Of course, his opinion on that would likely continue to fluctuate depending on how messy the dog proved to be.

"All right, yeah," he said. "I'm that crazy. But I like to have control over my house and I know you understand that."

Samantha did understand that. She remembered what Jace's house had been like. She'd known him for more than a year before he'd let her inside, and when he had, his humiliation had been palpable. It was the only time she'd seen her friend near tears—that moment he'd let her walk through the rubble that was his childhood home.

Through the trash his mother treasured more than she had her husband who'd left and her son who was slowly going insane living in it.

She stood and picked up her empty bowl, crossing to Jace's spot and taking his bowl too. "Don't worry, Jace, I'll be good," she said, bending down and kissing his cheek.

The moment her lips touched Jace's skin, she knew she'd made a big mistake. She didn't just go around kissing him on the cheek. She'd done it before, but she didn't make a habit of it. And for some reason, this time had sent a rush of heat over her skin, a flame through her veins.

Calm down, woman. It was a kiss on the cheek, not second base.

Her body didn't get the memo. Her lips burned and her nipples tightened, begging silently for attention because they knew she sure as hell wasn't going to beg for him to touch her.

Nope. She was not.

She cleared her throat. "I'll even do dishes."

She turned and headed toward the kitchen and Poppy stood and followed her, her tags jingling with each footstep. There was something perfect about this moment. Something so domestic and calm.

Except for the lingering crackle of fire on her lips. That wasn't calm at all.

This moment, except the crackle, embodied all the things she'd always wanted but never had. But she would have her own home soon. And it would have Poppy. It wouldn't have Jace, but he would still be in her life.

That was all that mattered.

For now, she had his big, beautiful kitchen. Spotless and perfect. Like everything else in his house. She'd always admired the way he'd transcended his upbringing. The way he'd made something so orderly out of the chaos he'd been raised in.

She was afraid she'd inherited her mother's transient, hippie dippy nature. And in terms of her taste in incense, she didn't mind. But the restlessness she felt, the dissatisfaction with her surroundings... those seemed to be ingrained deep in her.

But instead of moving, she bought a new lampshade and curtains. Her feet were itchiest when it came to jobs. She'd had more jobs than most people twice her age. Not because she couldn't do the jobs she got, and not because the businesses she'd started had all failed, but because she'd simply never found anything to latch onto.

But Mrs. Brown had taught her to bake. Survival skills, the older woman had said. And that had always been a part of her life. So when the bakery downtown had gone up for sale, Sam had scraped together her meager life savings and poured herself into her new project with a vengeance. When she was bored, she infused buttercream frosting with lavender instead of selling everything.

The next big step in defeating her restlessness was buying a house. And then when she needed a change, she'd paint a wall.

She was rising above like a mother effing phoenix.

Then there was her love life. Men didn't stick with her, much like she couldn't stick with a career. Or rather hadn't been able to. No men, same job for the past two years.

She deserved a trophy. The Deferred Orgasm Award for Excellence in Abstaining While Getting Your Crap Together. Yeah, she was on the upswing for sure. Except for this little hiccup. But as always, Jace had her back, so the disaster wasn't too big.

That was Jace. Steady. And neat. So many things she wasn't.

Which was why she needed him. One of the many reasons why.

"You don't have to do dishes," he said, following her into the kitchen. "You cooked."

She started rinsing the bowls, smoothing away stew chunks with her thumb beneath the running water. "I want to."

"Seriously, it's fine."

She glanced over at him. He was leaning against the counter, his relaxed posture at odds with the tension coming off of him. "Oh my gosh. You don't think I'll do a good enough job on the dishes, do you?"

"That's not it," he said, rubbing the back of his neck, a sheepish expression on his handsome face.

"No, it totally is. Jace Colter. You don't trust me to do dishes."

"You're scrubbing them with your thumb, Samantha."

"They're going in the dishwasher!"

"You have to pre-clean them correctly."

"Holy frick, Jace. Your issues can be perfectly adorable, especially when they culminate in you wiping my kitchen table off after we have dinner at my place, or you vacuuming my couch before you sit on it, but this," she said, holding up the bowl, "not so cute, my friend. It's going in scalding hot water that will disinfect everything. It's not like I let Poppy lick it."

"You wouldn't."

She arched a brow and took the bowl out of the sink, lowering it slightly. "You don't think?"

"Sam," he growled.

"Grrr. Jace is mad."

"I will put you on the hide-a-bed." He took a step toward her, his scent attacking her like a sexy beacon of temptation again.

She swallowed hard, tossing her head back, ignoring the lingering tingle in her lips. "Bastard. You have a bed with a down pillowtop and you would be put me on that abomination?"

He took another step toward her, his dark eyes clashing with hers, sending a little zing of heat through her. It was all that deferred pleasure business. This level of not-being-able-to-ignore-Jace's-hotness wasn't normal.

"If you let your dog lick my dish..." His tone was so menacing, his gaze so intense, and the tension in her chest was so tight...she snickered.

"That sounds like the world's sickest euphemism."

His lips twitched, as if he was trying very, very hard to hold back a smile. Or evidence of amusement of any kind over her shenanigans.

"Samantha, do not let your dog lick the bowl. And I'll let you do the dishes."

"Hollow victory, but I'll take it." She lifted the bowl back up out of Poppy range and turned to the sink. "You can do the breakfast dishes."

"Great. I'm going to go take a shower. Pick whichever room you want, but the dog cannot sleep on a bed."

"Fine. Fine. Good night, Jace the Grumpy Cowboy."

"Good night, Sam."

He turned and walked out of the room and she just kept washing dishes. She didn't even look at his ass.

Normal. Everything was back to normal. The kiss had inspired a bit of temporary insanity, but it was over now.

Totally over.

The next month was going to be just fine.

Chapter Three

Samantha cranked up the radio and ladled some more pancake batter onto the griddle, singing the octave above Blake Shelton as she got in touch with her hillbilly bone. Poppy barked along in no particular key.

Jace's kitchen was so big she actually had to take steps to the fridge to get more milk for her batter. In her old apartment she'd just kind of stretched to get everything. This was heaven.

When her bakery started getting featured on the Travel Channel and Food Network, 'cuz hell yeah it would, then she'd get rich and famous and buy a house with a huge kitchen. Testing recipes would be way more fun in here.

She started to do a little dance, using the batter-covered ladle as a microphone and giving an on cue "Yeehaw" as the song commanded.

"Samantha, what the f—"

Then she flung her arms wide, a motion started because of the music and made bigger by the very stern sound of Jace's voice, and came up against something solid, the pancake batter making a wet splat as it came into contact with its target.

She turned, her eyes wide and level with Jace's throat. And the spray of raw batter that started between his pecs and spread out like a gooey star.

She snorted a laugh and quickly took a step back, clapping her hands, one of which was still holding the ladle, over her mouth. "I'm sorry," she said through her fingers.

Little clumps of uncooked pancake tangled in his dark chest hair, which got her noticing the chest hair. Which got her following the thin line of it that ran down the center of his abs and to his very low jeans and...oh my.

She looked back up into very dark, very angry eyes.

"Good morning," she said, her smile wide. "I made breakfast. *Dammit!*" She turned and scurried back to the griddle and flipped the pancakes. They were only a little dark. Some syrup and whipped cream would cover that right up. "It's okay. The pancakes are fine."

"What the hell are you doing, Sam?"

"Cooking. For you, silly. Before you go out riding the range."

"I'm castrating calves today."

"Well...you know. Before you go cut off animal balls. I hear that really works up a sweat. Also, these are kind of a theme breakfast. They're round like...yeah, well, that's not appetizing."

Jace pulled a hand towel off the oven door handle and wiped it over his bare chest. She cocked her head to the side and watched intently, unable to help herself. It was like some kind of weird breakfast porn. And it was kind of fascinating.

Jace walked over to the radio and turned it off.

"Country music hour is sacred in the morning," she said.

"My sanity is sacred all the time. And I reserve the right to not be assaulted by breakfast."

"Who hasn't had a slight pancake mishap?"

He looked down at his chest. "Everyone?"

"Eh." She waved her hand. "Charming foibles aside, I've made you breakfast."

"Your foibles are possibly less charming than you think."

She shook her head. "Nah. I'm quirky. It's adorable."

"Is that what you call it?"

"Breakfast!"

She used the spatula to put a stack of four pancakes on a plate. Then she added syrup, chocolate chips, whipped cream and a cherry. And held it out to him. "Be mad at me while you eat this," she said.

"It's impossible," he said, sounding defeated as he took the plate and sat down at the small kitchen table, his bad mood lightening even more when he noticed the cup of coffee already in position for him.

"I know." She smiled and put a pancake onto a plate for herself, sticking to chocolate chips and whipped cream, and sat across from him.

He took a bite and moaned, a deep, guttural sound that echoed in her stomach and made her feel all strange and jittery.

"Good?" she asked.

"So good."

First the pancake batter show, now he was making sex noises while he ate. The man was a damned hazard to her health.

No, this wasn't the first time she'd been inappropriately

aroused by Jace. There was...well, all of high school. But he'd dated other girls, and she'd dated other boys. And then there were a few months of melancholy longing sprinkled throughout the next twelve years. But nothing she couldn't deal with. Nothing she couldn't ignore.

Like a few weeks ago when they'd watched that movie and he'd put the popcorn bowl in his lap. It had forced her mind to what was beneath the bowl. To whether or not he felt her reaching in the bowl. To what he might think of that.

But then she hadn't seen him for a couple of days due to work obligations, and she'd gotten her head on straight.

It was just that there had been two incidents in the space of a few hours and since she was living with him for the time being, there had been no blessed distance to make sure she could get her brain back in order.

The Jace lust had to end. It was just bad. Bad bad bad. If they were going to live together for the next four weeks she had to somehow manage it without drooling like Poppy.

"I've got to head out," she said, standing and stretching. "I need to get everything going at the bakery. Thank God I just make cupcakes and pies and not breads, or I'd have to be there at three a.m. Still, the meringue will not whip itself." She wiggled her eyebrows and reached down to the floor by her chair to retrieve her purse.

"What are you doing with your mongrel?" he asked.

"My purebred—" she bent and smooched Poppy on the lips "—stays home. I run a bakery. Unsanitary."

"You just made pancakes with *it* right there."

"*She's* not unsanitary to me. She's unsanitary per regulations laid out by the state of Oregon. I think she's a peach. But then, I don't really want hair wafting onto the cupcakes either."

"What am I supposed to do with her?"

"I'll take her out now and she can stay inside until I close up shop. That's what I normally do."

"You want her to stay in the house?"

"She can't stay in the van. It's cold. Sometimes I leave her outside, but not all day in the snow."

"She's a Newfoundland, Sam. Aren't they...waterproof like ducks?"

"Poppy is an inside doggy," she said.

"You're overindulging."

"Ah, Jace, you overindulge in bleach and I love you anyway."

"Bleach, unlike your dog, leaves things cleaner than before it blew through the kitchen."

"I was the one splattering pancake batter, not Poppy."

"Then maybe I should keep her and throw her owner in a snowbank."

"You wouldn't. I'm too cute."

Jace felt all the electricity that had flowed through his veins when she'd hit him in the chest with pancake batter now run toward his heart and encircle it, giving it a hard jolt. Dammit, she was too cute.

She was too cute to send to a mouse-infested storage unit. Too cute to throw into a snowbank. Too cute to have underfoot twenty-four hours a day because she was also just about too cute not to pull into his arms and kiss until neither of them could breathe.

Which meant it was time to go out and throw himself in a snowbank and then get his ass to work.

"Do whatever you want with Poppy. I have calves to de-ball."

She arched her brows. "As you do."

He gave her a halfhearted wave and walked toward the

front door. He grabbed his gloves from their place on the shelf that was just to the right of the door and the keys that were hanging on the hook below.

A place for everything, everything in its place. A simple fantasy he'd had in his childhood, one that had been unattainable.

Now he had it. And it really did make everything run smoother. He could get everything he needed for the day together in a matter of minutes. Muscle memory. Everything was right in reach, just where it was supposed to be.

No waste. No valuable moments spent searching for a tool that wasn't where it belonged. He didn't really care if Sam thought he was crazy. He was efficient. Crazy and efficient, but what the hell? He had control. He was the master of his domain.

He paused for a moment and put his hand on his hips, letting out a long breath that lingered in the air like fog before dispersing. He looked at the fields, covered in snow, to the mountains beyond them. The barns. The equipment sheds. It was all his, and it was all how he liked it.

Yeah, life was pretty damn good. And in a few weeks, Sam would be on the path to homeownership and out of his house. And things could get back to the way they were supposed to be.

With mild lust flare-ups that happened every now and then. But nothing like this seam-busting, perma-erection he was dealing with now.

He shook his head and kept walking. Spending the day removing the testicles from animals should serve as a decent libido crusher.

He'd never looked forward to the job so much.

～

"Holy shit."

Jace walked through the front door of his house and was greeted by the muggy, unpleasant scent of dog. Wet dog.

And then his eyes went to the floor and followed the little trail of cotton fluff balls that ran from the kitchen, across the entryway and into the living room, to the fireplace.

He half-expected to see a big black beast at the end of the trail. But he didn't.

Because the big black beast was on his couch. With the remains of the throw pillow that had been viciously attacked hanging from its jaws.

And its face was wet. It added to the gore of the scene. And judging by the puddles that led from the hall bathroom to the couch, the wet had come from the toilet.

"Hi, Jace! I brought cupcakes."

He whirled around. "Why is your dog on my couch? Why did it drink out of the toilet? And why in hell did it chew up my pillow?"

"What?"

"You heard me," he said, angry now, unreasonably so, maybe. No, not unreasonable. She'd come storming in yesterday and given him a fait accompli and now she was getting pancake on him and getting his cock hard and her dog was breaking his house.

"She never does stuff like that."

She crossed to where he was standing and her mouth dropped open.

"See?" he asked. "She did that. She did. She killed that throw pillow and she didn't even have the decency to consume the body. A pleasure killing."

"She never does things like that!" she said again,

running over to the side of the couch and kneeling down in front of Poppy. "Bad dog! Bad, bad dog."

She sounded like she was cooing at a newborn baby. Not like she was scolding a two-hundred-pound animal.

"You don't sound like you mean it."

"I'm in shock," Sam said, pushing into a standing position. "She doesn't chew things at home. She must have been confused about the boundaries here."

"Confused about the...she's a dog!"

Sam crossed her arms beneath her breasts, the motion tugging her shirt tight across them. He imagined her expression was fierce, but he was having a hard time motivating himself to raise his focus and confirm it. Angry eyes...perfect breasts. Frowning mouth...boobs.

There was no contest.

But at some point, he had to acknowledge that he'd passed from normal, expected male study of the female form to slobbering douche bag, so he had to no choice but to look up. Yeah, she was mad.

"Where do *you* get off being mad? Your dog chewed up my—"

"Ten dollar throw pillow."

"The money isn't the point. It's mine. And I like things where I left them and not desecrated by the hound of the Baskervilles."

"It won't happen again, Jace. Come on," she said to Poppy, genuinely stern now. "Outside."

She walked out with the dog and returned a few moments later without her. "She's thinking about what she did."

"No she's not. She's thinking about when she can kill again."

"Jace, I'm sorry. She really doesn't normally chew. She

does drink out of the toilet—I can't lie. But she doesn't have opposable thumbs, so we'll just make sure the bathroom door is closed and she'll go for her water bowl."

"She can't stay in the house, Sam. Not while you're gone. I can't have her in here. It would drive me crazy."

"Jace, what am I supposed to do with her?"

"She can hang out with me. That way I can keep an eye on her. She's never made a move toward any of the animals on the ranch before, so I'm assuming she'll stick close, right?"

"Well, yeah, but you hate her."

"I don't hate her, not any more than I hate the idea of any dog in my house and on my furniture. We'll be fine as long as she doesn't try to crawl in my lap like an overgrown puppy."

"She'll be a mess if she follows you around all day."

"I'll hose her off inside where I take care of the horses. She won't get cold. I don't mind mud out there. I mind it on my floor. There's a difference."

"Okay, thanks. I'm sorry we're being high-maintenance guests. That wasn't my intention."

He let out a long breath. "I know, Sam. We'll be fine. We just have to establish a routine."

"Well, in keeping with that theme, I brought more dessert."

"I like that routine."

Samantha felt a little glow at the center of her chest. She had no idea why Poppy had decided to go postal on the pillow, and she really did feel bad, in spite of the fact that protectiveness for Poppy made her a little prickly. So the idea that something about her was welcome in Jace's eyes was…nice.

"I'll bring out a tray of cupcakes. You sit down. We'll watch a movie. Your pick."

He muttered something about cupcakes being preferable to popcorn. "Sure, Sam."

"And Poppy can come sit by the fire. It'll make a nice domestic picture."

"Nothing with that much fur features into my version of a nice, domestic picture."

For some reason, his words made the glow vanish. Leaving her cold and a little sick. "Oh. Well, what does feature in your nice domestic picture?"

He shrugged. "Me by myself, I guess. Or with you over for a movie."

But living by himself. Not with a wife. Why did that bother her? She shouldn't care. If Jace had a wife she'd never get to see him. She'd long dreaded that day, really. The day when another woman became more important to him than she was.

But it hadn't come yet. And she was pretty thrilled about it.

Still, the idea that he was happiest alone...she didn't like that either. "Well, you pick the movie."

"*Die Hard.*"

"Ugh. Fine. I'll get the cupcakes."

"And a beer."

"Cupcakes and beer?" She made a face. "Instead of dinner?"

"It's my house. My rules. Beer. *Die Hard.*"

"Cupcakes. Manly."

"Put a piece of bacon on them and man them up."

"I think I'll pass."

"Great. You go get that stuff and I'm going to..." He looked at the couch, then at the fuzz on the floor.

"You're going to clean up."

"I know how to party on Friday night."

"You surely do show a lady a wild time." Their eyes met and she felt a tug that went down deep, from her heart to her stomach. "I'll just...cupcakes. And maybe I'll fry bacon for a side."

She turned and went into the kitchen. Where she could get a momentary reprieve from Jace's scent, his hot body and the looks that made her feel like she was being turned inside out.

Chapter Four

Saturdays were always slammed at the bakery. When Samantha got back to Jace's that evening she was carrying a box of unfrosted sugar cookies and a tube of red icing, and she was ready to fall over.

"You're late tonight," Jace said when she walked through the door.

"Tidings of comfort and joy!" she said, holding out the cookies.

"Busy day?"

"Yes," she groaned, setting the box on the sideboard that was just by the door. Then she took off her gloves, her hat and her coat and put them on the floor. "Where is Poppy?"

"I set her free. Back into the wild where she belongs. She should be making her way back to the Canadian wilderness as we speak."

"Jace, where is my dog?"

"In front of the fireplace. She had a busy day following me around. I think she's out of shape."

"Yeah, we don't do much in the way of ranching."

"I didn't figure. She did like playing in the snow though."

"Aw, fun. I'll have to go out with you both for a while tomorrow. Sunday, my blessed day of rest," she said.

"Holiday orders getting heavy?"

"Around Thanksgiving I made so many pies my fingers were curled into claws for days, and it hasn't slowed down much. Mince pies, apple pies, pumpkin pies. I have a special order in for a cherpumple."

His dark eyebrows locked together. "What fresh hell is that?"

"It's a pie inside a cake."

"That's wrong. You can't put a pie inside a cake."

"You can."

"It doesn't mean you should."

"Some power-mad baker decided to wreak havoc with the order of the universe, I guess. I don't know what to tell you," she said.

Jace took his hat off and smoothed his hair, his muscles shifting beneath his tight T-shirt. He and Poppy must have just gotten back because he rarely wore a hat inside. "I like things to make sense. To go where they belong."

He walked over to the coat closet and put the black Stetson up on the top shelf, then left the door standing open. A clear invitation for her to put her own stuff away.

She wouldn't even grumble about it. She picked up her coat and other accessories and brought them to the closet, placing her hat next to his, and then put her gloves on the shelf by the door, right on top of Jace's leather Carhartts.

She grinned at him in triumph. "I can adapt," she said.

"Good," he said. "Because I don't very well."

"Aw, be adventurous. Try a cherpumple."

"I'm letting a dog sleep by my fireplace. I think that's

enough adventure in my life for the time being. I'm not eating some unholy dessert mash-up."

"A cherpumple and a romantic comedy."

"A beer and *Die Hard Two*."

"Bah!" She smiled at him and her stomach tightened. She took a deep breath and headed toward the kitchen, scooping up the cookies along the way. "Hey, what do you want for dinner?"

"I made dinner," he said.

"You...made dinner?"

"Yes, you can have some."

"I thought you just got in."

"I came in and put chili in the slow cooker and then went back out for a while. I usually live on my own, you know."

"I know," she said. "But I kind of picture you being a little more helpless than that. Your kitchen doesn't look used."

"Clean. It looks clean."

"Ahahaha. Funny, funny. Where is this chili?"

"In the Crock-Pot, waiting for you."

Again she couldn't shake the feeling of the domestic. And a little bit of bliss. Domestic bliss. She'd been short on that in her life. She wasn't sure what she thought about feeling it now, in this situation, with Jace.

She hadn't ever felt this with guys she'd slept with. She'd never felt at ease having them in her space. Which, when you were in a long-term relationship with someone, obviously wasn't very good. And that was maybe why they'd ended up dumping her.

Man #1, Mike, had lasted for two years. Two years of dates, the occasional dinner and night in and then an unceremonious boot in the morning so she could get back to her life.

Man #2, Caleb, had lasted a fleeting three months and hadn't made it into her bed. Poor bastard. He'd always been called out at third base. No chance of sliding in home.

Man #3, David, had lasted a record four years. Until he'd wanted them to move in together. And the idea had felt so close to permanent it had given her the shakes.

Two years since that horrific breakup and she'd been sort of happily without.

So, in all honesty, she'd spent a long time avoiding domestic bliss. That she was liking it now, with Jace, was more than a little disturbing. Because Jace didn't want it. And making any move toward it might alienate the one constant in her life.

The simple truth was, she loved Jace. Not that she was in love with him or anything, but she loved him. He was like a part of her. So deeply ingrained she didn't know what she would do without him.

Which was maybe the root of some of her relationship trouble. Jace was the most important person in her world. That meant her boyfriends always came second. And they didn't like that.

And a husband couldn't come second to a friend. So that made things...impossible.

Just dating was almost impossible. David and Jace had not been each other's biggest fans. And it wasn't entirely Jace's fault. Or David's really. But David had been understandably iffy about his girlfriend going to another man's house, alone, late at night to watch movies. And Jace had been understandably pissed that David had suspected they would fool around behind his back.

And she'd been understandably pissed about it too, but

if she'd been in David's place she would have been a little suspicious as well.

That had just been a big mess. And while her attachment to Jace hadn't ended the relationship, it hadn't helped either.

She shook off her decidedly downbeat musings and headed toward the Crock-Pot, filling a bowl with chili, cheese and corn chips. "Nom," she said. "Thank you. It's kind of nice to have someone cook for me."

"Has anyone ever cooked for you?" he asked.

"Not really. Mrs. Brown used to bake for me. And she made us both cheese sandwiches for lunch."

"Oh...I remember those," he said. "Mayonnaise and cheese on white bread."

"It was nice to have someone care enough to feed me." She swallowed past a rising lump in her throat. "Anyway, it was nice then, and it's nice now."

"It's nice to have you here."

"I'm been making your life hell, but thanks for saying that."

"No. Really. It reminds of me of how things were. I mean, the good things. Because Lord knows there was a bunch of crap. But...there was good. And you were a huge part of that."

"Thanks. You too. For me, I mean."

"Tomorrow we should have cheese sandwiches with mayonnaise," he said.

"I'll pack them for lunch. I really do want to follow you around while you work for a while."

"Why?"

"Because I'm proud of you. Of what you have here."

"I had help getting it."

"And you were smart enough to take help. You should

be proud of that too. Neither of us had anything growing up. I had whatever tiny apartment my mom could get us into. Whatever food we could cook on a little individual burner in one pan. And hey, sometimes we just lived in cars. And then there was your house..."

"Yeah."

"We've come a long way, baby," she said.

"I know."

"I'm looking forward to seeing how things have changed since the last time I did an extensive tour. Normally I just come sit on your couch."

His whole face changed. Pride. Contentment. Oh, she loved to see all that there. He deserved it. "You'll love it. I'm experimenting with the best time of year to calve. These babies were born in October."

"And they're probably mad at you since you stole their testosterone."

"That's how it works," he said.

"You wouldn't be so cavalier if it was your testosterone we were talking about."

"Are you acknowledging I have it?"

"What? Naturally. Your chest hair doesn't come from your rampant estrogen, and I know about your chest hair since I tried to make a pancake on it yesterday."

"You did."

"Thought maybe I could cook it on your skin. 'Cuz you're so hot."

"Ha ha."

"See? I acknowledge your..." The light in his eyes changed and her sentence died on her lips. He looked so intense, so focused for a moment that she thought he might...that he might be intending to...

And now he was staring at her lips.

Oh no.

Oh yes.

No. No, no, no.

Her inner hedonist and her inner doomsday prophet were locked in an epic battle. One thrilled about the potential for a kiss. The other screeching about it bringing about the end of days. And unfortunately, the little bitch with the sandwich board was right. It was a recipe for doom. Dooooom.

"Your testosterone," she finished, kicking her brain into gear and taking a step back from him. "It is in full working order. Beer and *Die Hard Two*! Let's do this thing."

She stalked into the living room, her heart beating so hard her pulse echoed in her temple. This time, it was all Jace's fault. He couldn't look at her like that and expect her to maintain sanity and purity of thought. She was on a two-year sex hiatus. And he was hot.

And she was a red-blooded woman with urges and needs. Urges and needs that were going to have to calm the hell down because she was not, under any circumstances, going to kiss Jace Colter.

No, she was not.

She sat down on the couch and closed her eyes, waiting for Jace and imagining warm summer days spent on a grassy hill. Away from home. Away from the crazy for Jace. Away from the empty for her. And she thought of mayonnaise and cheese sandwiches. And how no matter what, Jace had been by her side. How he'd supported her through everything.

Nothing was worth risking that. Nothing at all.

Chapter Five

Jace blessed the cold air as it washed over his body. But he cursed the fact that Sam was with him. Because she was negating the effect that the frigid surroundings otherwise would have had on him.

He'd been harder than hell and bound up in one big knot since last night.

He'd almost done it. He'd almost leaned in and kissed her sassy pink lips. And damned if he wouldn't have regretted it. He regretted *not* doing it. And that was dumb as rocks.

But she'd gotten to talking about his testosterone. And then the pancake incident. The pancake incident that he should be irritated about. The pancake incident that made his blood run a little hotter and his pulse pound at an accelerated rate.

Because now, when he pictured the scene, batter all over his bare chest, he invited her to lick it off. A fair trade since she'd caused the incident. And then, when the altered memory went there, his chest wasn't the only thing she licked.

And that was just sick. Who had those thoughts about their best friend? He felt like a complete bastard having fantasies about her lips on him, but dammit, he had them. Lots of them. Explicit, erotic fantasies.

He redirected his thoughts quickly—a necessity because his jeans were starting to get tight—and turned to face Samantha and her big black shadow.

"So," she said. "What are we doing today?"

"We," he said, "are going to move the cattle from one pasture to another. We have to keep the rotation going, especially through the winter so they have plenty of grass to eat."

"We're going to herd your cattle? That's freaking awesome." Her pale cheeks and nose were already stained cherry-red, her hair frizzing around her head thanks to the moisture in the air. She had on a berry-colored hat and gloves, which should have clashed with her coloring but somehow didn't. She was so vibrant against the background of white snow and silver sky. The most beautiful thing he'd ever seen.

And it wasn't just his groin that tightened. It wasn't just his stomach that felt strange. It was his heart.

Well, damn. That was inconvenient. Feeling these inappropriate Sam feeling were bad enough when they were below the waist. Bringing his heart into the equation made it all worse.

"Yep," he said, his throat suddenly tightening up too. Oh good, his whole body was staging a rebellion.

"Get along, little doggy!" she said to Poppy, weaving back and forth in the snow, making uneven footprints. Poppy pranced behind her, lifting her feet higher, clearly excited by Samantha's exuberance.

And he couldn't blame her. Samantha had that way

about her. She was infectious. She'd always made him smile, even when there'd been nothing in his life to smile about.

She still did that to him. She did everything to him. *Dammit.*

"Calm down, cowgirl," he said. "We've got to saddle up some horses."

Five hours later, Samantha was muddy and exhausted, and so was Poppy. And Jace still wasn't done working.

"We're going to head back to the house," she said.

"Right. I'll be behind you in a bit."

She nodded and strolled from the barn back to the two-story home. She'd spent the whole day in the cold with Jace and his hired hands. And they'd eaten cheese and mayonnaise sandwiches, and her cheeks hurt from smiling so much.

Her butt hurt too, from riding the horse for so long. And she was pretty sure she would be walking funny in the morning. She didn't ride very often, and she'd never shadowed Jace on the ranch before.

It was incredible. To see what his hard work had earned him. To see how hard he worked every day. And it made him even sexier. To see him get dirty. Sweaty. To see him like she never normally saw him.

He really wasn't joking. He didn't mind getting dirty; he just cleaned up after.

He was like a walking fantasy. Tough and masculine, yet deeply involved with soap.

It wasn't fair.

She let out a breath and opened the door to the house,

cringing when Poppy bounded in and left several paw prints in the entryway.

"No," she whined, grabbing Poppy's collar. "Hang on." She marched the dog into the laundry room and got a towel to clean her paws. "You need a bath," she said. "Let's go upstairs."

Samantha wiped up the floor on her way back by the entry door, then marched Poppy up the stairs and into the guest bathroom, right next to the room she'd claimed as her own for the duration of her stay.

"Okay, chica, let's get this mud off you."

A half an hour later, she had a clean and mostly dry dog snoozing at the foot of her bed. And she had a bathtub with a dirt ring to contend with.

She grabbed the flexible shower head and started to spray along the edge of the tub until most of the ring was gone. Now there was just a bit of black hair sticking to everything. That was always the problem with bathing Poppy. The water drew out enough hair to build a whole new dog.

She hummed as she sprayed the tub, jumping when she heard Jace's voice.

"Did you bathe your dog in the house?"

She flipped the switch on the shower head and stopped the flow, diverting the water to the tub. "What? Yes. Did you want me to leave her muddy?"

"I bathed her in the stable yesterday. I didn't bathe her inside."

"Oh, for crying out loud, Jace. Unclench," she said, a rush of anger washing over her. Anger directed at him for being such an ass about the house. And for being so sexy. And so off-limits. And anger at herself for wanting him when she knew it was impossible.

She was suddenly very angry about all the things and there wasn't anything she could do to stop it from leaking out.

"It smells like wet dog in here."

"Does it? It's about to smell like wet cowboy." She flipped the switch on the sprayer again and aimed it at his chest, making a nice little damp spot right in the same place she'd smacked him with batter the other day, then turned the water off again.

"I can't believe you did that," he said.

"Believe it. I'll do it again too."

"Sam..."

She sprayed him again.

"Samantha."

Again, and she could have sworn he smiled as he crossed the bathroom, reaching out toward her watery weapon even though he was trying to give her his very best angry eyebrows. "No!" she shrieked, spraying him the whole time he was advancing on her. He grabbed her arm and spun her so that she was locked against his chest, facing away from him. And then she was unceremoniously disarmed, held captive against his wet chest, the sprayer against her breasts.

"You wouldn't," she said.

"You did."

"But I'm mean. And you're usually not."

"Nah, baby," he said, his voice low, resonating in his chest, vibrating against her back and sending a million little sparks through her body, "I'm a mean son of a bitch. And don't you forget it."

"You are not." She wiggled, her butt coming into contact with what was either a hard belt buckle or...or...oh my. She wiggled some more, not so much to get free as to identify just what all was hard back there. Because no matter how much she *shouldn't* want him to be hard against her ass, she kind of wanted him to be hard.

He flipped the diverter on the sprayer and a shot of cold water hit her between her breasts. "Dammit!"

"I told you."

"But I didn't believe you!"

"You pushed me."

"Yeah, well, you could use a little push, Jace," she said, pushing her butt against him again. "Lord knows you don't get challenged enough."

"You don't think?" he asked, his hold tightening on her, bringing him harder up against her ass and no, that was not a belt buckle.

"No," she said, her throat tight.

Good. Lord. Jace was hard for her. And what was she supposed to do now?

Ride him like you're not saddle sore!

Her inner hedonist was quick with an answer, while that ever more cautious part of herself whispered "doom" on a low hum in the background.

He lifted his hand, his thumb and forefinger bracketing her jaw, and he turned her head gently, so she could meet his eyes. She couldn't breathe. She couldn't think.

All she could do was want. She'd wanted him before, but not this badly and not when he was standing so close.

It was a recipe for disaster. Or tasty physical cake...

No. Disaster.

But he was looking at her, and his fingers were rough against her skin. Masculine. It had been a long time since a man had touched her. It had been...*never* since it had excited her so much. His jaw looked...scratchy. A full day's growth on his skin, dark and...and rough...and masculine.

She'd thought all those adjectives already. But it's because they were so true.

He pulled her closer, one arm still partly around her front and holding the sprayer, his cock getting harder at her back.

She couldn't help it. She moved against him. Not an accidental wiggle. A full-on, intentional arch against him. Oh. Yes.

And then her lips parted, her eyes dropping to his.

Kiss me. Please kiss me.

And her silent prayer went answered.

Because then, suddenly, and *finally*, Jace was kissing her. His lips were firm, purposeful, expert. And he smelled like him. He smelled like home. Spices, familiar and exciting at the same time. Like leather and sweat. Like Jace.

She couldn't get close enough to him.

She turned fully in his arms and he dropped the shower head, wrapping his arms around her and pulling her hard against his body.

"Yes," she whispered, parting her lips for him.

His tongue slid against hers, the friction sending her to the edge, the pleasure radiating deep inside of her. She ached. Everywhere. Her breasts, the apex of her thighs. If he actually touched her anywhere she might explode. Right now, his hands were on her lower back and he was just kissing her lips, but she felt like she was on the verge of an orgasm.

She wrapped her arms around his neck, sifting her fingers through his hair, kissing him back. Hard.

He growled and backed her up against the wall. She arched against him, trying to fit that tempting ridge of his arousal just where she needed it. She was a little too short to manage it.

She gave up for the moment and put her hands on his chest, skimming them over his body. He was as hard as she'd always imagined, his muscles clearly defined, even with the wet T-shirt fabric stretched over his skin.

Oh no, the fabric wouldn't do.

She ran her fingers down to the hem of his shirt and pushed them underneath, coming into contact with his skin. Lightning zipped from her fingertips through the rest of her body. He was so hot. And she was so hot *for* him.

There was no time to think or measure what response her actions might get. Measure what kind of consequences they might have.

And then her shirt was gone, so fast she hadn't realized he'd made a move for it. He lowered his head and kissed her neck, her collarbone, his teeth scraping the delicate skin there.

The water was still running into the bathtub, hot now, steam filling up the small room. Or maybe that was just them producing the steam. It was entirely possible.

She was mindless, but she knew it was Jace. It was the fact that it was Jace that made it so hot. That made it so perfect.

He pressed a kiss to the rounded curved of her breast, traced the edge of her bra with the tip of his tongue. She whimpered, holding his head to her. So good. So incredibly good.

He reached behind her and unhooked her bra. She pushed it down her shoulders. He pulled her up against him and claimed her mouth again, his chest hair rough against her nipples. She arched her back, increasing the friction, deepening their kiss.

He swept her up into his arms and stepped into the bathtub in his jeans and bare feet, her with her jeans still on, then set her down in the water, never breaking their kiss as he settled between her thighs.

He kept kissing her, and she moved against him, using the seam of her jeans and his erection to chase the release that was close. So close. So very, very close.

Jace kissed her neck again. She gripped his belt loops, urging him to move against her harder, faster. She locked her legs over his, the wet denim heavy and scratchy on her skin. She didn't care. She didn't care about anything but this. But the way Jace made her feel.

He put his hand underneath, on her lower back, pushing her up more tightly against him, increasing his movements. Harder. Faster. Yes. *Yes.*

He bent his head and ran the flat of his tongue over her nipple, then sucked her deep into his mouth. Her orgasm rushed over her. She held on to his shoulders, a hoarse cry escaping her lips, as her mind went blank and she surrendered herself. Utterly, completely.

Jace bucked against her, once, twice, then buried his face in her neck, his body stiffening as he found his own release.

Chapter Six

Suddenly, reality shot back into focus. And Sam was very aware of the fact that she was in wet jeans. That the water was still running. That she was half-naked in the arms of her best friend after having dry-humped...well, wet-humped maybe was the better term, all things considered. Whatever.

Gut-wrenching regret and humiliation were all the same no matter what you called the thing that brought them about.

She pulled away from him slowly, her eyes locked shut. She didn't want to see him. She didn't want him to see her. She wanted to sink beneath the water and hide until Jace left the room.

But she was frozen. Completely.

Jace was the one who moved first.

He stood, water pitching around them, splashing over her bare stomach, up to her breasts. She managed to open her eyes and look up at him. His jeans were molded to his legs, to the bulge right behind his zipper. Droplets ran down his chest. And up higher...up higher was what she really didn't want to see.

His eyes were shadowed, his jaw set. At his sides, his hands were clenched. He didn't look happy, that was for sure.

Well, she wasn't all that happy either. Considering the release she'd just had, she was battling between horror, anger at herself, anger at him and a sweet sort of languor that made her feel boneless and warm and wonderful. It didn't make any sense that satisfaction and terror could exist side by side.

But right now they did. Her body was all happy and smoking a cigarette. Her mind was completely freaking out.

It was quiet in the bathroom now. Except for the water that was still running. Cold now, and she was still in it as it got higher.

Awkward silence had passed to devastating silence, and they were just sort of staring at each other, letting it get worse.

Hell. It couldn't get worse. Could it get worse?

It was getting worse. He was still standing there, staring at her. And she was just staring at him. And she felt like she was looking at a stranger. Because was it really Jace who had taken her to heaven like that? Her best friend, the man she'd known since she was sixteen?

Yes. Yes, it had been.

And now, after speaking millions upon millions of words to the man with total ease over the course of the past fourteen years, she couldn't think of one to say after getting a mind-bending orgasm from him.

Not one.

Except maybe...

"Thanks."

"What?"

He didn't look happy that that was the word she'd said.

Damn. Bad choice. Yes, judging by the stormy look in his dark eyes, it had been a bad choice.

"I don't know," she said, sitting up, suddenly so embarrassed she thought she might die of it. "I don't know what I'm saying. I don't know what I'm doing. I don't know." She climbed out of the tub, her jeans stuck tight to her legs, and scrambled for her shirt.

"Why the hell did you...thank me?"

"Because the orgasm was good?" She tugged her shirt over her head. "It seemed polite."

"Polite?"

"I don't know. What's the protocol for this situation?"

"There is no protocol." He let out a string of curse words, each progressively more crass than the last, ending in a word combination she never could have conceived of. "There is no protocol."

"I was afraid of that. *Farmer's Almanac* has nothing? No? Okay."

Jace was still shirtless, still standing in the tub in water that hit him mid-shin. His expression was starting to resemble that of man who'd been punched in the stomach with the end of a two-by-four.

It was like watching him go through the stages of grief. Denial was the part that had him frozen in the tub, and she had a feeling anger would be next. But she didn't know whether the anger would be directed at himself or her.

And she didn't really want to stick around to find out. "It's been a long day," she said, starting to edge out of the bathroom, wondering if Jace would be pissed about the water on the floor. Too damn bad. She was not hanging around to clean it up. That was what had caused this mess in the first place.

It confirmed her deepest suspicion that nothing truly good ever came of housework.

"Yeah," he said, looking down, probably realizing he was still standing in the tub.

"I'm going to go to bed." It was five o'clock. Even she didn't buy her BS. But darn it all, she would huddle up in her room until Jace went to work the next morning if she had to. Because she couldn't deal with this just yet. Just yet or maybe never.

So she would do what she'd done when she was a kid and reality sucked. She would cover her head with a blanket and imagine she was somewhere else. Just like she'd done nearly every time they'd moved.

Or on particularly cold, frightening nights sleeping in their car.

As scary as that had been, she was pretty sure this was worse. Because this had rocked her foundation.

If she ruined things with Jace, there was no one else.

Mrs. Brown was in Florida. Her mother probably didn't even remember which city she'd left her only child in all those years ago.

And Poppy was wonderful, but she didn't make Sam watch *Die Hard* or drink beer with cupcakes.

She needed Jace. She needed this to not have happened.

"Good night," she said, not looking at him and as she walked out of the room, closing the door behind her.

Jace was still trying to catch his breath, and Sam was already gone. It was probably a good thing because the moment he caught his breath, if she was still here, he would have done one of two things. He would have started yelling. Or he would have pushed her back down into the water and wrestled those jeans off of her no matter how hard it was to peel wet denim from skin.

He breathed in deep, finally, his chest pitching sharply with the motion, and stepped out of the tub.

Dammit. What had he just done?

Years of pent-up lust had exploded, and it had gotten all over Sam. Had he been in a shower by himself, great, fine. He'd have guiltily jacked off to her image. And it wouldn't have been the first time.

Even those moments, moments of pure fantasy, made him feel like dirt.

But this was inexcusable. He'd expended his fantasies all over her. Well, the denim had caught most of it.

He winced. What kind of asshole did that to his best friend?

In fairness, she'd kissed him back. And she'd really seemed to enjoy everything that had happened in the tub. But he should have stopped. He should have known better. He should have done better.

He looked around the bathroom. It was a mess. Evidence of the dog's bath all over the place, and puddles from their water fight splashed across the floor.

But for some reason the thought of cleaning didn't relax him.

Whether he cleaned the bathroom or not, what had just happened would have still just happened.

Because no matter how much control he took over his surroundings, in this situation he had no control at all. And it made him feel like the entire theory for his life wasn't quite as sound as he'd always believed.

He had to figure out a way to get control. At the moment, a little dog hair was the least of his worries.

Chapter Seven

Samantha had scurried out of the house before he'd gotten out of bed the next morning. And she wasn't home when he got in from working the next afternoon.

It was so fricking cold outside he felt like his balls had been on ice all day, which, all things considered, was kind of helpful. Especially since he'd spent the whole night trying to ignore the hard-on from hell that seemed to be inextricably linked to a shame wave that threatened to wash him away the minute he wrapped his hand around himself.

He'd been awake most of the night, horny and unable to do anything about it. Because he was hard for Sam, and that was something he was ashamed about. Vicious cycle set on repeat.

Thankfully, punishing physical labor in weather that was pushing the negative numbers on the thermometer was helpful for that state. If he couldn't tame his nether regions he'd freeze them off.

He poured himself some coffee, needing the warmth in spite of the fact that it was past five in the evening, and added just a little bit of booze. To warm himself up. And to make the image of Samantha's breasts a little less clear in his mind.

He froze at the kitchen counter, his hand wrapped tight around the hot mug. Perfect, pale breasts with little pink nipples. So hard. So delicious. One taste and he craved more with everything in him.

He craved her flavor. Not just her mouth or her breasts. He wanted to bury his face between her thighs and…

Poppy barked and Jace jumped, sloshing his coffee and alcohol mixture over the edge of his cup.

He turned and looked at the dog. "You can read my mind, can't you?" he said, his tone hostile. Poppy looked confused by what she'd done to earn his anger, but he had no doubt that she knew. That bark was too well timed.

"I can have fantasies," he said. "It's my right as a man."

Poppy tilted her head to the side. Silently judging.

"Clearly you wouldn't understand. I guess you've never met another mutt who lit your fire. It's probably better in the end. This is all a lot more trouble than it's worth."

The front door slammed shut and Poppy jingled over to the entryway. He looked out the window and saw Sam's van parked out front, covered in snow. Oh, so that was why she'd been barking. Fair enough.

He stayed at the counter in the kitchen, cursing his own cowardice. He was avoiding her for the next thirty seconds. It seemed the thing to do. And if that made him chicken shit, then fine. He was. He owned it. But he was extending the moment between now and the awkward silence for as long as possible.

Then Sam walked into the kitchen, holding a cake and wearing a huge grin on her face. "Hi! How was your day? Have cheese sandwiches for lunch?"

"Leftover chili," he said, feeling a little stunned.

"Oh. Well, you know, 'cuz of the nostalgia and whatever." She laughed, a weird, high-pitched sound, and set the cake on the little table by the window. "I brought cake!"

"You're going to make me fat. It's going to go straight to my hips," he said, his tone dry.

Her cheeks flushed pink. "Ha!" Her fake laugh was as overenthusiastic as her fake smile. "Funny. Jace, that's...funny. Because you're a man and things don't uh...they don't go to your hips."

"Yeah, Sam, that was the joke. Thanks for explaining it."

"I'm going to make dinner."

"What the hell, Sam?"

"What the hell what?"

"You're fluttering around here chattering like a deranged chipmunk and trying to pretend everything is okay when you know damn well things aren't okay. You're trying so hard to act like everything is normal that you're acting like a nut job."

"I...I'm not." She crossed her arms under her breasts, then fidgeted and cocked her hip out to the side, uncrossing her arms and putting a hand on her hip instead. "I'm...fine."

"Really?"

"Yeah, why wouldn't I be?"

"Because of last night."

"What?" she said, her voice reaching heights that were almost only audible to Poppy. "That was...nothing. We made out."

He crossed his arms in return. "We made out?"

"Yeah, we kissed. So...so what? No big deal. I've kissed guys that I've only known for, like, twenty minutes. It's really only surprising that we've never kissed before. We've known each other forever. Not really a huge shock that we'd test the waters. Ha. Waters. See what I did there?"

He reached out and grabbed her arm, pulling her toward him. "Stop," he said, anger pooling in his gut. "Stop making it a joke."

"We kissed, Jace. Stop making a huge deal out of it. We don't need a postmortem. There's not even a body."

"Just a kiss?"

"Yeah."

He swore and released his hold on her, pushing his fingers through his hair. "Just a kiss? That's what that was to you? That's why you were digging your nails into my back like that? Do you kiss all your dates that way, baby? Because if so, I've been missing out."

Her whole face turned red. "Stop it."

"Why? You're determined to act like nothing happened! You're lying about it, to me, to yourself..."

"Because this is the alternative!" she shouted. "Screaming about it and freaking out about it because...because suddenly this bomb went off between us and neither of us could do anything about it. Because it scares the hell out of me, Jace. Because we went from best friends to having a mutual orgasm in a bathtub in about three minutes flat."

"Actually, Sam, it took fourteen years to get into the bathtub, but I get your point."

"Aren't you freaked out?"

"Hell yes."

"Then why talk about it?"

"Because it happened."

"But we can pretend it didn't," she said, her eyes shining. "Please, Jace, can we pretend it didn't?"

"How?"

"By not talking about it," she said. "I'm embarrassed."

"Why are you embarrassed?" He knew why *he* was embarrassed. Because, in his estimation, it was pretty obvious why it had been so easy for him to go from friend to bathtub buddy. It uncovered the fact that he had some serious not-so-latent lust where she was concerned.

"Because I...climbed all over you like a...hoochie mama."

He laughed, in spite of the situation and his own horror at it; he just couldn't help it. "Sam, that wasn't what I thought about you."

"Well, gosh, I don't know what you thought. I attacked you. I'm horrified. I literally have no excuse except...obviously—" she took a breath "—obviously I'm attracted to you, but the thing is, it's not really worth doing anything about."

He felt like he'd been sucker punched. "You're attracted to me?"

"No, Jace, I think you're a flipping ogre, that's why the minute you touched me I had a violent orgasm."

Heat streaked over his skin and his face got hot, not from embarrassment but from that same dangerous arousal that had overtaken common sense yesterday. He rubbed the back of his neck, trying to think of something to say.

"Obviously it's mutual," he said. "I sort of felt like *I* attacked you."

"I think I embedded a fingernail in your shoulder."

"I knew you...liked it," he said. "But I felt like I must have taken advantage of you and..."

"No. I felt like I jumped you. But it looks like we both sort of feel like the sexual predator and neither of us feel...preyed upon, so that's...good. And now we can move on. Hopefully we're both a little less...hair trigger now."

He laughed because the alternative was to say: *no, no I'm not, if you touched me right now I'd come on contact.*

"I know we avoid talking about this stuff, but it's been...a while for me. Since before the bakery. Since David...so...a long time."

"Right," he said, not sure he liked the explaining-it-away thing she was doing. But what was the other option? There wasn't one. Not really. The other option was to say it meant something. But...he didn't think he could have it mean something. He was sure she didn't want it to mean anything.

Burning attraction to your best friend only worked if you were also hopelessly in love with them. Which he was not.

And she definitely wasn't.

They were just, apparently, mutually hot for each other and in a mutual dry spell. So that explained things. That was the perk of explaining things away, he guessed.

"It's been a while for me too." Not that long, but a few months...like...eight now that he thought about it, which was actually a very long time.

"So see? There. Glad we talked." She patted his arm, then drew back quickly. "This was good. Now we can...be normal."

"As normal as we are."

"Yeah, well, normal for us. It will be enough." She smiled, but the smile still rang false. He smiled back, and he knew his was fake. "I'll make dinner."

"Seriously, you don't have to."

"Hey, I want to. I like this. I like being here with you."

The silence stretched between them, not really awkward but full. Of desire on his end, questions. A deep ache that he couldn't quite define. He wanted more. He wanted something else. Right in that moment he felt like he might want it all.

But there was a reason he was thirty and not anywhere close to being married. He liked his control too much. He liked his space the way he liked it too much.

It wouldn't make any sense to pursue something more with Sam. Not when it would ruin what they had. Because it would ruin it. Because he would go nuts about Poppy's fur. Because he didn't know how to live with someone. He didn't know how to share his space.

And then he would be left with the burned-out remains of the most important relationship he'd ever had. All because he couldn't keep it in his pants.

No. The longing and aching were just going to have to keep on longing and aching. Because he wasn't acting on it.

He and Sam were going back to normal.

"I'm going to go wash up then," he said. "Thank you."

She looked at him, the expression in her eyes unreadable. "You're welcome."

"Movie and popcorn after dinner?"

"Sure. As long as it doesn't star Bruce Willis."

"I'll let you pick."

"Then we have a deal. And I brought movies with me, so don't think you're getting off easy."

Interesting choice of words. And he'd learned yesterday that where Sam was concerned, there really was no *getting off easy*. Well, it was easy to get off. It was the after stuff that was hard.

But it was an important lesson learned.

"Great. I'll be down in a few."

"Great."

Yeah, things were normal now. And he was glad.

Sam was happily surprised at how easy dinner had been. And they were on to cake and a movie, and things were still easy. She'd picked a rom com because that was what she liked, and since she humored Jace's need for car chases and explosions on a regular basis, he had to deal with her love of slapstick and happy endings.

They were keeping a healthy distance between them on the couch, and yeah, it was a little healthier than normal, but that was probably good. Because clearly, things were a little more combustible between them than they'd realized. So taking precaution was a good idea, really.

The popcorn bowl sat in the yawning blank cushion space between them—not in anyone's lap. It was just smart to do it that way. As conscious as she'd been about what was beneath the bowl that last time it had ended up in his lap, she would be a million times more conscious of it now that she'd felt every hard delicious perfect inch between her thighs, taking her to heaven faster and better than any other man ever.

He'd had clothes on, and still, comparing the quality of the orgasm she'd received to what she'd experienced with her exes had been like comparing first class to economy. A superior ride in all senses of the word.

But she wasn't thinking about that. She was watching a movie and not thinking about it. Because she should be good. She should be satisfied and stuff because they'd gotten all the tension dealt with, so to speak, and now they were being normal.

She took a deep breath and reached for the popcorn bowl, and her fingers brushed against his. She jerked back like she'd been burned, turning to face him, her eyes wide.

Jace was staring straight ahead, his posture rigid, his eyes focused on the TV. He didn't look like he'd just been zapped by a rush of electricity.

And she immediately felt stupid because when did she react like that to him touching her hand? Never. So why start now? Because she knew how good that hand felt against her bare skin? Because she wanted to feel that hand on her bare breast, and her butt and...and...other places?

No. Surely not. So inappropriate. And she wasn't being inappropriate. She was being normal. She checked this time to see if his hand was in the bowl before she reached in and took another handful. She was taking no more chances.

The electricity between them was just hazardous. And she hated it. Because she couldn't deal with it. At least, she couldn't deal with it in a healthy, mature way that didn't involve throwing herself on his body and breathing heavy.

It was the proximity—it had to be. It was like cranking up the heat on something that had been on a low simmer for a lot longer than she would like to admit.

And last night it had boiled over.

She turned her attention back to the movie and tried to focus except...oh, that kiss on screen was getting very passionate. And...how had she forgotten this part? How? How had she forgotten there was a shower scene? Of all things.

It was so very bad. She and Jace had just had their own, less awesomely choreographed scene in a shower, and now this was just making her think of that. Well, she was already thinking of it so it was making her think of it more.

She didn't want to look at Jace. It would be awkward. But the more she didn't look at him the more awkward it got because she was so purposefully not looking at it him that it was getting painful.

Oh, geez. How had this happened? How had they gone from best friends to this? To her sitting frozen on the couch afraid to move and break the band of electricity stretching around them? Because if she did, she would either snap it and things would just fizzle all to hell with the uncomfortable tension, and he wouldn't want to sit next to her ever again *ever*. Or worse, she would set off a spark that would ignite them both and she'd find herself flat on her back again, riding the ridge of his arousal.

But she looked at him anyway, in spite of the inner voice screaming at her not to. She couldn't do anything else.

He was looking at the TV, his jaw tight, his hands clenched into fists. She looked back at the screen and her skin prickled. Some serious action was happening there, and she was feeling envious and edgy.

"It's going to get better, right?" she said.

She wasn't going to pretend everything was fine—not when it wasn't. She'd tried that earlier and the attempt had been laughable. He knew her too well. And she respected him too much to lie to him. She respected their friendship too much.

"This?" he asked, and she knew he knew she was talking about that invisible crackle of electricity, the one you couldn't see. But damn, you could feel it. "I don't know, Sam."

"It has to. How else are we going to...live together for the next month? How else are we going to be friends?"

"It'll get better."

"But you just said you didn't know it would get better!"

"I lied one of the times. Pick which one disturbs you less and call it the truth."

"It will get better."

"Yeah, I'm sure it will."

"Or we just have sex and get it over with."

Jace did a literal spit take with his beer, a fine sheen of moisture coating the TV screen. "What?"

"I don't know what I just said. I think I'm crazy. Don't listen to me."

"You said we should have sex and you think I'm going to just...not listen to that?"

"Well, I hope you'll write it off as temporary insanity."

"Like last night?"

"Yes."

"If we're still having insanity from last night, is it really all that temporary?"

"We're within a forty-eight-hour window. I think it is."

Jace looked at Sam, who was looking back at him with huge eyes, chewing on her thumbnail. A gentleman might let her take back what she'd said. A gentleman might get up and go to his room instead, take the offer off the table completely by removing himself from the situation.

But he'd proved yesterday that he wasn't a gentleman, and she was offering sex so he sure as hell wasn't about to start pretending he was one.

"It's not temporary for me, Sam. I wanted you before last night. I want you now. I don't know what that tells you, except maybe that, for me at least, it's not just going to go away."

"But what does that mean?" she asked. "Does it change things?"

He closed the distance between them and wrapped his hand around the back of her neck, drawing her to him and kissing her hard on the mouth. She was even sweeter than he remembered. "I don't know," he whispered, his voice husky. "Does it?"

She bit her lip, looking at him, so close it would be easy

to taste her again. "I don't...I can't think when you do things like that but I...I thought...I mean, wouldn't it be better to let things go back to normal? I thought we were being normal."

"Closing the gate when the horse already got out?" he asked.

"Maybe that's what it is," she said, looking down at his lips. Then she leaned in and kissed him, lightly at first, then deepening it, slowly, thoroughly. She slid her tongue against his. Her mouth fit perfectly against his, the rhythm and flow seamless.

It was nothing like other kisses he'd had. Nothing like kissing a woman he picked up in a bar who didn't know him. Who didn't know the steps to what he liked or the shape of his mouth. Nothing, even, like kissing a woman he was in a relationship with.

This was different. This was Samantha, and he was so acutely aware of that fact. Because she poured *her* into her kisses, and he knew her better than he knew anyone else on the planet. Her kisses were sweet, sensual, with bright spots and little points of quirkiness. Nips, licks, the way she sucked his lip between her teeth, things no one else would do.

Nobody kissed like Sam. Because no one else was Sam.

And it was Sam he craved. Had craved since he was sixteen years old and learning just how strong physical desire could be. Had wanted her every day, every hour, every moment since then, no matter how hard he'd tried to pretend he hadn't.

The freedom now, to kiss her, just kiss her, was like balm on a wound he hadn't known he'd had.

When she pulled away they were both breathing hard and her eyes were glistening, the confusion in her expression causing a wrenching his stomach. "I...Jace." She closed her eyes and leaned in, kissing him again. "I need you to promise me something," she said when she pulled away.

"What?"

"This won't ruin us."

"How could it?" he asked, even as he thought of a million different ways. But for him, their relationship was already changed. Because when her lips had touched his a moment ago he'd realized how much feeling he'd been holding back. And now that he'd seen it, now that he felt it, he couldn't go back to pretending it wasn't there.

It was too late for things to be unspoiled for him. And maybe it was selfish of him to want to push on through the feelings. If their friendship wasn't changed forever for her, then maybe he should keep it that way.

But he felt selfish. Completely and totally ungentlemanly. And he was okay with that. Right now, he was very okay with it.

"Sam," he said, "I care for you. I'm attracted to you. We'll follow through and see what happens. It can't ruin things. What we have is too strong."

"Just sex?" she asked.

"Yes," he said. And he hated the answer. Because he wished he could give her more. He wished he could have more. But he couldn't make those promises. And he knew Sam didn't want them.

Sex was one thing, but bringing emotions in—that was one gamble too far. Friendship and sex, a change to excise the wanting that was starting to take over his body, his life.

He was just now realizing that Sam was the reason he hadn't had sex in eight months. She was the reason none of the women in his life lasted for very long. He couldn't get over the longing. The what if. And if they could just do it now, if he could take away the mystery, then maybe he could get over that desire. Maybe he could go back to being the friend that he should be.

Yeah, somehow, in his lust-fogged mind, that made sense. A fix-it fuck. That was what they needed.

"Okay."

She leaned in and kissed him again, that deep, sweet kiss that was like getting hit in the face with all the things he'd always wanted growing up but never had. A home that felt like comfort, spice and love. Companionship. Understanding. A place he could stay and rest forever. A refuge from everything ugly. She was so beautiful, her kiss so intoxicating, there was no room for bad feelings.

He closed his eyes and let it all wash over him, through him. This was more than lust. More than want. More than the F word he'd thought of a moment ago. This was more than he'd bargained for.

And they'd only kissed. But it was a kiss that had altered his whole body, from the inside out.

She pulled away, extending her hand, touching his lips with the tips of her finger. "I didn't know how much I wanted this," she said.

"I knew how much I wanted it." He grabbed her wrist and tugged her forward, leaning back and bringing her with him so that she was astride him. She shrieked and braced herself on the couch arm behind his head. His erection was cradled by the heat at the apex of her thighs, her legs draped over his. He braced his hands on her hips and looked up at her, at her wide eyes and open mouth and he thought that if he died then, he could die happy.

Almost. It would be better if he could be inside of her first.

Just the thought made his blood pump hot and fast,

made him feel like he was on the edge of losing it. His control, his mind. Everything.

Sam put her hands on his chest and leaned back, tilting her head to the side, her hair spilling over her shoulder, red with gold fire around the edges in the dim lamplight.

The movie was still on, but he didn't care. He couldn't care about anything right now. Anything beyond what it felt like to have Sam touch him like this.

"I seem to have forgotten how to do this," she whispered. "It's kind of embarrassing."

"I'm at your mercy, Sam. If this is you forgetting how, I'm in big trouble if you ever remember your moves."

"Can we stop talking?"

"I'm in favor of that."

Sam's whole body trembled as she leaned in and kissed Jace, her breasts pressed against his chest, her pulse pounding like a horse's that had just escaped through an open gate. It was too late to go back. He was right. She would always wonder. She would always want.

And their little near miss, well, she hadn't missed and she was sure he hadn't either. They hadn't fully consummated, but they had pushed things past the point of no return. So maybe if they pushed further, they would do a full circle.

A little bit of sex, and they would be able to reset everything. Go back to how it was, with the mystery solved. Successful experiment done.

Or something like that. Logic was a tricky thing with Jace's hard cock up against her clit. Yes, yes it was. He even made her think words like that. Made her feel like a totally different person.

So strange that a man she'd known for almost half of her life was able to open up something in her she'd never found before. It made sense in a weird way, though. That sex with him would have a depth to it nothing else did. Because their relationship had depth to it that no other relationships in her life ever had.

She only hoped she survived this. More than that, she hoped *they* did.

Jace pushed his fingers beneath the hem of her sweater, his skin hot against her belly. His hands skimmed upward, cupping her breasts, not-so-expertly shielded by her lace bra.

"Oh...that feels..."

"Good?" he asked, his thumb sliding over her nipple.

She arched into him, the motion hitting all the right places between her thighs and thrusting her breast into firmer contact with his hand. "Oh...yes. Oh...how do you do that?"

"What?"

"You make me..." She couldn't say it. She didn't say things like this. During sex or ever. But this was Jace, and she was always honest with him. When she wasn't, it blew up in her face like it had earlier today. So she decided on honesty. "You touch me, and I feel like...one more little brush of your hand will make me come. Just like that. I don't know how you do it."

"It's not usually like this for you?"

"No. Finding an orgasm is usually like searching for the Holy Grail. Tricky. Hit or miss. Step on the right stones in the right combination. Either I get there or you step on the wrong stone and I throw a spear at your head."

He laughed, the vibration hitting her between her legs. "I hope to make it out without getting a spear thrown at me."

"Your laugh just did more for me than my first boyfriend could do with forty minutes and a vibrator."

"Do you have a vibrator?"

"Not with me."

"Damn."

"Jace!"

"What?" he grinned, wicked, sexy. Oh, he was so sexy it hurt. "You're the one who brought it up."

"But you're...straitlaced and tidy."

"When it comes to cleaning house," he said. "But I know how to get my hands dirty when I work. And I damn sure know how to get dirty in the bedroom."

He sat up and wrapped his arms around her waist, kissing her long and deep. He was the best kisser ever. It was official. She'd never enjoyed kissing so much. Because when it came right down to it, it was a little awkward and someone else's tongue was in your mouth.

But with Jace...it wasn't awkward. And she was happy to have his tongue in her mouth. More than happy.

He lowered his hands, gripped her thighs and pulled the heart of her harder against his denim-covered erection, still kissing her.

She pulled her mouth away, leaning back, trying to catch her breath, while he tried to prevent her from breathing by kissing a path from her neck to her collarbone.

He tugged her shirt up over her head and unclipped her bra. "Oh...yes." He leaned down and drew one nipple into his mouth, sucking hard.

"Mmm" was the only noise she could make. It sounded sharp and kittenish and she didn't care. He pinched her other nipple lightly between his thumb and forefinger and she made the sound again, kneading his back with her fingernail.

Poppy barked and they both froze.

They looked down at the dog, who was looking at them. "She thinks you're hurting me," Sam said, studying Poppy and feeling...embarrassed and somehow guilty for exposing her poor dog to her and Jace's sexual activity.

Poppy wagged her tail and approached the couch. Jace stood, cupping Sam's ass and holding her up against him. She flailed and wrapped her arms around his neck, trying to keep herself steady.

"Mine," Jace said, his voice almost a growl, the word directed very clearly at Poppy. "Stay down here and sleep on the couch if you want. I don't care. But she is mine tonight, and you don't get to interrupt."

Sam squeaked when Jace turned and started walking them toward the stairs, pausing for a moment to kiss her again, quick and hard. "I'm not sharing," he said, his tone hard.

It was so stupid, but she felt like swooning a little bit. Thank God he was carrying her because her knees had turned to jelly and she wasn't sure she would be able to support her own weight.

But Jace could. He carried her up the stairs and she was surprised by how much of a turn-on it was. Such a cliché, but it made her so conscious of his strength and size, of how much of a man he was. Of how much of a woman she was.

He carried her down the hall and to his room, and when he opened the door she was assaulted by the strangest sense of familiar and new colliding. She'd been in Jace's bedroom before. Lots of times. But she'd never been carried into his room and set down on the bed. She'd never been in his room while he was looking at her like she was dessert and he was a very hungry man.

That was the real difference. She'd never been in his

room when she was quite so conscious of the fact that he was a man and she was a woman.

A woman who wanted him. Very much.

There was something extra terrifying about the desire tearing through her because it was directed at Jace. And something comforting about it too.

The entire experience was an exercise in extremes. Good and bad. Terrifying and...well, terrifying. Because she'd never wanted a man like she wanted Jace right now. She'd never trembled with it, had never been so close to the edge from just kissing and a little touching.

He moved away from the bed and pulled his shirt over his head, his hands going to the buckle on his belt. She wanted to stop him. She wanted him to go faster.

Jace was a contradiction, like everything else about this situation. So familiar, yet a stranger. The lines on his face, a face she'd know anywhere, looked sharper, more drawn, his expression much more...dangerous than she'd ever seen it before.

And it was that combination, that contradiction, that thrilled her, that made her feel like she was going to die if he didn't hurry up and take those jeans off. And a little like she might die when he did.

And then he was pushing them down his lean hips, along with his underwear. And she was looking at her best friend, naked and aroused. For her.

And good Lord, he was the biggest man she'd ever seen.

"You'd think," she said, her voice scratchy thanks to her suddenly dry throat, "that after fourteen years of friendship, you might have mentioned that you were in possession of what must be record-breaking equipment." She tried to swallow and couldn't. All the moisture in her body had clearly migrated elsewhere.

"I doubt it breaks any records. But I didn't mention it for the same reason you never told me that you have the world's most perfect nipples."

"I might have mentioned it if I'd known I had the world's most perfect nipples."

"What assholes have you been flashing your breasts at, Sam? They should have told you." He got down on the bed with her, lying next to her, pulling her tight up against him, his erection hard and hot against her stomach.

He cupped one breast in his large, rough hand, squeezing her gently. "You are perfect."

She wanted to cry. And she didn't know why. Except that she was excited, and scared, and no one had ever looked at her like Jace was looking at her right now. No one had ever given her a compliment like that before. One so sincere and so deep.

It made her feel like she was being turned inside out. And in the theme of contradictions, made her want to run from him and cling to him all at the same time.

He moved his hands to the snap on her jeans and undid it, then pulled the zipper down slowly. He closed his eyes and paused, his expression pained.

"What?" she asked.

"I have to catch my breath," he said. "I...you don't know how long I've wanted to do this, Sam. What it means to be this close to touching you. I tried not to put you in the middle of my dirty fantasies, but baby, I failed miserably. And this? This is a big fantasy of mine about to come true."

Her heart felt swollen, achey. Jace had wanted her like this? He'd thought about it? She felt...honored by the realization. And strange too.

"I don't want to disappoint you," she said, her voice a choked whisper.

"Never," he said, his hand sliding beneath her panties. "Oh...damn, baby," he whispered as he slid his finger over her clit, down to the entrance of her body.

"Jace." She lowered her head, rested it against his shoulder as his hands created a path of white fire over her flesh, the pleasure so deep, so all-consuming she didn't know if she would survive it.

She shifted to give him easier access and he slid one finger deep inside her. She bit her lip to keep from making that kitten sound again, but she wasn't successful.

He moved his hand away from her, cupping the back of her head and kissing her deep. She pushed her jeans down her legs, suddenly unable to take any more barriers between them. No more rough denim. Nothing. She just needed him. Now.

"I'm on the pill," she said. "And I'm...clean. I haven't been with anyone in more than two years."

He nodded slowly. "You don't want to use a condom? I have them."

She shook her head. "I know you."

He let out a long breath, a pained expression on his face. "Sam..." He lowered his head and kissed her neck, her shoulder, her breast, down to her belly, below her belly button.

She jumped at the hot swipe of his tongue over the sensitive skin there. He eased her thighs apart and moved lower, his hands digging into her hips. He pulled her closer, his eyes intent on her.

Now, no man had ever, ever looked at her quite so intently. Quite so closely. It was a little intense, a little embarrassing. But she didn't have time to worry about the embarrassment because suddenly he was kissing her there, licking her, sucking her gently.

And all she could do was grab onto his shoulders and hold on tight. She was shaking, her entire body on fire with pleasure, too hot, too much, but she couldn't stop him. She didn't want to stop him, even though she wasn't sure she could take any more.

"Like eating a cupcake," he said, his tone rough. "You have to start by licking all the sweet stuff."

And he did. Long and slow with the flat of his tongue, like he was savoring her. Like he was having her for dessert. He pushed two fingers deep inside of her while he continued to taste her.

She couldn't breathe now, couldn't think, couldn't do anything but surrender to the violent need that was racing through her.

"Jace...I'm...I'm going to..." And before she could even say it, her orgasm broke over her, her internal muscles tightening around his fingers, her entire body shuddering with the force of her release.

It was Jace's cue.

He moved up her body, taking her mouth in a hard kiss while he thrust deep inside of her. She let out a hoarse cry and arched against him, the penetration on the heels of her orgasm so intense she could have wept.

And then she looked up at his face, into his eyes, and she really did shed a tear. Jace's eyes. His face. His lips.

Jace.

He started to move, thrusting hard, his motion matching the desperate light in those familiar eyes. And every time he entered her, she heard his name again, echoing inside of her.

Jace. Her Jace.

Making love to her like a god. Making her feel things, want things, no other man had ever made her feel or want before.

It was too much. Too intense. The well it opened up inside of her, deep, too deep to be filled.

"Samantha," he growled, looking at her so intently, like he saw that need in her, like he was trying to fill it. With his body. With himself.

She had to close her eyes. Had to turn her head to the side and focus on how good he made her body feel, on the climax that was starting to build in her. Impossible because of the strength of the one she'd had only a moment ago.

But no. There it was, close, so close.

Jace let out a harsh groan, stiffening above her, emptying himself inside of her. And it pushed her over the edge. Into that deep, never-ending well inside of her. She was falling, but warm, suffused with ecstasy, surrounded by Jace.

And she never wanted it to end. Because when it did, reality would hit. And she hated reality right now.

She clung to him as she fell, and when she landed, the mattress was beneath her, soft and warm, and Jace was above her, hard and hot.

She wrapped her arms around his neck and he rolled onto his side, holding her against his chest. She buried her face in the curve of his neck.

"Let's not talk," she whispered, a tear sliding down her cheek.

He tightened his hold on her, and she felt him nod his head.

They could talk later. Right now, she just needed to be held. She needed to crawl back out of that abyss and get the cover back on it.

There was no way she could live like this, not forever. Exposed and needy.

Jace had exposed her. And now Jace would hold her

until she recovered. Because Jace was her rock. He was her comfort.

A cold feeling entered her chest and she burrowed deeper into Jace's embrace, trying to escape the chill. Trying to shut out the destructive thought that she might have just put a crack in her foundation. One that she might never be able to repair.

Chapter Eight

Jace was awake the entire night, with Sam's naked body nestled against his, her breasts snuggled into his side—a serious distraction from sleep.

Unfortunately, he still did a lot of thinking.

About what she meant to him. About the fact that he was pretty sure he loved her.

Dammit.

Love. Had he always loved her? Probably. It was likely why there had never been a woman in his life that he'd wanted to keep more than Sam. Because when push came to shove with relationships, Sam had always been an issue.

No, he'd never said anything to her about it because, in his opinion, it wasn't her problem. But at some point, his girlfriends started getting touchy about her. Her place in his life, him going to her house to watch movies until midnight.

And some part of him knew that their jealousy was normal for the situation. But mainly, the conversation always ended with him getting pissed and telling them that if they wanted to mark their territory, he was the wrong guy for them.

Not one of them had enticed him to change his situation with Sam. Ever.

Because Samantha was always the most important. Samantha made his world spin. He was so attracted to her it hurt. He thought about her all the time—his first thought when he got up, his last before he went to sleep.

Yeah. So that was probably love.

Dammit again.

He got out of bed, leaving Sam there, soft and sleepy and so sexy. If he didn't move away from her he was going to jump her, and until they talked he didn't feel comfortable doing that.

He crossed the gray room, the sun still not up over the mountains, and went into the bathroom, turning on the water and waiting for it to warm up before stepping under the shower head.

Love.

How had it come to this? He wanted to tell her. And he wanted to hide it forever. Or at least until he figured out what he could do with it. What it meant for him. For them.

He pushed water back from his face, sliding his hands over his hair, leaning back against the hard tile. Love was elating and terrifying. Like a roller coaster. The climb to the peak was incredible, the free fall after...in Sam's arms...amazing.

It was the blind corners that were killing him. They'd survived everything behind them, sure, but he had no idea what was up ahead.

The door to the shower opened and he turned. Sam was standing there, naked and biting her lip, looking nervous and beautiful, so damn perfect it hurt.

"Mind if I come in?" she asked.

"Please," he said, his voice rough, not like his own at all.

She did, closing the door behind her, the moisture in the air clinging to her hair, which was completely wrecked after their activities last night. She wrapped her arms around her midsection, the action pushing her breasts up and together.

And he could only stare.

Had she always been *this* beautiful? How the hell had he survived looking at her for the past fourteen years without his head, or other parts, exploding?

Not the most romantic thought. But honest.

Right now though, it wasn't just his cock that was on the verge of serious injury. It was his heart. It felt like a fist was squeezing it so tight that his chest might cave in due to the pressure.

She didn't make a move to touch him, but she was here, in the shower with him, so that had to mean something.

"So, I was thinking," she said, her voice soft.

"Sounds dangerous."

"Does it?"

He shrugged, feeling a little like an asshole for trying to have a conversation while standing in front of her with an erection that was advertising the true contents of his thoughts. "I'm having trouble doing any real thinking right now."

She looked down. "Yeah. Well...I can see that."

"Sorry." He wasn't. Not really. She was there and naked. And he was crazy about her. If he was lucky enough to see her naked every day of his life for the next sixty years, she would probably always make him hard. That was just the simple truth.

"I was just thinking that...that there's no going back, Jace," she said. The way she said it made him feel cold. Like he was sure he wouldn't like the next words out of her mouth. "I can't forget last night or what happened before that. The only solution is to...is to keep going until we come out the other side. That makes sense, right?"

"I suppose," he said. Except he was right—he didn't like what she was saying. What she was saying made it sound like they were lost in the forest, muddling around, groping and falling into each other's naked bodies. But not to worry—they would find the other side eventually and all the groping could stop.

And that wasn't how he felt. He didn't feel lost. He finally felt like he'd found himself.

"While I'm living here...Jace, this tension isn't going to let up while I'm here. There's no freaking way. We've seen each other naked. We've...y'know, and we'll be sleeping down the hall from each other and...it's not going to work."

"I agree." Kind of.

"So, I think...as long as we want it, let's have it. While it feels right, we do it. And when it doesn't...we'll stop and never look back."

"Can you do that?" he asked, feeling like the wind had been knocked out of him.

"What other choice is there?"

There was another choice. One he knew she wasn't ready to address. One he was more than ready to take on.

If he said the L-word now, he would scare her away. But he could show her. He could make her fall in love with him before they got out of the damned woods.

He wrapped his arm around her waist, pulled her up against his body and kissed her. That was his answer. Because he wasn't agreeing to her terms, not really. He had his own agenda. And he wasn't about to give away his plans.

She didn't seem to want to talk any more, though. She was kissing him back, and his whole body felt like it was on fire, the stream of the shower not nearly enough to stop the flames from burning through him. Consuming him.

She was so soft. So perfect. Everything he'd ever wanted. Everything he'd never known he wanted.

The woman he loved.

He groaned and pushed her back against the wall, deepening the kiss, cupping her full breasts in his hands, her skin slick, sexy. Tempting. He leaned forward and licked the water droplets running down between her breasts, lowered his hands and sucked her nipple deep into his mouth, drinking in the moisture that had pooled on her body.

She shifted, opening herself up to him, and he reached down, gripping her thigh and tugging it up over his hip, testing the entrance of her body with the head of his erection.

He slid deep inside of her, his breath exiting in a gust, curling around his throat and pressing against his windpipe, making breathing an impossibility. But it was okay; he didn't need to breathe. He just needed her.

The feel of her, hot and wet, tight around him, the water hot on his back, her breasts crushed against his chest. It was too much, but it was perfect.

She gripped his ass and pulled him forward, burying him deeper inside her body. She had her eyes closed, her head back against the wall, her brows locked together, her lips parted slightly.

He leaned in and kissed her because in his mind, parting her lips just like that was an invitation to taste her. An invitation she'd made subconsciously for years, one he'd denied because he didn't want to ruin their friendship.

But he wasn't denying it anymore. Never again.

He slid his tongue over her lush bottom lip, taking in her

flavor, her texture. Like a crushed rose petal dipped in sugar. Sweet, velvet perfection.

He moved his hands over her curves, the water easing his way. Full breasts, slim waist, rounded hips. A fantasy. But no matter how those curves changed and reshaped over the years, they would still be a fantasy. They would always be his fantasy.

She would always be his fantasy.

He was lost then, in her body, in her sighs, in her nails digging into his back. He wrenched his mouth from hers and pressed his face to her neck. His orgasm rushed up over him, blinding him, making him feel like he was losing his grip. On his surroundings, on the world. So all he could do was cling to Sam.

She dug her nails deeper into his back, the pain a sharp spike of reality amid the pleasure, helping him stay standing as he emptied himself into her body, his thighs shaking, his whole body shaking.

It wasn't until he came back to himself that he realized he was biting her neck. Not hard. Just a little. But still. He moved away from her, examining the little mark he'd left there.

He brushed the back of his knuckle over the indents, regret slugging him in the gut. "I'm sorry, sweetheart," he whispered, leaning in and kissing her over her delicate, marred skin.

"Mmm." She tilted her head and kissed his cheek. "Don't apologize."

"I hurt you," he said, lifting his head and looking into her eyes.

"A little. But it was the fun kind. And no guy has ever gotten so into it with me before. You make me feel…different." She smiled, sweet and sleepy. "And the orgasms are pretty rad too."

"Rad?"

"Yeah." Her smile widened. "Got a problem with that?"

"Not at all." Hell, he was just glad he was in a position to give her orgasms. He wasn't going to argue with her choice of outdated nineties slang when expressing her enjoyment of them.

"Good." She smacked his butt and wiggled out of his hold as she stepped out of the shower.

He turned the water off and followed her out into the cold air. She was drying off and it should not be as hot as it was. He was sure he'd seen women dry off after a shower. He was sure he'd had sex in the shower before.

He just couldn't remember very clearly. Not because there had been so many or anything, just because...every other woman seemed indistinct in his memory now. Every other time seemed indistinct. Samantha was the definition of sexy to him. His life's sexiest moments were now made up of encounters that had happened with her, and all in the past couple of days.

"Baby, I could watch you do that...for another ten seconds and then I would jump you again," he said.

She smiled at him, hot and tempting. "Already?"

"You said no man had ever been like this with you, which proves what I already knew: you have dated assholes. But it also means that I have to tell you I've never been this way with any other woman. Ever."

Her cheeks turned pink and she tugged the towel up over her breasts. Funny what made her blush. And what didn't.

"That's nice of you to say. But you don't have to say it."

"I do. Because it's true. Because you're different. Because I bit you. I've never bitten a woman in my life."

"If you were Poppy, I would have smacked you with a newspaper."

"I'm glad you didn't."

She let out a long breath and hugged the towel closer to her body. She looked smaller for a moment. Unsure. And he wanted to grab her and pull her into his arms. He wanted to reassure her. But he didn't know if she wanted him to. He didn't know what was allowed in this little scenario of hers.

And he didn't want to push her too far. Not yet. Too much pushing and she would scurry off into those metaphorical woods without him and he wouldn't have the chance to make his case for forever.

His chest suddenly felt tight. Was that what he wanted? Forever? With her and Poppy in his house, screwing shit up and leaving hair and footprints everywhere?

Yes. Yes it was.

He'd spent most of his adult life protecting his space and his organization, prizing it above all else.

And it hit him then that if he kept on doing that, he wasn't any better than his mother. Loving his things more than he loved people. Of course, he was into neat and clean rather than piles of trash. But it was the same idea.

If he took on Sam, he had to let her in. Really. He had to let her have an equal share. He had to give up control.

And in that same moment, he realized he would give up anything, even a clean floor, for her. He would let her damned dog on the couch. He would let the damned dog in his bed. As long as Sam was there too.

Okay, he would get used to those ideas in stages. And maybe they could compromise.

But the sentiment stood.

"Yeah, well. Don't push your luck. Anyway...the cupcakes will not frost themselves."

"My cows won't take their own vitamins either."

"Or cut off their own...well."

"Yeah."

"Okay so...makeup is in the other bathroom and I..." She shrugged her pale shoulders and backed out of the bathroom.

He didn't know what had caused her unease, but she was definitely uneasy. He let out a breath and walked into his room, hunting for his clothes. He would have to follow her lead. To a point. Then he was going to do some pushing.

Because he was done hanging in limbo. He knew what he wanted now. He knew what he felt. He loved her. For better or worse, for chewed-up throw pillows or orderly house. And that meant he wasn't going to just hang back.

And she wasn't going to be able to avoid him forever.

Chapter Nine

Jace was so hot. Standing at the stove cooking her dinner. And he wasn't wearing a shirt. Just jeans riding low on his hips, the snug fit hugging his ass like a little denim-wrapped present that was just for her.

Ugh. Wasn't this supposed to be getting easier? Weren't things supposed to be less...lusty?

She'd spent the past week in his bed. And on his couch. And in the shower. Once on the floor in the hall.

Yes. It had been a busy week.

And she didn't feel any closer to getting out of the woods. Worse, she was forgetting why she wanted out.

Things were getting tangled. Jace her friend and Jace her lover weren't really staying as separate as she would have liked. Because sometimes they were talking and laughing, and she would picture him naked. And then sometimes they were naked and he would say something very Jace and make her laugh.

Muddled. It was muddled.

And her mind was muddled at the moment because of those jeans. Because of the sexy shift and bunch in his muscles as he stirred the pot of spaghetti sauce on the stove.

What she really wanted to do was walk up and kiss his bare shoulder. Trail her fingertip down the curve of his spine. Slide her fingers beneath the waistband of his jeans. Squeeze his butt.

But this was the problem with their little arrangement. She felt compelled to find the line during the times they weren't getting it on. Which meant acting like his friend and not his bed partner when they weren't hot and heavy.

Which meant no random shoulder kisses or proprietary ass grabs just before dinner.

But she wanted to.

That was sort of disturbing. It was line-muddling. And stuff.

But it might not hurt, either. Especially not if it was considered fore-foreplay. Because they would have sex later, of that she had no doubt. Because if every night over the past week was an indicator, they couldn't keep their hands off each other.

She crept up behind him and put her hand on his shoulder. "Hi," she said. He went stiff beneath her fingertips.

"Hi," he said.

She leaned forward and pressed her lips to his skin, just like she'd imagined, before tracing his spine, also like she'd imagined. And then she edged her fingers beneath the waistband of his jeans, skimming the top of his butt. She stopped short at squeezing, even though she wanted to.

"How was your day?" she asked, pulling away.

"Good."

"Did Poppy behave?"

He shrugged a shoulder, the one she'd kissed, and turned to face her. "Yeah, she was fine. She rode in the truck and did my errands with me. Then we did some ranch work. The hands like her a lot. I think she might have gotten a little spoiled with lunch scraps."

She made a face and looked down at the dog. "Greedy thing. They're going to make her fat."

"Her fur will cover it."

"Ah, yes, black hair is very slimming."

Their eyes met and he smiled. And her heart did some kind of weird melty thing it had never done before. Ever. In her whole life. It was strange and she didn't like it at all.

She cleared her throat and turned away. "Can I set the table?"

"Sure," he said.

She busied herself with the task while he finished cooking and dished their plates. They ate in relative silence with more small talk about their day passing back and forth. But mainly her eyes were glued to his chest. Why was he shirtless anyway? It was snowing outside. It was warm in the house, but she didn't feel the need to strip off her top.

It seemed like gratuitous male nudity. Which, if it also counted as fore-foreplay, was allowable.

She would just enjoy it then. Let it kindle her flame. Light her fire. Make her go up like a match thrown into a tank of gasoline.

Yeah, more that last one.

Because the man had the most perfect chest ever. And while she'd definitely noticed it before, even before the morning she'd smacked him with pancake batter, she was really, really noticing it now.

Now that she knew just how those muscles felt under her fingertips.

Now that she knew just how sexy he was.

"I'm suddenly hungry for dessert," she said, realizing she'd gone a little Marilyn Monroe.

"Are you trying to seduce me?" he asked.

"Yes," she said. "I am. And if you have to ask, I'm not doing a very good job."

He smiled and her heart did that thing again. Then he stood from his spot at the table and crossed to where she was sitting, kneeling in front of her and taking both her hands in his, his eyes intent on hers. "You have been seducing me since the moment I first met you. Pick-up lines appreciated but not required."

"I..." She blinked, trying to soothe suddenly stinging eyes. "How do you do that?"

"How do I do what?"

"How do you make me feel like I'm the only woman in the world?"

"Because you're the only one that matters."

She breathed out hard, fighting against the intense emotion rising in her chest. She didn't want to cry. There was no reason to cry. Jace was her friend so he was saying nice things. He was her lover so they were extra mushy.

That was all.

Nothing deeper.

"We should do dishes," she said. "I mean, before dessert."

He reached up and brushed his thumb over the corner of her mouth before straightening. "You really do know how to talk dirty to me. By talking clean."

"I know my audience," she said. "Most guys aren't so excited about putting their hands in warm soapy water."

"If you were in it, any guy would be."

"Oh..." Her cheeks heated. "Well, you...you..."

"Yeah. And you."

He was being gooey. And looking at her funny.

"You know," she said, "I'm easy where you're concerned. You don't have to try this hard."

"I'm just being honest."

"Okay."

She started running hot water out of the tap, scrubbing at the bowl idly with her thumb before realizing what she was doing. And then she realized he wasn't yelling at her. And that was weird.

"I'm washing the bowl with my thumb," she said, studying his face closely. "My thumb, Jace. I petted Poppy with these hands earlier. I grabbed your ass. This thumb was involved in said ass-grabbing."

He shrugged and smiled. "It's going to go in the dishwasher."

She squinted at him. "Are you high?"

"Never once in my life."

"No. You're too much of a control freak. Which is why I am suspicious of you now."

"I'm fine. I'm..." He looked down at her hand. "You did stick your hand down my pants."

"Yeah."

"Maybe you could use a cloth?"

She smiled and grabbed a clean dish towel from the counter. "Yeah, I could do that." There. That was more normal. Nitpicky Jace, who was freaky about his dishes, was strange but normal in his way.

"So what's with the trying to be relaxed about me manhandling your stuff?" she asked.

"I'm making an effort to be flexible."

"That's weird, man. I'm not gonna lie."

"You're staying here. And I shouldn't make you feel like an imposition."

"Huh. Well. For the record, you don't make me feel like an imposition, but thank you."

"But you wouldn't feel comfortable if you were staying here permanently."

Something strange and heavy settled in her chest. "No. But I'm not."

"No," he said. "But...if you were, I couldn't be tyrannical about everything."

"But I'm not," she said, feeling the need to affirm it.

"No," he said again.

She set the bowl down in the sink. "Stop thinking so much," she said, touching his cheek. "I can think of something that doesn't require thinking at all."

"Really?" The light in his eyes changed. It had been soft, almost sweet a moment ago. Not now. Now it was sharp. Predatory.

"Yes, really."

She reached between them and grabbed his belt, tugging him forward. She ran her hands over his chest, confidence filling her. Because Jace was the most enthusiastic lover she'd ever had. Because he made her feel confident. Beautiful. More aggressive. And safe. Even when he took her to the edge, Jace made her feel safe.

She skimmed her fingers over his abs and nearly whimpered. He was so freaking hot.

With one hand, she worked at his belt buckle, the other enjoying all of his amazing muscles. Then she got frustrated with her one-handed technique and attacked the belt with both hands, pushing his pants and underwear down to the floor, dropping to her knees in front of him.

They hadn't done this yet. She hadn't. Because...stupidly maybe, it seemed so intimate. And now she wanted to taste him so bad she was shaking with the need for it. To bring it back down to sex—that was why. To stop him from saying all these sweet things. To stop him from talking about her living here full-time, like that could ever happen.

She cupped him, sliding her palm up and over his shaft, squeezing him gently before leaning in and tracing the head of his cock with her tongue. He sifted his fingers through her hair, tugging hard when she took him into her mouth.

A harsh curse escaped his lips, and he tugged harder as she moved her hand in time with her lips and tongue. And she liked it. This was raw. This was sex. This was something she could understand.

It was Jace, her lover. The man who made her feel like she could do anything to his body and he would like it. The man who whispered dirty promises in her ear at night.

Not the man she ate cupcakes with. Not the man who hated dog hair and kept a small vacuum in his pickup truck to take care of dirt.

This was the easiest way to put a sharp divide between those two men, and she needed the divide. Without it, things were too dangerous. Without it, Jace was everything.

She pushed that terrifying thought away and focused on pleasuring him. On how hot and hard he was, on how perfect. On how this had never, ever been an arousing act to her before, but had her on the brink now.

"Enough," he growled, tugging lightly on her hair. She followed the motion, rising to her feet, breathing hard, her entire body shaking. "I need you," he said, his voice rough.

He wrapped his arm around her waist and gripped her thigh with his other hand, lifting her and setting her on the counter with one smooth motion. He pushed her skirt up to her hips, his hands rough as he pulled her wool tights and then her panties down her legs.

He held her open to him, thrusting hard inside of her,

kissing her deep, in time with his thrusts. His desperation fed hers, her heart hammering so hard she thought it would eventually come to a dead stop, too exhausted to beat once more.

He pulled away from her, then entered her again, slowly this time, his eyes on hers, intense, dark, predatory, but for some reason, the line between Jace, her friend, and Jace, her lover, blurred. And they became one man.

He became everything.

A choked sob rose in her throat and she wanted to close her eyes. To bury her face in his neck like she'd done the first time. To hide from what they were doing. From what she was feeling.

But along with the pressure, the emotion building in her chest was the climax building deep inside of her, tension that was winding tighter and tighter. A sob broke through her lips, and still she looked at him, at his eyes. And she saw the emotion there. Flecks of light breaking through that dark gleam.

Something that went beyond sex. Something that pulled hard at her heart, at all of the feelings swirling inside of her. That forced the desire, the building climax and all of the emotion into one massive knot that made it impossible to breathe.

Panic assaulted her, and she tried to fight it. Tried to fight everything. The feelings. The desire. But it was too late. She was too far gone.

"Oh, Sam," Jace said, his voice rough, broken as he thrust, harder and faster. And his voice, her name on his lips, his heat and hardness around her, in her, pushed her over the edge.

Everything shattered around her, shards digging inside, splintering the knot that had built into tiny glass slivers that burned through her, stuck into every part of her. Pain and pleasure in equal parts. A tear slipped down her cheek as the wave of her release washed through her, soothing the burn left behind by the emotion.

But only for a moment. The wave was salt on a wound, leaving her feeling raw, in pain, in the aftermath of the most incredible, devastating release of her life.

Jace lowered his head, kissing her, desperate, intense. It wasn't sexual, it was something more. A bid for connection, for an even deeper closeness. When they parted he kissed her forehead, her cheek. "I love you," he said, his voice broken. "Samantha, I love you."

Chapter Ten

She shook her head and tried to look away. "Samantha," he said again, cupping her chin, redirecting her focus, forcing her to meet his eyes. "I love you."

"No," she said. "No."

"Sam..."

"No!" She pulled away from him and got off of the counter, panic surging through her, her entire body shaking. She pushed her skirt down her hips, covering herself.

"I do," he said.

"Stop it. That's not what this was. This wasn't supposed to change anything."

"Too damn bad. It changed everything."

"But I didn't want it to!"

"And what, Sam, you honestly believed it wouldn't? Honestly?"

"I don't know. You're a guy and..."

"I am your best friend, Samantha. I would never use you that way. Ever. How could you not know I had feelings for you?"

"Because you said," she began, her voice shaking, "you said we'd just get it out of our systems."

"I thought maybe it was possible," he said, his voice unsteady too. "But not after. Not after it happened."

"I can't do this."

"Why?" He moved closer to her, still naked, his expression stark, raw. Painful. "Why can't you do this with me?"

"I don't know if I can ever do this with anyone."

"But why not me, Sam? Don't you feel something for me?"

"Jace...you are...you're my rock. You're my...everything. And me and men...it never works. I don't know how to have that kind of relationship. I don't like it. I don't...do well with it."

"Bullshit."

"I don't! It's never worked."

"It was never me."

"Like that would really change anything?" she asked, regretting the words as she spoke them, panic driving her on. "My mom left me, Jace. My mom left me here and never came back. She didn't even care. I don't...people don't stay with me."

"And I've only stood by you for fourteen years. Not much of a guarantee."

"It's different. I...Jace...." She took a deep breath. "I have had so much...so much loss. And not a moment of stability, until you. I need you. Don't you understand? I need you where you were. I need my friend. My support system." She put her hand on his cheek. "If I don't have you here to hold me up, my whole world will crumble and I can't risk that for sex, for...for this idea of love when I've never, ever seen that version of it last."

Jace stumbled back like he'd been punched in the stomach, and she felt the impact in hers.

"Tell me you understand," she whispered.

He nodded, a muscle in his jaw jumping. "I understand."

"Thank you," she said.

"I understand, but I'm not going to do it."

"What?"

"I'm not going to be your fucking support system," he said, his tone hard, even. "I am not here to prop you up. Stand on your own damn feet, Samantha. You aren't a child. You're a grown woman, and I'm a man. I'm not going to be half a person to you. Just here to fill your needs. Because I want everything. I want to be your friend. I want to be your lover. I want to be your husband."

She felt like her world was falling away, the ground disintegrating, slipping from beneath her feet. "Jace..."

"You can't have me only on your terms."

"So, I can only have you on yours?" she asked, a tear sliding down her cheek. "That's not fair. That's..."

"Put your dog on the couch. Let her drink out of the toilet, wash the dishes with your thumb, bake pies inside cakes—that's fine as long as I can have you. I want you, Sam. But I want all of you. Not half."

"Maybe...maybe you feel like that now. And maybe you want me now. But in five years? I don't...I don't think you will. And it's not worth it to me. There's too much risk and I...I can't."

She regretted the words the moment they left her mouth, as she watched them hit Jace with the force of a slap. He swallowed hard, the expression on his face so pained it tore into her guts.

"Great. Then that's...fine. But I'm going to need you to go somewhere else."

"Where? I can't...where?"

"Then I will. I'm going to a hotel."

"You can't leave your own house."

"I'm not staying here with you."

He bent and picked his clothes up off the floor, putting them on as quickly as possible. He walked away from her into the living room, grabbing his T-shirt off the back of the couch.

Poppy lifted her head from where she was sleeping in front of the fire, unperturbed until that moment.

Jace flung open the closet and pulled out his hat and coat, putting both of them on before going to the door and picking up his keys and wallet.

Horror crept over her, along with the realization that he really was leaving. "Jace!"

He turned to look at her, waiting for her to speak.

"You won't really go. We're friends...we..."

He shook his head. "No. Text me when you figure out somewhere else to stay that will take Poppy."

"Your animals..."

"I'll come back to take care of them. We won't run into each other."

He put his hand on the doorknob and anger shot through her, rescuing her from dissolving into tears. "You're throwing away fourteen years of friendship because of sex?" she spat. "Then maybe what we had didn't mean as much as I thought it did."

"No, Sam. You're throwing away love because of fear." He opened the door, a shaft of cold air bursting through the comfortable warmth of the house, and then he slammed the door behind him. And he was gone.

Really gone.

Her legs wobbled, gave out beneath her, and she went to her knees, to the floor, too numb to cry. She heard his truck motor. Heard the vehicle roar through the snow and out of the driveway.

Poppy got up and wandered, not to where Samantha was on the floor, but to the door, whining, the high-pitched sound hitting Sam right in her heart, pain splintering outward.

She moved over to where Poppy sat, wrapping her arms around the big dog, and she buried her face in her fur. And then she cried like she'd lost her best friend.

Because she had.

Jace hated motel rooms. They weren't his, and he hated that feeling. But it seemed to fit right now because his body didn't feel like it was his either.

It was numb. All of him was. And for now, he was thankful for that fact. Because like any good physical injury, once the shock wore off it was going to smart like a son of a bitch.

He wasn't looking forward to that.

Fortunately, he could prolong the moment by downing some whiskey. And then, in the morning, maybe, just maybe his head would hurt more than his heart.

He popped the top on the bottle and debated pouring a glass, then decided against it. He raised the bottle to his lips and took a long drink.

Class act. But who the hell cared? No one. Apparently, no one cared.

Not Sam.

He replayed the scene in his mind. Every ugly word that had flown between them. He'd done the right thing by leaving. He had. Because if he had stayed, he would have to watch her finally find the guy who melted her reserve. The man who would make her want to take a chance on things she clearly didn't want to take a chance on with him.

"*You can't have me only on your terms.*"

"*So, I can only have you on yours?*"

Was that what he was doing? His way or the highway?

No. She wanted him to be her damn crutch through life, and he deserved more than that.

You love her, but you're taking yourself out of her life completely as punishment for not feeling the same way? For being afraid? Asshole.

So what? He took another drink. He deserved more. He deserved more than a mess of a house and a mother who loved garbage more than she loved people. He deserved more than a friend who loved safety more than she loved him.

And maybe she deserved more than a love with conditions.

He took another drink and stared out the window at the snow. He had a feeling his heart and his pride were going to do battle tonight.

And he had no idea who was going to win.

Samantha slept on the floor by the fire with Poppy. Well, she didn't really sleep. She tossed and turned, her entire body aching.

She hadn't known heartbreak was physical. Hadn't known she would really feel like a part of herself had shattered. She'd imagined she'd felt heartbreak before, but she'd been wrong.

Nothing was like this. Nothing.

Being in Jace's house without him was a special kind of hell. She needed to find another place to stay, but she didn't want to. Because it smelled like him here.

She wanted to crawl into his bed and inhale his scent, wrap herself in it.

But she denied herself. Because she didn't deserve it.

She kept replaying her own words, hearing how small they sounded. How pitifully meager in light of what he'd offered.

She pulled her knees up against her chest. She'd lost him now. In every way. As her support. As her lover. As her friend.

She wanted to be angry. To scream at him and say this was why she couldn't do it. Because losing him would hurt too much.

Because it did hurt too much.

So much. So much she didn't know if she would survive it.

He left because he offered you his heart, and you asked him for something else. You didn't offer a damn thing.

A tear rolled down her cheek and she squinted, the light from the fire blurring into orange stars, the heat on her face doing nothing to heat the chill in her soul.

It was the truth. He'd laid it all on the line, and she'd rejected it. Rejected him.

Because she'd been afraid. But not of what she'd thought.

The realization made a sob catch in her throat. Jace was already everything to her. No matter what she'd let herself think. No matter what lies she'd told herself.

She hadn't needed to share his bed for him to have her heart. He'd always had it. Always. It was why she'd never let her relationships progress past a certain point. It was why no one had ever been important enough to replace him in her life, to come between the two of them.

She loved him. She'd always loved him.

He was her everything. Not just her support, but her *everything*.

And what would happen when he realized that she could never be his? That was her real fear. That he would suddenly look at her and see what her father must have seen when he decided to walk out. What her mother must have seen when she'd let her teenage daughter stay behind in a different state.

That he would realize at some point she wasn't worth all that emotion.

She closed her eyes and scooted closer to Poppy, resting her head on her dog's shoulder. "What did I do?"

Chapter Eleven

Sam's fingers were stiff by the time she raised her hand to knock on the motel room door. Her heater had decided to crap out in her damned van, and she'd been driving all over Bend, checking every hotel in mad pursuit of Jace, with Poppy in the back, happy as a clam among the pies. And the cherpumple, which, epic broken heart or not, she had to deliver today.

But she hadn't opened her bakery today.

She had priorities.

She'd been to eight motels already and it was only seven-thirty in the morning. Because somewhere between midnight and the gray light of dawn, she'd made a decision.

Fear was a dumbass state to live in.

She was hiding from possible heartbreak by giving herself certain heartbreak.

More than that, she was being a lousy friend. Because Jace had never lied to her. He had never let her down. And she was judging him based on other people's track records, and not his own.

And dammit, she loved that man, and she wanted him. For always. For keeps.

She stuck her hands in her armpits and waited. No one came to the door, but the front desk man had been certain that Jace Colter was indeed staying here and in this room. And when she'd given a little eyebrow wiggle and said she wanted to surprise him, the man had immediately given over a room number.

Because men were very predictable that way. And of course, he was not going to block Jace out of a potential lay. It was bad security.

But the motel employee letting his penis do the thinking was currently her best friend, so she wasn't complaining.

She extricated her hands from their place of warmth and knocked on the door again. "Jace!" she shouted for good measure. She knocked again; the cold, combined with the hard door, made her feel like she was in danger of splitting her knuckles open.

Fine. She'd knock 'til her hands were bloody. She didn't care.

Finally the door opened, and there was Jace. Shirtless and scowling, a blanket wrapped partway around his shoulders. He winced against the light. Hungover. She recognized his hangover posture well.

"Mornin', Superman," she said. "Nice cape."

"What the hell are you doing here, Sam?"

"I came to see you."

"Why?"

She laced her fingers together, squeezed them tight, tried to ease some of the nerves, the adrenaline that was rushing through her body. "Because. Because I was stupid last night, and while I lay by the fire crying like an infant for half the night, leaving a snot trail on your rug, I realized something."

"What's that?" he asked, leaning against the door frame.

She drew in an unsteady breath, releasing her hold on her hands and shaking them out. "I can't stop you from being everything to me because you already are. I thought the key was keeping sexy Jace and buddy Jace separate so I couldn't fall in love with you, but here's the thing. I loved you without the sex. I have loved you from the moment I met you. But I was afraid you could never love me. So it was safer to forget the attraction part. To lean on your strength, to be your buddy. And I counted on you, and your presence in my life, so much that I never, ever wanted to take a chance of losing it. But everyone in my life has walked away so easily, Jace, so I was afraid of upsetting anything. Afraid you would be like everyone else, not because there's something wrong with you, but because of me."

"Samantha," he said. "That's not..."

"It wasn't fair. Because never once have you ever let me down. You've never lied to me. You've never disappointed me. How dare I question you? You didn't deserve that."

"That stuff is hard to shake," he said. "I know. I'm the king of the bleach bucket, right?"

"Yeah, I know."

"I was wrong, Sam. To ask so much of you all at once. To walk away when you couldn't give just what I wanted."

"You didn't ask anything of me. You gave. I'm the one that shoved it back at you and asked for different. And you were right—it was all because I was scared."

"So what is it you want now?"

"Everything." Her chest burning, a tear sliding down her cheek that she didn't bother to wipe away. "Your friendship. Your heart. You, all of you. Your love, every kind of love. That everyday friendship love that makes me excited to see you. That deep intense love that makes all the pieces of me ache a little bit. Makes me want to cry over its beauty. The kind of love that makes my body burn for yours. Every emotion. *Die Hard* and romantic comedies. Every. Damn. Thing."

He dropped the blanket and walked out of his room on unsteady feet, wrapping his arms around her and pulling her up against his body, his breath hot on her neck. "I want it too," he said against her skin. "The way you kiss me and make me feel like I'm finally home. I want your mess in my house. I want you to take some of the control from me. I want your dog and your dishes in my sink to frustrate me. I want you so that I can feel that kind of happiness only you make me feel. You're my smile, Sam. You always have been. Until you walked into my life fourteen years ago, I'd forgotten how. And when I walked out last night, I thought I would forget all over again. But now you're here." He tilted his head back, and he smiled. "It feels easy now."

"I love you, Jace."

"I love you. Forever. No matter what. Do you believe me?"

She nodded. "Yes. I do."

His heart on the verge of bursting, Jace looked at Sam standing outside of his hotel room door, backlit by the early morning light, snow piled high behind her. She looked like an angel.

"Now why are you standing out there doing a dramatic reenactment of the Little Match Girl?" he asked, his smile widening.

"I thought my best friend might take pity on me. Because I was an idiot, and I hurt him. And he was right about me. I was a coward. But I thought standing in a snow-drift looking pitiful might earn me a little compassion."

"I'm all out of pity. How about love? The deep, ever-lasting kind?"

"I would take that."

"And a place in my house, permanently."

"You know, Jace, every other time I've thought about putting down roots with someone, or, until recently, even when I thought of putting them down alone, I panicked."

"Are you panicked now?"

She shook her head, hazel eyes glistening with tears. "No. I'm home."

"You're at a motel."

"No, silly. I'm with you. And that means I'm home. I think that's why you always felt like my foundation, why I could never settle anywhere else. Because I was supposed to be wherever you were. With you."

"Welcome home, baby," he said, kissing her nose. "I'm so glad you came." A hard knot loosened in his chest, emotion flooding through him. Joy. Contentment. Love.

"Me too."

"So come in and stay a while."

"Eek. Can't."

"Why?"

"It's cold and I have Poppy in the van. And a cherpumple."

"The pie cake thing?"

"Yes. I have to deliver it."

"Give me a minute."

He joined Sam out at the van a moment later, fully dressed, his hat doing something to keep the sun from making his headache worse. Really, his heart felt so good the hangover didn't seem that bad.

"Okay, Sam, let's take that sugary abomination to its rightful owner." He got into the van and closed the door.

"What about your truck?"

"I'll come back for it."

"You seem so relaxed about all this spontaneity. We're practically being unruly! Disorganized, in fact."

"The most important thing in the world is in place, Sam. Nothing else seems to matter that much."

"Not even throw pillows?"

He looked back at Poppy, sitting between the racks of desserts, gazing at him and wagging her tail. "Sam, she can chew up one throw pillow a day for the rest of her life and I'll give thanks for every damn fluff of cotton I sweep off of my floor, and do you know why?"

"Why?" she asked, smiling that sweet, special smile.

"Because it'll mean you're there. And I would rather have you and a little chaos than a clean but empty house."

She leaned over and kissed him. "Now I know you love me."

"More than anything, Sam. More than anything."

Her grin turned wicked. "Enough to let me make a cherpumple for our wedding?"

"No."

"A true representation of blending lives by blending desserts."

"Sam, I have my limits."

"Come on, baby," she wiggled her brows, her voice getting breathy. "Blend desserts with me, you dirty pastry-mixing boy."

"When you put it that way," he said, "it sounds kind of hot."

"Just wait. I have even better ideas for mixing butter cream frosting and...skin."

"Well, hell." He sat up straighter, arousal pulsing through him. "If that's what I get for letting you experiment, you can have a wedding cherpumple *and* a wedding turducken for all I care."

She smiled, and his heart melted. "Stick with me, baby, and it'll be a fun ride."

"It always has been. And I'm sure it always will be."

If you enjoyed Imagine Me and You - check out Dallas!

Also by Maisey Yates

The Bull Riders

Colt

Maverick

Standalones

Happy After All

The First Witches Club

Short and Sweet

Imagine Me and You

Her Little White Lie

Crazy, Stupid Sex

Lessons in Dominance (Multi-Author Series)

Rustler Mountain

Rustler Mountain

Outlaw Lake

Lonesome Ridge

Books For Characters Mentioned in Dallas

Luke & Olivia - Smooth Talking Cowboy
Wyatt & Lindy - Good Time Cowboy
Bennett & Kaylee - Untamed Cowboy (Where Dallas makes his first appearance)
Grant & McKenna - A Tall, Dark Cowboy Christmas
Dane & Beatrix - Unbroken Cowboy
Sammy & Ryder - The Hero of Hope Springs

Excerpt from Colt

Chapter One

Colt

No guts, no glory, at least that's what they say.

I've always had plenty of guts, but glory in the way I want it has eluded me. If my stepsister could hear me say that, she would punch me in the shoulder. She'd say I've had nothing but glory my entire life.

I guess that's true. In some ways. But I've never made it to the ultimate championship and won. It's the one thing that I haven't managed to get, and that makes everything feel like it doesn't matter. I'm on a mission this season to get myself back to the bull riding championships and to win.

I lost last year to my best friend, Dallas. And then he retired, which I think was kind of a dick move. Because if my win is going to count, I feel like it has to be against him, and I feel like he quit just so it never could be.

That's not really fair. He quit because he fell in love. He quit because suddenly he found something that was more important than this.

I don't have that.

Nothing is more important to me than this.

Everyone thinks I don't care about much of anything. But they're wrong. I just don't want to scare it away by showing it my true feelings.

Because what I am, is fucking intense. In a way that I know no one can really handle.

No one but the beast.

I'm standing outside the chute at the arena, looking through the slats in the metal at the blue merle bull. He's huge. Big, blunted horns, his snot dripping out of the front of his nose. A mean bastard.

I'm glad that I drew him.

Stone Cold. And I know that he is. That's what I need. A killer.

I need a killer, because I need a good ride. Hell, it's not enough to be good, it's got to be a bang. At this level, it's not enough to just stay on for eight seconds.

"Are you going to give me a good show?" I ask, tapping my fist against the chute, getting a reaction out of the bull, who kicks at the side of it.

"Yeah, buddy."

I climb up the side of the chute and sit on the top, waiting for the right moment to get on the bull's back.

I get a signal from the gate attendant and get down over the top of him. He jerks underneath me, and I tighten the strap around my hand, adjusting everything, getting a feel for where I'm sitting. I can feel him breathing underneath my thighs.

"All right," I say. "We are one, buddy." I lean down and

pat the bull on his shoulders and feel them twitch beneath my palm. Hot and revved up, ready to go. "We're doing this together. You and me. We're taking this all the way to the championship."

He kicks the side of the chute aggressively, and I pat him again.

"Twenty-five years old, here in Central Point all the way from Gold Valley, Oregon, folks, over one million dollars in winnings, been to the championships three years in a row, it's Colt Campbell."

The music starts, and I know the gate is about to open. I grab on as tightly as I can, not at the gate attendant, and it bursts open. The bullet is all energy. Lightning and thunder as we rumble out into the arena. I maneuver and try to get my body into the best position to find my groove, but I can't quite seem to get it.

He's bucking, rolling, and then I realize he's moving right toward the wall.

Fuck, if that bastard smashes me up against the cement...

But then he moves in an entirely different direction, and I find myself flying through the air. It's been so long since I've been bucked off, I can't accept what's happening even as I'm sailing down toward the ground. But I don't hit. Not the arena dirt, anyway. All of a sudden, there's a sharp pain in my ribs, and I realize the fucking worst has happened. Stone Cold whips his head underneath me, catches me, and flips me back up into the air.

Then, as I'm coming down again, he lowers his head, grinding my midsection down into the arena dirt as I hit. This isn't a benign shaking off of the rider. This is intentional destruction.

He comes down on me as he lowers his head and shakes

his horns against me again. I feel something hot and wet on my face. For some reason, I think it must be bull snot, until I put my hand there and it comes away dark red, and I realize this motherfucker is tearing me to pieces.

I look up into the stands just for one second, as he continues to ravage me.

I'm getting killed in front of my family.

My guts are about to be all over the arena. With no glory to be had.

Preorder now!

„Er ist ein de Ware", sagte sie, als würde das alles erklären.

„Oh ja, er ist ein de Ware. Wenn es zu kalt wird, findet er ein Weib, das ihm das Bett wärmt. So wie ich."

Für diese Bemerkung kitzelte Linet ihn. „Ihr", verkündete sie, wobei sie auf ihn kletterte und ihn auf die Nase küsste, „seid böse." Sie küsste seine Stirn. „Und eingebildet." Sie leckte ihn am Ohr. „Und primitiv." Sie biss ihn am Hals. „Und anmaßend."

Duncan vergaß seine Eigenschaften, während sie eine nach der anderen aufzählte und erst als sie sich selbstsicher mit gespreizten Beinen auf ihm wiegte, wobei ihr heißer Po auf seinem Bauch saß, bemerkte er, dass sie seine Handgelenke mit der Kordel der Gardine an dem Bettpfosten festgebunden hatte.

Seine Augen wurden dunkel. „Weberknoten?"

Linet grinste ihn an wie ein Wolf sein Abendessen. Duncan erschauderte erwartungsvoll.

ENDE

VIELEN DANK, DASS SIE MEIN BUCH GELESEN HABEN!

Hat es Ihnen gefallen? Wenn ja, posten Sie bitte eine Bewertung, damit Andere sie sehen können! Sie können einer Autorin kein größeres Geschenk machen, als die Liebe für ihre Bücher weiterzugeben.

Es ist wahrlich eine Freude und ein Privileg, dass ich meine Geschichten mit Ihnen teilen darf. Zu wissen, dass meine Worte sie zum Lachen oder Seufzen gebracht haben oder eine geheime Stelle in Ihrem Herzen berührt haben, ist das Salz in der Suppe und gibt mir den Mut, weiter zu machen. Ich hoffe, dass Sie unsere kurze, gemeinsame Reise genossen haben und dass ALLE Ihre Abenteuer gut ausgehen!

Wenn Sie mit mir in Kontakt bleiben wollen, können Sie sich gern für meinen monatlichen, elektronischen Newsletter unter www.Glynnis.net anmelden und dann erfahren Sie als Erste(r) alles über meine Neuerscheinungen, besondere Rabatte, Preise, verkaufsfördernde Maßnahmen und viel mehr!

Wenn Sie mich im täglichen Leben begleiten wollen ...
Freunden Sie sich mit mir auf Facebook an
Liken Sie meine Autorenseite auf Facebook
Folgen Sie mir auf Twitter
Und wenn Sie ein Super-Fan sind,
werden Sie Mitglied des Campbell – Leser Clans

Vorschau auf ...

MEIN KRIEGER

Buch 2 der Reihe
Die Ritter von de Ware

Cambria träumte. Ihr Vater lächelte und kam über eine sonnige Wiese mit ausgestreckten Armen auf sie zu, um sie willkommen zu heißen. Aber als er näherkam, erschien ein großer grauer Wolf mit riesigen Pfoten und durchdringenden Augen plötzlich aus dem Nichts zwischen ihnen. Das wilde Tier öffnete sein Maul zu einem traurigen Heulen, während ein großer schwarzer Schatten über den *Laird* fiel.

Sie wachte auf und hätte fast geschrien. Ihr Herz raste, während sie versuchte den Albtraum einzuordnen. Sie legte ihre zitternden Hände wieder an ihren feuchten Kopf. Die Träume kamen jetzt immer häufiger und störten ihren Schlaf – Träume, die scheinbar die Zukunft vorhersagten. Sie war sicher, dass dieser eine Warnung war. Der Wolf war ein schlechtes Omen für ihren Vater.

Aufgewühlt stand sie mit wackeligen Beinen auf und ging zum Fenster um hinaus zu schauen, wobei sie die Felldecke hinter sich herzog. Verflucht! Die Sonne stand bereits hoch. Katie hatte sie wahrscheinlich aus Liebe zu lange schlafen lassen – Cambria war bis nach Mitternacht wach gewesen und hatte ihre Rüstung poliert – aber gerade heute konnte sie es sich nicht leisten, zu spät zu kommen. Sie fluchte und warf das Fell zurück aufs Bett.

Ein lauter Knall echote durch die Flure und brachte den Eichenboden zum Beben, wobei sie sofort hellwach war.

Das Rufen unbekannter Stimmen ertönte von unten und sie hörte das fieberhafte Bellen der Hunde. Ihr Herz raste. Sie kroch über das Bett und griff nach ihrem Breitschwert an der Wand. Hektisch kämpfte sie sich in ihr Unterkleid und fluchte, als ihr wirres Haar im Ärmel hängen blieb. Der Knall von geworfenem Steingut und die entsetzten Schreie von Frauen drangen durch die Luft, als Cambria endlich ihre Zimmertür öffnete und hinauseilte.

Sie rannte den langen Flur entlang, als sie das unmissverständliche Klirren von aufeinanderprallenden Klingen hörte. Sie eilte nach vorn und lief die spiralförmige Treppe hinunter, die zu der Galerie über der großen Halle führte.

Oberhalb des Treppenabsatzes erstarrte sie.

Die Szene vor ihren Augen wirkte wie eine Reihe grausiger Bilder, die sie nicht miteinander verbinden konnte, damit sie einen Sinn ergaben: Bunte Wappenröcke voller Blut, Diener, die in der Ecke kauerten, weinten und sich entsetzt aneinander klammerten, fiepende Hunde, die auf dem mit Schilf bedeckten Steinboden krochen, leblose und verdrehte Körper der Gavin Ritter, die ausgestreckt in ihrem eigenen Blut lagen und Malcolm und der Rest der Männer, die wie Tiere aneinander gefesselt waren. Betäubende Kälte legte sich um ihr Herz wie eine Rüstung.

Als ihr Blick von den umgeworfenen Tischen zu den abgeschlachteten Rittern und den kauernden Dienern wanderte und sie versuchte, das Durcheinander vor ihren Augen zu verstehen, barst diese Rüstung in eine Million Teile.

Der *Laird*. Wo war der *Laird*?

Panik überkam sie. Sie veränderte ihren Griff am Knauf ihres Schwertes und suchte fieberhaft nach ihrem Vater. Wenn sie ihn finden könnte würde alles wieder gut sein. Der *Laird* würde ihr alles erklären. Er kümmerte sich immer um seinen Clan.

Mit zitternden Fingern strich sie sich über die Lippen. Verflucht, wo war der *Laird*?

Kurz darauf traten zwei Jungen aus einer Seitenkammer hervor, wobei sie mit dem Gewicht der grausigen Last die sie trugen, kämpften.

Nay!, schrie Cambria lautlos, als sie den Wappenrock ihres Vaters erkannte. Nicht der *Laird*!

Ihr blieb das Herz stehen und doch wagte sie zu hoffen, dass er noch lebte. Aber sein Körper war schlaff und blutüberströmt und als sein Kopf nach hinten fiel, starrten seine glasigen Augen blind nach oben in Richtung Himmel, wo seine Seele jetzt wohnte.

Ihre Totenklage durchdrang ihr Herz und verließ ihre Lippen. „Nay!", schrie sie und eilte die Treppe hinab. „Nay!"

Weder Freund noch Feind versuchte sie aufzuhalten und die Jungen, die ihren Vater trugen, setzten ihn vorsichtig auf dem Steinboden ab und traten beiseite.

Cambria ließ ihr Schwert fallen und schüttelte den blassen Körper, da sie die unmögliche Stille des *Laird*s nicht akzeptieren wollte. Er musste aufwachen. Der Clan brauchte ihn.

Sie strich ihm über die Stirn, aber er zeigte keine Reaktion. Sie ergriff seine große Hand, aber sie war so schwer und schlaff wie ein getöteter Hase. Blut durchtränkte ihr Gewand und verschmierte ihre Brust, während sie die stille Gestalt umarmte.

„Nay", flüsterte sie, „nay."

Er konnte nicht tot sein. Es konnte einfach nicht sein. Sie hatte bereits ihre Mutter verloren. Er konnte sie nicht auch noch allein lassen.

Und doch lag er da so still wie ein Stein.

Ein elendiges Schluchzen stieg in ihr auf und sie erstickte fast daran. Ein messerscharfer Stich durchbohrte die leere Stelle in ihrer Brust.

Der *Laird* war für immer für sie verloren.

Heiße Tränen liefen über ihre Wangen auf ihren Vater hinab und vermischten sich mit dem Blut des Gavin, der jetzt nicht mehr da war. Sie weinte eine Zeit lang und um sie herum tuschelten die namenlosen Eindringlinge weiter und wischten in aller Ruhe das Blut von ihren Klingen, das Blut der mutigen Gavin-Männer, die sie getötet hatten. Durch ihre wilden Haarsträhnen schaute sie den obszönen Feind an, der ihre Leute abgeschlachtet hatte.

Wer waren sie? Wer waren diese Mistkerle, die in einem blutigen Augenblick den Gavin-Clan zerstört hatten?

Ihr Herz zog sich voller Hass zusammen. Nay. Sie weigerte sich, es zu glauben. Diese Fremden hatten den Gavin-Clan nicht zerstört. Niemand konnte den Gavin-Clan zerstören. Die Gavins gab es schon seit hunderten von Jahren. Sie würden niemals sterben. Sie lebten in ihr. Sie war jetzt das Lebensblut des Clans.

Mit der Rückseite ihrer Hand wischte sie die Tränen weg und umklammerte den Knauf ihres Schwertes wieder fester. Sie trat ihr Gewand von ihren Knöcheln weg und warf ihr Haar über die Schulter. In einer Drehung hob sie ihre Klinge und stellte sich ihrem Feind. Viele der Diener bekreuzigten sich, als sie sich den Rittern mit dem Zorn einer Wahnsinnigen zuwandte.

„Ihr Mistkerle!", schrie sie. „Stellt Euch dem Zorn des Gavin."

Die Augen des Vogtes Malcolm weiteten sich. Cambria würde getötet werden. „Nay, Mädchen!", brüllte er von der Ecke des Raumes.

Für seinen Schrei bekam er einen Schlag von einem der Ritter, die ihn festhielten, aber das hielt ihn nicht davon ab, an den Ketten an seinen Handgelenken zu ziehen. Er beobachtete hilflos, wie die Tochter seines besten Freundes sich auf einen Kampf einließ, den sie sicherlich verlieren würde. Die Muskeln an seinem Hals zuckten schmerzhaft. Er hatte bereits seinen *Laird* verloren. Er konnte nicht zuschauen, wie Cambria ebenfalls starb.

Aber sie konnte ihn nicht mehr hören. Das war offensichtlich. In ihren Augen war nur noch Vergeltung zu sehen. Wie ein Racheengel hob sie ihr Schwert mit beiden Händen hoch. Mit einem Schlachtruf griff sie den Feind an und schwang ihre Klinge in einem weiten Bogen wie ein Bauer die Sichel bei der Kornernte.

Ihr Stahl blitzte wild, während sie versuchte, es mit einer ganzen Kompanie aufzunehmen und die Ritter stoben auseinander, um ihrem Breitschwert auszuweichen. Zu Malcolms Zufriedenheit waren die Engländer einen Augenblick von diesem zierlichen Mädchen, das sich ihnen so kühn stellte und kampfbereit war, verwirrt. Sein Kinn bebte vor Stolz. Ihr Vater und er hatten die kleine Löwin gut ausgebildet.

Sie schlug hin und her und umklammerte den Knauf ihres Schwertes mit beiden Händen um ihren Schlägen Kraft zu verleihen. Zwei Männer, die sie unterschätzt hatten, erlitten ernsthafte Verwundungen, für die sie vielleicht später büßen müsste.

Aber das Überraschungsmoment würde nicht lange von Vorteil sein. Obwohl Cambria sie mit den Mitteln, die sie ihr beigebracht hatten, kurz in Schach hielt, war ihr der Feind bei weitem zahlenmäßig überlegen. Zwei der Ritter ergriffen sie schließlich von hinten und drückten ihre Handgelenke, bis sie das Schwert fallen ließ, was dann laut klirrend auf den Boden fiel.

Malcolm überlegte erleichtert, dass die Engländer zumindest keine Frauen kaltblütig umbrachten.

Halb wahnsinnig vor Zorn kämpfte sie, um sich von dem Griff der Männer an ihren Armen zu befreien.

Malcolm fluchte. Warum war das Mädchen nicht in ihrer Kammer geblieben?

Der Ritter mit dem schwarzen Bart zog ihren Kopf an den Haaren zurück. Sie fletschte die Zähne in seine Richtung und kniff die Augen zusammen wie ein in die Enge getriebenes Tier.

Plötzlich öffneten sich die unbewachten Türen der großen Halle. Ein riesiges schwarzes Pferd mit einem Ritter mit Helm galoppierte wie der Donner über den harten Boden. Er wurde von mehreren anderen Reitern begleitet, die ihre Pferde auf dem Steinboden zu einem Halt brachten. Überall flog Schilf herum und die Ritter hatten Mühe ihre Pferde in den engen Räumlichkeiten unter Kontrolle zu bekommen.

Cambria wurde von ihrem großen dunklen Fänger auf die Knie gezwungen und angesichts des aufsteigenden Staubes kniff sie die Augen weiter zusammen.

Der goldene Ritter stammelte überrascht und verneigte seinen Kopf vor dem Neuankömmling. „My-Mylord."

Spannung hing in der Luft, während er auf Antwort wartete, aber die Stille wurde vom Schnauben der Pferde, dem Quietschen des ledernen Zaumzeugs und dem Schniefen der Dienerinnen unterbrochen.

Cambria atmete tief durch und versuchte sich zu konzentrieren. Sie spürte, wie ihr Körper der Bewusstlosigkeit entgegentrieb zu einem Ort, wo ihr nichts passieren könnte, aber sie widerstand der Verlockung und klammerte sich verzweifelt an die Realität, indem sie sich immer wieder ins Gedächtnis rief, dass sie jetzt *der Gavin* war. Sie drückte ihre Fingernägel in ihre Handflächen, um sich davon abzuhalten in Ohnmacht zu fallen und konzentrierte sich auf den ersten Reiter, der mit seinem Pferd näherkam.

Der Ritter setzte sein riesiges Schlachtross in Bewegung, indem er nur ganz wenig Druck mit einem seiner gepanzerten Knie ausübte. Das Pferd schüttelte stolz den Kopf und ging vorwärts. Der Mann und sein Tier bildeten zweifellos einen beeindruckenden Feind in der Schlacht und sie zeigten eine heldenhafte Haltung.

Mit herrischer Arroganz ließ der Reiter das Pferd bis auf einen Fuß an den goldenen Ritter herantreten, bis es seinen Atem in die Augen des Mannes schnaubte.

Cambria bedachte den Ritter mit seinem Helm mit einem finsteren Blick. Dies musste das Ungeheuer sein, das den Mord am *Laird* befohlen hatte. Einen Augenblick lang wankte sie vor Übelkeit und erinnerte sich an den blutigen Surcot ihres Vaters und seine toten, glasigen Augen. Sie schluckte, um ihre Übelkeit zurückzuhalten.

Sie betete um Kraft, dass sie aushalten würde, bis Hilfe kam. De Wares Ritter sollten heute eintreffen und der englische Lord hatte sein Wort gegeben Blackhaugh vor allen Feinden zu beschützen. Er würde verpflichtet sein, diese Mörder zu fangen und zu bestrafen. Sie hoffte, dass der Wolf ihnen ein Gliedmaß nach dem anderen abreißen würde.

Der Ritter nahm seinen Helm ab und warf ihn seinem Knappen zu. Er zog die Kettenhaube über den Kopf und fuhr sich mit der Hand durch seine dunklen Locken.

Ihr blieb das Herz stehen. Sie beobachtete ihn und konnte sich weder bewegen noch sprechen. Ein schweres Gewicht schien auf ihre Brust zu drücken machte es ihr unmöglich zu atmen, als sie sein Gesicht sah.

Er war so gar nicht der Schurke, den sie erwartet hatte. Tatsächlich war er der bestaussehendste Mann, den sie jemals gesehen hatte. Sein Gesicht war perfekt gemeißelt und er wäre schon fast hübsch gewesen, wären da nicht die gerunzelte Stirn und die Narben aus vielen Schlachten gewesen. Sein Haar war schweißnass und erinnerte sie an die dunkle Farbe gerösteter Walnüsse und es fiel ihm verwegen um seinen kräftigen Hals. Er hatte ein festes, resolutes Kinn, aber etwas an seinem Mund zeigte an, dass er bei weitem nicht herzlos war.

Am auffälligsten waren jedoch seine Augen. Sie hatten die Farbe der Tannen in einem Wald in den Highlands und wirkten ein wenig traurig vom Anblick von Gewalt und dem Leid, das sie gesehen hatten. Diese Augen sorgten dafür, dass ihr Herz nur unregelmäßig schlug und sie war sich nicht ganz sicher, warum das so war.

Er richtete sein Pferd mit einer weiteren Bewegung seines Knies aus und hob eine Augenbraue in Richtung des goldenen Ritters. „Seid Ihr fertig, Roger?" Seine Stimme war leise und kräftig und hatte einen ironischen Unterton.

Der goldene Ritter betrachtete ihn mit unverhohlener Feindseligkeit. „Aye, Mylord. Sie haben Widerstand geleistet, aber ..." Er zuckte mit den Schultern.

Der Ritter bewegte sich in seinem Sattel und atmete lange aus. Das Blutbad vor seinen Augen war unentschuldbar. Wie er bereits vermutet hatte, als er an diesem Morgen los ritt, um Rogers Angriff zu unterbinden, stimmte irgendetwas nicht. Er hätte Roger Fitzroi niemals vertrauen dürfen. Offensichtlich verstand der Mann nichts vom richtigen Einsatz von Gewalt. Wenn man die verblassten Schilder der Besiegten, die in der großen Halle an der Wand hingen, betrachtete und die zerfransten Gewänder der Gavin Ritter in Betracht zog, hatte dieser arme Clan wohl kaum eine Bedrohung dargestellt. Verflucht, es waren noch nicht einmal viele an der Zahl, dachte er, als sein Blick auf die Toten fiel.

Dann sah er sie, wie sie zu Füßen seines Ritters inmitten all dieses Chaos kniete und ihm stockte der Atem.

Sie war ein Engel. Nay, berichtigte er, während er in ihre Augen starrte, die zu wild waren, ein Kinn, das zu kantig war und Haare, die zu dunkel waren. Sie war kein Engel. Sie war eher eine Elfe. Er war an die fleischigen, trägen Frauen bei Hofe gewöhnt und fand das exotische Aussehen dieses Mädchens so erfrischend wie ein Bad in einem kalten See.

Er konnte den Blick nicht von ihr abwenden. Sie sah aus, wie er die Frauen in seinem Bett aussehen ließ - mit offenem Haar, zitternden Lippen und geröteten Wangen - und er sehnte sich danach ihr über die zarte Wange zu streichen, mit seinen Fingern durch ihre etwas zu dunklen verhedderten Locken zu streichen und die Stelle an ihrem Hals zu küssen, wo ihr Puls sichtbar schnell schlug.

Das Weib starrte ihn finster aus ihren kristallklaren Augen an und er war fasziniert, dass ihr Widerstand nur minimal unter seinem Blick ins Wanken geriet.

Sie erinnerte ihn an eine Wildkatze, die er bei seinen Ritten durch das Moor einmal gesehen hatte und die in einer verlassenen Falle gefangen gewesen war. Bevor er das Tier befreit hatte, hatte es ihn genauso angesehen – verängstigt, hasserfüllt und argwöhnisch. Plötzlich hatte er die lächerliche Sehnsucht ihr wie bei der Wildkatze den Schmerz zu nehmen.

Ariel bewegte sich leicht unter ihm und stampfte ungeduldig mit den Hufen und brachte ihn zurück in die Wirklichkeit. Verdammt, dachte er und schüttelte den Kopf. Sein neues Leben als fauler Herr machte ihn weich.

Er schaute finster in das Gesicht des Mädchens. Dann wanderte sein Blick weiter nach unten. Ihr Körper drückte gegen das dünne Leinen ihres Gewandes und er konnte deutlich einen perversen dunkelroten Streifen über ihrer Brust sehen.

Verlangen wurde durch Entrüstung ersetzt. Er zischte Roger zu: „Habt Ihr angefangen, Unschuldige anzugreifen?"

Roger antwortete streitsüchtig. „Es ist nicht ihr Blut, Mylord. Es ist das ihres verräterischen Vaters, dem *Laird* Angus, aber diese Unschuldige hat zwei meiner Männer verwundet!"

Holden schnaubte ungläubig. Ein kleines Mädchen aus dem Grenzgebiet war wohl kaum in der Lage, die großartigen de Ware Ritter zu ängstigen. Zweifelnd schaute er wieder auf sie herab, um zu sehen, ob er etwas übersehen hatte. Es tat ihm leid, dass der Vater des Mädchens gestorben war, aber wenn der *Laird* ein Verräter gewesen war, wäre es nur eine Frage der Zeit gewesen, bis er für seinen Verrat hingerichtet worden wäre. Vielleicht war es besser edel mit einem Schwert in der Hand zu sterben.

„Wer ist der Nachfolger Eures Vaters?", fragte er sie ruhig.

Das Mädchen hob Mut mutig ihr Kinn und antwortete: „Das bin ich."

Er hätte es wissen sollen. „Euer Ehemann?"

„Ich habe keinen Ehemann."

„Euer Verlobter?"

„Ich habe keinen Verlobten. Ich bin ... *der Gavin*." Ihre Stimme brach, als sie dies sagte. Er konnte sehen, dass sie mit den Tränen kämpfte.

Einige seiner Männer grinsten bei der Idee, dass eine junge Frau Anspruch auf eine Burg erhob, aber er wusste, dass das in Schottland nicht ungewöhnlich war. Er starrte das Mädchen mit einer Mischung aus Mitleid und Ekel darüber an, dass der *Laird* ein solcher Narr gewesen war, dass er seine Tochter unverheiratet und daher ungeschützt zurückließ. Er schwor, dass er die schottischen Traditionen niemals verstehen würde.

„Ich verschone Euch", sagte er, „wenn ihr den Lehenseid vor mir ablegt."

Zu seinem Erstaunen schaute das Mädchen ihn an und schüttelte einmal fest den Kopf. „Selbst jetzt in diesem Augenblick wird die Burg von der Armee des Königs umzingelt", verkündete sie. „Ihr werdet nicht lebendig davonkommen."

„Mädchen", rief ein kräftiger alter Gavin Mann aus der Ecke, aber sein Fänger zog an seiner Kette und befahl ihm, still zu sein.

Er blickte finster auf das Mädchen herab und hielt eine Hand hoch, um seine Männer zum Schweigen zu bringen. „Des König ... Edwards Armee?"

„Aye", zischte sie und ihre Augen funkelten wie Saphire. „Lord Holden de Ware wird Euch für die Morde, die Ihr begangen habt, töten! Er ist ein mächtiger Krieger und ist für seine Wildheit als der Wolf bekannt und er hat geschworen diese Burg zu beschützen!"

Er starrte sie erstaunt an. Ihre Augen glitzerten siegessicher und sie hob ihr Kinn selbstsicher und stolz. Er hasste es schon fast, dass er ihre Hoffnung zerstören musste.

Aber er musste es tun.

Er begegnete ihrem Blick und erklärte leise: „Ich bin der Wolf. Ich bin Lord Holden de Ware."

Melden Sie sich unter www.Glynnis.net an und erfahren Sie als Erste(r) alles über Neuerscheinungen.

ÜBER GLYNNIS CAMPBELL

Ich bin eine USA Today Bestsellerautorin von verwegenen, abenteuerlichen, spannenden, historischen Liebesromanen mit über einem halben Dutzend preisgekrönter Bücher, die bereits in sechs Sprachen übersetzt wurden.

Aber bevor ich die Rolle der mittelalterlichen Heiratsvermittlerin übernahm, habe ich in der Mädchen-Band, „The Pinups", auf CBS Records gesungen und meine Stimme den MTV-Animationsserien „The Maxx", „Blizzard's Diablo" und den Starcraft-Videospielen und Star Wars-Hörbüchern geliehen.

Ich bin mit einem Rockstar verheiratet (wenn Sie wissen möchten, mit wem, kontaktieren Sie mich) und habe zwei Kinder. Ich schreibe am Liebsten auf Kreuzfahrtschiffen, in schottischen Schlössern, im Tourbus meines Mannes und zuhause in meinem sonnigen Garten in Südkalifornien.

Ich nehme meine LeserInnen gern mit an Orte, wo kühne Helden liebenswerte Fehler haben und die Frauen stärker sind als sie aussehen, wo das Land üppig und wild ist und Ritterlichkeit an der Tagesordnung ist.

Glynnis Campbell

Ich freue mich immer wieder, von meinen LeserInnen zu hören. Schicken Sie mir daher gern eine E-Mail an glynnis@glynnis.net. Und falls sie ein Super-Fan sind und Teil meines inneren Kreises werden wollen, melden Sie sich an, um ein Mitglied des Glynnis Campbell Leser-Clans auf Facebook zu werden. Dort können Sie hinter die Szenen blicken, erhalten Vorschauen auf noch nicht erschienene Bücher und besondere Überraschungen!